F
G56   Goldman, Alex J.
         The rabbi is a lady.

Temple Israel Library

Minneapolis, Minn.

Please sign your full name on the above card.

Return books promptly to the Library or Temple Office.

Fines will be charged for overdue books or for damage or loss of same.

The Rabbi Is a Lady

The Rabbi Is a Lady

Alex J. Goldman

Hippocrene Books
New York

Acknowledgments

I would like to thank my literary agent and friend, Bertha Klausner, and my editor and friend, Jacob Steinberg, for the help they have given me.

All characters in this novel are fictional and any resemblance to any living person is purely coincidental.

For information, address: Hippocrene Books, 171 Madison Avenue, New York, NY 10016

ISBN 0-87052-306-6

Printed in the United States of America.

For my wife, Edith —
She paints and sculpts in
  her studio.
I think and write in my
  study.
Together we create and are
  fulfilled.

The Rabbi Is a Lady

Chapter One

THE HOUSE WAS CROWDED. The clutter was there even before the people began to arrive. Books were everywhere—sacred and profane—in the floor-to-ceiling bookcases lining the walls, on tables, even on the floor. The magazine racks were bulging with back copies of *The New York Times*, *The Jewish Spectator*, *Commentary*. Rabbi Sam had been a prodigious devourer of printed matter. The soft, floral, cotton covering on the sofa was the worse for wear, as were the two lounge chairs whose hardwood frames needed a coat of varnish. And yet visitors found the place inviting. It was a house where people lived.

Rabbi Sam, as he was affectionately known, had died after a brief illness. His heart gave way, and members of Temple Shalom responded instantly, converging on the Weintraub home to offer their condolences. Sara, who with her husband had served the prosperous, suburban Long Island community of Wilmette for fifteen years, received the visitors stoically, though she was on the point of collapse and wished nothing more than to be left alone to cry. For years, at Sam's side, she'd visited the bereaved, urging courage upon the grieving. She couldn't very

1

well dissolve in tears in the presence of all those people who came trooping to the house.

During the decade and a half, Sam and Sara had developed close friendships with many of the congregants. They enjoyed the reputation of being "regular guys," and were considered friendly, outgoing, responsive. The sudden tragedy sent shock waves through the Temple Shalom congregation.

Preparations were made for the funeral, and honorary pall-bearers were selected. The city government participated officially. Rabbi Weintraub had been an important force in the community, having served on innumerable civic committees.

On the day of the funeral, long before the service began, friends and worshippers packed the synagogue for the simple service. They walked past the closed coffin, some in tears, others with a prayer. Then they paused briefly before the widow, offering words of condolence. Sara, who felt now that her life was shattered forever, gathered her two children around her and held on to them. It was as though they were the last fragile support she possessed in the world.

They sat on a bench; Carol almost sixteen, a pretty girl with long black hair, her lively black eyes the image of her father's; Simon, twelve, trying to hold back his tears like a man. Sara occasionally reached out, touched the shoulder of one or the other, speaking words of consolation. "It will be all right," she kept repeating, sounding stronger than she felt. "We'll work it out." They nodded in tears.

But really, after the crowds had gone and she was alone, she could not imagine how she would survive without Sam. But now she wanted not to let Sam down by sobbing and carrying on in what she felt would be an unseemly manner. She remained composed, blinking back tears as she nodded, listening to others urging courage and strength upon her.

Sara's knowledge of the mourning ritual equaled that of the man for whom she was now mourning. She had a table set up in the living room and placed food on it. Hard boiled eggs were required by tradition, symbolizing the continuity of life. Juda-

2

ism, in its wisdom, held that one should eat. This was to prove that life was stronger than death. The Meal of Condolence, it was called.

Sara sat on a lowered bench provided by the funeral directors. She was not sure this practice was necessary. But people were creatures of custom, some of it surely outmoded, and one had often to be most concerned with the attitude of man. One of the women brought her a cup of coffee and a bit of food. Mourners, according to Jewish tradition, are not allowed to serve themselves during the seven-day *shiva* period; it is a *mitzvah*, an obligation, to assist. Sara tasted the coffee, nibbled at the food, and wondered when the ordeal would end.

Three temple officers huddled in the corner of the living room. They watched the rabbi's widow.

"She sure has guts," said Don Shapiro, the temple president, shaking his head admiringly to emphasize his disbelief. "I have to hand it to her."

"Unbelievable," agreed Harold Kaplan. "Amazing. I was very close to Sam as well as Sara and the children, especially after my wife died. But I never thought she had all this . . . courage."

"A special woman," Don affirmed. "Such dignity and bearing. She sure has class. One in a million I'd say. If the rabbis in America sponsored a Mrs. American Rabbi contest, she'd win hands down. She'd certainly make a great rabbi."

Harold Kaplan and Sidney Weinberg stared at him.

The members of the board of governors, confronted by the customary pre-holiday problems, were facing a new one—what to do about Sara and the children. Summer is the time of planning for the High Holy Days. But how could they interview a new rabbi? Sam's grave was still warm, his presence was still pervasive. And then there was the problem of the state of Sara's finances; it could be safely assumed that Sam had not left much money. Perhaps he had left a mutual fund, a little insurance, a few stocks. Hard decisions could not be put off. The holidays would not wait. And again, what about a new rabbi?

The congregation was lost without their rabbi. Sam had been captain so many years, and Sara had been his adjutant. They had worked marvelously together. She had inspired and even pressured him into social action, and the two of them had led their community to support Soviet dissidents, Ethiopian Jews, and, on the secular scene, the Equal Rights Amendment. But in spite of the many decisions for which Sam had been hailed later that she had helped formulate, Sara was content in the congregation to live in her husband's shadow.

But it was only in Wilmette that Sara consciously played a secondary role. This had nothing to do with the women's movement. It was rather that Sara would not compete with her husband for recognition. Local organizations, civic and Jewish, were aware of her national reputation, and they tried to persuade her to lecture and become involved. She persistently refused. "No exceptions. There's only one rabbi in our family," she reminded them.

But outside Wilmette, Sara was a favorite on the lecture circuit. Though family was her primary responsibility, Sara cleverly managed travel time during the week. She lectured for many well-known Jewish welfare organizations. After the Yom Kippur war of 1973, she was deluged with calls. Sam encouraged her. "You must help wherever you can," he said. Sara could galvanize a community. She would never forget the time when, in a Connecticut town three days after the war began, people had literally rushed towards her in an outpouring of love and patriotism. She'd been standing on the podium imploring the crowd to help fellow Jews in Israel. The result had awed even her.

She recalled the man who, despite his dark skin, turned ruddy-faced with enthusiasm. With fiery zeal, yet deliberate understanding, he had shouted: "I vow every last penny to Israel. I'm donating my entire savings account!"

And then there was the young boy who brought his piggy bank to her and offered it gladly. A teenager asked his father to write a check he would pay back, so he could answer Sara's plea. She had kissed him, she recalled fondly. There were even two kind nuns in the crowd among those who gave freely.

"If we talk about unity let's mean it," she cried. Her voice was strong, unwavering. "We thank God that *we've* made it—now let's share our blessings with Israel!"

A hushed silence had descended over the crowd. Then suddenly, there was a rush of people—inspired, determined. They showered applause. And she had roused all of it. But in Wilmette, Sam was the rabbi. Sara would have it no other way.

When the seven days of mourning were over, Sara wondered when the board would meet to plan what could no longer be put off. Sam was dead; Sara was no longer adjutant. And no longer a wife, she realized as a rush of adrenalin filled her with fear. What would the community do? Would they force her to leave her home? Would she have to find a job immediately? Inevitable questions emerged at first in hushed whispers and small gatherings. Then the questions were out in the open.

Two weeks after the funeral, Donald Shapiro dropped in on Sara. Don had been president of the temple for two years. He was a prosperous Wilmette women's garment merchant who was enjoying robust middle age (though he was overweight), and who played a passable game of golf and a fairly good game of tennis. He had abundant energy and only one child, and spent most of his leisure hours on the affairs of the synagogue. Don had been devoted to Rabbi Sam and Sara. He felt the loss of the rabbi keenly. He now sat opposite Sara in her living room, uneasy, wondering what to say and how to say it.

The house was deep in stillness even though the days of shiva were over. Don heard footsteps upstairs, but they were muted. Radio, stereo, and television sounds were absent. He missed them. Rabbi Sam's house had been a lively place.

Sara, sensing his dilemma, came to his aid and said, "There are matters that need talking about." She spoke out of a strong need to make certain that even though Sam was no longer alive, the things that had to be accomplished would be done. Don looked closely at Sara's pretty, olive-skinned face. He noted her handsomely flowing dark brown hair, and watched the full sensuous lips moving. Her large brown eyes widened eagerly. Don was aware that there were matters that needed to be discussed. This was in fact the real reason he'd come now. But he had not expected Sara to allude to them. How could her mind be on synagogue matters with Sam dead only a few days? "You don't have to concern yourself, Sara," he said with empathy. "Just take care of yourself and the children, and if there's anything I can do . . ."

"Thanks, Don. I appreciate your kindness."

Don nodded, anxious to get to the business at hand. He hesitated, then said, "What worries me, Sara, is how we'll get some one to take Rabbi Sam's place. Who can measure up? Sam was the best."

Sara almost cried. "Sam *was* the best," she echoed almost in a whisper. "But there will be others, Don. Good men are graduated from the Seminary all the time. As Sam would say: *"You don't lie down and die!"*

"That's right," Don said with a faint smile. "The question is, where do we go from here?" It was a rhetorical question and he didn't expect Sara to answer it. Don wondered himself why he'd asked. It was as though he expected Rabbi Sam's spirit to answer him. So he was a little surprised when Sara remarked, "I'm sure, Don, you've considered the advisability of calling a board meeting soon. There are the High Holy Days. Sam was just beginning to prepare for them. A new rabbi will need time to get ready. Don't you think you'll have to find one soon?" She choked down a sudden swell of tears.

Don nodded, furrowing his brow. He didn't like to talk about a new rabbi, not in Sara's presence, at any rate. Too many questions were involved, not the least of them the problem of Sara and the children. Where would she go to live? What would she do? Putting off was one way of avoiding the hard decisions. But it seemed that she was making it easier for him. What a woman, he thought. She *is* different.

"Sara, I've decided right here and now to call a board meeting for a day after tomorrow," he said, slapping his thigh nervously. "Yes, I guess that covers it. I won't bother you with any more details." Rising, he held out his hand stiffly. "We'll keep in touch. And don't worry about a thing, Sara."

"Don, do you want me to come? It might make it easier."

Embarrassed, Don responded. "Thanks," he shook his head negatively. "It would make it harder." He walked out after a brief good-bye peck.

Outside, he started the large Lincoln-Continental and maneuvered it onto the road. It was a soft, mid-summer's night, with breezes drifting off the bay. The sky was studded with stars. Don was pleased with the visit. Dammit, why did I expect her to cry? he mused. She'd been a rock. Diplomatic, good for a man's ego, he could see that. And pretty too. Don turned left and accelerated. He felt guilty thinking about her as a woman. But what's so reprehensible? He defended himself. Sara is pretty, different, she's got a nice figure, all woman. Don cleared his throat as though he'd been caught in an irreverent act, quite unseemly for the president of Temple Shalom. First thing tomorrow he'd call the men for an urgent meeting.

Sara's apparent calm shattered when Don left. As in a trance, she moved into the living room and crumbled onto the couch. Tumultuous feelings pressed against her mind and her heart. Memories, she said to herself, memories flow, but does one really remember? Is there truly a reliving of experiences? Only in the mind. Then it is gone, unsustained.

Fifteen years here with her husband. Now he was gone. The snap of a finger had compressed the span of a decade and a half. A burst of heartbeat, then tears, then reality took over. I've got to get hold of myself. I can't give way. I can't submit to fear. I have a family to take care of. Simon and Carol need me to be strong.

And then the thought of her own family, meandering into the past, growing up. Father, daughter, the picture of her father, the rabbi. The image of a richly bearded grandfather, with small, penetrating eyes, plunged into her mind. She looked around. How things had changed. First a young bride here, now a

7

widow. The past caught up. My husband, no more. I'm a widow, alone.

She leaned back and allowed her mind to roam. Her first meeting with Sam. Having grown up in Chicago. The old west side of Chicago. Meyer Levin's country. And then on to college where she had naturally been drawn into Hillel. In a Hillel Foundation on a college campus, anything goes. She had wanted to help the rabbi with services. Services were in her blood. She enjoyed the experience, even met Sam as he was listening to her. Love at first sight.

She had often said to him, "I could be better, Sam. The sermon was okay—weak in the beginning, strong in the middle, the conclusion was too long." What had impelled her? she wondered. What moved her to criticize, to challenge? She tried to think of the picture that was forming in her mind. And then suddenly an unanticipated and unexpected thought flashed through. Had I wanted to be a rabbi then? *Do* I want to be a rabbi? Did Sam die so that I could become one? She shook her head. God works in strange, mysterious ways, to be sure. But this is wrong. How macabre, how terrible even to think it. She tried to throttle the thought. Am I glad that Sam died? She fought it, then struggled with a long suppressed wish for his presence, for his love to overwhelm the concerns of the present, of the future. Then guilt moved in. "God knows," she called out. Uncontrolled thoughts kept coming back. Yes, yes, yes! She tried to fight back. But she knew what was coming and she was losing. Could it be that her whole subconscious past was all coming through now? At that she jumped from the sofa. She was drenched. She wrestled with the conflicting thoughts as the telephone rang. A voice from the deep recesses of her mind persisted: Death is my salvation. Sara felt instantly repelled, then relieved. Her heart pounded as she answered the phone.

The call was from Sara's younger sister Ruth, who at Sam's funeral had patched up a decade-long estrangement from Sara and her family. Now she phoned Sara nearly every day, sensing

8

that the two sisters shared a new and lonely bond in being unmarried women. Sara was impressed with the way Ruth seemed to have changed over the years. Two unhappy marriages followed by nasty divorces must have sobered her. Yet Sara was still cautious in her conversations with her sister. She refused to forget that Ruth had once lived in Wilmette, where she had caused Sara and Rabbi Sam many embarrassments with the way she behaved in the community. But what caused the family disaster was the scandal Ruth caused when she divorced her first husband, Barry, and openly admitted having an affair with a married man. The adultery was bad enough, but when Ruth announced that she was going to marry the Italian restaurant owner from the next town, Sara wanted to disown her. "You're so out of it," Ruth had protested. "Vinny's part of the younger generation, and he doesn't hate Jews the way you think." Sam had been livid, Sara choked back strangled sobs, then finally swore at Ruth, including words worse than "damn." Afterwards, she had quietly asked Sam to see Ruth out, instructing her younger sister that she never wanted to see her again.

Now Ruth appeared a little more subdued, though the crowd she associated with in New York was still rowdy, hard-drinking, and foreign to Sara. Their Orthodox father certainly would not have approved of Ruth's weekends of gambling in the Caribbean. But the two sisters avoided talking about men, money, and sex. Tonight Ruth wanted to know if Sara wanted to look for a job. Sara, already shaken by the events of the day, told Ruth that she wasn't ready to decide. She was just too tired to think, she said.

But sleep was elusive. Grief and exhilaration were an ironic mix, Sara thought. She tossed and turned. Though the room was cooled by air conditioning, Sara felt her entire body damp with perspiration.

Mourn Sam . . . hope to be a rabbi. . . . How could she have these feelings simultaneously? Her thoughts reeled ın confusion. Unable to sleep, she sat up, switched on the bedside lamp, then began pacing like a mad woman. "Is this how psychosis begins?" she asked aloud. The remark frightened her. She continued to pace, head throbbing with conflict and doubt. It's no use, she told herself. You've got to get some rest. Unsure, but resolute at the same time, she headed for the medicine cabinet. Sara had taken tranquilizers only once before, right after Sam's heart attack. The doctor had advised her to use them moderately and she did. But this was a most trying time. Swallowing them quickly with a glass of warm, gritty-tasting tap water, she marched back to bed, ordering herself to sleep. Because she was unaccustomed to medicines, the pills took effect almost immediately. She drifted into a sound sleep, but then later entered a hazy, twilight stage.

Yet it had all been real. There was Sam, looking trim and stylishly handsome in his tuxedo. They were already in the hotel room, but hadn't had time to change from their wedding attire. Sara languished in the short but delightful bath, the warm water massaging her muscles. She could even smell the fragrance—honeysuckle. When she came out, demurely dressed in a simple, yet elegant peignoir set (a bridal shower gift) Sam was waiting for her, clad only in pajama bottoms. She didn't remember blushing. Instead, she went right into his arms, letting him smother her with kisses.

He eased her onto the bed, smoothly, effortlessly. She remembered a sensual, yet clean crisp smell to the sheets. Chocolate mints wrapped in gold foil were placed atop the ruffled, satin pillows—a hotel nicety, she remembered. The fresh-cut flowers in a crystal vase were in full view, as was the bottle of champagne, leaning on its side in the ice bucket. Sam poured two glasses. They sipped, just looking at each other for what seemed a terribly long time.

Kisses and embraces returned, and with increasing fervor. The peignoir was off, then the nightgown. She lay naked in her husband's embrace, ready and happy the moment had arrived. She remembered the warmth, a loving, wonderful silky feeling, heard Sam whisper sweet, private affectionate words—then remembered it happening all over again. More enjoyment, more awareness, a sure feeling that she loved this man and always would. Other scenes drifted in and out of the dream—the first years together, the delicious almost wildly uninhibited love-making until their first-born, Carol, arrived. Sara was sitting up in her hospital bed, and there was Sam grinning, slim, with dark full hair and a bouquet of roses. And then the nurse brought Carol in. She saw the glitter of tears in Sam's eyes. "A miracle," he exclaimed. She reached out, he crushed her in an embrace . . . the way he held the baby was so tender, so loving.

And then even later, after ten years of marriage and another child—still so intimate, so fulfilling. The hair was graying now, Sam had gained weight, but the love, the love was the same. Even stronger.

Her dreams took on a turbulence she couldn't control, mixing elements of the past and present. It seemed to her they were making love on a balmy spring evening, a full year before the heart attack. The air was fresh with lilacs she could smell from the open window. She felt Sam's body unusually heavy; in a moment the weight lightened. She remembered it now. Suddenly bony, ice-cold fingers clutched her heart, chilling her blood, letting her smell the fear. She lurched forward. "Sam!"

She was blinking in the darkness, a cold sweat bathing her face. He'd been *here!* Sam *was* here! She groped around to the other side of the bed. Cold, dark, empty. But he'd been here, she was sure!

She switched on the light. Now it was only she, alone in bed. Sara hung her head. Her painful sobbing continued until dawn.

Chapter Two

THE BOARD OF GOVERNORS, called into special session, gathered in the temple lounge. It was a stifling July evening, and the air conditioner worked only in fits and starts. By eight o'clock almost every member of the board was present. A number of them had returned from vacations in fashionable resort areas to be on hand for the important meeting.

Don took his seat at the table. He wore a beige summer-weight suit, a white knit shirt, no tie. A heavy man, he perspired profusely. The men, and there were only men, scattered in the lounge, looking grave. Some had pained expressions on their faces. Stuart Lodell, who owned a drug store, had closed his business early—something he seldom did—in order to be present. As secretary, he sat on the president's right. Treasurer Harvey Pearson, one of Wilmette's most prosperous real estate brokers, sat on the president's left and gazed through thin glasses as though Don were seated a mile away.

Don pounded his gavel, calling the session to order. "Gentlemen, you all know the purpose of this meeting," he announced, as he shifted his six-foot-two frame in the chair, unable to be comfortable.

He asked for a moment of silence. The men all stood. Silence enveloped the hall, violated only by the wheezing of the air conditioner.

Don brought the gavel down hard. The men sat. "Gentlemen, we have some important problems to consider. I'm damn sorry to be president during this trying period. But we've got to meet the situation head on. Let's face it: we're just two months away from the High Holy Days. The New Year will begin soon, what with Hebrew School and Sunday School and everything else. Rabbi Sam always made his detailed plans at the end of July. That's a week from now." He paused and shook his head dolefully. "But now there's nobody to do these things for us; we have only ourselves to depend on. We have a duty to the congregation and to ourselves. And Temple Shalom must carry on." He shrugged helplessly. "Where do we begin? Let's have some suggestions."

Harold Kaplan raised his hand. A tall, solemn-faced handsome man in his middle forties, bordering on six feet, his hair slightly gray, his sideburns long and luxuriant and revealing a healthy firm face, he was one of the pillars of the temple. Hal had been president for two terms, remaining active even after he'd ceased holding office. Kaplan was one of the few in the community who commanded respect, even awe. His affluence (he was head of a prosperous import-export business in New York) and deep concern for Judaism had led him to the higher echelons of major Jewish organizations. When Kaplan spoke, Jewish leaders listened. A widower whose wife had died two years before, Kaplan lived by himself in a large house on Summit Hill. He took care of himself, jogging regularly to keep trim, or if the weather was bad, jumping rope in his living room. He could have been quite a catch. But though the bait was out for Hal, and had been for some time, he refused to nibble. He and Judy had been very friendly with Rabbi Sam and Sara. And

13

after Judy died, Hal grew even closer to the Weintraubs. The rabbi's children knew him as Uncle Hal and were extremely fond of him. And Sara always had reserved a special feeling for him.

"Hal has the floor." Don knew he could count on Hal to set the stage for discussion.

Hal Kaplan rose, an aura of success about him. "There are many weighty problems facing us," he said in a slow, deliberate voice. "The holidays, plans for the year, a new rabbi. But not least of all . . . our responsibility toward Sara and the children. I, personally, will always cherish Sam's friendship. He and Sara helped me more than I can tell you, when Judy passed away. So there are these two matters that need our immediate attention. We should discuss ways of helping Sara and reach some decision at this meeting. As for a new rabbi, we need to write to the Rabbinical Conference of America and their Pulpit Commission for a list of available rabbis. We must insist, in this letter, that they act as promptly as possible."

The recording secretary had his hand up. After Don recognized him, Stuart said, "Excuse me, Harold, but I was just wondering why we should send a letter, the mails being what they are? You're in New York, so why don't you call them from your office? I'm sure they know who you are."

Hal Kaplan nodded. "All right, I'll call them. But I need instructions from this body. For example, how much are we going to pay a new rabbi?"

"Pay?" Don said. "There should be no problem on that score. Let me see . . . Rabbi Weintraub's salary was $50,000 a year, plus retirement, his house, insurance, and Blue Cross. If we offered a new man $45,000, we might get someone who could grow with us, like Rabbi Sam, though I know we won't get another Rabbi Sam. How does that sound?"

"Wait a minute," called out Jacob Abrams, an aging man with an Eastern European accent. He was the wealthiest member of the congregation, and a survivor of Dachau.

"Yes, Jack. I recognize you." Don said.

"My point is this," said Abrams, rising. "If we offer a new rabbi, a young man, I mean, $45,000, how much will we have left for Sara and the children? Five thousand? That's *bupkes*. Do you men have any idea what it costs to run a house nowadays? I'm sorry," he retreated. "Of course you do."

"Then what do you propose?" the president demanded.

Arnold Peskin, owner of the drive-in on Oak Road, secured the floor. "I propose we start this new man with a smaller salary . . . or we'll have to raise the budget . . . and the dues."

"Raise the dues?" The first part of the statement was lost in the shouting reaction.

"What are you talking about?"

"The dues were raised six months ago!"

Don banged the gavel. "Order, please."

Peskin continued. "I object to raising the budget or the dues," he said. "We raise dues every year. If we raise them any higher we'll put ourselves out of business. Our dues are already higher than any other synagogue on the Island. If we call for another raise, members will drop out left and right. They can get it cheaper elsewhere. People will shop for synagogues, let's not kid ourselves. We all know they're breaking ground over at Four Corners for a new temple, with an indoor Olympic pool. And they're building squash and racquetball courts too. Go compete with that! Remember, we don't have Rabbi Sam to draw them."

"Arnold is right!"

"That's the way it is!"

Harry Servell, who owned one of the largest automobile agencies in town, raised his hand. "This is not a simple matter," he said. "As I see it, we have very little choice. If we don't get a good man, we'll lose members. We've built up a reputation on the Island and the only way to mantain it is to get a top man. So I suggest we authorize Harold to tell the Pulpit Commission of the R.C. that we are ready with an offer of forty-five thousand as a start."

"What about Sara?" Don put in. "I'm for giving her everything we can. By that I mean the rabbi's salary for a year or two, till she gets on her feet. Maybe even let her keep the house. We just can't ignore her, wash our hands of her. Not after what Rabbi Sam meant to us."

Jacob Abrams said, "I move we give Sara the rabbi's salary for the next year."

"What? The whole thing?" a member sitting in the rear demanded. "That means at least an extra twenty thousand to be raised! The budget's passed already. How are we going to change it? We don't have a contingency fund. You're out of your mind!"

"We'll get the money, somehow," responded Alan Steinberg, an accountant. "We'll have a few special fund-raising affairs, maybe a little bingo or a Las Vegas night, a Purim Carnival, a raffle, you know. If we tell people why we're doing it, they'll come across. I have faith in our members."

"Let's get back to finding us a new rabbi," a voice was heard from the rear of the lounge.

Don banged his gavel. He was perspiring heavily, and he reached for a handkerchief to mop his brow. "Now wait a minute. Let's do this thing in order. I'd like a little order, if you don't mind. We have two problems to solve. Let's take them up one at a time. First, the question of Sara. We have a motion on the floor. All in favor of the motion. . . ."

"Read the motion first," Robert Smiler, the caterer, demanded. "I like to know what I'm voting for."

Don turned to Stuart. "Read the motion, Stu."

The secretary read: "Jacob Abrams moved that we give the rabbi's wife his whole salary for the next year."

"Any seconds?"

Someone said, "Second."

"Any discussion?" Don said. "Anybody have anything to say? Say it now. Don't keep quiet and go out of the meeting to complain later. That's one thing I don't like and you know it."

"Question, call the question."

"All right," Don said, annoyed. "Take it easy. You'll live longer. All those in favor of the question that we give Sara Rabbi

16

Sam's salary for the next year signify by raising your right hand."

He looked over the heads of the board members anxiously.

A number of hands went up.

"All those opposed?"

Only two hands were raised in opposition. "The motion is carried," Don said, relieved. "Now let's turn to the next question. Hal made a suggestion—I think it's a good one—that we contact the Rabbinical Conference tomorrow morning about a rabbi. What'll we offer for salary? We want a good man and we'll have to pay! Any bright ideas?"

"We have no choice," Abrams declared. "To get a good man, we have to offer forty-five thousand as a start. I so move."

"Any second?"

"Second."

"Any discussions?" Don asked, mopping his large creased forehead.

Several hands shot up. Gil Cowen, who ran the Luscious Bakery on Rice Street declared, "It appears now we'll have an outlay of at least $95,000 a year, fifty for Sara and forty-five for a new rabbi! Now I see the justice of this, but from the practical viewpoint . . . I mean how the heck will we raise it? I mean, be reasonable."

"Gil is right!" said several men in unison.

Don grimaced. "Can't somebody get hold of the custodian and get the air conditioner fixed? It's so hot, I can't think straight."

"Ninety-five thousand is beyond our means," Gil maintained.

"Maybe we'll only have to do it for one year," Don pleaded. "How about it?" He gazed at the perspiring faces of his colleagues, searching their eyes for a clue. "Look here," he said, a note of pleading in his voice. "We Jews are known as good givers; we have the highest reputation where giving is concerned."

"That's all well and good," Gil Cowen said, "but you can't take water from a stone."

17

"Who wants the floor?" Don asked, barely able to conceal a note of reproach in his voice. There was a long pause, then Sidney Weinstein asked to speak. In his middle thirties, his hair contoured conservatively, and eyes actively eager, the youngest member of the board, Sidney was the owner of a successful advertising agency. He was the temple's man in the gray flannel suit. He wrote poetry during his spare time and was rumored to have a manuscript of a novel in his drawer at home, detailing the seamier side of small-town life. "I've got it!" Sidney cried, as though he'd conceived a brilliant notion for an ad.

"Let's hear," Don said hopefully.

Sidney's eyelids fluttered as he tried to put the idea into words.

"Why engage a rabbi and pay him forty-five thousand, assuming you can get somebody for that kind of money, and then pay Sara? The temple would go broke for sure." His voice became surer, more confident. Deliberate. "Why doesn't this congregation join the twentieth century, get with it . . . and ask Sara to become our rabbi? Save yourself a pile and at the same time put Temple Shalom on the map . . . we'll get a million dollars worth of publicity. . . ."

Sidney said a good deal more, but his words were drowned out by a chorus of objections. The voices rose to a near frenzy. There was a great deal of talking, though no one was really listening. "You're crazy," someone shouted.

"Are you out of your mind?" another cried.

"What the hell's going on here?" a third groaned. "What's this synagogue coming to?"

Don rose, waved the gavel, and called for order. It took a full five minutes before he regained control. In the meantime, his gavel banged the table viciously.

Dr. Phil Elkind, the gynecologist, was on his feet. "It's true we live in a new age," he began. "And women's lib is here to stay, for a while anyway. Now I'm not opposed to women's lib. Women are my best customers, as you all know." He paused for an appreciative chuckle that failed to materialize. "But as for

Sara being our rabbi—the only question in my mind is, is she *qualified?* Sidney dangles the million dollars' worth of publicity before our eyes as though that were the most important thing to consider. We need a *rabbi*, not sensations! Sara is a nice person, an attractive woman. I might say she's warm and loving. I have no criticism of Sara as a human being. But what do we really know about her? We hear that she's a great speaker from everywhere except Wilmette. Have you ever heard her? Any of you? Is she qualified? That's the question bothering me."

Sidney was on his feet, crying, "I object! We do know about her. You have all gotten reports from relatives and friends on how she speaks. 'She's great' is what I always hear. Personally, the more I think of it, she'll make a very good rabbi. Who knows? Maybe another Sam. She knows Hebrew, her father was a rabbi, and so was her grandfather. She studied the Talmud, was president of the Sisterhood three times and helped Rabbi Sam write some of his best sermons. She's sincere. She's warm. She has a lot going for her. She *relates* well to people. She's written books. She's not bad looking either. The Lutherans and Episcopalians have ordained woman ministers, and the Methodists are going ahead with it too. The Catholic Church isn't ready yet, but some nuns went to Italy to pressure the Pope. See how nuns dress today? It'll happen. The Reform people just recently ordained another woman rabbi. So why shouldn't the Conservative branch of Judaism be innovative? I want to say this—for those of you who are still clinging to the shreds of your male superiority. Bear this in mind—Golda Meir was a woman!"

There was a scattering of applause when Golda was mentioned, but it was apparent that most of those present were not impressed.

"I just can't see it," Jack Richards exploded. His neck bulged red. "Women? On the pulpit? Telling *me* what to do? Ethics and all that. Frankly, I'll be thinking of something else if I see a woman on the pulpit. Dammit, the Orthodox are right. I won't have my mind on prayer."

Stan Stein supported the attack. "I've never heard anything like it. *Anywhere.* I mean, boy, the world is going crazy with this feminism crap!"

"Yeah, where'll it stop?"

"It's against Jewish law," fumed Lester Rosenberg, angrily. He was considered the most knowledgeable and the most observant of the board members. He attended minyan every morning, helped with coffee and the thousand-and-one chores afterwards. He was the closest thing to a sexton. "Never heard of it," he repeated his reaction. "Traditionally, women are not permitted with men . . . at all!"

"But, we've broken with that, haven't we? Women *do* sit with men. So what the hell's the difference?"

"I just don't know," Rosenberg shook his head. He shrugged his shoulders and his eyes popped. "I can't believe what I'm hearing. My God, what will you think of next?"

"The hell you don't know, Rosenberg," Alfred Harris simply couldn't contain himself. "Hell, no. I'm against it. I'll be damned if I can see a goddam woman standing at the funeral chapel delivering a eulogy. I'm not letting any woman Bar Mitzvah my son. And if Helen has a little boy, this . . . this . . . woman rabbi will officiate at the *bris? She'll bris* my grandson? Hold my grandson's . . . that's where sexual abuse starts from. Hell, no, I say. My God! My father, *olov hasholom,* who founded this synagogue, will turn over in his grave. What the hell's this world coming to?" He sank in his chair.

Don shouted, "Hey, watch your language. Where do you think you are?" His hand hurt from pounding the gavel.

Disregarding Don's reprimand, Rosenberg was back on his feet.

"How about Jewish law? The Torah. It's against Jewish law!"

"Where does it say that?" Sidney Weinstein, the proponent, challenged. "Where does it say that women can't be rabbis? Nowhere! Nowhere!" he emphasized and looked around at each member. "It doesn't say it, *anywhere!*"

"I don't know exactly," Rosenberg answered, "but it does say. Check it out."

"Come on," Don pounded vehemently, "cut it out. Let's talk like *menschen*. We're all here for one purpose. The temple. Cool down." He was breathing heavily and it was obvious that every board member was worked up.

"How do you know she'd even accept?" Phil Elkind demanded, changing the subject. "Hal, you're a friend of the family, what's your opinion?"

"My opinion?" Hal questioned, rising and turning to face the men in the back rows. His controlled response calmed the meeting. "Frankly, the notion of Sara carrying on Rabbi Sam's work intrigues me. I'm sure she's qualified. She's dynamic. But there are other questions. Like stamina. The job of a rabbi is a killing one. And Sara, if she's offered the position and accepts, *will* give herself. It's in her nature. But she has two children to raise. We all know she's done a magnificent job in that sector, but can she be a good rabbi and a good mother at the same time? Isn't it asking too much of a human being?"

"Then in your opinion, Hal, she will not accept?"

"Your guess is as good as mine," Hal replied.

"She *should* be asked!" Sidney Weinstein declared, jumping to his feet, not bothering to ask Don for the floor. "What have we got to lose? Our male superiority? I say give Sara a chance and she'll surprise us all, everyone! Remember Rabbi Sam teaching us about Jewish women? About Sarah, Rebecca, Henrietta Szold, Beruria? They were great women. They weren't called rabbis, but if they'd had the title then, they'd surely have been addressed as rabbi. So let's get with it! As for the practical aspect of it, we'll save ourselves a nice piece of cash."

The debate resumed. "Have a heart," Don pleaded. "We'll all roast unless somebody calls for the question."

"What are we voting on?"

"Whether we should ask Sara if she wants to be our rabbi," Don said.

"I move instead that we empower Hal to get in touch with the R.C. and ask them to recommend a rabbi, a male, if you please," Alan Steinberg said.

Sidney Weinstein was on his feet. "An amendment to the motion . . ."

"State your amendment, Sid."

"That we get in touch with Sara and sound her out regarding being our rabbi. It is exploratory, you understand. If she refuses, we'll be in the clear. It will have been a magnificent gesture on our part, a progressive move of the first importance. The papers will pick it up right away, I guarantee you that."

"Any debate on the amendment?" Don asked.

The debate was brief and acrimonious. But Sidney Weinstein's amendment carried by a close vote.

Customarily, after a board meeting, the men piled into Biggie's for a cup of coffee or an ice cream soda. But tonight they scattered as they left, as though they'd had their fill of one another.

Chapter Three

DON SAT IN THE WEINTRAUB LIVING ROOM. The sun shone through the French windows. In the past, he'd derived a great deal of satisfaction sitting in this book-cluttered, cheerful room. He had expected, before entering, that he would find it funereal and empty. But Sara had greeted him with a smile and offered her cheek, which he kissed. Perhaps, he thought, his task would not be so difficult after all. "We had a meeting last night," he said, without any preliminaries, "and we came to some decisions."

"Oh, I'm glad, Don," Sara said, sitting down on the sofa. She wore a light purple dress, a good deal longer than the length she had seemed to favor when Rabbi Sam was alive. Her eyes were eager and her warm smile disarming and friendly.

Don gathered his courage. "Well, first, for the time being, until something else turns up, the board voted to pay you Rabbi Sam's salary."

"I appreciate that more than I can tell you Don." Tears welled up in Sara's eyes at the offer. "But I must decline," she replied.

"What are you talking about?" Don interrupted, flushing, his voice rising. "I know Sam didn't have a whole lot of savings in the bank. The few stocks he had don't amount to much. His insurance policy, I know what it adds up to. So what do you mean you *decline*? You *can't* decline. You need money to tide you over. Later on, you'll see."

"The temple can't afford to support us . . . and a new rabbi," Sara said calmly. "I was thinking, instead, of taking the children and going to live in the city."

"What are you saying?" Don demanded. "With the New York City crime rate? Tell me, do you want to go, really?"

"It's not a question of wanting to, Don. Wilmette is where Sam and I made our lives. This is the place our children love. But we're adaptable, we'll. . . ."

"Out of the question!" Don cried, waving his huge arms. He looked anguished.

"I can type. I can get a job teaching Hebrew; I can go on the lecture circuit. I've done that. Maybe I can pick up the kids and go live in Israel altogether. You know how often Sam and I argued that to live a *totally* Jewish life, you have to go to Israel."

"And get killed by some fanatic Arab? No way. We need you here in Wilmette, Sara. . . . But I'm not finished."

He shifted in the chair, tugged at his tie, straightened it unconsciously, adjusted it again, pulling his neck over the collar. He wondered how to approach the next point. Should have asked Hal to do it, he thought. But he was stuck with the job of telling her and he meant to do it. "We talked about the High Holy Days and the need to get a rabbi," Don said. "So we authorized Hal to get in touch with the Pulpit Office of the R.C. about it. He's supposed to see them today."

"Well, I'm glad," Sara said with a nod. "If I'm here I'll help the new rabbi as much as I can. I mean, if he *wants* help."

"What do you mean if he wants?"

"Some men resent when a woman offers to help. They're intimidated. They don't like to think a woman knows something they don't. So I don't intend to stick my two cents in unless I'm asked."

24

"You'll be asked," Don replied. "You can help a whole lot, Sara. Being married to Rabbi Sam so many years, you learned plenty from him. It's no big secret that you wrote some of his best sermons. We know, Sara. We know more than you think."

"You have no proof of that, Don," Sara protested smartly, a smile emerging. "The most I ever did for Sam was type his sermons."

"Don't be so modest, Sara," Don countered with a smile. "Your modesty is becoming, but it isn't true. But that's neither here nor there. The holidays are coming, and we don't have a rabbi. In other words, we're stuck."

"But Hal is going to ask for one. . . ."

"Asking and getting, as you well know, are not the same, Sara. The chances of having a rabbi for the holidays are slim. I mean, a good rabbi. Most of the top men are grabbed up in spring."

Sara nodded thoughtfully. "I thought of it myself, last night, and it made me sick. Why, it's inconceivable not to have a rabbi for Rosh Hashanah and Yom Kippur. Oh, Sam, Sam . . . but never mind." She gazed at Don, smiled faintly and said: "As you were saying, Don. . . ."

"We may need you to step into the breach, Sara," Don said. "Sam always said you'd make a good rabbi. Some of us have said it often, especially Hal."

Sara's thoughts froze.

What did they really know? Sara wondered. She had grown up in an environment where study was intense; she had attended religious school four hours per day, six days a week. And as she had seen teenage boys accorded primacy in synagogue and home, she had felt a resentment that snowballed into a driving rebellion against the secondary role of women. She had been a challenging, demanding firebrand, occasionally even railing at the injustice with her father. "That's the law, Sara," he always shrugged.

"We've got to change it, change the whole damn thing," she once yelled. Her father slapped her, not for her thinking, but for the use of the word "damn." "Not in my house," he fumed, a rare response from such a gentle man.

"Some day," she stormed, wanting the last say. "Some day, I'll be a rabbi. You just wait. I'll show them."

Her father was amused. "When the Messiah comes, you'll be a rabbi," he chided.

Undaunted, she developed her secret longing, an unheard of, wild idea in the '50s. Now, women's roles had changed, but she recalled the hotbloodedness of earlier days and the long cherished but diverted dream.

It had been natural for her to marry a rabbi. And through the years, she had lived the role vicariously by helping, guiding, and assisting in sermons. But for herself the urge had been suppressed. She loved being a mother and wife. But as the children grew up, she felt a growing compulsion to express both areas of her life. She would accept engagements to speak, arrange for the children's care, and then make sure she was home for the Sabbath. She worked hard in each role, aware of tensions within her, tilting at times one way and other times the other way. Outwardly she was a happy woman. Inwardly she was not completely fulfilled.

Now with Sam dead she was no longer a rabbi's wife. She was no longer a wife. She was now only a mother . . . and a widow absorbed in empty thoughts.

"What's the matter?" Don pressed. "You changed colors!"

His words had struck a raw nerve. At the possible mention of her becoming a rabbi, she had gone hot and cold all over. "No, I'm fine. Just fine," she answered, struggling to regain composure. She suddenly wished Don would leave. She had to think. The suggestion pained, yet excited her. *I have my chance now!* Almost immediately the betraying guilt invaded again: *Am I glad Sam died?*

She tried desperately to expunge the thought, sure that Don sensed something amiss. But the thought kept intruding.

Don studied her intently. "Something's wrong, Sara. Your eyes are glazed . . . you're not here!"

"What? Of course I am. I'm grateful to you. I can't believe how wonderful the people are."

"I'm not joking. We had this meeting last night and the board voted to ask you to. . . ."

"To what?" She leaned forward eagerly, hoping her anxiety didn't show.

"To ask you to help us out . . . to be our rabbi, for the time being. If you like, to stay on, if. . . ."

"I don't believe it," Sara stammered defensively. "W-why, the whole thing is absurd. Me? A rabbi! Why, I never heard such a fantastic notion in my life!" Suddenly tears were in her eyes and she was laughing!

"Sara, it's not a joke. We voted to ask you."

"Well, it's very kind of you, but my answer is *no.*" She herself didn't understand the refusal.

"Why not?" Don demanded. "Your husband was a rabbi, your father was a rabbi, your grandfather. You know ritual, you know the Talmud, the Bible, you know Hebrew."

"I know all that," Sara conceded, "but to get up in front of a congregation . . . as a rabbi. It's *chutzpah* . . . to think I could take Sam's place. Don, to be a rabbi is a calling only for the great and the gifted, for men like Sam, like my father. I look upon the rabbinate as the noblest of callings."

"Are you hesitating because you're a woman?" Don asked.

"No, Don. I do sometimes think women should be given a chance to be rabbis. Some women I've known would make really great rabbis. But I'm . . . I'm not qualified. And I'm not ordained. And I have two children to take care of."

"We took all these things into consideration, Sara. I still think we are doing the right thing in asking you. Why don't you talk to the children about it? Talk to Hal. What I mean is . . . don't give us an answer now. Think about it. Think of what Rabbi Sam would want you to do. Think of the congregation. Sleep on it."

27

"Thank you, Don." She rose and held out her hand, then changed her mind and kissed him on the cheek. "And thank the board. I really do appreciate it. It's the most flattering gesture they could make . . . I don't know of anything they could have done to flatter me more. But . . . it strikes me funny. Me take Sam's place? And by the way, have you thought what the Pulpit Commission and the Seminary will say about this?"

"We've delegated Hal to sound them out. He's seeing them today, as I said."

"I'm sure you'll get a resounding *no*. And that should solve this problem for all of us. Goodbye, Don, and thanks again."

When Don left, Sara's turmoil returned viciously, tumultuously. The incredible truth had emerged, and she could look at her secret. The nerve had been pricked and now the excitement and depression, the exultation and thrill, climbed and plummeted like a roller coaster.

Opportunity! So soon? Am I glad he died? Now I have my chance. No, it can't be. I *loved* Sam. I didn't want him to die. It isn't worth it. But it *is worth it. It isn't. It is.*

She tried to exorcise the thought. And—but he's *dead.* That's a fact. I'll take it from here. I'll start again. I *will* be a rabbi. Now it *can* happen. It's what I've always wanted—to be fulfilled. God certainly works in mysterious ways. The children will learn. The community will accept me. I'll work and I'll prepare and I'll study. My opportunity has come! But how do I do it without giving away, without revealing this unfulfilled quest?

After dinner, Sara asked her children to come into the living room. "There's something I want to discuss with you," she said. The two looked at each other quizzically. "What's the matter, Mom?" Carol asked. "What's up?" Simon repeated.

When they were seated on the couch, Sara carefully weighed her words. The only time she was ever really cautious was when she discussed Carol's and Simon's roles as rabbi's children. In other areas, she was always free and easy.

As rabbi's children they *were* different. People watched them. The sons and daughters of rabbis and ministers were a breed apart, not allowed the privileges of other children. Though Rabbi Weintraub knew that the children would be violating certain traditional laws, he had not wanted to make his children oppressively different from others. They were given a larger measure of freedom than the Orthodox rabbi allowed his children. Yet they were still expected by others to be more religious, observant, honest, moral, kind, and better. Like angels. They were always to be careful. While some inhibiting resulted, Sara's children really did not mind too much. There were compensations. Sara was aware of a recent novel about a rabbi's daughter and her retaliatory disposition to sex. She had wondered why the author had to select a rabbi's child as the protagonist, until she rationalized that people were insatiably curious about rabbis and their families. This was one kind of book, she had said to her husband, that encourages rabbis' children to flee Judaism and seek anonymity as people, rather than as congregational stamps.

She began to speak. "When Dad passed away, we were all shaken and hurt, but you helped me over this hurdle. It wasn't easy, you know. Dad made all the money for us, helped us with our home and everything. Now that he's gone, it's my job to make a living and take care of you. Women should always be prepared, but all I can do is teach Hebrew and lecture. That's not enough. I haven't thought the whole thing through yet. It's too soon. But I do know that the temple has to do something. The people need a rabbi and I know it's hard to picture another rabbi on the pulpit, taking Dad's place. Hard for you and hard for me to be in the congregation and watch someone else take over what Dad built. No, I have to be realistic about it so I suggested to Mr. Shapiro that he call a meeting of the board and decide what to do about a new rabbi. The High Holy Days will be here in less than two months and it all takes time, meetings and trial sermons, and so on. I told Mr. Shapiro not to worry about us, but to take some action."

The children were trying hard to understand. Even in their apparent maturity, they found Sara's words incomprehensible.

"Mr. Shapiro did call a meeting. It was held last night. He came to see me this afternoon. He told me that the board had talked about the whole matter very seriously last night and decided that they were going to make some inquiries of the Rabbinical Conference, Dad's organization. They also decided something else, kids, which I think is so wonderful, and shows the kind of people they are." Sara paused, took a deep breath. "They decided that we don't have to worry about money for a while. I think it's a great tribute to Dad, don't you?"

Sara reached for a handkerchief and blew her nose, and dried her tears.

"And one more thing. Someone came up with the idea, and this is what I want to tell you, too, that," she hesitated . . . "the temple talked about asking me to be their rabbi."

She stopped. Sympathetic and appreciative, the children blinked their eyes and looked at each other.

"*You*, Mother?"

"You, a woman-rabbi?"

Sara laughed. "I know it sounds foolish. But I wanted to tell you because it's all over town. Or will be soon. Your friends will certainly tease you. Mr. Shapiro told me that Uncle Hal would be in New York today and that he'd call the R.C. to talk to them about it, just to see how they respond to the idea. It may be crazy, I'll admit, but who knows. . . ." She shrugged. Her thoughts strayed.

"What will I call you?" Simon asked. "Mother-rabbi?" He laughed out loud and they all laughed.

"What did you call Daddy, Daddy-rabbi, or Father-rabbi? No, you'll call me *Mother*."

"Oh, boy, wait until the girls hear about this," chimed Carol. "A woman rabbi. They'll think it's real neat."

"Say, my mother, a rabbi?" Simon wondered. His eyes opened wide. He wasn't sure.

30

Sara tried sleeping. But her thoughts raged on. She was back
in the kitchen. Could they be serious, these men on the board?
They were mad. Whose bright idea had it been? She suspected
it was Sidney Weinstein's. A typical ad man's notion! She did
not judge him harshly. She'd heard it said that he was probably
the only member of the temple who helped his wife do the
dishes after supper. But Sidney—if that was who it was—had
only made the suggestion. The entire board voted and approved. What had been their motive? Suddenly she had it, *to
save money*. Kill two birds with one stone; since they would
pay her Sam's salary, they might as well have her as a rabbi too.
Cheaper, more practical, novel. Then she grew furious,
seething. "Bastards," she exploded. Bathed in perspiration, she
instantly regretted the sound of the word. She was not given to
swearing. But this was different, she assuaged herself. Yet, the
other side of the coin revealed itself—opportunity! It suddenly
struck her that the thing to do was to take the children and run
away from Wilmette. She shook her head furiously. What's the
difference! She put an empty cup in the sink, rinsed it, and
went upstairs to her bedroom.

The room was simple but furnished with taste. Utilitarian, no
frills, like the rest of the house. She turned out the light for the
third time. This time she would sleep. But almost as soon as she
pulled the sheet to her chin, Sara knew she would not sleep.
"Sam, what should I do?" She muttered. She was going out of
her mind. Talking with the dead? What did everyone want of
her? Hadn't she served them loyally for fifteen years, given the
congregation her full measure of devotion, as the saying went?
"Help me, Sam. . . ." She opened her eyes and stared into the
dark. Had it not been for the proximity of the High Holy Days,
they wouldn't have asked her. A portion of her ego was bruised.
She recalled how every year they—she and Sam, of course—
prepared meticulously for the Holy Days. She knew the ritual as
well as Sam. So why was she frightened now? Why the equiv-
ocation? Wasn't half the battle won? But knowing and *doing*

31

were two different things. How would she look standing on the pulpit, the lady rabbi?

But she reflected further. "I think you should know about me," she had said to Sam, "all my life I've wanted to serve. Maybe that's one reason, only one, I might say, but an important one, why I married you, a rabbi." This confession she'd made on their honeymoon, in the Catskills. At one time, just out of college, she'd planned on becoming a nurse, going to India. To give herself wholly, completely. Become a Jewish saint. It was part of an age; materialism was denounced, and possessions meant little. Then she'd toyed with the notion of going to a kibbutz in Israel, where she could subsist on little, giving of herself, like Golda Meir. Serving. But was there ever a time more propitious to serve than now? Was the world ever in such dreadful shape? What was happening to the cherished values? "If we could only interest the youth!" Sam had said to her more than once. "This is a golden opportunity, Sara. I believe Judaism can help save what seems irretrievable. Our values, properly presented, are the solution for what ails the world today. We must go to the youth, work against poverty, help stop the wars, speak out for racial equality, save our kids from the cults. The missionaries are going wild. It's big business. There are twenty-five hundred cults in America, seventy of them vying for our Jewish college and high school youth. Stand guard! Watch! Denounce! Give our children the knowledge to confront them. If we only could!" Sara felt bathed in perspiration.

Some of the causes that Sam espoused proved unpopular among a few of the wealthier members of the temple, but the rightness of his cause was incontrovertible, his success impressive. Had Sam lived. . . . She sat up, turned on the light. You owe it to Sam, the thought struck her. Then she chuckled out loud, struck by the absurdity of the notion. Did we have a deal, Sam? You die, leave me, and then say I owe it to you? No, if I do, it's not because of you. It's because of me. Me! Me! Do you hear? She willed the tormenting thoughts out of her mind.

Could she handle some of the functions of a rabbi—counseling, funerals, weddings, Torah readings? Could she take part in all the ceremonies of a male rabbi—circumcision and *Pidyon Haben?** Would the woman in her have to be suppressed? Could she, as rabbi, go swimming wearing a bikini? She could hear it all in the whispered dark. "Look at the rabbi in the bikini!" or, "She's hot stuff, that rabbi of ours." She was rather pleased with her body and had enjoyed exposing it to the sun. And to Sam. She always relished Sam's enjoyment of the exposure. He'd smile. He was, after all, *bosor vodom,*a human being. In Judaism, the flesh is a blessing. Nor did she consider it a sin if men observed and admired her. God created beauty. She felt blessed. Would she have to drape her body if she became a rabbi? What kind of swim suit would she finally select? Problems large and petty. "What am I going to do?" she pleaded out loud. A thought struck her. The notion that Hal might come back with a rabbi made her feel momentarily as though a burden had been lifted! The decision was out of her hands. Was she sorry now? She was beginning to enjoy the challenging idea. "I hope he fails," she heard herself say.

She parted the drapes and raised the blinds. It was almost dawn.

*Redemption of the First Born

Chapter Four

RABBI MALCOLM FRIEDMAN, secretary of the Rabbinical Conference and head of job placement, was adept at handling community representatives who besieged his office, seeking rabbis. Each community expected and demanded the best, most eloquent, handsomest man. A rabbi was supposed to be experienced in every phase of synagogue life, a brilliant and provocative orator, a fund raiser, educator, and representative to the non-Jewish community.

Sitting in Rabbi Friedman's office now, Harold Kaplan was impressive, with the look of a serious executive stamped on his face. He seemed relaxed, which would make it easier for Friedman to deal and reason with him.

"As you were saying about Rabbi Weintraub's death, Mr. Kaplan. It was a great loss to all of us. We have made a notation of this tragedy. Our Committee on Tributes has arranged an appropriate memorial at the next Rabbinical Conference in November."

"I'm pleased to hear that, sir," Kaplan said. "I'll convey this information to Sara Weintraub, whom I believe you know." He

34

paused, took note of Rabbi Friedman's affirmative nod and went on. "Well, Rabbi, as to my reason for being here, our board of governors met last night in emergency session to discuss the urgent problems arising from Rabbi Weintraub's death. One decision reached, which I would like to mention in passing, was to give Mrs. Weintraub a year's salary. Rabbi Sam received approximately fifty thousand annually."

Rabbi Friedman nodded approval. "You're very considerate, Mr. Kaplan. Please tell the people on your board that this is most unusual. Communities, by and large, take a limited interest in the rabbi's family. People forget, you know."

"That's the kind of temple we have, Rabbi Friedman," Hal declared. "And that's why we're looking for a good man, one who will grow with us. I mean, sir, a top man."

Rabbi Friedman regarded his visitor with an amused air, his earlier impatience tugging at him. He had heard it all before. As though rabbis could be turned out a dime a dozen. Out loud he said, "Of course. Unquestionably."

"You think you can get us one, sir? We're willing to start at forty-five thousand."

"Generous of you, though not munificent, what with inflation and things. I assume you need a rabbi for the holidays?"

"Yes," Hal declared, a note of urgency in his voice. "You see, Rabbi Weintraub made rather an elaborate thing of the High Holy Days and . . ."

"But the High Holy Days are almost upon us, Mr. Kaplan," Rabbi Friedman protested mildly. "You want a top man and you want him pronto. An impossible order. Will you consider a stop-gap arrangement, someone for the holidays, if a rabbi can be found? It's a little late."

"On that score," Hal replied, "talking about stop-gap arrangements, which may in the end be our only solution, the board considered the notion of Sara Weintraub to . . . eh . . . officiate . . . be our rabbi . . . for the High Holy Days and maybe, if it works out . . ."

"Really?" Rabbi Friedman said, unable to conceal his surprise. He was prepared for all sorts of fantastic notions, but this was the most novel of all. "If anything, you people in Temple Shalom are most innovative."

"What is so innovative, Rabbi? The Reform movement has been doing it for years. So have the Reconstructionists."

"Let me remind you that we are not Reform, Mr. Kaplan, not by a long shot. We're Conservative and proud of it. Our emphasis is on tradition. Jewish law is our basis; we live by it. All our rabbis, for ordination, must study at the Seminary. The Seminary has very exacting requirements for admission. We're a million miles away from it so far as Mrs. Weintraub is concerned."

"I understand that, Rabbi," Hal said, trying to mollify Friedman. "It's just that here we have this emergency and Sara Weintraub is available. In the opinion of the board she is highly qualified. She always worked very closely with Rabbi Sam and even helped write some of his best sermons. She's a popular lecturer everywhere except in Wilmette, because she refused to compete with her husband. Moreover, she comes from a rabbinical family: her father, grandfather. Of course, if you come up with a few good recommendations, I have a feeling the board might give up the notion of Sara as a rabbi."

"Excuse me, Mr. Kaplan," Rabbi Friedman said, calling his secretary. "Florence, please bring me the dossier on Rabbi Sam Weintraub." When the dossier was brought, Rabbi Friedman scanned its three pages, his brow creased as though he found the whole process painful. The information he read, recorded almost fifteen years ago and updated only recently, revealed that Sara Weintraub had grown up in Chicago, where her father had been a rabbi. It said that she possessed a fine voice and had sung solo in the high school glee club. She had attended Herzlia and the Beth Abraham schools. Her awards included honors in Bible and history. Interested in Talmudic literature, she had written an essay on the Prayer Book when barely twenty. "H'mmm," Rabbi Friedman grunted with approval. "Commendable Jewish background, solid," he said out loud.

"Let me tell you about this Sara Weintraub," Hal said, sensing a breakthrough. "She's a marvelous person, kind, a heart of gold, very popular, confident and knowledgeable,too."

"I have no doubt, Mr. Kaplan," Rabbi Friedman said, putting away the dossier. "There are many popular and kind individuals. But that does not necessarily qualify them for the rabbinate. A woman rabbi? I don't know. We've never had one. Oh, by the way, is she willing to accept?"

"She owes it to Rabbi Sam to accept," Hal replied.

"But you're not certain."

"Yes, I'm certain, Rabbi. However, if you come up with a suitable choice we don't anticipate any trouble. But we need a rabbi without delay."

Rabbi Friedman rose. "I'm fully apprised now of the urgency of your problem," he said, slightly annoyed at being pressured by this man who was obviously a supersalesman not beyond trying a little arm-twisting. "Perhaps it would be best if I sent you an application. You people at Temple Shalom fill in all the pertinent data and return it to us. Our committee will then evaluate the requirements of your temple and send you a list of men available, at this short notice."

"And, as for Sara Weintraub?" Hal demanded.

"That's kind of a sticky problem," Rabbi Friedman replied. "As I said earlier, the Conservative movement has not confronted the issue officially. My guess is, it isn't ready to confront it. But since one of our synagogues is actively considering it, we owe it to you and to ourselves to discuss the matter. So why don't I explore it with some of our people? I think if we worked this at both ends, we'll come up with a mutually acceptable solution."

"I hope so," Hal said, shaking Rabbi Friedmen's hand and taking his leave.

Rabbi Friedman reached into his drawer and popped an antacid into his mouth.

A woman rabbi? he thought. Reform Judaism leaned to the

left so there was no problem there. Most of the historic laws and traditions were no longer considered relevant to the Reform group. And in Orthodox Judaism, with its traditional separation of the sexes, the problem would simply not come up. But for Conservative Judaism, the middle-of-the-road force in Jewish life, still rooted in tradition and Jewish law, the issue could well demand a major decision. It was going to be a history-making confrontation.

The Executive Committee met at ten o'clock in the morning, as scheduled, in the Seminary, in a large airy room with a long mahogany conference table and confortable leather chairs. Representatives were present from the entire Eastern seaboard. The unusual topic on the agenda had created a flurry of excitement. On the West Coast, a miniature Pulpit Commission stood by in the event consultation was necessary.

You could tell that these men were rabbis. Imposing edges of pomposity touched each. Uplifting in bearing, most had either mustaches or beards in a variety of styles. Their sonorous, deep, animated voices, enunciators all, were further reminders of their profession. The look was there, skull caps of all colors, shapes and textures, some coordinated with suits, some perched precariously on large, hairy heads. Hair was salt-and-peppered, or sometimes totally lacking. A bit pale, some with middle age paunches, it was clear that for the group, exercise was not part of the daily regimen. They were serious, dedicated people, committed to their heritage, from which they derived incredible satisfaction if not wealth. They could jest about some aspects of their religion, but if challenged they rose as a unit in Conservative Judaism's defense.

"Seems everybody's here," Rabbi Friedman said to Rabbi Hoberman, chairman of the committee. "Shouldn't we start?"

Rabbi Stanley Hoberman, a tall stout man with a carefully trimmed, chin-hugging jet-black beard, nodded. He rose and announced to the assembled rabbis, "Gentlemen, I'm impressed by the turnout. Please, let us begin." Rabbi Hoberman quickly filled them in on the details of Hal's meeting with Rabbi Friedman.

"Now the hot potato is in our hands. To be quite frank, the issue poses a very serious problem for us. We have never discussed this thing to any degree; we haven't been forced to do it. But we can't postpone it any longer; we have to arrive at a decision for Rabbi Friedman. Anyone want to begin?"

Rabbi Morris Sohn, spiritual leader of the most prestigious synagogue in Riverdale, was the first to speak. He had an angular face, with grave, deepened lines reflecting middle age. With slow and measured delivery, as though each word had a significance of its own, the rabbi said, "I believe we have to establish first of all that there has never been in Jewish tradition, so far as I know, any decision about whether a woman can or cannot be a rabbi. That's number one. Number two—the notion did not even enter the minds of the sages. They thought of rabbis in a very different context than we do today. Rabbis then were only teachers and interpreters of the law. So women could not have been considered. Women, let's be honest about it, did not distinguish themselves in the academic world. A few, perhaps; but most were busy with home and family. It should also be kept in mind that women had—and from the Orthodox point of view still have—certain . . . eh . . . limitations that hinder them."

Rabbi Sholom Panzer, who at forty was the youngest one present, sought a point of clarification from the previous speaker. "What do you mean *limitations*, Morry?"

Rabbi Sohn gave his younger colleague a tolerant smile. "I had no idea it was necessary for me to spell it out," he said. "We're Conservative, middle-of-the-roaders who, as you well know, don't get involved in questions about menstruation, women's uncleanliness, purification, and all that. It's not that we have ever taken a legal stand on whether the *mikveh* is or is not outmoded. We sort of let the issue fade away, except for converts, you know. Now, whether we should have or shouldn't have—that's another matter; I don't want to get bogged down on it. I'd like to go on."

Rabbi Sholom Panzer asked to be recognized. "I'm for going on," he said. "But I reserve the right to come back to the subject later."

Rabbi Hoberman nodded. Rabbi Sohn continued, "Women were not really involved in communal activities because of this . . . physical disability. Now, this means that we can't find any explicit instruction or guide from our sources on the role of women as rabbis. It doesn't mean that we have nothing to look for in our heritage for guidance. It seems to me we can evaluate our position from sources dealing with women being called to the Torah, giving women an *aliya* in the synagogue. We can use that as a springboard."

Several hands went up, among them Rabbi Panzer's. He looked puzzled. "How does all that help us, Morry?" he demanded.

"Well, I think we can check out the sources," Rabbi Sohn replied patiently. "We've made some studies on that. About six or seven years ago, correct me if I'm wrong, one of our men asked for clarification about calling a woman to the Torah and giving her an honor. The rabbi who sought clarification . . . his name was. . . ."

"Mort Landerman, out in Bay Shore," Rabbi Friedman, who prided himself on his phenomenal memory, said.

"Thanks, Mal," Rabbi Sohn said. "Now, Mort subsequently did a study on the issue and found what I think is related to the problem we're confronting. In fact, it would be a good idea if Rabbi Friedman had his office make some copies of that decision so you each could study it. In fact, I so move." He turned to the presiding rabbi.

Rabbi Hoberman nodded. "Good idea," he said. "Okay if your office mails out the copies for the next meeting?"

"Of course," Rabbi Friedman said, jotting down the instruction, a note of resignation in his voice he could barely conceal.

He remained seated. "Gentlemen, it's all very well to talk about making copies of responsa and planning future meetings to discuss this or that, but what do I do *now*? What should I tell Temple Shalom? The holidays are coming, the temple has no rabbi. They want to put in Sam Weintraub's widow, who, I don't have to tell you, is not ordained. What do I do? I need specifics. I need a yes or a no answer."

"I'm leading up to it," Rabbi Sohn addressed himself to Rabbi Friedman. "Nothing in life is cut and dried. *This* matter certainly is not a simple one. To get back to the subject of . . . eh . . . women. While there must have been some views disfavoring women from being officiants, the rabbis in the Talmud did hold that women *could be called to the Torah to recite the blessings.* It's all there, black on white. However . . ." Rabbi Sohn paused, cleared his throat and let his gaze rest on the room crowded with his colleagues, "the sages set certain limitations, like insisting that women not be summoned from *outside* the sanctuary to recite the blessings, in order to avoid embarrassing the men who were incapable of reciting it themselves. So we can conclude that there were times in Jewish history when women *could be called to recite the blessings.* In fact, nowhere in Jewish law is it stated that a woman *cannot* be a rabbi."

"What you are saying, Morry," Rabbi Hoberman said, "is that the sages were in fact more *liberal* than Orthodox rabbis are today, regarding women, I mean? Do I read you right?"

Rabbi Sohn nodded. "I would say so."

"Then what happened to make the change?"

"Well, there was this passage about not being 'respectful to the community' and some people seized on that and argued that calling women up to the Torah lacked propriety. I don't think dress or modesty had anything to do with it, because the Talmud says specifically that dress does not relate to the issue in any shape or form." The double-entendre brought an amused smile to a number of the rabbis.

Rabbi Joseph Stein from New London, Connecticut, asked for

the floor. A short, corpulent man in his late fifties, he spoke clearly: "With all due respect to Rabbi Sohn, whose legal mind I admire and whose many responsa are models of scholarship, I cannot see that his dissertation is leading us where we want to go. Mal, here, is seeking guidance. But are we helping him? After all, we know that the law states that women cannot be witnesses to legal, *religiously* legal documents, such as a marriage contract, and that they can't blow the *Shofar* on High Holy Days or act as judges. But if there is no need for them to be witnesses, objections fade. Now, what you're doing, Morry, is focusing on one area and suggesting to us that since there was a time women could be called to the Torah, a woman can be a rabbi. I frankly don't see it."

Rabbi Hoberman found it necessary to come to Rabbi Sohn's defense. "Joe, you're not giving Morry a chance to develop his thesis."

"Because, with all due respect, I think he's on the wrong track," Rabbi Stein declared. "If we find that it's okay for Sara Weintraub or *any* woman, one who is qualified, I mean, to be a rabbi, we can find enough sources to justify our stand. I have the feeling that in our Law Committee we're trying to be Reform rabbis through law. Let's lay the issue on the table. This is not a Law Committee; it's an Executive Committee. Are we or aren't we going to recommend Sara Weintraub as a rabbi? Or for membership? Leave the legal aspect of it to the Law Committee."

"Would you care to state an opinion, Joe?" the chairman queried. "On whether we should or shouldn't recommend, I mean?"

Rabbi Stein shrugged, then nodded. "Might be worth a try," he said with a smile. "I find the idea tantalizing. It'd bring down on us the wrath of the Orthodox rabbis and earn us applause from the Reform side. As for ourselves, it might do us good. Some of us men stand to learn a thing or two from women rabbis."

"Gentlemen!" Rabbi Sohn was on his feet. "Gentlemen, if I

agreed to making a decision *first*, and then look for reasons to support it, I would be remiss. This is *not* the way to approach an issue of such importance. Now if the R.C. plans to approach it in this fashion, then I belong with the Orthodox. They, at least, approach it from the point of view of Halakhah. And we're committed to Halakhah as I understand it?"

"I respectfully disagree," Rabbi Stein declared. Stein had the reputation of being a left-winger. "The Orthodox gentlemen are in the same boat we are. It's just that we tend to act quicker than they. Whatever we do, they get around to emulating, eventually. We found a way of getting confirmation in, they did too. We sit together with our women in synagogue. Was this ever discussed? No, it wasn't. Reform started it; we emulated them; now the Orthodox, or many of them, are doing it. And they'll sit in restaurants and eat broiled fish, even on *treife* dishes."

"Again, I say this is all well and good," Rabbi Friedman said, interrupting the previous speaker. "And again, I plead for specifics. I have to be in touch with these people from Wilmette tomorrow. What do I tell them?"

Rabbi Murray Bronstein, tall, red-faced and wearing thick horn-rimmed glasses, who had deemed the meeting important enough to come in all the way from Ithaca, rose. "I don't see how we can give a direct answer in such a short time," he said. "The concept of a woman rabbi is a new and revolutionary one. It takes time to come to a decision. Let's not go out on a limb and make recommendations in any way. Mal is authorized to recommend only men, *ordained* rabbis, who have applied for positions. However—and this is an *out* for us, in view of the fact that every synagogue affiliated with the Federated Synagogues of North America is independent and is never asked to account for its actions except regarding clearly unethical or immoral practices, it can make its own decisions."

Rabbi Bronstein's remarks elicited some scattered applause. "Murray hit the nail on the head," a rabbi at the far end of the table said.

"Of course, if they want to discuss pension with Mal," Rabbi

Bronstein went on, "or disability insurance, you can make it clear that these cover only members of the Rabbinical Conference and this lady is not a member."

"In the meantime," Rabbi Hoberman suggested, "we should ask the R.C. to convene a special session to discuss this case."

"What if Temple Shalom asks us to issue a statement of approval, Stan?" Rabbi Stein asked.

Rabbi Hoberman shook his head. "That's setting policy, and we have no authority to do that. It's the job of the convention."

"We'll sure be spared a lot of headaches if this lady turns down the offer," Rabbi Bronstein observed.

The chairman disagreed. "Whether or not she accepts," he declared, "the question must be raised. If it isn't Sara Weintraub, another woman will come forward. We must be prepared to cope. Our Women's League is beginning to press. Where have you fellows been? The subject is all around us."

The rabbis seemed pleased with the results of the meeting, except Rabbi Friedman, whose task was to get in touch with the people representing Temple Shalom. What was he really going to tell them?

Hal Kaplan began to speak emphatically on the telephone. "You know, of course, why I'm calling so soon, Rabbi Friedman," Hal said. "The board is getting pretty anxious. There are all the holiday preparations to make. Anything to tell me, sir?"

Rabbi Friedman shifted uncomfortably in his vast black leather swivel chair. He turned, gazed briefly at the expanse of Riverside Park, stretching below like a green carpet blackened with dirt, but saw nothing else. He swivelled back to the desk. "I wish I had something *specific* to tell you, Mr. Kaplan. But to be quite frank with you, I haven't. Our Executive Committee met yesterday, but we didn't come up with a definite solution."

"How's that?" Hal demanded.

"We couldn't, Mr. Kaplan. Please understand . . . we're not authorized to *make* policy. And this issue does involve policy."

"And who makes that?" Hal demanded, frowning.

"The Rabbinical Conference. The Executive Committee met and recommended a study of the issue. We always follow that procedure. A committee is then appointed to study and issue a responsum."

"What's that?"

Rabbi Friedman took his time replying. He wondered how it was that Sam Weintraub had not even taught his officers such a basic word. "A responsum means an answer," he finally said. "It's the traditional Jewish method of creating law in our day. Matter of fact, it's been the method for a few hundred years. Someone poses a question, it is studied, in terms of Jewish history, Talmudic literature, codes and all that, and then a decision is reached."

Hal asked warily, "And how long does that take?"

"It all depends on the issue involved. No one can really say. But I know this—a problem such as you posed, which bears on the entire Jewish community, which involves overall policy, will take a little time."

"But, Rabbi, that's precisely what we don't have, *time*. Something has to be done soon."

Rabbi Friedman shrugged. "I can't even guide you today, Mr. Kaplan. Maybe in a few days I can help you out."

"Why not today?" Hal demanded. "Can't you do better than that, Rabbi?"

"If it'll be of any help, Mr. Kaplan, your temple could act as your people see fit."

"What do you mean by that?"

Rabbi Friedman told him how every congregation is empowered to make its own decisions.

"You're saying in effect that Sara Weintraub could be named rabbi by us?"

"Not really. What I *am* saying is that you can make any arrangements you wish."

"Sounds like double talk to me. If we elect Sara and she accepts, will you recognize her as a rabbi? Will she be admitted to the Rabbinical Conference?"

45

"Now wait a minute, Mr. Kaplan," Rabbi Friedman stressed, spreading his palms upward. "One thing at a time. The question you are asking can only be answered by the Law Commission."

"I see," Hal reacted, understanding the tactic. "In the meantime, we can go ahead with Mrs. Weintraub? Or have you a rabbi in mind for us for the holidays?"

"We're looking, Mr. Kaplan."

"But you haven't found any prospects, I assume?"

"Not yet. At any rate, we should have the whole matter cleared up after the holidays. Oh, by the way, has Mrs. Weintraub accepted your board's offer?"

"We don't see how she can turn it down," Hal replied. "She owes it to the temple and to Rabbi Sam to accept. But it won't help matters, Rabbi, if she feels that the Law Committee and the Rabbinical Conference may turn her down in the end."

"It's in God's hands, Mr. Kaplan."

Chapter Five

TEMPLE SHALOM was one of the most impressive synagogues on the East Coast. Built by one of the world's leading synagogue architects, Sanford Raskin, it attracted tourists, Jews and non-Jews alike. A Raskin synagogue possessed a character of its own. Temple Shalom, as most of the others Raskin built, prided itself on its small inconspicuous dome and half-barrelled rotundas over the entrance. Evenly chiseled stony mountain rock gave the exterior a strong-looking character. The sanctuary was large, hewed out of brown wood, exuding warmth. The wood-sculptured Ark stood in the center of the pulpit like a sparkling jewel in an exquisitely wrought crown.

Rabbi Sam had indulged in a walk-in Holy Ark so structured as to contain twelve Torah stalls, on two levels, each housing one scroll, silver ornaments shining through the transparent covers. He had seen such an Ark in a synagogue in Europe and had fallen in love with it. Entering this Torah room gave one a feeling of being surrounded by sanctity.

Six stained-glass windows, rising up thirty-two feet from the floor, told Judaism's story. Rabbi Sam had divided the windows into two categories: concepts and expressions. The concepts dealt with three underlying principles of Judaism: God, Israel, and Torah. The expressions reflected the three roles of the synagogue—House of Worship, House of Assembly, and House of Study. Some had criticized Rabbi Sam for the windows, which, they said, would distract the worshippers; but fears proved unfounded. In fact, many believed the symbols enabled the mind and the spirit to take wing jointly.

The seats were comfortable. Two pulpits graced the *bimah*. A large one, on the left, was for the cantor and for the reading of the Torah. The other pulpit was for the rabbi, the symbol of a lion pressed on it. Four larger leather chairs stood behind each of the pulpits, the rabbi's being the closest to the Ark.

Sara entered the sanctuary on tiptoe, as though she meant not to be caught in the act of visiting. The place had a majesty that sent her pulse racing. She had never ceased marvelling at Sam's calm manner in the sanctuary. She'd never seen him excited; a flush had never risen in his cheeks. But it seemed to her now if ever she had to stand on the pulpit, graced by that gorgeous imposing lion, if she had to face the congregation and speak to them, her words would profane the place. Doubts of her dreams assailed her. Lecturing was one thing; preaching in an official capacity was quite another. It struck her that she could not utter words that would measure up to the imposing aura of the sanctuary. One had to be immensely gifted to hold one's own in this hallowed place. She was small, a pygmy, an interloper. The accident of death had brought her here. They were using her because of Sam's salary . . . the proximity of the High Holy Days, and the temple's inability to secure a new rabbi on short notice. "But why me?" she muttered.

"And God tested Abraham." She remembered the Biblical phrase. She was being tested. But why had she been chosen? By some cosmic design? Would someone explain it to her? She was utterly alone. The lion on the pulpit intimidated her. The Ark, still a mystery, made her tremble. Why are you afraid? she demanded of herself. Hal Kaplan had come back from New

York, discouraged about the slowness with which the Rabbinical Conference was acting on their request. "And it's altogether questionable whether the R.C. will approve our choice," he had said to her. "If they disapprove," she had answered, "I withdraw. I won't oppose them." But now she was sorry she had said it. Why be submissive? Then Hal had brought up the word *autonomy*. Each synagogue was free to make its own decisions. "So why don't you take it, Sara? For the holidays, at least. If you turn us down, we'll have nobody. Besides, it may take months before the R.C. acts on our request. In the meantime, you could prove your mettle. Prove yourself to yourself."

"And God tested Abraham. . . ."

She'd waited, after her initial discussion with the children, to hear their opinions. Carol was mature for almost sixteen, and Simon was only several months away from being Bar Mitzvah. But Simon was a handful since his father had died. He'd been good, cooperative, a fine student in school, excellent in Hebrew, but now he was acting up. She had to be careful about Simon. "Children, they want me to take Daddy's place, as rabbi. Should I do it?"

"Do you want to, Mother?" Carol had asked.

"Yes and no. I'd have to be away on temple matters, at meetings, Bar Mitzvahs, funerals, communal affairs. What'll we do about time together?"

Carol, small-boned but full-bosomed, her long hair tumbling over her shoulders, her face so startlingly her mother's, said, "Don't worry about our time together." A sophomore in high school, an honor student whose interest in the theatre and acting had recently been replaced by a new passion, women's rights, she was eager for her mother to accept the offer. "You take it," she declared, "and we'll manage."

"*How* will you manage?"

"You can be a rabbi and a mother," Carol had said, "just like Daddy was a rabbi and a father. Besides, I like the notion of my mother being the first woman Conservative rabbi. It'll prove women can do what men can. Men have been discriminating against women long enough!"

"Power to the women!" Simon had said.

To the children it seemed a lark, an adventure. Even to Simon. But how long before Simon would begin to give her trouble?

Other worries rose to the surface. If the R.C. approved and if she was ordained as a rabbi . . . would she remarry . . . eventually? The fleeting thought shocked her. Forgetting Sam so quickly? She shook her head as if to erase the thought. Nonetheless, it persisted. Would she remarry—eventually? Another rabbi? Two rabbis in one family again? Would it be a businessman? Ascending the three steps, she was on the *bimah*. Stopping at the side of the rabbi's pulpit, she felt a moment of dizziness. She had stood on the pulpit several times, but never alone, as when she had participated in Carol's Bat Mitzvah and Sisterhood Sabbaths, when she read the prayers in Hebrew. It wasn't the ritual that intimidated her, but doubts about her ability in this new role. Perhaps her Talmudic knowledge was required these days to minister to a congregation? "Talmudic erudition," Sam had said many times, "regrettably is no longer the criterion of a successful rabbinate." Even Orthodox congregations placed little emphasis on Talmudic scholarship. So far as Wilmette's synagogues were concerned, the rabbi as well as the members were concerned with interdating, intermarriage, anti-Semitism, drugs, and fund raising for Israel and local Jewish agencies.

She turned to face the Ark. She walked towards it, aware that her knees were shaking. A woman at the Torah Ark. . . . She was the first at this temple. If she touched it, she feared her flesh would be seared. Fantasy! Memories of her Orthodox father! What if someone came in and caught her? Would she be accused of desecrating the Holy Ark? What nonsense! Why couldn't a woman touch the Ark? Where was it written that a woman couldn't? "Thank you, God, that I was born a man, not a woman. . . ." These lines in the morning service had not been written by God, but by man. Many things needed changing. And she might well be an instrument of change, chosen to serve.

"And God tested Abraham." Men's prejudices die hard. Two days ago, a colleague of Sam's, an Orthodox rabbi, friend over a period of many years, had come to see her. Rabbi David Hollens was one of a new breed of Orthodox rabbis. A different yarmulke to match each outfit—as if *that* was the recognition of modernity. "Sara, there's a rumor about town that your synagogue is considering you as rabbi."

"It's true, David."

"How can it be?"

"I wonder myself. How can it be?"

"You know, of course, that it's against Jewish law."

"No, David, I didn't know. Where does it say?" Sara challenged.

"It doesn't say directly, Sara. But it has been assumed to be against Jewish tradition. And that's good enough. . . ."

"Good enough for whom, and for what, David? The patriarchal society in which we grew up?" she flared.

"No, Sara. What I mean is that women have never been religious leaders among the Jews."

"What about Deborah and Beruria?" she demanded, flushing.

"But there have never been women *rabbis*."

"And before Golda Meir, there had never been a woman prime minister either."

"But you don't have ordination and Gemara. . . ."

"Few Conservative rabbis and no Reform rabbis have traditional ordination."

"What about the Talmud?" he demanded.

"How much do you have to use the Talmud, David? How many people come to you with questions on ritual matters?"

"It's important for a rabbi to know and be prepared for any question that might come up."

"I grant you this."

"And Torah readings? And how about the problem of men-

struating women? They're not allowed to come in contact with
men!"

"That's not fair, David!" Tears pressed against her eyelids. She
had not expected such a relentless attack on the part of a friend.
And only because she was a woman. He knew very well that
Conservative Jews did not accept this principle relating to menstruation. "I'm shocked and puzzled by your attitude, David."

"I owe it to you to be quite frank, Sara. If you take this
position as rabbi, I cannot have any *official* association with
you."

"Oh, I'm sorry. You mean you won't stand within four cubits
of me, like I'm excommunicated."

Hollens disregarded Sara's words. "The Rabbinical Conference will never approve."

"I'm terribly sorry, David."

David's assault had left her defenseless. She had decided after
his visit to call Don Shapiro and Hal Kaplan and plead with
them to let her withdraw. Coming as this assault did, from a
friend, she could well imagine how others in Wilmette felt
about her being offered the position Opposition to her must be
legion. Not a few of those who opposed her must be women,
though men were doubtless most outspoken, as they felt threatened by her invasion of what had always been their private
preserve. Although she had been led to believe that a majority
of the members of Temple Shalom favored her for the post, she
suspected that many who were allegedly for her lay in wait for
her to make the first wrong move before they would pounce
with the cry: "You see! Always knew a woman wasn't up to
doing the job!"

Now she raised her hand and pulled the Ark cover. She
closed her eyes for an instant, as though fearing she would be
blinded by the glorious sight of the twelve scrolls. Her hand felt
heavy. "What have you done?" she thought. She stood petrified,
waiting for some dreadful calamity. But nothing happened. She
opened her eyes and gazed lovingly at the scrolls, each one
ornamented like princesses, possessed of a beauty to blind the

beholder. It appeared to her that they were beckoning. Here in these scrolls, she mused, was the splendid secret of Israel's survival. She felt an overpowering desire to embrace the scrolls and kiss them.

She stepped back exhausted, still facing the Ark; one did not turn one's back on it. Then she sat down in Sam's chair. A sudden peacefulness descended upon her. Affection for the sanctuary, the scrolls, the pulpit, flowed from her heart. She felt like a lover, ready to give herself, to serve. What she lacked in Talmudic knowledge, she could make up in love, in giving herself fully. She owed it to Sam, to the temple, to herself. She could not let them down. What Sam had started so nobly, she must finish, or at least continue. She felt sure she could make some contribution after all.

But in the next moment she was shocked at her audacity, her *chutzpah*. You'll die, she mused, the first time you stand up here and face the congregation, *your* congregation. She rose with a start, aware she'd been too comfortable in Sam's chair. She was assailed by guilt. Her opportunity to prove herself had come only because of his death. "Then what should I do, Sam?" she demanded, hurling her voice at the empty sanctuary. "Forget myself? I have needs too. Tell me . . . guide me. . . . Help me, Sam . . . God. . . ."

A crushing silence descended on the sanctuary. Then words were whispered—austere yet comforting. She wasn't sure if the voice came from within her or from a spirit in the room. "Welcome, we need you. What must be done will be done."

She nodded and repeated in a barely audible voice: "What must be done will be done." She knew her silent gratitude was heard by God and Sam too. Suddenly, she was no longer afraid. Sara left the holy site feeling a sense of exaltation, as if she'd been reborn to a new purpose in life. It was going to be all right.

Chapter Six

SARA FELT COMFORTABLE about becoming a rabbi. Even her children encouraged her. But her confidence as a woman had not surfaced since Sam had died. At least not until she slipped out of her clothes that evening to shower and relax after the experience in the synagogue. Walking to the shower, she caught a glimpse of herself in a full-length mirror. She stopped as she rarely did.

"Me? A rabbi?" she asked herself. She scanned her body and a look of proud confidence stared back. She liked her body. Every part of it. Her full breasts were evenly distributed and her nipples balanced projectingly. She eased one leg over the other, lowered her head, and a furtive, demure, yet seductive glance responded in the mirror. She enjoyed the self-admiration.

"Rabbi? I'm still beautiful!" But would women give her a jealous going-over, ever comparing her to themselves? In her new role how could she express her physical desires? Desire was an easier word than lust. Yearning, sex, had not seriously crossed her mind. It was so soon. But as she saw herself naked, the thought persisted, then moved to sexual fantasies. Recollections of love-making with Sam. Fondling; it was welcome, missed. Sexual yearning begat doubt. Give it up? Caution? How conservative would I have to be? Hide this God-given beautiful body because of people, congregants, jealous women? Every man's visual undressing, lustful gestures, roaming eyes?

Will this body ever be held again, loved, caressed, kissed, desired? Do I really want to give up femininity for a role? Will it be worthwhile in the long run? Will I be able to make love again? Am I binding myself? Don, Hal, and other men's bodies somehow drifted into her thoughts. With them edged a hot tinge of guilt. She renounced the thoughts, then rationally admitted their honesty.

She laughed but with a touch of sadness. Who would really want a woman rabbi as either wife or partner? She bounced the question back and forth in her mind. And why not? Why wouldn't I be wanted or needed? I *am* attractive. Suddenly she blinked. What am I thinking of? God, what am I doing here? Why do I think of Don in bed with Sue, now? And why do I think of Hal, alone, and I'm alone?

She tried to erase the thoughts. But she enjoyed them too much as she surveyed her body. It was a new experience. She had kept slim. Flowing dark brown hair rounded her face, falling deftly into place. True, she said to herself, the Talmudic dictum that hair creates temptation. I can understand it. And a voice of positive assertion came through: Good, let it be! So there. "Mirror, mirror on the wall, who's the prettiest rabbi of them all?" she laughed.

"Thank you, God, who has not made me a woman." That's what men say in the morning blessings. God! a slight prayer almost fell out of her mouth. What nonsense! What are they missing! Your creation, all this, and she slowly rolled her hands over her breasts and they tingled down over her stomach and onto her thighs. The gestured merriment gave her the power to be assertive as new words formed in her mind. "Positively and certainly, I will be a rabbi," one dimension said. "I will be a woman," added the other dimension. She had never exhibited herself brazenly or allowed herself this kind of self-indulgence while Sam was alive. Why not? Her life with him had been warm, loving. Am I freer now? Released from the mental bond of marriage? Can I attract other men, clothed? Yes, the decision process rolled on, I will be a woman rabbi and dress as a woman. She stood transfixed.

The euphoria locked out the soft knocks on the bedroom door. She did not hear the gentle call, "Mother." Carol, unable to sleep, had surmised from the light at the edge of the door that her mother had fallen asleep with the lamp on. Not hearing a response, the girl slowly opened the door.

Her gasp punctured Sara's reverie. "Mother!"

Sara turned to see a wide-eyed Carol, one hand flying up to cover her gaping mouth. Both stood frozen, embarrassed. Carol had never seen her mother nude. Carol started to close the door. Sara grabbed her slip. Covering herself, she rushed to the door. "Wait. Carol? Come back."

"It's all right, Mother." Her tone was defensive. "I'm sorry. I'll see you tomorrow."

"No," Sara pleaded. "Please, come in."

Sara took Carol by the hand. Following her mother's pull, Carol kept her eyes lowered, her face red, her shoulders hunched. Sara left her standing. "I'll be back in a minute." She ran to put on her nightgown.

"I'll be out in a second; please sit down," Sara coaxed. Carol couldn't sit down. What does this mean? she wondered. My mother? In front of a mirror? It's not like her. On second thought, she pondered, Mother has a pretty figure. She had not thought of her mother as one interested in her body. A mother was just, well . . . a mother takes care of whatever one needs. And here was her mother, her mother. . . .

Sara was out of the washroom quickly. "Sit down, Carol." Sara's face revealed no embarrassment now. Subconsciously she was glad that someone else had seen her as she was. She took Carol by the shoulders, and with one hand lifted her head slowly, looking deeply into her eyes. "I am a little embarrassed," Sara said, moving her face to catch Carol's shifting eyes. "I think you're even more embarrassed," she continued. Carol raised her eyes slowly. In a split second she looked into her mother's face, then lunged into her arms. Sara held her tightly, patting her older child lovingly on the back.

"I didn't mean to intrude," Carol began, "I just thought we could talk. I couldn't sleep. When I opened the door I . . . I . . ."

"There's no need for defense," Sara helped. She spoke more rapidly. "I made a decision today, Carol. You and Simon helped me. I went to the temple and into the sanctuary to think of myself in your father's place. I had to feel sure that you would be proud of me, that people would be proud of me, that I was needed, and that I would respond to that need. I spent a long time there, walking up the steps, standing in front of your father's pulpit. I walked over to the Ark. I opened the door. I drew open the curtain. I looked at the Torahs. I was there, Carol, all alone, and I knew that if I could go there all alone and picture myself standing there, you would be proud of me, and I knew that I could be a good rabbi, but that I'd also have to be a good mother and I'd also have to be a woman. I came home fully convinced and I was going to shower and lie down. I walked past the mirror and I saw myself; I don't usually walk nude you know. . . ."

"I know," Carol faltered, still not fully composed.

"I began to wonder, what am I doing? I'm a woman, a mother, I'm not bad looking. 'What'll happen to the children,' I said to myself, and, Carol, I learned a great lesson. How wonderful God's creation is. God created you and gave you a beautiful, lovely figure. God created us all and I decided I *would* be a rabbi, *and* a mother without sacrificing the woman I am. I would be myself. That's what you want, isn't it, Carol? My clothes would have to be feminine. I wouldn't hide my figure, and I would be proud of me. Do I make sense, Carol?"

"You do, Mom, you really do. We'll all be proud. Just be

yourself. You're beautiful, Mother, and I love you for being you. But please promise me, you won't become pompous like some other rabbis."

"I promise, Carol, if I ever begin acting pompously, remind me of how you surprised me in my bedroom." They smiled at each other, and said good-night.

Sara watched Carol walk out of her room. She felt encouraged and stimulated. The synagogue visit had nudged her on towards the crucial decision. Now Carol's understanding was supportive. But she still felt a bit of a void; an absence continued to gnaw her. Her decision was, thus far, all from within. How about beyond? Beyond the synagogue and the family. What would they think? But was it really important? She had to know. Where could she find out how others felt?

She thought of Don, friend, gentle, interested. But he was, after all, the president. He had a responsibility that might color his view. Then she thought of Hal. Yes, that would help. Why do I turn to him so frequently? she wondered. She thought of herself in front of the mirror and her hands suddenly covered her mouth as if caught in sinful thought. Her heart pounded. What am I thinking? He must never read my thoughts.

She dressed quickly in the morning and moved hurriedly downstairs to prepare breakfast. At 8:00 A.M. she dialed. Harold Kaplan answered. Unaccustomed to telephone calls in the morning, he was startled to hear his name.

"Hal? Sara."

"Sara?"

"Sara Weintraub."

"Sara? What's the matter, Sara? What's up?" His voice rose in concern.

"Nothing, Harold. Nothing's wrong. Only I thought I'd call you before you went to the city. Harold, could you give me a little time, today, tonight?"

"Come on, Sara," he pressed. "What's the matter?"

58

"Nothing really, Harold. Only I need someone to talk to. You've been so close to the family. I have to talk this whole thing out."

"Sure, Sara, sure." He paused, hesitated, "Let me call you back. I'll check my schedule and get back to you. Maybe we can get together this morning. I'll see."

"Thanks, Harold." Sara was relieved. She had done the right thing. Strong and firm in her decision, it would be valuable nonetheless to have another opinion.

The children rushed down to breakfast chattering, unconcerned. The morning was bright and cheerful. Sara was preoccupied. But when Carol cast a knowing look and wink at her, Sara responded. She smiled and returned the wink.

The telephone rang. "Sara? Harold. I can take a later train if it would be helpful. No problem."

"Thanks, Harold."

"It's O.K. Anything I can do, you know. You can count on me."

"Who was that, Mother?" Carol asked.

"Uncle Harold, Carol."

"Uncle Harold? So early in the morning? What's the matter?"

"Yeah," Simon chimed in, "what's the matter?"

"Nothing's the matter. He's coming over to talk with me. He's been very close, and I need someone to help me."

"You, Mother? Need someone to help you?" Carol's eyes opened wide, "I thought. . . ."

Sara laughed. "Everyone needs a friend. I think Uncle Harold can help me."

Disappointment spread over Carol's face. "Didn't I help you last night?"

"You certainly did, Carol. You helped me a great deal. But I want to talk to someone who is a little older than you, who's outside the family and has had more experience."

"O.K. Mom, if that's the way you want it."

Simon listened and shrugged his shoulders.

"I've purposely stayed away, Sara, because I didn't want to influence you," Harold began when they sat down in the living room. He had been there many times, but never so formally. It was different now, he thought. It was more restrained, uneasy. "It's your decision to make."

"I know you've been talking with Don and Rabbi Friedman," Sara said. "Now that the time is coming close and I have to make it definite, I need help. I mean, I need someone to encourage me, to say, 'Sara, we need you, take the position.'"

"I thought you've already made up your mind. Don told me you did."

Sara laughed. "Of course, I did. Outwardly, that is. But, inside I'm still unsure."

"You? Unsure?"

"Yes, Harold. Me, unsure. It's not easy, you know."

"It'll take a lot of guts, Sara," Harold agreed. "It won't be easy; you're right! You'll have your hands full. And the children. . . ."

"What do you really think? I mean, can I do it?" Her eyes pleaded for encouragement. She caught herself staring. Was she being forward?

"Sara," Harold began slowly. "I'll be very honest with you."

Sara waited. The moments were long, his voice was certain. "I'm sure you can do it. I'm sure you can succeed. I think you'll serve well. And what's more, Sara, I'll do everything in my power to help. I'll be with you. All the way, Sara. You can count on me."

Relieved, Sara felt tears welling into her eyes. "Thanks, Harold. That's just what I need. I needed those words of encouragement." She dried her eyes by blinking and smiling.

"Thanks," she repeated, feeling drawn to him. "Thanks for coming."

"I have to catch a train," Harold said, looking at his watch. Sara led him to the door and kissed him. For Harold, it was a friendly kiss. For Sara, its memory lingered.

Chapter Seven

SARA'S DECISION had to be reported to the board of governors. Don and Hal discussed her acceptance and decided that the board should be summoned as quickly as possible, not only because of the oncoming holiday season, but also because rumors had begun to spread in the community. At bridge games and swim clubs, the topic of conversation was Sara. Some women challenged the decision, arguing the pros and cons. Men surprisingly defended the position of the board. "Look what it will do for you women! Isn't that what you've been fighting for? It will give you equality."

"We're not interested in that kind of equality," some retorted. One woman went so far as to say that it reminded her of female policemen assigned with men to tour the night spots and protect citizens. And a second one reminded the other women sitting around the swimming pool that the navy had finally agreed to accept women on ships. "Of course," she said sarcastically, "there'll be separate quarters. Millions of dollars will be spent to create new and different facilities, but you know what'll happen. We all know." Don personally wrote letters to members of the board asking them to come to the crucial meeting on August 13th. Not more than four or five weeks had passed since the stir in the Wilmette Jewish community had occurred. There were repeated discussions and arguments between husbands and wives, husbands and husbands, men and men, and women and women. Don himself did not have the most positive response from his wife Sue, who intimated that he wanted Sara to be a rabbi, not only because she was Sam's wife, but because Don was somehow taken with her.

"You want to be close to Sara," Sue insinuated.

Don responded angrily, "I don't know what you're saying. What are you trying to create, Sue? There's nothing between Sara and me."

On the night of the meeting some members of the board were jolly and vibrant; others, it appeared, had been persuaded by their wives on how to vote. Don surveyed the members as they came in, and could almost count the votes, pro and con, and predict the decision by the way the men looked.

Don had asked Hal to come earlier to prepare for the proceedings. He noted that the air conditioning had been fixed and that there ought to be no interference to prevent the board from making the appropriate decision. When Sidney Weinstein formally made the motion, Don recommended that the decision be positive and made with dispatch.

"Wait a minute," came a cry from the side of the room. "Don't railroad this through. You've got to have a discussion, Don, and I want to discuss. I want to talk against the motion." Don looked at a raging Phil Elkind in surprise. A change of atmosphere descended like a pall. Elkind stood up, his face scarlet. "Don't railroad this thing through, Don. I'm against the motion."

"All right," Don said shaken. "Any discussion?"

"Yes!" the gynecologist exclaimed. "I'm against the motion because I'm against Sara being our rabbi. Or *any* woman rabbi. I've been thinking about this since our last meeting. I grew up in another world, and I just don't believe in it. Women don't belong in the pulpit. Women's places are in business, in the homes, and in stores. I'm not against them getting greater opportunities. They should get good salaries. But I just can't see one as my rabbi. Call me a chauvinist. I don't care, I just can't see it. Now you're going to ask me what's wrong with it. I may not know the answers rationally, but I feel that we're going off on a tangent. If we have a woman rabbi, we can't be honest with her. We can't fire a woman rabbi. We have to be more careful. We have to be more delicate. We have to be more gentle. I can't see Sara standing on the pulpit and preaching to me. I can't see Sara officiating at a funeral. I can't see her at a *bris*. You know what I mean."

He was interrupted by Gil Cowen, who was also on his feet. "I want to second what Phil said. He's right. We're going too fast. We have to take this thing very seriously. Now my wife's against it too and I've talked to a number of women who said to me that they don't want a woman rabbi. They simply won't be able to look upon Sara as their rabbi. They go to the same butcher shop, or they'll play bridge together with their rabbi, Sara? It's ridiculous!"

Don banged the gavel. "Now wait a minute, men, let's take it easy. We have a responsibility. If you're against the motion, say so. Let's discuss it calmly. I happen to have another feeling. I think it would be beautiful for us. You know that Sara is capable. She's strong and she'll lead with real force. I'm convinced of that. We ought to at least give her a chance!"

Elkind responded heatedly, again rising to his feet. "What do you mean give her a chance? You know once a woman takes over, that's it." He was sorry he had made the statement, knowing full well that it would reach his wife's ears.

Don turned to the others. "Any other comments? We have to make a decision. I'm not going to force you one way or the other. What do you say, Hal?" Hal stood up slowly, and said calmly: "I really don't have anything to add. I've already said what I believe to be true. I've known Sara for a long time. Even in the Rabbinical Conference they look upon her with admiration. They are not able to ordain her, at least not yet. They haven't made a decision, but they will. I am confident that once they reach the decision that a woman *can* become a rabbi in the Conservative movement, Sara will be the first to achieve that recognition. That means a great deal to me. We have to break down our prejudices."

Elkind responded, "It's not prejudice. It's a gut feeling I have. Right here. I'm even worried about how Sara will react. She's a woman. Maybe she'll be much stronger than we want her to be. Maybe she'll rock the community. Break down the good relations we've had with our Christian neighbors. Maybe she'll want to show the community that *because* she's a woman rabbi she has to be stronger than the average rabbi and she'll do things that will get us into trouble. She'll give us a bad image. Wouldn't it be better for us to get someone temporarily-like, and take our time about deciding on such an important step? Let some other community break the ice. Why should we? Once they do it and recognize women as rabbis then we'll go along. I'm not ready to be a martyr and I don't want my synagogue to be a martyr. You can take it or leave it. I only hope that some day I won't have to say I told you so."

"Any other discussion?" The debate went on, until Don said, "I don't hear any new ideas in our discussion. Are you all ready for a vote?" He sensed the positive results and confidently asked, "All right. Now remember, men, that this is a very important and historic decision. Remember that everyone in our synagogue, including our wives, will know who voted *for* and who voted *against*. When you vote, do it because you're committed to whichever position you decide is the right one, not for yourselves and not for your wives, but for the temple and for the Jewish community. All right, all in favor of Sara being our rabbi, raise your hands." Don glanced around the room and saw that the majority raised their hands. "The motion is carried," he announced, a broad smile creasing his perspiring face. He banged the gavel. "Any other business?"

"What's the vote?" Phil Elkind asked. "I want a count!"

"All right, let's have a count. Hands up again, please."

Don counted. "All right, eighteen to five. That's a pretty good majority. The motion is carried. Thank you very much, men."

"Move we adjourn."

The board members had already risen. Chatter as well as backslapping accompanied the decision.

"Good luck," Phil muttered to Don, sarcasm rippling through the words.

Chapter Eight

THRILLED AND ANXIOUS at the same time, Sara felt the weight of her new role. She sat transfixed in her lounge chair trying to project her future. Uncertainty, mixed with determination, enervated her. Awakened out of her thoughtful mood, she eased slowly up the stairs, her thoughts confused. She saw a light under Carol's door. She knocked.

Carol, sitting up in bed, was writing in her diary. She had a way of sitting up, propped in front of the pillow, her upper shoulders unsupported. Her legs were drawn up, her knees forming a writing surface. She wrote first resting on one leg and then on the second, her penmanship changing with each shift. She heard a faint trudging up the stairs, looked up at the knock, and softly called out, "Mother?"

Sara heard the whisper. "Yes, Carol. Aren't you sleeping yet? It's after ten."

"Come in," Carol called, patting the bed. She lifted herself up, one hand grasping the diary, and shifted to allow room for her mother. Sara sat down on the edge of the bed. Carol moved over, whispering. "On the bed, Mother, not halfway." Sara sat on the bed, below the pillow, her legs on the floor.

"Want to take your shoes off and put your legs up?"

Sara shook her head. "No, it's all right here."

"Come on, Mom," Carol urged.

Sara complied. Carol looked and said admiringly: "Pretty legs, Mom."

Sara blushed.

"Little tired, Mom?"

Sara nodded, hesitated, then spoke haltingly.

"Carol, Mr. Shapiro and Uncle Hal were just here. We talked about . . . you know . . . my becoming rabbi of the synagogue." She continued, "Uncle Hal has been in New York and has spoken to the Rabbinical Conference people. It's going to create quite an upheaval all over the country. Maybe even the world," she corrected herself. "And a decision has to be reached soon, with the holidays coming."

Carol looked more mature than her years. For the first time, she felt her mother was including her in a major family decision. She furrowed her eyebrows intently.

"What did you decide, Mother?"

"Well, the board tonight elected me their rabbi. I accepted."

"You did? I'm so glad!"

"Are you surprised?"

Carol hesitated, then drawled. "Not really. I sort of felt that you would. Only, I somehow thought that it was just, well, a passing idea. You know."

"No, Carol. But I was more confident before I accepted."

"And now?"

"Well, I'm still serious, but a bit more anxious and concerned now that it's here. I'm confident that I can be a good rabbi and I guess I'm not bad looking." She blushed as she looked at her legs, remembering Carol's comment. She hesitated. "What I'm wondering about, is how long I'll be able to do it. And what about the future. And you and Simon. I'll have to be out evenings with meetings and calls and so on. It won't be easy for any of us. It sounds so fascinating and challenging at first. But after the flush of excitement has worn off, like they say, after the honeymoon period, what then?"

Carol, not knowing how to respond, remained silent.

"But you've decided," she finally said. "I can't see why it wouldn't be all right. What difference does it make, man or woman, as long as you can be a good rabbi?"

"It's never happened, Carol. I'm like a guinea pig."

"So what?" Carol responded.

"I really don't know. But it's something new and there are laws against it. So the laws have to be changed. . . ."

"Why should there be laws against women being rabbis, Mother? Why? Aren't women as good as men?"

"Yes, of course they are. But. . . ."

"Discrimination, isn't that it, Mother?"

"No, it's not discrimination, Carol."

"It *is*! It *is* discrimination. And it's wrong. Women can be as good rabbis as men. Better." She affirmed the last word with an air of complete confidence and a facial gesture of "So there!"

Sara laughed, amused. "In history, life develops one way, rolling along merrily, lackadaisically, and then, when a new period comes, we rethink our values. Perhaps in this society, the Jewish pulpit will also undergo a radical change."

She continued with a chuckle, "This too may be part of the anarchy of this age. I'm afraid I'm not logical." She rethought her comparison. "A little tired. And it's late. I'll be going to bed. We'll talk more, Carol. You're really growing up now."

"Night, Mother Rabbi."

Still tired but lighter in mood, Sara smiled as she left Carol's room. What would the future bring?

Andre's beauty salon was not the last word in chic, but it had its charm. Andre was reliable. The morning of a Bar Mitzvah, the evening of a wedding, no matter what time, Andre would make his appointed rounds at the homes of his suburban clients. Like a doctor making night calls, Andre made his beauty calls. On occasion, Sara visited the salon but usually preferred to do her own hair.

So on this morning, with all Wilmette buzzing about the history-making decision, a group of middle-aged women converged upon Andre's like locusts attacking a rice field.

"Do you believe it?" Sue Shapiro tittered, her hair foaming with soap. "What do you think, Sandy?" The question was directed towards the woman sitting next to her, who was critically surveying her own reflection.

"Think of what?" Sandy eyed Sue's buxom figure. She knew Sue dyed her hair the minute the first sliver of gray appeared. Everyone knew everybody's business, especially when they came to Andre's.

Sue gazed into Sandy's large intent eyes. She's got a bad complexion, Sue thought. But she could change that long face with makeup. "Of Sara, of course."

"Sara? Sara who?"

"Didn't you hear? Sara Weintraub is going to be our rabbi."

Sandy jerked her head with such abruptness, Andre nearly jabbed her with his scissors. "Are you kidding?" she cried.

The smile was smug. "No. The board voted her in last night eighteen to five. Don told me."

"I heard a rumor, but I didn't pay much attention to it." She paused. "Well, I'll be damned," she said. "I don't believe it."

"It's true." Sue replied. "I think it's crazy, wild. Boy, did I let Don have it. He and Hal were behind it. Well, you know Hal's been friendly with Sara. I mean, very friendly with her. . . ."

Sandy turned again. "Look Sue, one shock is enough in a day, but two? You know what you're saying? You're saying um, uh. . . ." She looked at Sue, trying to extract a response.

"Yes, I know what I'm saying," Sue countered. "I wouldn't dare breathe a word to Don, and Hal would kill me. But I see. . . ." Her head bobbed up and down.

"See what?"

"Well, all of a sudden, things are changing. They're having meetings. More meetings than Rabbi Sam had. Don tells me they're all necessary. There are major decisions that have to be made, helping Sara," she added smugly, "but they're always in her home."

"I know, but you can't really believe. . . ."

"Yes, I can," Sue responded. "I know Don's been there many times, talking with her every day. *President* he said. How do I know about that? And how do I know about Hal, nice and friendly and all that. But look, I mean let's lay it on the line— Judy passed away, she's gone, he's been alone all this time, you know, and lonesome and I can guess Sara's feeling the same. Two plus two equals. . . ." Her voice trailed, slyly.

"I don't believe what you're suggesting, Sue."

"You don't have to; it's only what I think."

"What a way to become a rabbi," Sandy said. "Three strikes against you. Your gossip is enough to kill her."

Sue shrugged, "I don't like the idea of women rabbis. They just don't belong on the pulpit. Can you picture a woman up there, standing in front of the Ark? Nobody's going to be looking at the *rabbi*. Every woman will be looking at her dress, her hairdo, her makeup. Every man's not looking at a rabbi, but is looking at her figure, her behind. You know what they'll be thinking!" She felt righteous.

"Oh, come on, Sue."

"What do you mean, 'come on.' When you look at a woman, what do you think of? If you look at a more beautiful woman, aren't you jealous? I mean come on, be honest! I am. Look, I'd like to be Elizabeth Taylor, or Bess Myerson, but I just can't. But that doesn't mean I don't *want* to be. I'd love it, and if I were beautiful, slim, and proud, I could take this Sara. She's not *bad*—you know."

"What do you mean, she's not bad?"

"Well, she's tall and she's slim and, I don't mind telling you, she's got a very pretty figure and she has a nice face and she can really do a come-on."

"Sue, let's be fair."

"No. Maybe I'm more critical than you are, but I know men.

70

You know, it's like the Bible says, looking at a woman is temptation. I wish more men would look at me as a temptation. So up there in the temple, a woman is standing on the pulpit looking at the Ark or walking around, and you know temptation. We'll have a congregation of lusters after the flesh, like Jimmy Carter said, and that's why the Hasidim don't walk behind women. We'll have to have Yom Kippur and confessions every day, for temptations."

"Aw, you're exaggerating, Sue."

"No, I'm not. You don't think so? What happened to all those policewomen that were assigned with policemen? They said nothing would happen, that everything would be all right. Don't tell me that no hanky panky went on there. Now, you can't tell me that there's not going to be some fooling around there. I don't have to tell you. You're a big girl, Sandy."

Sandy looked at Sue's flushed cheeks. Andre looked at both and said to them: "I don't think you ladies are being fair. I don't know Mrs. Weintraub very well, but you're certainly convicting her before the trial has even started."

"Right," a strong voice echoed from the side. The opinion belonged to Barbara Moskowitz, a long-time friend of Sara's. Barbara was also a Hebrew teacher. She had been for women's rights long before the movement was invented. She'd always combined family and career.

"We all know why you're defending her," Sue protested. "You've always gone against tradition anyway. But I'm against it! What about the Sisterhood? Why weren't they consulted? After all, they run the synagogue. They make more money for the temple than anyone. If we'd been consulted, we would have voted it down!"

"Right," Sandy chimed in. "Oh, I know equal rights and all that—but deep down women believe something else. Women don't admire other women. They're envious. I think it'll be hell for Sara. If I were her, I'd say no. Only the men will bail her out. I don't think women will help her."

"Well you're certainly not," Barbara snapped. "Not with your medieval, narrow-minded views."

She slapped a bill down on the counter and stalked out. "Jealous, prejudiced old bitches," she muttered.

"See what you've done, Sue," Sandy chastised.

"Done?" Sue answered. "What have I done? I was only giving you my opinion, that's all."

"That's all? You've tried to knife Sara in the back."

"I'm sorry," Sue responded. "What am I supposed to do, keep quiet?"

"You could be more discreet."

"Even here? We're supposed to be open and free, you know. Let it all hang out, as they say."

The response at Andre's contrasted sharply to that of the Sisterhood. Their meeting was scheduled later that day. As the women's arm of the synagogue, they planned the year's activities. In the past, older women had dominated, but the torch had been passed to a younger generation. Many of these pretty and slim suburban women were tennis players, golfers, and racquetball enthusiasts. They were accustomed to taking winter vacations, but were also ethnic-conscious. Israel's wars had sharpened their closeness to their Jewish heritage. Suddenly being Jewish was important, and these women stressed religious education. Almost compulsively, religious school became as important as Boy and Girl Scouts and tennis and hockey and piano. The feminist movement also contributed heavily to the mosaic of the composite Sisterhood leadership. The young women were spirited in their emphasis on women's rights. They were part of the new era, and had achieved equality in ritual. They were called to the Torah and were counted in the minyan, unheard of recognition a decade ago. Many Sisterhoods were envious of this group of younger people.

Professor Hyman Yedelson of nearby Stonybrook University had been invited to speak that day. His assigned topic was "Israel and Religion." But as Maxine Stein, the president, turned the meeting over to the head of the program, she allowed facetiously, "Perhaps Dr. Yedelson would like to talk with us about the board's decision last night, engaging Sara Weintraub as our rabbi. Or about women rabbis." Before the program director could make her presentation, which included providing biographical facts about the speaker, Dr. Yedelson said, "I'd be very happy to."

"Would you?" Maxine asked, looking at the women, seeking an eager response.

"Of course," he said. "Let's talk. I mean all of us. Let's exchange our views and feelings, O.K.?"

"Wonderful," the women cried all at once.

"We're in a synagogue," Dr. Yedelson began. "I walk into the synagogue, I look at the pulpit, and I see an Ark. I see a woman standing up there. Someone says to me, 'Hey, that's a woman rabbi,' and I say 'Woman rabbi? What is she doing on the pulpit? She doesn't belong on the pulpit. I don't believe in women rabbis.' What do you think?" Responses came rapidly in clusters.

"I think you're wrong. If she's qualified, if she's outstanding, if she's studied, more power to her. I would feel for her spiritually as I would towards a male rabbi." Marlene Standard was the first to react. Dr. Yedelson pressed a position.

"That woman up there, I don't think her hair is done well and I don't know whether I like the yarmulke on her hair. I just don't think a woman should wear a yarmulke."

Joan Winston said, "I think that most men regard women in sexual terms. When I sit up on the pulpit, men say, 'Isn't that wonderful, her skirt is the right length,' or 'she looks so nice up there, etc.' They wouldn't comment that way about a man."

"Why is that?"

"Only because we're not used to seeing women on the pulpit. The more we see them, the more comfortable we'll feel."

"Meaning that if men saw women more often in all types of job roles, they would be less conscious of sex?"

"Yes."

Yedelson continued, "When you look at a woman, a woman

rabbi, do you look at a woman, or do you look at a rabbi? Would you look at the woman part or would you look at the rabbi part?"

"Well, if there were more of them, we would treat them as rabbis, not sex objects."

"But what do you think of a woman conducting a *bris*, standing with the father and with the mohel when they are ready to circumcise the baby? Will you react differently? Can you picture that?"

"Why not?"

"Don't answer 'why not.' I want a positive answer." A number of positive answers poured forth.

"What if she becomes an ordained mohel? She's called to circumcise a baby boy. Is there a precedent for a woman being a mohel?" As one woman asked this, the others laughed.

"Yes, there is," Dr. Yedelson said. "In the Bible, Tzipora, Moses' wife, circumcised their two sons."

"I didn't know that," a surprised chorus of voices responded.

"You, for example—let's say, Joan. You have a problem and you want to talk to a rabbi. You wouldn't have hesitated talking to Rabbi Sam. But if Rabbi Sam were a woman, do you think you would have the same ease in talking with her . . . as a rabbi?"

"It depends on the individual, but I think if a person has shown compassion and has some understanding it wouldn't make any difference. I as a woman would have no trouble. I don't know about a man; a man might have more problems."

"Do you think that women might be concerned about a woman rabbi and her relationships with the board of trustees?"

"No."

"Being involved on a close, intimate level with an officer?"

"The officers would be women. It's already hypocritical that *this* synagogue has no women on its board."

Dr. Yedelson expressed shock. "You want it all?"

"It won't be smooth. Any woman who decides to be a rabbi will have to recognize that it's going to be hard for a while. I think that women rabbis haven't taken congregations yet because they've all gone into teaching."

Dr. Yedelson interrupted, "There's one rabbi, incidentally, out in the west, who was sent out to be interviewed. The first question she was asked was, 'What would happen if you become pregnant?' and she objected to the question as blatantly discriminatory. They didn't like her answer but they engaged her anyway. She did have a baby and she took a pregnancy leave . . . and afterwards felt that the congregation was so prejudiced that she resigned from the rabbinate."

Joan defended, "Because the pressure was on her. She probably wanted to resign anyway."

"What would you say of a woman rabbi who dressed in a tight, black slinky dress, low, low-cut in front and back, high slit front and back, wiggling and rocking-and-rolling with all kinds of gyrations? How would you react?" The women grew pensive, agreeing that the picture would not be flattering to the rabbinate. Someone asked, "How much of a slit would she have on the side?" The young members laughed.

"My position really is," continued Yedelson, "that if a woman wants to be a rabbi, and if she hides behind the image of the rabbi, she'll never make it. She cannot totally submerge her femininity. You see, there's a certain set image of a rabbi, whether we like it or not. I don't know whether women are going to make it; maybe it's a fad. So far, no woman rabbi has actually made it. They're nice kids, nice girls and all that, but they haven't blazed the trail to give the position stature . . . and meaning." Despite Yedelson's pessimism, the meeting ended on a note of exhilaration. The Sisterhood generally liked the idea of a woman rabbi.

Word spread quickly in the non-Jewish sector of the community. Episcopal church women applauded the selection. They had been in the forefront of selecting a woman as a priest, and had even split the Episcopal Church. A number of Catholic women called on Father McHale to tell him that the Jewish

75

people had selected a woman rabbi. Might it not be the time to press for the election of a woman priest as was decided at a convention in Baltimore? A delegation had even been sent to the Pope.

During dinner that night the topic in Jewish homes burned on everyone's lips. Children's questions were penetrating: "Mommy, can a woman really be a rabbi?"

"Dad, does she have to wear pants like Rabbi Sam?"

"Mother, for God's sakes, I can't talk to her like I talked to Rabbi Sam. She's a lady, Mom. Gee, Mom, how can I tell her anything?"

"Dad, will she wear a yarmulke, like mine?"

"Is she going to wear a V-neck gown, Mother?"

"Mother, what will I do about the wedding? Is she going to marry Bill and me?"

Mothers and fathers throughout the community were hard put to provide answers. They had hardly had time to form their questions when the issue was decided.

Sara, as yet unaware of the furor she had caused, was determined to be as successful as she possibly could be. She would fulfill her dream and fulfill herself. Nothing now would stand in her way.

Chapter Nine

WHERE DOES ONE BEGIN? They ushered her into Sam's study. Two beige telephones rested on the large glass table. There was another telephone on the conference table, and a half dozen upholstered, throne-like chairs. Bookcases lined the walls, trophies lay scattered on shelves. Sara had never felt at home in the place; it was too big, too crowded, too masculine for her taste. On the wall, facing the rabbi's chair, were several photographs. One was an autographed one of Menachem Begin, inscribed to Rabbi Sam for his fund-raising efforts on behalf of Israel. Near it stood photos of Theodore Herzl and Abraham Horner, Chancellor of the Seminary. Sara admired Dr. Horner more than any other living person. She'd read all his books on theology, had heard him speak at conventions, and had been introduced to him once, a thrill she would never forget. *His* photo she would surely keep.

The sound of the buzzer startled her. She didn't know which button to press. Each time someone called her "Rabbi" she winced. I'll simply have to get used to it, she told herself. Her thoughts were jumbled. She could no longer put off planning for the High Holy Days. Then there was the religious school. She shifted religious school to the top of the list; it must open before the High Holy Day season and teachers had to be engaged, though she knew that Saul Edelstone, the education director, was handling the school program capably. But she herself would have to get involved in the school. Children balked at coming there three times a week, complaining that the Christian kids had to go only once a week, and only for an hour. Sam had never ceased wrestling with the challenge of how to interest the young, how to win them over to Judaism, how to keep them in the fold. It was a staggering problem Sara would have to face. With the adults she foresaw other problems; but she felt more secure about them—they would not desert the tribe.

The Bagel Breakers' Breakfast on Sunday mornings was a solid institution that would endure. She would have to relinquish some of the community activities. But could she drop the Ministerial Alliance? Sam had served as president. Presiding over twenty-six ministers was regarded as a sign of success in the American Jewish community: to be Judaism's spokesperson to the Christian community was an achievement highly regarded.

The ecumenical spirit was strong among the religious leaders in Wilmette. Somehow that unity had cooled over the past few years, when not all the Christian clergy condemned anti-Israel terrorism. Neither the National Council of Churches nor the World Council of Churches was pro-Israel. Rabbi Sam, in an unusual statement, had accused the clergy of insensitivity and hypocrisy. Yet with the passing of time cordial relationships were reestablished.

Almost as soon as the newspaper announced that Sara had been named rabbi of Temple Shalom, community leaders reacted. Reverend Harold Jenks (who every year at Passover would receive wine and matzohs from Sam, which he would use for the eucharist in his church) telephoned Sara to say he hoped she would continue the custom to which his parishioners looked forward. Reverend Barton Palmer of the Methodist Church said he'd enjoyed working with Rabbi Sam on the United Fund Campaigns and encouraged Sara to involve herself in fund-raising projects. "I'd be privileged," she said, "if you'll have me."

Reverend Palmer, who thought he detected a note of help-lessness in her voice, had replied: "Why, of course, we'll have you."

Dr. Servis Vocelle, Superintendent of Schools, phoned to congratulate Sara and said he hoped she would carry on Rabbi Sam's good work and that he would appreciate being informed about Jewish holidays and matters affecting Jewish students.

Dr. Henry MacLeary, minister of the large Faith Baptist Church, wrote expressing the hope Sara would bend her efforts toward interracial work. By the time Father McHale called, Sara was exhausted.

The phone buzzed and Ginny, the secretary, announced that members of the executive board of Temple Shalom had come. Would the rabbi see them now?

"Yes."

They came in; a half dozen men. She longed to see one woman, at least one, to take her side. She felt alone, abandoned, in this world of men. But her thoughts were hidden. "I have to lead with strength," she said to herself, as if reciting a mantra. Don pointed to the conference table, and the men, having shaken hands with Sara, congratulating her on her selection, sat down, leaving the imposing leather chair at the head of the table for her. She sat down with seeming confidence, put a pad and pencil on the glass-topped table, and gazed at the men whom she had considered friends in the past—kind men, good to their wives and children, honorable men. Now formal. She read challenge in their eyes. Did she see their wives' doubts reflected in their eyes? Were these men waiting for her to make a false move so that they could justify their male prejudice with which she suspected even the best of them were afflicted? "I will lead with strength," she repeated to herself, as if rehearsing a self-assertiveness lesson.

"I'm glad you're here," Sara began. "You've put your confidence in me. The High Holy Days are almost here. There are many things yet to be done. Where do we begin?" She surveyed the table.

Harry Katz, a heavy-set man in his middle fifties who owned the town's largest kosher butcher shop, came to Sara's aid. He detailed aspects of preparations and continued, "As for the Torah and Opening the Ark honors, that's been taken care of, too."

"How do you mean, Harry?" she asked barely above a whisper, surprised to hear herself asking.

"Why, we've passed them out. Always do, early in August."

"To whom, may I ask?" Her voice was clearer.

"I don't have the list here," Harry replied, looking perplexed. "But our committee met and went over the membership list and sent out notices. We couldn't wait. Naturally, you know."

"Are new members included in the honors? Will they be?"

"No, we felt we should give the honors to members who've been active over the years. They're entitled to honors."

"Of course they are," Sara agreed with a nod. "But would it hurt to involve new members? Or even some of our active women?"

"In honors?" Harry asked in surprise.

"If a woman is a rabbi, why can't one be given an honor?"

"But Sara—I mean, Rabbi." The word didn't sound right. "We've already given out all the honors. Maybe next year."

"Sara's right," Don interjected.

"Can't we add a few more?" Sara asked.

"But we already have about one hundred now."

"Let's add twenty or thirty more," she said. "I can add without any problem." As she said the words, she thought, Here I go, in hot water before I start. What's the matter with me? But she couldn't help herself.

The men looked at each other, but they didn't challenge. Sara went on to other issues on the priority list. By the time the issue of the religious school was brought up for discussion, Sara was tired. She yearned to bring the meeting to a close, but one subject, discussed earlier, troubled her. She shouldn't have let it pass. It was the matter of engaging a policeman to stand at the door of the synagogue, checking the tickets. She had faulted Sam for his insistence on such a practice during the High Holy Days.

"We've been doing it for years," Jack Rogoff, the stock broker, remarked. "If someone doesn't demand tickets, people will come in free. They'll pray for nothing. It's a matter of the temple's survival."

"Still, why don't we try it once, *without* a policeman?" Sara coaxed. "We're a synagogue, after all, not a rock-and-roll show or a disco. It's unseemly. Besides, I think we're turning our youth off by seeming materialistic. If we lose them, who will carry the torch of religion?"

"That's all well and good," Jack Rogoff countered. "It *sounds* right, but anyone will come in. Is that what you want?"

"People should have the opportunity to come to the synagogue on our holiest days," she replied. "Yes."

"But they have a responsibility to the synagogue, too, Sara. If they stay away all year long, and don't support the temple with dues and contributions, why the hell should they be entitled to our services?"

"Because we are a *synagogue*." Sara straightened her back.

"But we have expenses," Jack Rogoff said. "We need money to finance the place, to pay for maintenance, heat, our teachers and staff . . . and to pay *your* salary."

The first impasse was reached. "If I told you that I'd rather see my children go hungry than have a policeman at the door, you'd probably call me crazy. But that's the way I feel." Sara said. But she saw that she had lost this battle.

After the meeting, the members of the executive board filed

out of the rabbi's study shaking their heads and shrugging their shoulders. Some took a second look at Sara, who remained seated. "I think she's crazy," Jack Rogoff said to the others.

"If she has her way," Harry Katz said, "honors won't mean a damn thing. And giving honors to *women!*" He didn't see the inconsistency of hiring a woman rabbi, however. "Don, I think the board made a terrible mistake. We'll pay for it, yet. Mark my words."

"Wait and see," Don said. Inwardly, he smiled. Good for her, he thought.

On the following day, exhilarated from her first encounter, she began to work on her first sermon. She would not allow her excitement to dissipate.

How did one go about doing it? She'd written some sermons for her husband but now that she was confronted with writing her own, she drew a blank. What was she to talk about? Drugs? Israel? Women and their place in Judaism? Issues affecting Jewish life in America? She could begin with some innocuous subject that would not give offense. But aside from the subject, there was the matter of delivery. As a lecturer, she was supremely confident. Sermons, however, had to have a different ring. Would they expect a sermon from her as carefully thought out, as masterfully delivered as Sam's? Obviously not, she reflected. But why are you down-grading yourself, undermining your own confidence? she thought. Do the best you can.

What about pulpit dress? To the rabbi, minister, or priest, one's appearance on the pulpit represents an image. Priests and ministers have worn gowns for centuries. Sara's father used to wear a large prayer shawl, yellow with age. Should she wear a white gown Friday evening and Sabbath morning, and a white on the High Holy Days? Should she put on a prayer shawl? Only men traditionally wore prayer shawls. Was there a law against women wearing a Talit? As she recalled, a renowned authority forbade it only if it were worn promiscuously or for purposes of exhibitionism. It was not against religious law. Sara decided, however, not to wear her husband's gown; the congregation might resent it. Then she upbraided herself for worrying about the subject. In the end, she decided to wear a simple white gown and a smaller prayer shawl. Respectful but equal.

She rose, sharpened her pencil, and went back to her sermon for the New Year. For a few days, the page remained blank.

Chapter Ten

THE EVE OF THE New Year arrived. Sara and her children were getting ready. "Don't worry, Mother," Carol said. "I know you're nervous. I'll bring Simon; you go ahead."

Hal Kaplan rang the bell. Sara opened the door, glad to see him. He looked handsome in his Brooks Brothers suit, blazing red Italian tie and Gucci shoes. His sideburns were tinged gray, adding the right touch of distinction. Not a hair was out of place. If one did not know Hal as well as she did, with his interest in painting and love of books, one would take him to be a stuffed-shirt conservative businessman. However, there was a mischievous twinkle in his eye, behind the solemnity, which only those on intimate terms with him knew. He bent over, kissed her on the cheek. "I'll walk you to the temple," he said.

"Thank you very much, Hal. You couldn't have come at a better time."

They started out.

His proximity, as she held his arm, gave her courage. God! she thought. It's only two months and here I am walking with an available man.

He glanced at her, noting with approval the dress she wore. It was soft and full and loose, laying little stress on her splendid curves and swellings. As for her sensuous mouth, how was she going to conceal that? She was really too exciting physically to be a lady rabbi, Hal thought. A definite drawback. Hal found it necessary to clear his throat, as if to expunge his thoughts.

"I feel as though I were going to my execution," Sara said, smiling wanly.

"You're joking."

"If I come out of this alive. . . ." She paused, then said, "Hal, sit in the front row, center, please, where I can see you. Near the children. I'll feel safer."

Cantor Jerry Markow, barrel-chested, pink-cheeked, angelic when he raised his eyes to heaven, his voice the envy of all who heard him sing, was on hand when Sara came in. The sixteen members of the choir looked bright and cheerful. She could tell at a glance that they had slept well. They were testing their voices. Some were sucking Sucrets and cough drops, clearing their throats.

Sara, the only one really on trial, was tense. Collapsing in a chair, she reviewed her notes.

Cantor Markow exuded good-will and self-confidence. "The place is filling up nicely," he said. "You look nervous."

She nodded, too weary to comment.

"Being nervous is nothing out of the ordinary," the cantor calmed her. "Sam was always nervous on the holidays. It *is* different. Don't think you're the only one." He regarded her critically and said approvingly, "You look nice." She had on a white robe, a white collar, with a shawl draped over it. A small white skull cap sat smartly on her hair. "Very nice," he added. "You'll be all right."

"Where's Don?" Sara asked anxiously. The president always sat on the pulpit.

"He'll probably be right in. Don always comes in at the last moment, just as you're ready to walk on the pulpit."

The door burst open and Don rushed in perspiring. "Made it!" he cried triumphantly. He stopped, regarded Sara with approval, patted her wrist, and declared, "You look great, Sara! A little flushed but you'll do just fine. You ready?"

Sara rose. She was aware of the door of the sanctuary opening, the organ making the sanctuary tremble, the faces below, eyes riveted on her. She felt as if those waiting eyes would consume her. She thought she would never, ever, reach the pulpit to which Don was leading. His was not only a gallant gesture, it was a merciful one. Then she remained alone at the lectern, the spotlight on her. She'd never felt so lonely and stood transfixed for a moment. The organist finished the prelude. Sara's eyes swept over the congregation. She swallowed hard, looked down at her prayerbook and said with strength, "We begin our service, this New Year's eve, as we read the opening prayer together, on page two." Would the microphone amplify her voice? The Hebrew words were blurry, but she knew the ritual by heart. Her pulse was beating so wildly she wondered if it could be heard. She began the prayer, slowly, to control a possible quiver, enunciating each word distinctly. With each passing moment she felt that she was mastering her emotions, and that barring unforeseen obstacles, she would make it to the end. The congregation, she sensed gratefully, was on her side. The cantor's chant blended well with her words. Finally, she reached the mourners' prayer, breathed a sigh of relief, and relinquished the pulpit to Don Shapiro.

Don remarked that he was proud to be the president of a synagogue in which a woman rabbi was making history. Sara's confidence was restored. The congregation rose for the benediction. Sara was about to raise her hands in priestly fashion but changed her mind. Raising of the hands in blessing was traditionally in the male's domain. She would not be abrasive. "*Leshana tova tikatevu.*" She almost sang out on a note of triumph. You made it . . . she thought. Thank you, God. See Papa? The Messiah has come.

There was a good deal of handshaking and embracing. People were wishing one another "A Happy New Year!"

She walked out eagerly with Don. The world suddenly brightened. She could see again. Smiles greeted her. Hands reached out. "You were great, Sara!"

"You were wonderful, Rabbi!"

"More power to you!"

"Thank you. Thank you." Tears brimmed in her eyes; she shook them off. If only Sam were here. In the next instant, the irony of that thought cut through her. It was precisely because Sam was *not* here that she had triumphed.

She gathered her childen and started for home. Hal Kaplan caught up with them. He was on the point of congratulating her, but when he saw the tears in her eyes and the agitated expression on her face, he said quietly: "You really made it."

"Thank you, Hal, for being there."

Hal gave her a thoughtful look. Suddenly he felt terribly alone. As he glanced at Carol and Simon, the loneliness deepened.

Sara, who'd been silently observing, kissed Hal on the cheek. Startled, he looked at her with affection. Goodness, he thought, am I attracted to Sara, our new rabbi? Admit it, he told himself. You thought Sara was a very attractive woman for a long time now. Way before she'd been named rabbi.

"Thanks for helping Mom," Carol and Simon echoed. They too gave him friendly kisses on the cheek. But what had been the meaning of Sara's? He warned himself to stop thinking about her. Of *course* hers was just a friendly kiss.

As they neared Sara's house, she invited Hal in. "I'm making something for the children. Please join us," she encouraged.

He wanted to say yes, but felt torn. "No, thank you, Sara. I should be getting home." As she nodded her understanding, he barely felt her squeeze his hand. "And thanks again, Hal—for everything."

After Carol and Simon went to bed, Sara sat up thinking. The evening had been a fairly simple affair. The real test would come tomorrow, when people would be more critical. Her thoughts slipped back to Hal. He certainly made a more than acceptable appearance. In fact, Hal was downright attractive. What's more, he was so eager to help. An intelligent, successful man with a kind, compassionate heart. A nice man, a good man. Perhaps even sexy. Stop it! her conscience condemned. Sam hasn't been gone long enough.

But he *was* gone, Sara reminded herself. She also knew Sam had never indulged in self-pity and didn't like those who did. Images of wailing, breast-beating widows were unseemly, perhaps even a touch insincere. Sara had mourned, weeping her heart out within the private confines of her bedroom, *their* room. She had suffered a silent, private hell, a grief too deep and too heartfelt for public display.

Sam would want her to be happy, she reasoned. And what about Carol and Simon? They still needed the guiding hand of a male parent. Then her conscience declared, You're getting carried away with yourself, Sara Weintraub! How do you even know Hal feels the same way?

She directed her thoughts back to the congregation. Yes, they would surely be more critical tomorrow. Better get some sleep.

She rose early, dressed quietly, and tiptoed downstairs. The children were still asleep. While drinking coffee, she went over her notes, interpretations, and sermon. She hoped the day would pass quickly.

The day was bright, a little on the warm side for the time of year. The weather somehow relaxed her. But as she neared the temple, her pulse quickened. Entering, she greeted several older congregants who were holding minyan. She wished them Happy New Year.

From their warm responses, it seemed as if she'd passed a test. Even they had accepted her.

Cantor Markow was in the study, behind the pulpit, when she

came in. "You were good last night," he said. "Not a Rabbi Sam yet, but good. You had the audience with you. I heard one man say, 'Not only does she know what she's talking about, but she's pretty in the bargain.'"

Sara put on her white gown, and gazing in the mirror, adjusted her skull cap. Don came rushing in, late and breathless as usual. "You're looking great, Sara. Ready?"

She took charge from the start, keeping to a time schedule. "How long did your services take?" was asked more frequently than "How inspiring were your services?" If a service proved a little long, the rabbi was blamed. "He didn't let us out till 2:10!"

The tyranny of the clock troubled her, and late arrivals disconcerted her. But soon she became absorbed in her task, the reading of the Torah. She watched the cantor taking Torahs from the Ark and listened to his rich chant of Israel's Affirmation of Faith, the Shema. Now the procession of the scrolls was at hand. Should she take her place *behind* the cantor and the scroll as he led? Or should *she* lead? Women did not take part in the Torah processions traditionally. She felt suddenly rebellious, defiant, in no mood to compromise. Falling in behind Cantor Markow, she walked down the aisle, stepped forward in front of him, startling him, her face radiant, her voice joining his. Her eyes scanned the faces of the male congregants, trying to gauge their reaction. Did they resent it? Some men simply turned their heads aside; others did not follow the custom of moving forward to touch and kiss the scrolls. I'll probably hear about it later, she mused. She silently rejoiced at being the instrument of defiance, the breaker of archaic traditions. She walked straighter now, statuesque. Carol would approve when she realized what her mother had done. But how far should she go?

The procession wound through the sanctuary, returned to the pulpit. The Torah mantle was removed for the reading.

Sara paused over the Holy Scroll, as though waiting for someone to challenge her right as a woman to proceed. Patiently and lovingly, she explained the procedure of Torah honors, the pattern, number, hierarchy of significant Torah honors.

Next came the sounding of the shofar, the ram's horn, dating back to the days of Abraham. Only the select, she had believed as a girl—those chosen by God—could make themselves heard on the shofar. It was not an easy instrument to sound. Her father had been among those chosen. Each time he blew it, Sara would tremble with awe, expecting the heavens to open and the Messiah to appear.

Cantor Markow was adept at the shofar. He could sound the *tekiah*, the long blast, the *shevarim* with its three broken sounds, the *teruah* with its nine staccato sounds, and each was clearly enunciated, deliberately crude but lyrical, presaging the end, heralding the beginning. Prior to each sound, Sara explained its meaning. Her voice blended with the shofar, her whole being caught up in its rhythm. For her it was the summit; she could go no higher. She had trod where only men dared. But someday, perhaps next year, *she* would sound the shofar.

Her sermon traced Jewish history. She spoke of Abraham, Isaac, and Jacob; and also of Sarah, Rebecca, Rachel and Leah, the matriarchs of Israel, their devotion to their husbands and to their religion. She could almost see Carol nodding approval as she spoke of the lives of Miriam, sister of Moses; Deborah, the prophetess and judge; of Yael; of Esther, who saved the Jews from catastrophe. She touched on Talmudic times and reminded her audience that women were credited with maintaining the faith of Israel. "God gave Israel the Torah," she said. "Because of women. The Talmud says so. I believe it."

It was an auspicious day. "All beginnings are difficult," the rabbis say. How bitter yet sweet the struggle.

Chapter Eleven

THE CONGREGANTS OF TEMPLE SHALOM had nothing but praise for Sara's performance. But she was vaguely dissatisfied with her work. Her triumph was delicious—and it felt good to earn money and provide for her children—but there was the question of relevancy. It was Carol's favorite word, and Sara took it very much to heart that her daughter did not find her mother's work sufficiently relevant. "Where were the young people during your services?" the girl demanded. Sara sat on Carol's Mexican bedspread, comb in hand, doing her daughter's hair.

"But we can't change the world overnight, honey," she defended. And yet, she knew that Carol had a point. To say that one could not change the world overnight was a cliché. The world had to be changed, if it was to survive. And what would help save it? A vibrant, relevant Judaism, the Judaism of Jeremiah, Isaiah, of Abraham Horner? But what could she, one person, do? She was already spreading herself too thin, attending to her rabbinical duties, religious school, and the community with its Ministerial Alliance and a score of other projects. There was scarcely time left for sleep. She hardly ever

91

saw her children. She had not been to Andre's beauty salon for weeks and it seemed to her she had gained a little weight. She simply had no time to watch her diet, what with meetings, dinners, and late snacks. She had been proud of her slim figure, size eight; sometimes she could wear a six. How many women of forty could say that? It had not been easy to avoid cakes and ice cream and sugar-rich sodas. But it had been worth it.

"What in your opinion must I do to be considered relevant?" she earnestly inquired of her daughter.

"Take a stand against poverty, help for the minorities and homeless, support women's rights to choose. Then you'll get the young to come hear your sermons."

"All that?" Sara sighed, putting down the comb. "Where does one get the time and energy?" She had a tiger by the tail and couldn't let go.

Rabbi Sam had reserved for himself instruction of the confirmation class. If he could only, he used to say, open a few doors to Judaism and show the young how relevant Judaism really was, they would embrace it. "The demands of college students," he would tell the young people, "of the blacks, the civil rights advocates, are not new to Judaism. You'll find them in the Bible and in the Prophets. As for poverty, this isn't new either. It has been with us throughout history; the Bible inveighed against it." He would reach for the Bible, thumb through its pages and, finding the desired sentence, would read: " 'If you have a field and you glean the corners of the field, don't go over it, leave it for the poor.' " Then he would find another quotation to buttress his argument: " 'If your brother is poor, and oppressed, strengthen him, raise him up, help him.' Now isn't that what's going on today? To help the poor is a mitzvah."

In the confirmation class, Sara was confronted by twenty-two teenagers between the ages of thirteen-and-a-half and fifteen-and-a-half. Carol, almost sixteen was the oldest. Sara's first impulse was to run. There was a disturbing uniformity to the appearance of the students. They all wore jeans and "unisex" tops. Sara knew that most attended against their will, prodded and sometimes bribed by insistent parents. A new car for the sixteenth birthday, a trip to Europe, were not out of the realm of many of the parents. The bribes kept the teenagers coming. But their attitudes were lackadaisical, negative.

What is the problem? Sara asked herself. Is it *my* generation? Have we kept pace with them? Is Carol part of this milieu?

"Let's come to attention, please," she called out. "I guess you know that I'm the new rabbi of Temple Shalom." There was a jeer from the back of the room. Sara stopped. Her voice returned, crisper: "One of the duties I intend to keep is that of teacher of the confirmation class." She glanced at Carol, who looked straight back without emotion. "I know many of you are not exactly wild about coming to religious school, so I want to make these sessions as interesting and as exciting as I possibly can. I can't do it alone, and I'm not going to try. I am going to suggest that we talk together about things that you're thinking about. I can assure you that there is a Jewish position on almost every theme, but you'll have to help me, first by listening, second by being respectful, and third by your own input. I want to talk about *now*, today, what's going on in the world and how we're all affected by it. We may not have all the answers. We may not even have one answer. We may not even know the questions to ask. But at least we'll know we're talking about matters that affect us as Jewish people.

"What are some of the subjects you want to talk about?" She looked around for a response. All heads were down. Many of the students held pencils; others were doodling. Sara knew they were testing her. She repeated, "Are there any subjects that you want to discuss?"

Stephanie Kornblatt was the first to respond. "Let's talk about abortion." Sara was startled, and the others chuckled and looked at each other.

"Abortion?" Sara asked. "Is that something you're really thinking about?" She tried to conceal her bewilderment. Were other questions like this going to arise?

"How about interdating?" came the next question. And then

the flood of subjects flowed like a dike burst open.

"Poverty."

"Cults."

"Gays."

"Israel."

"A.I.D.S."

"Sex."

"Sex," repeated a second.

"Yeah, that's good, let's talk about sex, or drugs, or contraceptives." Sara's head jerked toward this last speaker. Billy Elkind's father was the town's leading gynecologist. The thought ran through Sara's mind that it was natural that of all teenagers, Billy should think of contraceptives. An automatic embarrassed look at Carol caused her daughter's head to lower. Could she talk of these subjects with her own daughter in class, or should she have someone else, another teacher perhaps, discuss them? Yet, the challenge had been cast. In a matter of seconds she regained self-control.

"Any other issues? I'm just jotting them down, then we'll start the discussion." There were no other suggestions. "All right, I think we're off to a good start. Let's zoom in on one or two as we get to know each other." The teenagers sat up and looked at each other. This lady rabbi meant business.

"What do you think about abortion? What do you *know* about abortion?" she asked. "What *is* abortion? We have to know what we're talking about." No response. "Stephanie, you mentioned it, didn't you? Why did you bring it up? Is it something teenagers talk about?"

"Sure it is," Stephanie said, hesitatingly at first. "Of course, we talk about it. It's all over the place, in the papers, on television, everywhere. We know all about it."

Sara looked at Stephanie. Suddenly the girl was mature. Was Carol also grown up in that sense? Strange, we never talked about it. Was she really close enough to Carol, or was she too much the unreachable mother figure?

"And while you're talking about that," Billy interjected, "let's talk about birth control and contraceptives." In her generation, Sara had never discussed these subjects openly. Here suddenly these issues were not only matters of common knowledge, but common subjects, out in the open. Should I discuss these things? she wondered. What about their parents? Is religious school the place?

"Sure, and while we're talking about abortion and contraceptives, let's talk about sex," added Bill Kahn.

The teenagers snickered and smiled. "I have to be honest with you," Sara said. "I really didn't expect these questions. You know what I expected? I thought you would ask about Israel, about the P.L.O., about poverty, about drugs maybe, but I didn't expect this."

"Will you talk about them?" The question was serious. The students waited.

"Yes," she said. "I will. But I really want to have time to prepare the Jewish position. I can tell you briefly now that Judaism is liberal in this area. Some believe that life begins at conception. You know what conception is?" She tried to be humorous but the response was a howl. Stephanie exploded with a "Do we know?" There was persistent snickering and a shifting of seats. "Wow," came another response. Sara blushed, but continued.

"Judaism is liberal because we don't believe that life begins at conception. That's why there are many instances in which Judaism doesn't really oppose abortion. That's a very general statement, but I'll stick by it, and, incidentally, I should tell you that the Bible talks about it."

"You mean the Bible speaks about abortion?"

"Of course. A passage in the Bible is the basis." She reached for a black book marked Holy Scriptures and thumbed through a number of pages. "Yes, here it is—Exodus 21: 22." She read slowly. "When men fight, and one of them pushes a pregnant woman and a miscarriage results but no other damage ensues, the one responsible shall be fined according as the woman's husband may exact from him. . . . But if other damage ensues, the penalty shall be life for life." She raised her head. "We'll talk about this next week. And also let me tell you that, yes, we believe in birth control. Oh, I know that you've heard that we're against it. No, we're for it, in certain cases."

"And about sex?" Bill asked.

"Well, we find . . . how shall I put it?" Carol's head lowered; she was not ready. "We find in Judaism no . . ." she hesitated, "no opposition to, what should I say, the enjoyment of sex, for married people, that is. You'll find Judaism to be most understanding in this area. By the time the year is over, I hope you'll come to me and say, 'Rabbi, I understand my religion and my heritage so much better now.' All right, any questions?"

"Boy, Rabbi," said Stephanie, "I think this is going to be great; don't you think so, kids?"

"Yeah. Oh, yeah, this is good stuff."

"Don't forget, everybody: sex is great." Stephanie had the last word.

When class was over, Carol was among the few who encircled Sara, and, much to her surprise, Carol kissed her mother on the cheek. "Thanks, Mom, that was good." Sara walked out with a cluster of girls who had gathered around Carol. All Carol heard was, "She's great, Carol. Your mother's great. She's beautiful."

"Hey, Steph," Bill said as they walked out, "Hear what the rabbi said about sex? Ummmm."

Melted into confusion, Sara returned to her study. Had she been too blunt? Would there be a reaction? She remembered that several years ago Sam had taken an antiwar stand on Latin America in the confirmation class. As she thought about it, she remembered that Dr. Elkind had raised a furor. His son, Billy's older brother, had come home and had reported that Rabbi Sam was against providing American aid. Elkind, in addition to being a gynecologist, was also a past commander of the Wilmette American Legion. Furious because he felt Sam was unpatriotic, he had complained to the board of governors that Rabbi Sam took a stand and expressed his position to teenagers. Elkind never forgave Sam for what he considered an attack against the President of the United States. He had threatened that some day he would even the score with the rabbi.

What did Carol really think? Sara wondered. Carol had expressed herself maturely, with understanding, before Sara had assumed the job. She was encouraging and yet Sara never really thought of her as grown up. It seemed that Carol was taking the controversial issues in stride. What did I really miss? I've never talked to her about these subjects. Carol didn't seem embarrassed. She kissed me afterwards. Said thank you. Was that her way of telling me that she was mature, that we are both women now? My little girl? A woman?

Carol didn't say a word about the class during dinner. Sara thought Carol looked somewhat sheepish. Should abortion be discussed with children? And at what age? What of sex and condoms and other devices? Can parents honestly be expected to discuss these subjects with their children? But where else may information be gained? Is public school the place? TV ads were now beginning to advocate the use of condoms; with the A.I.D.S. epidemic, sales had soared twenty-five percent. Was it the role of the synagogue or church to teach these subjects. She remembered a recent book designed for Jewish confirmation classes—the book graphically illustrated and described every part of the human body and described the sex act. Although the subject matter was dealt with from a Jewish point of view, Sara suddenly realized that she hadn't thought it proper for a confirmation class group. But now the subject was no longer academic, it had struck home. And soon she'd have to worry about Simon too. He's twelve-and-a-half. Is it time to talk with him? He'll be Bar Mitzvah soon. Can I? Shall I ask a man, maybe Don or Hal, to talk to him. Do boys really respond better to adults of their own sex? It's not going to be easy either way, she thought.

After the dishes were finished that evening, she asked Carol to sit with her in the living room. Sara began, "Carol, I think we have to talk about what happened today."

"Okay, Mother, let's. Let's talk."

"I was shocked to hear the members of the class speak so

bluntly about things that I never planned to discuss with them."

"I know, Mother; that's what you said. But, why not? Where have you been, Mother? I'm sorry, I don't mean to be disrespectful. It's all over. On television, in the papers, everybody talks about it. We just don't hide things anymore. We talk about everything."

"I just didn't expect it."

"You haven't seen movies, Mother, or television, and they're the subjects of every movie. It's all love and sex and abortion and violence and rape. I don't understand you. We go to parties and we dance. What did *you* do when you were a girl? We don't hold hands, or play spin the bottle or post office anymore."

Sara seemed startled but looked straight at Carol. "I know you don't hold hands, but you dance."

"Sure we dance, but we're more honest. We've got feelings, and we express them. We want to have meaningful relationships with each other and understand each other and feel good about it."

"I don't understand what you mean, Carol." The phrase *meaningful relationship* seemed to mean free sex.

"Well, Mother, we're more mature at our age than you were. You were sheltered. We've seen so much more. We've grown up quicker. We're very open about everything and we're not ashamed of it."

Sara looked at her daughter and saw in her the maturity she hadn't realized. "And I hope," Carol continued, "I hope you'll be honest with the kids. If you have to talk about sex, you have to talk about sex."

"I can't talk about sex like that, Carol. I mean, how detailed or how explicit can I be?"

"I don't know what you call explicit, Mother, but we're frank and anything you say is all right. Of course you don't have to use four-letter words." Sara fleetingly recalled her father's slap when she had said "damn."

"I guess I've been out of things," Sara replied. "I hope that it doesn't lead to more problems if you're that unashamed."

"I don't know what there is to be ashamed of," Carol said defiantly.

"I didn't mean ashamed. I meant, well, how do I know what you do when you're with your friends?" Sara spoke hesitantly, trying to conceal her anxiety. "I don't know; I hope that you're moral."

"Moral? Of course, I'm moral."

"I know, but I mean, *moral* moral."

Carol laughed. "Mother! If you're thinking that I'm not a virgin, you're wrong."

Sara almost keeled over and whispered, "Thank God," but quickly decided it would be best not to remain silent. In split seconds she could picture Carol and her friends lying around, free, open and unashamed, letting it all hang out, as Carol had said. Sara looked squarely into Carol's eyes and relaxed. "Frankly, I'm glad. I hope that you understand that it's not in the best interests of a young lady to . . . you know, to be indiscreet, shall we say?"

Carol looked at her mother with equal firmness. "Maybe it is and maybe it isn't, but it's my choice to make. I'm grown up, I'm almost sixteen, and I'm mature and I have a nice body and I can do what I want with my body because it's mine."

"I know, Carol, but there are rules in society and Judaism, and we live by certain standards. By Jewish standards, we rather discourage relations until people are married." Sara felt an overwhelming frustration and inadequacy as she spoke. "I wish you were somebody else's daughter. It would be easier for me to talk."

"Of course, Mother, I understand. Somehow parents don't believe that their children are what they are. They think we don't understand. But we grow up. We grow up naturally with the same physical characteristics that parents have. I look like you. Do you remember when you were looking in the mirror,

Mother? I've looked at myself in the mirror. I've seen my body. I've seen my breasts and I've seen my, my you know, and I've seen my figure, and I find myself very attractive. Didn't you say that it's God's blessing? Well, if it's God's blessing, maybe I ought to use God's blessing with boys who are blessed too. They're blessed the same way, but a little differently."

Sara sat back, genuinely surprised. "I don't believe it; I don't believe, Carol, that you're talking this way."

"You mean, Mother, you never thought that I would know. Or grow up. You kept me sheltered but you and Dad were busy with the synagogue, with other people and other things. I just learned by myself. I've seen movies and read books and, you know, Mother, that drugstores have magazines. Like *Playboy, Playgirl,* or *Oui,* and *Penthouse.* We're not living in a secret society anymore."

Sara fell silent, taking in Carol's words. She wondered if Carol had already experimented with some of the things she was talking about. Or was thinking about it.

"We're just more aware of things," Carol continued. "And we've learned how to take care of ourselves. If we have to do something to protect ourselves, we have to do it. We have to learn. That's why it's your responsibility, Mother, to teach us not only as a mother but as a rabbi. That's your job. You don't only have to talk about Jewish subjects. Abortion has nothing to do with being Jewish and sex has nothing to do with being Jewish."

"What are you saying, Carol? It does. It does because Judaism has always been concerned with life, with every part of life. Every part of life is part of our heritage, our culture. . . ." She paused. "It will take me some time to realize that my little girl is so grown up, but if I'm going to teach you as a rabbi, you've taught me a great lesson, too. You've taught me that I have to be honest. I'm not going to be very explicit. I can't be; that's not my job. I can't discuss those parts but I'll tell you about Judaism and its position on all these subjects."

"That's why I kissed you at the end of this session. Because I knew you would. I'm sorry that I got excited now." Sara accepted Carol's explanation.

"You've grown so in the last two, three months, Carol, I hardly recognize you. Let me ask you. What will some of the other parents say?"

"I really don't know, Mother," Carol answered thoughtfully. "I guess some of them will be happy and some will be angry. Those who are ashamed or can't talk about it, they'll be glad that a rabbi, who is also a woman, will be able to teach their children."

"I'm not so sure," Sara said. "I wonder whether some of the parents might not be angry that we're discussing these subjects in religious school."

"Why should they be? You've said that Judaism is interested in every part of life. Aren't we supposed to learn about our heritage?" Carol was bouncing Sara's words back at her.

"You're logical, Carol. But most people are not logical; they're emotional."

"Well, if I were you, Mother . . . if I were you, I would just go ahead and stand by your ideas, and I'd fight, because you're the rabbi and you can't be afraid of what people think, as long as you think it's right. The kids'll admire you for it, and they'll come to services because of it. You'll see."

It was not one of those conversations that could end. The ideas lingered. The experience hung like a canvas suspended over Sara's mind. Everything she did—every letter she wrote, every visit she made, and every conversation she had with the school principal and with her own secretary—was colored by the evening's exchange. She couldn't shake it from her mind. Don had even asked her if she was feeling all right.

"You seem a little far away," he said. "Something bothering you?"

"Oh, no," she answered. "Just a number of things on my mind, and I somehow have to work them out."

"Like what?"

"Oh, not yet, Don. When I think I need some help, I'll discuss it with you. They're rather confidential now. You know, a rabbi has to maintain confidences."

"You mean people have already talked to you about problems?"

"Oh, yes, I've already met some families to talk about their problems."

"I didn't think they would come to you that quickly."

"Well, let's say that there are problems that are occupying my mind right now. I'm trying to work them out."

But Sara felt that she *did* need to talk it out. After services on Saturday she asked Hal to walk home with her. Carol walked ahead with Simon. When the Sabbath lunch was over, Hal and Sara remained at the table drinking tea. After speaking in generalities, Sara said, "I have to tell you something, Hal. I was very disturbed this week."

Hal laughed, "It's already begun, has it? Honeymoon over?"

"I guess," Sara answered. "I guess the problems had to start sooner or later."

"I know what you mean."

"What do you know?"

"All I know is that something must be bothering you. You looked like you were far away today at the temple. Don noticed it too. You're tight and strained."

"I was going to talk to you about it. Of course, it's confidential."

"Of course."

"You know I'm teaching the confirmation class."

"Yes, I know."

"I only had one session with them and, frankly, they startled me and I really didn't know how to handle it."

"What do you mean?"

"Well, I described the nature of the course and asked about topics they might want to talk about, and they rattled off a number of subjects that I didn't expect."

"Like?" Hal asked.

"Like abortion, for example."

"Abortion?"

"Yes, and love and sex and birth control and other subjects too. It really surprised me. I said a few words, though I wasn't sure whether I should have or not. Then, that night I had a long talk with Carol and she really let me have it, Hal. She was so frank. I guess I haven't been close enough to her generation."

"Well, I'll be damned," Hal said. "I guess I've been away from it too. Two old fogies," he laughed.

"I knew you'd be surprised. It's a real problem. I'm wondering if I should teach these subjects, and how? I'm concerned about the reaction of parents. They might be furious."

"Well, if they're furious with you, Sara, they'll simply have to be furious. You have to be honest with the kids. You're their rabbi now and it's tough to be a rabbi sometimes. And the parents? Can you really be afraid of them, Sara? In the final analysis, you have to decide whether you are going to play your role or not."

"That's what Carol said."

"That means that both old men and young children think alike."

"You're not that old, Hal," Sara protested.

"No, but I'm not exactly sixteen."

"You're not an old man," she cajoled.

After a second glass of tea, Hal rose as Sara escorted him to the door. She thanked him for helping her. "You always help me so much, Hal. I really appreciate it."

"That's all right," Hal answered. He turned to Sara and some- how found her lips. The kiss was brief but the impact was electric. It caused both Hal and Sara to look at each other. A moment of hesitation and then Hal wound his arm around her waist and crushed Sara in an embrace. His kiss was deeper— probing, seeking more. Sara didn't resist. She surprised herself by returning the kiss with a sense of yearning.

"You're a special woman, Sara."

She flushed. "Shabbat Shalom, Hal. And thanks again." As if she were a schoolgirl, the pink in her cheeks deepened. She was thanking Hal for the kiss as well.

She leaned against the door after he left. The warmth of Hal's body and the sensation of his kiss lingered.

Chapter Twelve

SARA SPENT MUCH OF THE FOLLOWING WEEK in the temple library, researching material for the confirmation class. Temple Shalom was proud of its Molly Abrams Memorial Library, one of the most extensive on the island. Rabbi Sam had insisted that the temple collect reference material, so that people would not have to go to the city. The library consequently had the finest possible collection of Judaica. Jacob Abrams, the wealthiest congregant, had donated a large sum of money in his mother's memory—thanks to Rabbi Sam.

Sara found many books catalogued under Religion and Contemporary Issues. During the course of the week, she read many scholarly journals and texts.

The teenagers were seated before the bell rang. Their chatter was animated. As Sara walked in, a quick glance gave her the feeling that a different attitude prevailed. More serious, she surmised. She surveyed the classroom. The kids looked like normal teenagers. Their designer jeans were skin-tight and revealing. Some of the girls wore multicolored jerseys with decorations across their breasts, part of this year's craze, designed to draw attention. Stephanie's shirt shouted the declaration, "Thou Shalt . . ." over one breast, "Thou Shalt Not . . ." over the other. Melanie's projection read "Touch me, touch me not." Sara realized she had not kept pace. The girls seemed more brazen and fully endowed than she remembered. The boys took the girls' aggression in stride. Or did they?

"Are we really going to talk about those subjects, Rabbi?" Sara looked up, glanced at Carol, who exuded confidence. Her daughter's nod was encouraging.

"Of course we are," Sara said. "I promised last week that I would teach you, and I plan to do just that."

"What are we going to talk about first?"

"Abortion. I gather you all know what it is, and I assume that you know what pregnancy is." There was a snicker but it passed quickly.

"I have prepared some material, and I want to distribute these outlines," Sara said. "It will be much easier for you to understand what we are talking about, and you can then appreciate how much debate and discussion went on all through history about this subject."

"Let's take this in order," Sara continued. "Let me explain that there is only one place in the Bible that speaks about abortion. Everything comes from that source, that one passage. And that's in the book of Exodus. Last time I read you the section that says 'when two men fight and one of them pushes a pregnant woman and there is a miscarriage, but no other damage, then the one who is responsible has to be fined by the decision of the woman's husband.' That means that the husband has to be paid. 'But if there is other damage, then the penalty is life for life.' What this passage really means is that if the fetus is destroyed, the husband only has to be paid. But if the *woman* is killed, then the penalty is 'life for life.' This means that the *fetus* itself is not considered a life, a human being. If it *were* a life, then the penalty would be 'life for life.' And that is what Judaism bases its position on—that a fetus is not considered a life for which a penalty of murder is imposed. Judaism believes that the only time the fetus has an absolute right to life is when it is in the process of being born."

Sara looked around and saw some embarrassed faces, though most were intent, interested. She continued. "Once the major part of the baby's head is out, the child too has a right to life. Before that, the mother's life takes precedence. Everything must be done for her. If the mother's life is threatened, the fetus can be taken out limb by limb."

Richard Blum asked, "Does that mean that if the mother's life is in danger you can take the fetus out?"

"That's right."

"What if the mother just doesn't want the baby? Not when the baby is coming out, but before. Can there be an abortion?"

"Well, yes and no. We hold that until forty days, the fetus is considered *maya b'alma*, 'a water substance,' and it can be removed. After that, the mother's life has to be threatened. And if the. . . ."

"That's double talk, Rabbi."

"Now, wait a minute, let me finish. We call an abortion *therapeutic* because the mother's life is at stake. But Judaism has also begun to consider abortion an option when the mother is *mentally* endangered. That too is a therapeutic abortion."

"Do all Jews believe that?"

"I would say so, yes. As Conservative Jews, we follow Jewish law, like the Orthodox. The Reform do not follow traditional Jewish law—they must use whatever reasons they deem important. But *we* believe that therapeutic abortion is permissible. As a matter of fact, if you look at the last column of the photocopy I gave you, you will see a statement made by Rabbi Isaac Klein who says that 'where abortion is therapeutic, there can be no objection to it because like any other surgery we sacrifice the part for the whole.' There are some rabbis who believe that there are other instances where abortion is permissible—for example, in rape cases. Some rabbis call these abortions therapeutic, because the mother, the girl, is mentally anguished. And in some cases, if a baby is going to be born deformed, an increasing number of rabbis will say that abortion is permissible. Recently some rabbis have also held to the same position when a fetus has the genes for Tay-Sachs disease, a condition that is eventually fatal. It is not that the mother has a right over her body, because every body belongs to God, but that God has given us the mind to think. In that way we can determine what to do with our bodies."

Sara finished, sat back, and waited.

"I want to ask one question, Rabbi. How about life itself? When does life begin?"

"A good question, Steven. I can only answer you in this way. We have to go back in time and understand where the sources came from. You have heard of Plato and Aristotle and the Stoics. Plato, and the Roman Catholic Church follows his position, holds that life begins at conception. Aristotle says that life begins when the fetus is forty days for a boy and eighty days for a girl. The Stoics say that life begins at birth. I guess that Judaism may have adopted a blend of Aristotle's and the Stoic positions. We believe that the fetus is alive, but it is not a viable life. That begins at birth. As a matter of fact, if a baby dies before it is thirty days old, there is no funeral. A baby is not considered viable, that is, able to live without the mother, until it is thirty days old.

The teenagers sat back and looked at each other. Steven made the comment, "That's not bad. I think I understand. I think it's liberal, Rabbi, and I like it."

"Jewish law is based on reason. We have to find reasons for whatever decisions we take, so that when we do interpret Jewish law, it should be relevant. O.K.?"

"O.K." they responded. Sara watched them going out, a more subdued group. It appeared that they were thinking, trying to understand what they had heard.

This time Carol did not go up to her mother. Walking out with the others, she winked, and Sara winked back, smiling. Both turned to the group as a voice was heard: "Thou Shalt, Thou Shalt Not." Stephie's voice rang out, "Cut it out, cut it out."

Feeling successful with the confirmation class, Sara turned her thoughts elsewhere. She had had no contact with either the Rabbinical Conference or the Seminary. She had allowed Hal and Don to negotiate and she felt now, on the crest of success, that she ought to initiate a relationship. The next day she called the office of the Rabbinical Conference and asked for Rabbi Friedman. His secretary buzzed and announced, "Sara Weintraub."

Rabbi Friedman responded, "Sara Weintraub? I knew this was coming. Here we go." He picked up the telephone and after the usual exchange of amenities, Sara said, "Rabbi Friedman, I'd like to talk with you some day about my role in the Rabbinical Conference or at least the Seminary. I haven't been ordained and I'm not a member of the R.C. Is there something we can do? Can we work out a plan of study so that in some way the Seminary might give me, you know . . . recognize me, ordain me?" The question came rapidly, nervously.

"Exceptions are sometimes made," Rabbi Friedman responded, a little overwhelmed. "It's not up to us. You know that. The Seminary has to make that determination. Maybe you ought to talk with someone there—perhaps Doctor Horner himself."

"I thank you for that, Rabbi Friedman, but I thought you might pave the way for me. If you would be good enough to tell the Seminary that I did call, that I am interested, they might be more responsive."

"I'll be glad to do that too, Sara. Let me talk to someone."

"I would like to do whatever I can, Rabbi Friedman. I'm in an awkward position. I'm recognized here, but I want *real* recognition. However you feel, I can do a great deal for Judaism as a rabbi. I'm committed to it. I'll do everything I can, everything in my power to make my congregation, my community, and my people proud of me and their heritage."

"I'll get in touch with you, Sara," Rabbi Friedman said. He was feeling the pounding of her rapid, staccato, jab-like assertions. "I'll call and we'll stay in touch. In the meantime, good luck."

At the end of the conversation, Rabbi Friedman called Rabbi Hoberman.

"Maybe you *ought* to speak to Rabbi Horner, Mal. I think it's a good idea. Why not go right to the top? He's a liberal, understanding man. He may very well give it his personal attention."

"O.K. I'll call him. I'll let you know."

Chapter Thirteen

THE IRATE DR. PHIL ELKIND was the first to call Don. "As president of the board of governors, you ought to know this, Don. My son Billy, who is in the confirmation class, came home yesterday and told Beverly that Sara was talking about wild subjects. Completely out of place."

"Subjects like what, Phil?"

"Well, subjects like . . . abortion and . . . and sex."

"Sex? Sara talking about that?"

"Yes, she is. I wheedled it out of Billy. What I heard I find hard to believe. And I don't like it. What kind of school are we running? Are we running a sex school? That goddam rabbi."

"Hey, wait a minute, Phil. Watch your language."

"I won't watch my language, dammit. She's not much better than her husband. Remember him? He's the guy who made those unpatriotic statements and embarrassed me in front of everybody. When people heard that . . . that Sam was speaking against the government, that we had no right aiding Latin America. . . ."

"One thing has nothing to do with the other," Don interjected.

111

"No, but they're made of the same mettle. And I warned you, remember? I said I'd get even with him, and by God I'll get even with her too."

Phil hesitated, then angrily continued, at times incoherently. "Well, my son is a kid and I don't think it's the job of the religious school to talk about those subjects. Now, I'm gonna make a big fuss about it. I'm gonna raise a big stink. I'm not gonna let this go by the board. I'm gonna fight it and I know a lot of people who are already against it, and I know that others . . . and you watch, Don, unless you do something about it and stop her from teaching these things that don't belong in a religious school, I'm gonna fight this right down the line. I promise you." Don's ear throbbed.

"Now, hold on, Phil. She's just starting. Give her a chance."

"I will *not!*" Phil thundered. "I'm gonna nip this in the bud because I told you at the board meeting that once these women get the job, we'll never be able to get rid of them. And I'm. . . ." Phil choked on his own rage. Don heard Beverly call out: "Phil, take it easy; you'll have a heart attack."

"You keep quiet, you, you . . . and your women," he yelled at his wife. "You were for her and you shouldn't have been. I told you she's gonna cause us trouble and I'm determined to get rid of her."

Don tried to calm him. "Easy, Phil. Easy. I'm not going to jump to any conclusions. I'm not going to do anything rash. I'm going to sit down and talk with Sara and see what's it all about."

"Are you doubting me?" Phil demanded.

"No, I don't doubt your word, but I'd like to be sure. Don't forget that Carol Weintraub is in the same class, and it's not easy for, for a mother—I don't care whether she's a rabbi or not—to talk about abortion in front of her own daughter. And if her daughter isn't embarrassed, she's probably treating the subject properly."

"I'm not going to let this die out. Now, you take care of it, or you've got a big problem with me," Phil threatened.

"And if I don't solve it to your satisfaction?" Don threw the gauntlet.

"I'm gonna quit. I'll go to another synagogue, and there'll be a lot of people leaving with me."

Don was losing patience. "Are you threatening me?"

"Call it what you want. I'm not going to let this synagogue have a rabbi who openly encourages immorality. And to children to boot. I'm simply not going to permit it. I'm gonna fight you all the way."

"All right, Phil. We'll see. Calm down. I'll take it from here and get back to you."

Don sat back exhausted, muttering. Yet he was cool enough to wonder why Phil Elkind was so violent. Should we have a Board of Education meeting? he wondered. Parents could discuss the propriety of these subjects. Good idea, Don thought, satisfied, his agitation soothed.

Among the teenagers themselves, a new feeling emerged towards their heritage and towards Sara. They spread word among their peers. Many of the non-Jewish children were deeply impressed. Some even asked to attend synagogue. Some confirmands suggested they come to Friday night services to show Sara their appreciation. Sara was delightfully startled when a group came dressed in their best. She felt good as she looked out over the congregation and felt their admiration and respect.

"The subject we talked about last week," she began at the next meeting of the class, "was of interest to you. You hear about it, you said, and you read about it. It's all over; it's not something that's swept under the rug nowadays. So I decided to continue today on another subject. It's related, but it's another subject." She drew a breath.

"We say that sexual intercourse should be reserved for people who get married. But why do we say that? Because the greatest goal of a man and a woman is marriage. In our thinking, marriage is a holy achievement. It's called Holy Matrimony. We

113

believe that two people who fall in love and get married are reaching out for the greatest happiness two people can have; and the greatest expression of that happiness is sex. Not just, well, the playing around, but the meaning of having a close intimate experience. As people grow up they become aware of each other, and sex is primarily a growth process. We can speak objectively about it. In Judaism, marriage is called *Kiddushin*. Kiddushin means sacredness. It means two people fall in love and they vow to be together all their lives, and that they'll retain their original fascination for each other."

"That's all changed, hasn't it?" The question broke the monologue.

"What do you mean 'that's all changed'?" Sara asked.

"It's changed because of so many divorces. It's like people really don't care. They get married and when they don't get along they just divorce."

"Unfortunately you're right," Sara said. "But our ideal still is that two people who marry promise to stay together. They can make marriage beautiful. Judaism holds—it's in the Bible and the Talmud and everywhere else—that marriage and sex bring happiness." Sara suddenly stopped. What am I saying? she thought. Am I being carried away? They're fifteen, sixteen. Am I making another mistake?

"What do you think, kids?" she asked.

One or two of the girls lowered their heads in embarrassment. Not hearing a response, Sara backtracked. "Am I being too frank with you? I thought you were adults."

"Maybe we aren't." Stephanie said. "We kid around, but maybe we're not really all that grown up. Oh, I think you're right. I think it's good to know what Judaism says about . . . about sex."

"You hesitate saying it. I thought you were grown up," Sara countered.

"We are, but Rabbi, we didn't think you would talk about it like that. Abortion is something else, but we didn't think you would talk about sex and love."

114

Billy Elkind sat up straight. "I don't see anything wrong with it. I think it's good. But when I went home last time and told my mother that you talked about abortion, you know what she did?"

"What?" Sara asked.

"She slapped me."

"She slapped you?"

"She said I shouldn't talk about that. It's wrong and that it's not for kids. She told my father and my father was furious." Billy was at the edge of the seat. "He says that he's gonna do something about it."

"What do you mean?"

"He went wild. I thought he'd take my head off. If I tell him that now you're talking about sex, and said it was good . . . boy, I don't know what's gonna happen."

"Wait a minute," Sara said. "Don't take what I said out of context. I mean, don't go home or even amongst yourselves take one phrase and blow it out of proportion. You have to explain *everything* I said. If you don't, you're not being fair to me. You'll . . . well, you'll be getting *me* into trouble. Not that I'm afraid. I think what I'm doing is right. I should be able to talk candidly to boys and girls of your age. You know, a great part of the Bible deals with sex. Abraham, Isaac, and Jacob and the book of Leviticus consider which relationships are right and wrong. There are rules and guides of life that Judaism stresses." She looked supportingly at Billy.

"You can tell your father what I said, but be honest and tell him *everything* I said."

"I don't know," Billy said, his head swaying slowly.

"Didn't your father have to learn all this to become a gynecologist? Well, you tell him that anyone who wants to be a rabbi has to understand this part of life. It's a great part of Talmudic literature. It's not something to be ashamed of or to hide. Students at the yeshiva start studying the materials not when they're fifteen or sixteen but when they are eight, nine, and ten."

"Are you kidding?" Stephanie asked. "Eight and nine?"

"Yes," Sara emphasized. "Perhaps they don't understand everything completely, but they certainly study it. In the Talmud, two sections deal with marriage contracts. And sex is included. There's no shame to it," she repeated.

The teenagers filed out more subdued than ever. Carol came to her mother. "That was rough, wasn't it, Mom?" she commented.

"Yes, it was, Carol. I'm afraid I got carried away."

"You did very well. When the kids think about it, they'll agree. I just think we're sort of shocked that a rabbi said it. Or maybe because you're a female rabbi. Maybe that's why they were surprised."

"I don't think so," Sara disagreed. "Because children learn more about sex from their mothers."

"I don't know. Maybe." Carol added. "Maybe they're not as grown up as you and I thought. I'm really the oldest in the class, down deep, that is."

Sara had a premonition of a storm brewing.

A synagogue president is deemed to have a hold on the rabbi. As he picked up the receiver for the first call, Don could hear a quick argument, "Let me tell him!"

"No, no, I'll tell him, I'll tell him."

"No, you won't, I will." Don sat down to steady himself. It was Beverly Elkind who won the battle, who plunged her mouth into the phone, and spoke in spurts.

"Don, Phil called you last time, and you've done nothing about it. You promised that you would talk to Sara and now it's happened again. It's worse this time."

Don defended himself. "I haven't had a chance. I've been busy; Sara's been busy."

"You haven't done a damned thing. Do you know what Sara's done this time?" Beverly didn't wait for an answer. "This time she talked about sex. She talked about how beautiful it was."

"What's wrong with that?"

"What's wrong with that? These are kids, Don. Children."

"Are they? Your Billy is no angel, and he's not a child."

"I don't want a rabbi talking about sex. It's *my* job."

"If it's your job, Beverly, then you must have failed."

"How dare you! I haven't failed. I want my children to learn about sex from me, not from *her*. She must have a sex problem."

"It's not really that bad, Beverly. It can't be."

"It's terrible! She's getting these kids all excited."

"You're exaggerating, Beverly, but I'll talk to her about it."

"No, it's too late, Don. You're *not* going to talk about it. You promised before. Now *we're* going to talk about it. I told Phil and he's furious. He's already talked to some of the others. We want to meet with her."

"I'll take care of it. Let me give her a chance."

"I'm sorry. We've decided to meet with her to tell her exactly what we think. We just want you to know how we feel, that's all."

"All right, if you want. Let me talk to Sara and I'll get back to you. Then we can set up a meeting."

"People are not going to take her meddling lying down. I promise you. You know something? I'm broad minded and all that, but I was against her as a rabbi. Maybe because she's a fresh widow, still misses the. . . ."

"All right, Beverly, let's stop there. Either we discuss this intelligently or we're not going to talk at all. I'll talk to Sara and I said I'll get back to you. Now let go. The way I see it, maybe she's made a mistake; maybe she's overstepped her bounds."

"You don't know women, Don. You're wasting your breath."

"Trust me, will you please? Sara's no revolutionary. She's a sensible person."

"All right, all right," Beverly succumbed.

"And she'd be the last one to say things that would unnecessarily excite our teenagers." Don insisted on having the last word.

That evening, Don went to Sara's house. He thought her face looked terribly drawn. "Get enough rest, Sara?"

"Sure, sure. How's Sue?"

"Fine. She took up golf. By the way, have you thought of a hobby for relaxation? I know how strenuous this has been for you."

"Thanks, Don, not yet. I enjoy my work very much."

"I had the impression you're taking too much on yourself."

"What do you mean?"

"Well, all the things you're involved in, for instance, in synagogue matters, that is. I know you're going to be getting involved in communal affairs also, and, well, you've got two children to raise."

"I went into this thing with my eyes open, Don."

"Let's be sensible, Sara. Some of the chores really should be delegated. You don't have to do *everything*."

"I wish you'd show me what I don't have to do," Sara replied earnestly.

"Well, we do have a paid staff. We pay our teachers twenty-five dollars an hour. Edelstone, of course, gets more, so why can't Edelstone teach the confirmation class, for example? You're entitled to have some time for yourself, or perhaps to oversee the school."

Sara shook her head, not realizing Don's intent.

"But Sam, busy as he was, insisted on having the confirmation class. He put his life and soul into the younger people."

"I know, Sara, but you know the old saying, 'Rome wasn't built in a day.' "

"Rome wasn't built in a day," she repeated. Then she looked quizzically at Don. Her eyes widened with comprehension.

"Is that why you've come to see me? Has someone complained about what I discussed in the confirmation class?"

Don nodded. "There was a complaint last weekend, and just today, something else was criticized."

"You mean about abortion and sex?"

"Yes, Sara. There's been . . . well . . . a . . . uh . . . an explosion. They say you have to stick to religion. Some of the parents are violently opposed to what you said. The children are coming home and telling their parents that you said that abortion is O.K. and sex is beautiful, and all that. They're afraid that you're telling the kids to go out and do whatever they please."

"I never said that, Don. You know that. They're purposely misconstruing what I said."

"Sara," Don pleaded. "You've got to learn that what you say and how people interpret your words are two different things. These are sensitive subjects."

Sara was adamant. "I still think children should learn about them. The parents aren't opposed to it being taught in school— why should religious school be different? Why shouldn't we give them a Jewish point of view?"

"Sara, I'm not in the class. I don't have a child in the class. But you're talking out there to parents who are angry. I might as well tell you. They want to meet with you."

"All right, let's meet," she pressed.

"Sara, you have to tread very carefully; they engaged you."

"Are you saying I've got to agree?"

"No, but just try to remember that they *are* the congregation."

The threat jabbed her. "I'll remember everything," she answered coolly. "But I will *not* give up my sense of values as a teacher or as a rabbi."

"I'm not asking you to!" Don implored. "Oh, no!" he groaned under his breath. "Looks like we got more than we bargained for."

Sara's head began to throb when Don left. She wondered if she were going about it the wrong way. But I can't let a few narrow-minded congregants dictate policy to me, she reasoned. After all, I *am* the rabbi.

But waning confidence gave way to self-doubt. Without thinking, she found herself dialing Hal's number. "Hal? It's Sara."

"Hi. Glad you called. It's been a while."

"Hal, listen. I need some objective advice."

"What's wrong, Sara? You sound tense."

"I am. Don was just here. It seems some of the parents are complaining about what I'm teaching the confirmation class. They've taken a few things I've said out of context and have misconstrued the entire meaning. Don was suggesting that I give it up."

"What? That's ridiculous. One of your strongest points is knowing how to talk to kids. Don't you remember the terrific response you got at the rally for Soviet Jews? You were fantastic! You had all the kids with you."

Her voice dropped. "This is different, Hal."

Hal, ever sensitive, quickly responded: "Don't move. I'll be right over."

"But. . . ."

"No buts. I'm coming over."

Hal insisted that Sara dispense with serving coffee. He demanded to hear the problem at once.

"I'm sorry, Hal. Maybe I shouldn't have called you. Perhaps Don thought this was supposed to be confidential."

"Why? So no one would defend you? Does he think that the matter will be quietly swept under the rug?"

"No, not exactly. Oh, Hal! I've no right to keep bothering you with these problems."

"You've every right, Mrs. Weintraub. Every right, indeed." Sara blushed. After all, she'd been "Sara" to him for years. By deliberately calling her Mrs. Weintraub, he was underscoring the affectionate familiarity he felt for her.

"All right. I think Don wants me to resign from the religion class. Maybe even the synagogue."

"Why?"

"Some of the parents feel I'm teaching improper subjects. I *am* talking about abortion and sex—but all within the realm of Judaism, and, heaven help me, within the bounds of morality." She paused. "Some of those parents must have terrible guilt complexes. Anyway, in my opinion, the teenagers want and

120

need to know more about these subjects. I think they appreciate what I did, even if it will take awhile for them to truly comprehend. Emotionally that is."

"I think that's fantastic, Sara. It's about time. What's wrong with those parents? Of course you handled it properly."

"I wish everyone agreed."

"And I just bet I know which one of the parents is making the biggest stink of all."

"Who?"

"Phil Elkind, the quack."

"Quack?"

"Yes, quack. Judy went to him a few times. Prescribed all the wrong things. Was no help at all when we found out we couldn't have children."

Sara's voice was quiet. "I'm sorry, Hal."

"No, it's all right."

"But why is Phil so vehement about this issue?"

"You knew about Phil's vendetta against Sam, didn't you?"

"Hal, do you know what you're saying?"

"I sure do. Phil had it in for Sam and never got his chance to get even. So he's taking it out on you."

The pair grew uncomfortably silent. Somehow, the mention of Sam and Judy strained the conversation. Sara felt an overwhelming pressure. Sam gone, Phil's vowed revenge, Don's unfairness, her long suppressed dream possibly squelched forever, the worries over Carol and Simon . . . everything seemed to come crashing down around her.

Instinctively, Hal gathered her into his arms. "Oh, Sara, this is so damned dumb. Do you know how many times I've wanted to comfort you, to share with you, to. . . ." His lips found hers as he pressed closer. She returned the kiss with a passion that surprised Hal. He massaged the knotted muscles across her back and shoulders, murmuring against her ear. "I think I'm falling in love with you, Rabbi Sara. What do you say about that?"

Her heart pounded. It was still new; she was so unsure. But she couldn't hide the smile tugging at her lips. Hal saw it and felt content. There was plenty of time. They moved apart.

"Mother, I. . . . Oh, Uncle Hal, I'm sorry; I didn't know you were here."

Sara reddened more than Carol did. Did her daughter catch her in a compromising situation?

"No, that's all right, Carol," Hal said tactfully. "I was just leaving." He searched Sara's eyes, suddenly finding them unreadable. His gaze didn't waver as he continued: "And don't worry about that problem, Sara. You're doing the right thing. Don't give up."

"Good night, Hal. And thank you."

"What problem, Mother?" Carol asked.

"About the religion class, dear." Sara was not exactly prepared to talk about what Carol probably had just witnessed, but she would do so if her daughter questioned. Practice what you preach, she thought wryly.

But the girl chose to ignore it. "What problem with the class? I thought everything was going just fine."

"Some of the parents don't agree. They think some subjects shouldn't be taught."

"How ridiculous. You're so liberal, Mother. A shame that no one wants to appreciate it. But I certainly do." Carol's words had an ironic ring. Was she hiding something? Instinctively, Sara knew something was wrong. But what?

As Sara entered the auditorium, conversations abruptly stopped. With utter poise, she waved to some, smiled at others, then walked to the front of the room where a table was set. It seemed that every parent was present. A quick survey of faces told her that they were concerned. Some appeared hostile.

Sara welcomed the parents warmly, saying that she was delighted that they had exhibited such interest in what appeared to be an important matter. "The important thing to remember," she began, "is that I'm as concerned about your children as you are. I'm prepared to work diligently and seriously. I want you to be frank." She drew a breath.

"I understand that a question has been raised about some of the subjects I've been teaching in the confirmation class." She looked directly at Phil Elkind. "Dr. Elkind, I know that you've been annoyed. Do you care to express your opinion in the presence of all the parents?"

Phil Elkind, embarrassed at being caught off guard, rose slowly and began. "Yes, Sara, uh, Rabbi, uh . . . I . . . uh . . . was very angry when I came home last week and Beverly told me. She only told me a little bit and I had to draw the rest out, that you spoke to the children. . . ."

Sara corrected, "To the teenagers."

"Yes, to the teenagers, about subjects that . . . uh . . . I don't believe belong in the synagogue."

"Like what, Phil?" Sara was determined to elicit every fact and nuance.

"Like . . . uh . . . abortion and birth control and sex. Last week you talked to them about abortion and told them what the Jewish position was and . . . uh . . . when Billy came home and told us, I was furious. I really was, because, first of all, I don't think a subject like abortion and certainly not sex has to be discussed in religious school."

"Why are you so opposed to it?" Sara was the prosecutor. "What have I really done that is against the law or against any sense of moral values that you hold?"

Phil looked at Beverly and Beverly rose. "I don't think it's your place, Sara . . . Rabbi, to talk about sex to my son. That's my job and his father's."

"I agree with you," Sara answered, "but have you really discussed these things with Billy? If you have, then you're right and I'm wrong. Let me ask all of you a question. May I ask for a show of hands—we have about thirty-five people here—how many of you have discussed some of these subjects with your children? Let's see . . . four, eight, and the rest? Thank you. You see, Phil. You and Beverly may be the exceptions. How about you. . . .?" Sara looked at the others.

"Wait a minute, Rabbi," Nettie Kornblatt was standing, angry. "I don't know whether I want you to challenge me. I didn't come here to be put on the spot." There was a murmur of agreement. "I came to tell you, just like Phil and Beverly, I came to tell you that Stephie came home and all she talked about was, wow, sex, and that the rabbi said it was beautiful."

"Nettie, have you ever talked to Stephie about sex? She's a very pretty girl and she's grown up." The last phrase struck a familiar chord. "The boys in the class are grown up too and they see Stephie and some of the other girls. They're not blind, you know. You allow them to wear tight-fitting sweaters, and on their jerseys, 'thou shalt' and 'thou shalt not' written on their breasts." The parents squirmed at Sara's frankness.

"Wait a minute," Nettie called out again.

Sara continued. "Before you challenge me, how can you let them wear revealing clothes and then say that we can't talk about it? You haven't talked about it. Shouldn't they learn, somewhere, that there are moral positions in life, that Judaism says something about them?"

"That's not what we are against!" Nettie protested but Phil interrupted. "Oh, let me tell you," he said. "I think that *religion* is your job, Rabbi. Not sex. You teach religion. Leave the rest to us."

"And how about the cults? How about the Moonies, and Jews for Jesus? And drugs? And subjects like that? And business ethics? Nursing home scandals? Don't you read the papers, doctor? Nettie? Mr. Cowen? Don't you read the papers, and don't children read them, and don't you watch television, and haven't you seen the latest motion pictures with all the sex, killings, and violence? You're hiding your heads! Haven't you seen the commercials about contraceptives and vaginal douches? I'm surprised!" Sara's demeanor exuded confidence. "Now, I'm a woman and I'm not ashamed to talk about it. You say talk about religion. What's the Bible all about, Dr. Elkind? Male and female! God created them! Remember? All the episodes with Abraham and Sarah and Jacob and Rebecca and Leah—these are all human life stories, and therefore they are part of religion. I'm not encouraging your children to go out and try sex. Let's be honest about it." Sara heard mumbling in the crowd.

She went on. "I think that somewhere along the line they should understand what and who they are. We are all parents. We can't hide. Every study shows that parents are generally not capable, don't want to, are ashamed, or are embarrassed to discuss these things with their children. Now, I know that there was a recent study in which even the parents of the sixties generation, you know after the Vietnam war. . . ."

"There you go with politics," Phil blustered. "Now don't talk about politics to me because I'll never forget what your husband did to embarrass me. He called our government immoral when I was Commander of the American Legion post."

"We're not talking about that. We're talking about life and sex." Phil stopped short, his wings clipped. "I want to finish," Sara pressed. "Every study shows that parents today are not very different from parents of ten, fifteen, twenty years ago. It's just as hard for them to discuss subjects like premarital sex and contraceptives and homosexuality and abortion. I believe that somewhere these kids should learn a Jewish position. I'm not trying to excite them physically."

"You're wrong, Rabbi, I know you're wrong." It was Frances Solomon. Eyes turned to a handsome, stately woman. Frances had studied psychology in college days and had only recently decided to go back for her master's degree. Her manner was diplomatic and sincere. "When you talk about certain subjects, people, especially teenagers, think about it. They talk about it; they have to act it out. They play games. They jostle each other. They dance. Sara, they're human too, and they have to simply, well, express their feelings. They get stimulated."

"I'm not saying that they shouldn't express themselves," Sara defended. "I don't go as far as you seem to imply. Here's an example of what I don't do, even though it's in a Jewish textbook. I just brought this book to show you that Nachmanides, in the thirteenth century, wrote that the act of sexual union is holy and pure. He said that the Lord created all things in accordance with His wisdom, and that whatever he created cannot possibly be shameful or ugly. This letter, incidentally, explicitly describes the genital organs and says that when a man is in union with his wife, in a spirit of holiness and purity, the divine presence, God, is with them."

"That's not bad, Rabbi," someone snickered.

"I'm not going to read the letter. Just as you and I believe that when a child asks about sex or when a child asks 'Mommy, where does a baby come from' he will accept the answer you give him on his level, teenagers, too, ought to understand, on *their* level, what life is about. Abortion and sex can be discussed in a detached way. Should we be afraid to say it? Better here than television. Television teaches sex like no one else does. It teaches violence like no one else. Television and the commercials—did any of you write to the station when they advertised a condom, showing a boy and a girl going off into the woods?" The parents sat up, their faces awakening. Where did she learn all this? Sara responded to the alert look. "I'm a human being, my friends. I was a wife. I had a husband who loved me too. Sex was part of our life and it was a happy and active part and I'm not ashamed of it." She suddenly felt enervated. Was she too frank, revealing?

"I'm not satisfied," Phil said. "The religious school isn't the place for all this. They have so little time. They ought to learn how to read Hebrew, how to pray, the rituals, the holidays. That's what they should learn. About God, and the Bible, so they can answer questions and defend Judaism."

"Of course you're right on those counts," Sara conceded. "And I assure you, they will learn all that. Rabbi Sam covered some of it. But that still doesn't take away from the demand to know about these other subjects. They really want to learn and understand. Some of these kids are already quite mixed up. The world is a different place than it was when we were their age."

A fleeting look of doubt crossed Phil's face, as if Sara had struck a raw nerve. He looked at his wife. They exchanged whispers and then Beverly looked up. "Maybe you've got a point, Sara. But I don't know." She seemed less angry.

The exchange of opinions among the parents grew repetitive. Some seemed only to want to hear themselves speak. When the meeting finally ended, Sara's doubts persisted. But at least the parents were still willing to give her a chance.

Chapter Fourteen

THE LOCAL NEWSPAPER, the *Wilmette Courier*, carried the story of Sara's challenge to the parents. The headline read, "Rabbi Challenges Parents on Sex Subjects." The brief account mentioned Sara Weintraub and noted the Conservative Temple Shalom.

Sandy Shane, a local resident who was a reporter for the Long Island Supplement of the Sunday *New York Times*, sent the item to Isidor Schaeffer, the unofficial reporter for news stories about Jewish organizations. Noticing the item from Wilmette, Schaeffer wondered, Is there something that I don't know? Woman rabbi and Conservative? There may be something to this story. He sought out Rabbi Friedman.

"Where did you get this story?" Rabbi Friedman asked.

"Do you have a rabbi on your roster by the name of Sara Weintraub?" Schaeffer returned.

"No," Rabbi Friedman answered. "We don't."

"Well, then, what's the story? Is it a mistake?"

Rabbi Friedman knew that the proverbial moment of truth was at hand. If Isidor Schaeffer wrote the story for the *Times*, the Rabbinical Conference would be embarrassed. He would either have to deny or admit the story, and he wasn't ready. Bad publicity was detrimental to the Seminary. "I'll have Rabbi Hoberman call you. I'm not authorized to make a statement on every subject, you know."

"Doesn't sound right to me, Rabbi Friedman. Level with me. Is there or isn't there a woman in the wings?"

"You'll hear from Rabbi Hoberman."

"I'm going to watch you, now," Schaeffer warned. "I promise you. I think something is going on."

Friedman didn't say anything. Instead he quickly called Hoberman. "We'd better get on with it," Hoberman responded. "We'd better take it up. Sara was right. . . . Call Dr. Horner and get him into the picture. He really should know what's going on. It doesn't look like the problem is going to go away."

Rabbi Friedman went to visit Dr. Horner and outlined the history of events involving Sara. Dr. Horner had not been aware of the details and Friedman cautiously suggested that Dr. Horner might want to consider all the ramifications of the difficult issue. Perhaps he would call Sara in himself. She might be persuaded to resign and thereby avoid embarrassing the Seminary. Or perhaps she would be more determined to justify herself in the rabbinic role.

"Are you suggesting that I may go beyond mere talking to her?" Dr. Horner eyed his younger colleague.

"No, I'm only saying that we're going to have to meet the issue head on, and I don't want the Seminary placed in an embarrassing position," Friedman answered. "At least talk to her. Who knows what might result. We may avoid a problem altogether, or we may not. It's a chance." Dr. Horner was already envisioning the unknown. He stroked his short beard, nodding absently. His speech was deliberate. "It sounds like a good idea, from what you tell me. She's been dynamic, forthright. She's come out stronger than many of our colleagues, and she's fearless." Rabbi Friedman watched quietly as Dr. Horner mused. "Woman prophet?" He enjoyed the thought.

"I wouldn't say she's fearless, Dr. Horner," Friedman broke the reverie. "But it's true, she's excited the community and she really lays her heart on the line." Dr. Horner hardly heard the words.

"It's very commendable. Let me think about it. I admire any person, man or woman, who leads our people with such strength. It's refreshing."

Sara could hardly contain her exuberance when she received a written invitation to meet Dr. Horner at the Seminary. She was thrilled yet confused. Why? she wondered. Why does he want to see me? To make me resign? Is it possible that he will encourage me? Warn me? Why should he? She called Don. To be summoned by the Chancellor of the Seminary was a distinct honor, no matter what he wanted to discuss.

"Will you come with me, Don, I mean, as president of the synagogue?"

"No," Don answered. "You're the rabbi now, Sara. We have confidence in you."

"Not everybody does," Sara said. "Least of all me. Not now."

Sara called Hal and asked him to escort her.

"I don't think so, Sara. It's best for you to go on your own. You're strong, Sara. Don't weaken," he encouraged.

"I need you." Sara felt suddenly alone. Had her strength been a facade, a defense?

"It may be easier, but I don't know whether you want it to be." Sara paused to consider his meaning. But Hal added, "I'll be glad to drive you in, if that will help. I'll take you to the Seminary. I'll meet you later, if you want."

"Yes. Thanks very much, Hal, I'd appreciate it." She felt relieved. She was going alone but Hal would be there for her later.

At dinner, Sara sat with her children and showed them the letter from Dr. Horner. "What does it mean, Mother?" Carol asked.

"I really don't know," Sara answered, her eyes sparkling. "All

I know is that one of the most illustrious Jewish leaders in the world has invited me to come speak with him. It's a great honor, and I'm ecstatic."

"Does it mean that he's going to talk to you about being a rabbi?" Simon asked.

"I think so," Sara felt positive. "I would suspect that he is."

"Do you think that he might want to ordain you?" Carol and Simon sounded eager.

"No. That's hardly possible. After all, I'm not a student at the Seminary. I haven't studied. . . . No, I don't think so. That hasn't even crossed my mind."

"Maybe he heard about you, Mother," Simon said. Carol agreed.

"Maybe, Simon. Let's wait and see."

On the morning of the meeting, Hal met Sara at her home. Sara had slept well. Strangely, the anticipation had calmed her. Confidence strengthened her. Carol and Simon had rushed off to school with a cheery "Good luck, Mother." The sun shone brighter than usual, or so it seemed to Sara as she waited. "It has to be a good day," she thought, and added, "Please, God."

Riding next to Hal, Sara felt young and vibrant, as if she were on a date. It had been years since she felt so invigorated. Was it the enchantment of her forthcoming meeting, or was it the man sitting next to her? She was afraid of succumbing to guilty thoughts. But Hal seemed to take everything in stride. She began to talk about her experiences, even repeating herself.

"You're really on a high," Hal said, smiling. "I like that."

"It gives me confidence."

Crisscrossing the Long Island highways, they drove silently for a while. Nearing the city, Sara began to steel herself. She spoke of how she challenged her problems, and how the complaining members reacted. She talked about the achievements she had attained, the friends she had gained. She had a good feeling about the first few months of her new career. "You'll do okay," Hal said. "I have confidence in you. I have more than confidence in you—I'm proud of you." He winked.

"Thank you, Hal." Sara squeezed his arm. "You've been very, very sweet to me and you're the one who really kept me going, more than you think."

Hal glanced at Sara and then turned back to watch the road. "You've meant a great deal to me too," he said quietly.

"I guess we've helped each other," Sara added, pausing, "because we've needed each other."

When they reached the Seminary, Hal drove into the grand entrance, opened the door for Sara, and helped her out. He kissed her cheek and said, "Call me at the office when you're finished. We'll have dinner before we go home, O.K.?"

"Thanks so much, Hal. See you later." She watched him drive away. With a lilting bounce, she headed for Dr. Horner's office. The Seminary building reminded her of the western wall of Jerusalem. Heavy blocks of stone exuded a feeling of solid strength. The substantial, overpowering elevation into the sky reflected power, stature, and influence. Photographs of the great leaders of the movement, almost all bearded and saintly, looked watchfully upon visitors entering the lobbies. Ancient and modern religious symbols were displayed everywhere. There was no mistaking that this was a religious institution. Dr. Horner's offices were on the seventh floor. As the elevator opened, Sara felt as if she were in the presence of God. It reminded her of the experience in the temple's sanctuary before she reached her decision to become a rabbi. The recollection, she thought, was a good omen.

She did not wait long after announcing herself to the solemn-looking middle-aged secretary who had a brown bun on the back of her head. Walking nervously into Dr. Horner's office, Sara felt overwhelmed. Dr. Horner's office was more like a study. The walls were panelled but the panelling was roughly hewn. Five or six desks were spread about, each with a telephone and a pile or two of papers. In the far right corner near a large window sat Dr. Horner, as imposing as she had imagined him to be, as impressive and as saintly. He looked up from his desk, smiled, and rose slowly, gently. His tall and solid height seemed too large for the study, she thought. He had a trimmed rounded beard, white hair, shocked on either side of his face. A sharply outlined nose and mouth accentuated deep blue, penetrating eyes. The quick, easy break of his smile broke the aura of austerity. He stretched out his hand as his head tilted charmingly. He pointed to one of the chairs in front of his desk. Sara was almost frozen with fright.

Aware of her anxiety, the Chancellor kept speaking. "These are all my desks," he said. "I work on many projects at one time. Each desk represents a different program. Today I'm working on an understanding of God by Abraham. It's not a very easy subject, you know." His smile was encompassing and helpful. "Sit down, please, Mrs. Weintraub."

Sara had not heard herself addressed as Mrs. Weintraub for some time. She had become accustomed to *Rabbi* Weintraub. Was Dr. Horner giving her a message? Was the purpose of the visit to tell her that she was still a Mrs. and not a rabbi? She was glad to sit down.

"You probably wonder why I invited you here," Dr. Horner said, looking at her evenly but not without compassion. She nodded. "It's a good question, and I really wish I knew the reason." Sara waited, her heart starting to beat erratically. She felt her face flush.

"I understand that you've created quite a stir, an impact, in your community. Rabbi Malcolm Friedman told me, and others have mentioned this to me in the past weeks, past month, month and a half." He paused. "You know, we hear many things and we can't give credence to everything we hear. There are times when we have to pause and say there's something that we should research, to see what's happening and how it is affecting our movement and the total Jewish community. Do you understand what I'm saying, Mrs. Weintraub?"

"Yes, of course," Sara mumbled, expecting Dr. Horner to continue. "I'm honored that you have asked me to come."

"You don't have to be modest, my dear. I'm aware of many of the events and challenges which occurred in your community.

133

They get into the papers, and I have enough good friends here who keep me informed. I'm not here to judge you, but I thought I would talk to you about you as a woman, if I may."

Here it comes, Sara thought.

Dr. Horner smiled. "Just because you have been given a pulpit and a title by your board of trustees doesn't really establish a fact. Do you understand what I am saying?"

"Yes, of course I understand," Sara said, feeling her confidence rising, and her tension dissipating as she listened. The Chancellor was being careful not to hurt her feelings. "And you are correct. The members of my congregation have given me a pulpit. They *do* call me rabbi. A moment ago you addressed me as *Mrs.* It's true I'm not a rabbi. I haven't been ordained. I'm not a member of the Rabbinical Conference, though I hope that, please God, this will come to pass." Sara felt comfortable now.

"That's exactly what I want to talk about. May I call you Sara?"

"Please, by all means."

"Because of you, if I may be frank, there will be questions raised in the Rabbinical Conference, in other synagogues. So you are really involved in an important issue, and we will have to deal with it seriously." Dr. Horner pondered his next statement. "If I had the power, if I had the clear conscience. . . . Frankly, I would ordain you."

O God! Sara's thoughts exploded. "Ordain me?" Her voice rose. "Why? I don't have the knowledge. I don't have the . . . the . . . background. I was going to speak to Rabbi Friedman about it and maybe to your dean. . . ." Dr. Horner was already pleased with Sara's response.

"I appreciate your honesty," he said. "You're made of real mettle. If I could, I would take the bull by the horns and invest you with the title of rabbi. But that would create a great controversy in the Jewish world. The Conservative movement would say that I'm an autocrat, acting without authority, without consultation. The attack of the Orthodox would be damnation. The fact is that I can't, not now." The last two words hung.

134

"You mean, there's a possibility?"

"Well, I don't know. Let's let that go for a little while. You see, Sara," Dr. Horner was shifting to a new subject, "we've developed a theory about rabbis and men. For women to be rabbis, they have to be like men. There's pressure everywhere for equality. I'm not sure that there is such a thing as equality, in its finer sense. But let's assume there is. A woman has to be a woman, and from her own self, from her own being, she has to become; she has to achieve. So women rabbis, if there are to be any, shouldn't imitate, impersonate, or mimic men."

"But do we have any criteria for a rabbi other than those that apply to men?"

"You've got a point. There are no other criteria. Rabbis were different years ago. They studied Jewish law and they taught. Today, a rabbi has to be a master of all trades. In addition, heritage or roots is an important thrust these days. Everyone is looking, trying to find some connection with the past. We do the same thing about rabbis. Rabbis were students, scholars, private figures, anything except what they are today. So that if a woman wants—if she studies and has the knowledge—she can, without a doubt, be that kind of a rabbi—a student, a scholar, a private figure. You see I'm avoiding the question of a woman rabbi as people conceive it. Then again, what are we to do? A large percentage of our people are traditional. They believe in the Halakhah, in traditions and customs. What are we to do with them? They are the backbone of Conservative Judaism. Certainly you wouldn't want us to disregard them. Certainly we can't forget them. Or you might say, let's take a chance. It's fashionable these days to say, let's take a risk. Let Israel take risks for peace, give up the West Bank or Gaza. Or let's establish detente with Russia again and take risks for peace. I myself hesitate to risk a cleavage, a clash. Furthermore, you must know that the great leaders and scholars of the Seminary, while advocating Conservative Judaism, are essentially Orthodox. They are committed to firm tradition. What would happen if the Rabbinical Conference, for example, or if I act unilaterally, and these leaders say that they cannot be a part of a movement that violates this tradition? No matter how you try to rationalize it, if our Seminary teachers say they cannot accept it, what will happen to the Seminary? And then what will happen to our movement? I will not have it on my conscience that I had a part in any action that undermines the Seminary.

"I'm also concerned about disunity in the Jewish community. Some will say I am submitting to pressure and fear of the Orthodox community. Perhaps. We are all Jews and I am determined to avoid any break if possible. So, you see, Sara, these are important issues. The Rabbinical Conference will be discussing it, and the Executive Board and the Committee on Legal Interpretation will be evaluating the issue. I believe I know what their ultimate decision will be. I daresay they will decide in favor and will adopt a resolution saying that women should be rabbis. I say this for a number of reasons. First, because they're probably afraid that some of the women in their congregations will accuse them of prejudice. It will take great stamina for rabbis to withstand the demands for equal rights. However, from my point of view, I really have to look ahead, beyond what's going on today to what will happen in five months, six months, and even in a year or two. Will a decision to approve women rabbis be good and positive? What would it achieve besides satisfying some women that their sex is also recognized? Will the decision bring more people to Judaism? Will more come to the synagogue? Will Jews be more ethical? More observant? Will more people become active in Jewish life? Will more Jews understand their heritage and practice it? That's the question. So you see, Sara, it's easy for a congregation's board of trustees to say 'you're a rabbi'; that's easy, but they don't have the Halakhic authority. That's where the dilemma is." He stopped. A heavy silence fell over the study.

"Do you want me to think about it and respond?" Sara asked.

"Yes. By all means. God knows, you may be the first if it comes about."

"Is it a possibility?" She leaned forward eagerly.

"I didn't say there *was* a possibility. I said *if*. I may suggest, as a friend, that you speak to Dean Kahn of our Rabbinical School. Ask him about a private course under his tutelage that could help you study some of the basic required courses. It may be helpful in the long run." Sara thought she detected a wink hiding in his eyes. He rose to indicate that the interview was nearing an end. "Let's stay in touch. I shall be watching what you do, as will almost every rabbi in America. And Sara," he added, "I trust that our conversation, for the time being, will be confidential."

Sara left Dr. Horner's office and walked slowly to the elevator. She was perplexed. The sonorous voice lingered, as did the memory of his gentle smile. What was he really saying to her? *Was he asking me to withdraw? Signaling me to avoid creating problems by trying to be a rabbi? Didn't he suggest that I might be responsible for a major break in the Conservative movement or the cause of undermining tradition of more than a million people? Was he imposing guilt? The insinuation of ordaining me, was his mentioning the word "ordination" like throwing me a bone? He did say, speak to Dean Kahn about studying. Is Dr. Horner thinking of making an exception of me? Ordain me personally, just to show that it is an exception? What did I accomplish by coming here, and what did he accomplish?*

Sara's bemusement and perplexity continued. She did not recall telephoning Hal to say that the interview was over and that she'd be waiting for him at the entrance. She looked at the ancient ironbound fence and felt spewed-out and dismissed.

"You sounded so far away, like you were in another world," Hal said, as he drove in and opened the car door.

"I'm so glad to see you." Sara breathed easier in the car, her color returning. "I didn't know where I was, I was so overwhelmed. I still am. I don't understand what this was all about. I looked forward with such great anticipation to meeting Dr.

Horner. He's brilliant, charming, delightful, and I know why he's the leader of our movement. But I still can't figure out what he wanted."

"Let's talk about it," Hal offered. "Why don't we go out and have lunch at a nice restaurant, sit quietly, and you'll tell me all about it? Maybe I can help you understand."

"I'd like that," Sara responded.

They headed for the Tavern on the Green in Central Park. Sara had not been there since it had been remodeled. Its decor, blending with the green perennials outdoors, added to its natural setting. Like a secluded nest, it exuded a feeling of detachment. As they walked toward the entrance, Sara took Hal by his arm and felt lighter in spirit. A breeze swept her face as the gloom disappeared. Her cheeks glistened.

"You look better already," Hal said, as they walked jauntily.

"I feel better," she replied. She turned and looked at him with a broad smile. She was already different. She felt young, alive. They walked with long strides, her hair flowing in the cold gusting wind, her radiant smile bursting through frostbitten cheeks. In the restaurant, Sara's face grew warm. "It's so refreshing," she sparkled, "away from the grind."

"I'm glad. It's good to see you alive again," Hal responded approvingly. "You have to do this once in a while, Sara, to get hold of yourself, to see where you're going."

Sara reviewed the interview, surprised that she remembered it so well. Hal listened attentively, his eyes riveted, scanning her eyes and face. He analyzed as he listened, saying he viewed the experience positively. It seemed to be an omen, he said, a signal for her to study, to continue to work hard, to show the stuff she was made of.

"He's looking for a way to take a positive stand," Hal added. "He needs a basis so he invites you to come and he encourages you by telling you that you've brought pride to the movement. He's about ready, I think, to talk about it to the Seminary faculty. He needs also to show, to prove, that you've taken the role very seriously, that in spite of hard work, you are also studying, with

Dean Kahn. He's giving you a sign, Sara. It's really up to you. That's how I read it."

"You think so?" Dare she hope?

They visited the Jewish Museum in the afternoon, seeing photographs of European and early American Jewry. They walked over to the Metropolitan Museum after that, and had dinner in one of the small cozy restaurants on Madison Avenue.

They reached Wilmette about nine o'clock. Sara thanked Hal for his warm friendship. Hal hesitated, then said resolutely: "I want to be more than a friend, Sara." Sara placed her finger on his lips, saying, "Ah . . . no more, don't say it." With a smile he kissed her fingers. She paused and fell into his arms, her head nestling under his chin. She looked up and after a moment they kissed, the second kiss deeper than the first. As they embraced, a car drove by, slowed down, then sped on.

"I wonder who that was?" Hal remarked.

"Oh, it's nothing. People drive past, seeing someone at the door; that's all." Sara answered. She gave Hal a final peck on the lips.

Coming into the house, Sara instantly sensed something amiss. Books were scattered across the coffee table and a boy's jacket was tossed over the sofa. It wasn't Simon's. Radio sounds and a strange, sweet smell drifted down the stairs.

"Carol, Simon," Sara called. She began to mount the stairs as she heard a rapid shuffling sound coming from Carol's room. She knocked. "Carol, it's Mom. I'm back."

"One second, Mother. I'll be right out."

Sara noticed Simon's door ajar. She peeked in but didn't see her son. Just then, Carol came into the hallway. The figure behind her more than mildly surprised Sara. A tall boy wearing a scruffy T-shirt with the name of a rock group stepped out, smiling. "Hi there, Mrs. Weintraub." The voice was not terribly sincere. "How are you?"

Sara recognized the boy then. He was Bruce, the son of neighbors. But he wasn't the way she remembered him. Bruce used to be a shy, clean-cut boy. The transformation was unsettling.

"Hello, Bruce. Carol, where's Simon?" She asked worriedly.

"He said something about going over to Danny's house. I think he was invited there for dinner. Did you eat in the city?"

"Yes, as a matter of fact I did."

"With Mr. Kaplan?"

Sara noticed a slight smirk on Carol's face. Or was she imagining that? "Yes, dear, with Mr. Kaplan. We had lunch out also. At Tavern on the Green."

"How very nice."

"Uh, Carol," Bruce said, "I think I should be going."

"Sure. I'll see you downstairs."

As the two descended the stairs, Sara walked into Carol's room. It wasn't something she normally did, for she believed that Carol deserved her privacy, even if she was still a teenager living at home. But Sara felt she had the right to know what was going on, if anything was going on at all.

Sara breathed a sigh of relief at the sight of the unruffled bed. You're a terrible alarmist, she scolded herself. Glancing down, she saw that the "activity" had been taking place on the floor. There was evidence of pretzels and soda and a few record albums scattered about.

Sara smiled to herself at the innocent teenage rendezvous. But the smile vanished instantly as she noticed a magazine next to one of the albums. She picked it up with dismay. "Principles of the Jews for Jesus Movement," she read. Sara turned her head and saw the remnants of burning incense in an ashtray. Good Heavens! This was even more unsettling than her first suspicion.

"Mother!"

"I, ah, I'm sorry, Carol—but I've never seen Bruce here before. I just thought that, well . . . I *am* your mother, Carol."

"Yes, and I always thought you respected my privacy."

"I do. And I'm sorry the need even arose to come into your room without your knowing, but Carol—what is this?" Sara

waved the magazine before her daughter's eyes. The demand
was urgent.

"Bruce and his family aren't religious in the traditional
sense," Carol answered calmly. "In fact, Judaism doesn't much
appeal to Bruce at all. He's into this new movement. That's just a
sample of some of their literature."

"Carol! How can you say that? It's like a cult. Like the Moonies, Hare Krishne or Divine Light Mission or a hundred others
that have sprung up in the last few years. Do you have any idea
what they preach?" Sara was becoming more exercised. "They
preach that you can be Jewish and believe in Jesus. That's
nonsense. It can't be. It *just can't be.* You can't have it both
ways. One is either Jewish or he is a Christian."

"Mother!" Carol stammered.

"Don't mother me, Carol. What I'm saying is true. This group
uses every technique to convert Jews. They appeal especially to
young unknowing, unsuspecting Jews. They say that it's not
conversion. But, my God, it certainly is. Do you know what and
how they maneuver? Here on Long Island, in Miami, California,
everywhere?"

Carol shook her head automatically.

"They're very clever. They give the impression that what
they're doing is Jewish, to attract Jewish people. They publicize
and sponsor Onegi Shabbat, Havdalah services, Purim programs, Passover Seders. Then they casually bring Jesus in. They
have a Friday evening Sabbath service at a midtown hotel where
the announcement on the bulletin board reads Kehilat Yeshua.
Now, you know that the words sound Hebrew. They *are* Hebrew.
Most people who don't know would believe that it is something
Jewish, a Jewish service. But it means Jews for Jesus. It's not
honest, Carol. Let them be Christians. That's fine with me. I
admire, I applaud Christians who are true to their faith. But,
God, don't manipulate Judaism for your own purpose."

"It's a free country," Carol said cooly.

Sara's heart hammered. "Carol, for God's sake! You're a rabbi's
daughter!"

141

"Does that mean I can't have friends who are entitled to their own opinions? Who don't believe in Judaism the way you do?"

"Carol," she choked, "I can't believe this is you! Don't tell me that you believe in this, this nonsense! Why even a number of Christian churches have condemned the movement, not just the Jews."

Carol eyed the floor. "Maybe. But I don't know why you're getting so excited. We were only *talking* about it."

"Carol, have I done something to hurt you?" Sara asked guardedly.

Carol looked up, surprised. "Of course not. Why do you say that?"

"Well, you're behaving as if I deserved some sort of punishment for something I've done. What is it, Carol?"

"Nothing." She wasn't deliberately trying to be dishonest, but just didn't understand her own ambivalence. "I'm sorry if I've upset you, Mother. Did you and Mr. Kaplan have a nice time?"

So *that* was it, Sara realized. It was Hal. "Yes we did, honey. But that's not why I went to New York."

"Oh, Mother! I'm sorry. I forgot about your meeting with Dr. Horner. How did it go?"

"Fairly well, I think. There are still some things I'm perplexed about. He mentioned something about ordaining me."

"Mother!" Carol's enthusiasm was genuine.

"Now it's nothing to get excited about. It might never come to pass; too many obstacles in the way. What's more, I would have a tremendous amount of studying to do."

"You could do it."

"Maybe." Sara leaned over and kissed her daughter on the head. "I think we both could use some rest. What do you say?" At Carol's nod, Sara heard the front door open and close. "Simon?"

"Yeah, Mom. It's me."

As Sara heard Simon moving about downstairs, her concern shifted to her son. She hadn't been spending enough time with him lately either. She sighed deeply. Could she do it all?

Mother, teacher, rabbi, student? Her thoughts suddenly turned to Hal. Lover? Wife? Her shoulders drooped. Perhaps it was all getting to be a bit much.

Ten days later, a large parcel arrived from Dean Kahn's office. Sara eagerly snipped it open and discovered books dealing with Jewish theology, law, philosophy, Bible, and history. They were sent at Dr. Horner's suggestion. He's serious, Sara thought with a grateful surge. She stared at the books for a moment, envisioning the goal. Yes, she thought determinedly, she would do it!

Chapter Fifteen

THE CONFIRMATION CLASS had become Sara's sounding board. She felt especially flattered when one of the students remarked: "The class is really interesting, Rabbi. You're not old fashioned, you know. You don't give us the hell, fire and brimstone stuff." Sara laughed. But as the class filed out, Sara noticed a deep frown on Carol's face.

"Something wrong, honey?"

"No, Mother. Why do you ask?"

"You look terribly sad."

"Do I? I'm not. Probably just worried about my exams."

"Anything I can do to help?"

Carol opened her mouth as if to unburden herself, but drew back.

"Carol, something has been bothering you these past weeks. What do you say we have a nice long talk about it? Just you and I?"

"But you're so busy—the class, your studies, the synagogue, Mr. Kaplan."

Sara looked at her daughter. "Carol, you never behaved like this before. And you never called Uncle Hal Mr. Kaplan. Is something bothering you about him?"

The look in Carol's eyes stirred to life. Sara understood. "We'll have that talk right after dinner. I insist."

After the dinner dishes were cleared away, and Simon went upstairs to do his homework, Sara and Carol settled into the sofa for their chat. Sara began slowly. "It's Hal, isn't it?"

"Well, yes," the girl admitted. "Frankly, I don't understand why the two of you spend so much time together."

"But Hal has been a friend for a long time. Even when Dad was alive."

A sadness swept Carol's face. Sara forced herself to bear her daughter's grief, allowing the silence to endure for a moment. "Do you want to talk about it?" Sara asked softly.

"What?"

"Dad's passing. We never did, you know." She paused, drawing a breath. "But I think I can handle it now, if you want to."

Gripped by a surge of unanticipated anger, Carol jumped up and threw a pillow on the floor. "Damn! It's not fair!" Tears flooded her face.

Sara wrapped her arms around her daughter. "There now, honey. It's all right. I understand."

Carol gulped back sobs. "It's not fair, Mommy, not fair." The little-girl quality in her voice broke Sara's heart. She held Carol tighter. "Go ahead, honey, let it out."

"I, I have so many questions. I don't know how to. . . ."

"Take your time."

Carol dried her eyes and blew her nose. She sat back down and inhaled deeply. "I know God has a reason for everything and that without faith our lives are even harder—but I, I. . . ."

"Go ahead," Sara pressed.

"It was so sudden, Mommy! We didn't expect it. Dad wasn't sick. No warning, nothing!"

Conflict warred in Sara's thoughts. She had felt the same thing. The unfairness, the shock. But Sara's faith hadn't been broken. If there was ever a time to test her convictions it was now. "Carol, honey," she said slowly, "would God be fairer in your eyes if He had allowed Dad to suffer a long and painful illness? Would that have been better?" The girl shook her head. "I know that still doesn't explain what happened," Sara continued, "or take away the hurt, but if we don't trust God's judgments, whose do we trust?"

Carol lifted her eyes to search Sara's face. "When you're alone, at night, in your bedroom there without Dad, what do you think about? Don't you get frightened?"

"Of course I do, sweetheart. The nighttime is the most painful time."

"That's when I mostly think about Dad. When I'm alone in my room, late at night. I try to sleep but can't. All these questions, Mom. I miss him so much!"

Tears brimmed in Sara's eyes. She hurt for Sam, for Carol, for Simon. Her children's grief was as hard to bear as her own, even harder. She squeezed Carol's hand. "I know, baby," she whispered. "I do too."

Carol's face darkened with accusation. "You do? Then why are you spending so much time with Hal? Have you forgotten Dad already?"

The indignant words stung Sara like a slap. She had suffered her own guilt feelings; she didn't need Carol to remind her. She tried to keep her voice even, aware that treacherous emotions could tip rationality the other way. "Hal is a good friend, Carol. If he can help me, should I stop him?"

"As a friend, no. But he might become more, isn't that so?"

Sara bowed her head. "Maybe."

Carol turned away angrily. A suffocating silence filled the room.

Sara felt an eternity passing. Slowly, Carol faced her mother, a questioning look clouding her face. "If I need you, Mother, if I. . . ."

Guilt assailed Sara. She hugged her daughter. "Oh, Carol. Of course I'll be here. I'm sorry if I haven't been here enough. I. . . ."

146

"It's not the time, Mother; it's how we spend it."

"You're right. I promise to make amends." But she knew she had only encountered the tip of the iceberg. A cauldron of emotions was still seething beneath the surface.

"But I must ask you something now, Mother." Carol's voice had returned to normal. "Are you in love with Harold Kaplan? Are you thinking about marrying him?"

The stark frankness of the question unnerved Sara. "I, um, I'm not sure, honey. I like Hal; you know that. But I don't think. . . ."

"I'm honest enough to admit, Mother, I always liked Hal, but I can't see him taking my father's place. Not yet anyway. I've got to work through these unsettled feelings first." Unexpectedly, Carol's face lit up. "But if you need love and companionship I can certainly understand that. It's all right if you have an affair with him, I suppose."

Sara gasped. "Carol!"

"We're only human, Mother. Even you . . . Rabbi." She winked, not unkindly.

Had Carol's maturity blossomed overnight? Sara wondered. Or had it been there all along, slowly growing and developing but only coming to the forefront after Sam's death? She looked at the young woman, feeling an overwhelming rush of love. She hugged her tightly. "Will you help me, too, Carol?" The girl's silent nod comforted Sara. Just then, Simon bounded down the stairs rather loudly.

"And where do you think you're going, young man?" Sara asked.

"To Danny's house."

"Finish your homework?"

"Yup."

"O.K. But be home by ten." From the corner of her eye, Sara saw a disturbed look on Carol's face. "Something wrong, Carol?"

She didn't answer, but looked straight at her brother instead. Simon squirmed. "Aw gee, Carol, do I have to tell Mom?"

147

"Tell Mom what?"

Carol fell silent. Simon knew she would not tell. Somehow, that made him confess. "I, ah, got into a little trouble with some of the kids the other day."

Sara's voice dropped. "What kind of trouble?"

"Aw, Mom, all the kids do it."

"Do what?" She grew anxious.

"Play by that old lot down on Higby Street."

"So?"

"Simon," Carol warned.

"Aw, O.K. Some of the kids are in a gang. One of them, Joey Stafford, well, he got arrested for car theft."

"What!"

"He's not really one of my friends, Mom. He, um, he's sixteen and, well, I don't know. Some of the guys I was playing with just happened to know him, that's all."

"And where did you meet such young men, Simon? You never had 'friends' like this before."

"I dunno. Around, I guess."

"Around where?"

"Gee Mom, what is this, the third degree? It wasn't as if I was arrested, you know."

"But you said you got into trouble with some of the boys."

"Well, not really. Just that the police asked us all a lot of questions and stuff. I guess because they know that lot is where the tough kids hang out."

Sara's head throbbed. She imagined the headlines of the *Courier*: First Woman Rabbi's Son Arrested with Teenage Gang." She looked at Simon. "Have I failed you too, Simon?" Her voice was the merest thread of a whisper.

"You haven't failed anyone," Carol adamantly declared.

"I'm sorry, Mom. I didn't mean to upset you," Simon's voice was low.

"Simon, I don't want you playing with those boys. What happened to your old friends?"

The boy hung his head. Sara sighed. Simon probably needed

to talk also. But somehow, he seemed harder to reach than Carol. Of course he missed Sam terribly. Another rush of guilt assailed Sara. "Simon, I've been talking to your sister about Dad. I think one day, and soon, we should all sit down and. . . ."

"No!" the boy cried. And with that, he dashed out of the house. Sara slumped. It wasn't enough to come to terms with her own grief. She would have to help her children too.

The ringing phone jolted her thoughts.

"Hal? Hi. What? Yes, I'm O.K., a little tired maybe."

Carol rose from the sofa with an enigmatic expression. She went upstairs. Noting this, Sara's voice betrayed her uneasiness.

"Sara, what is it? What's bothering you?"

"Oh, Hal. Here we go again. Me unburdening myself on you. It's not right."

"And why not? If I can help you, why shouldn't I?"

"Because I'm always the one with the problems."

"Don't be a martyr, Sara. Come on now. If I needed someone you'd be the first helping hand."

Sara smiled in spite of herself. "O.K. you win. It's Carol and Simon, although with Carol I'm sure things will work out. She just needs time to take it all in."

Perceptive, Hal said quietly: "I'm part of the problem, right?"

"Oh, Hal. They've never fully come to terms with Sam's death. And I'm afraid Carol is jealous of you." She sounded weary, exasperated.

Hal paused for a long time, carefully weighing his words. "Carol's a bright, sensitive young woman, Sara. She'll come around—with your help. About the part of being jealous though. . . ." Hal hesitated, wondering if he should continue. "Well, about that I don't know. That's up to you. *Does* she have anything to be jealous of, beyond the fact that her mother has a friend?"

Sara's head began to swim. It was all getting to be a bit much. Here she was, a rabbi, a spiritual leader and counselor to her people, suffering such anguished doubts and fears herself. "Hal! I'm human too, for goodness sakes. Don't push."

Hal understood and instantly regretted the implication. "I'm sorry, Sara. Of all people, I should understand. When Judy died . . . well, I know the period of adjustment isn't easy or brief. I'll be patient. Now, what about Simon? Has he complained?"

"No, but I wish he would. I'm afraid he's acting out instead. It's got me terribly worried."

"What's he doing?"

"Spending time with a very rough crowd. It's so unlike him. You know, you read about the very serious problems of teenagers today. It's reached epidemic proportions, but you still think 'no, it will never happen to my children.'" Sara laughed bitterly. "*My* children. Funny isn't it? Particularly ironic in my case—a rabbi-mother raises delinquent." She choked on her last words.

"Sara, get hold of yourself. Simon's a good boy, a little mixed up right now, that's all. Maybe I could help."

The idea had crossed Sara's mind as well. She agreed with psychologists who believed that the most unhappy children are those without enough supervision and guidance. Kids need restrictions and limits put on their actions. They don't know where to draw the line. They need to be told. She was trying, but Sam's death was acutely felt in this case. The boy needed a strong male figure in his life.

"Would you, Hal? I'd be so grateful. You know, I think Simon always liked you. Even before Sam died." Her voice trailed.

"Sh . . . sh. I understand. I'll talk to Simon. Now get some sleep. I'm sure you have a lot of work scheduled for tomorrow."

"I do. Thanks so much, Hal. You've been a real friend. I mean it."

He started to say good-bye when a catch in Sara's voice stopped him. "Hal?" she asked, a bit unsure, "I, ah, when will we see each other again?"

Hal smiled into the receiver. "Scon. Very soon. I promise."

Chapter Sixteen

A T DINNER, after the confirmation class, Carol's enthusiasm spilled over into animated conversation.

"Mother is really great, Si. The kids in class really like her. They all talked about it afterwards."

Sara had discussed drugs and their effect on people. She had offered the Jewish view which forbids the taking of foreign substances that alter either mind or body. "The body," she had said, "belongs to God, and God's possession must not be harmed." For the teenagers it was a refreshing approach.

"That's great," Simon responded. "I wish she would teach our class. The older kids get all the breaks," he pouted. "They get all the good teachers."

"Why Simon, are you calling me a good teacher?" She was thrilled.

He nodded. "Everyone thinks so, except Jerry."

"Jerry?" Sara asked.

"Jerry Simpson."

"Jerry Simpson, the blind boy? Leo and Barbara's boy?"

"Yup."

"Why doesn't Jerry think I'm a good teacher, Simon?"

Simon hesitated. "I don't know, Mother. I don't know."

"Come on, Simon. You've got to tell me. Why's Jerry different?"

He paused, "You won't tell him I told you?"

"I promise."

"O.K. He's worried about his Bar Mitzvah."

"Why?"

"Well," Simon spoke slowly. "Because Dad was working with him on it, he's sort of alone now. He's been going over his Haftarah portion every day, but he's only got two weeks."

Sara was taken aback. "I *am* sorry, Simon. It's my fault. I should have thought of Jerry earlier. I remember Dad working with him. I *am* sorry," she reiterated, chastising herself. "I'll call."

Sara called the Simpsons later that evening and arranged to meet their son.

Jerry came to see Sara at the appointed hour, a bit hesitant. Sara could see the hurt and anxiety on his face. She welcomed him warmly.

Cherubic, with straight brown hair neatly in place, Jerry had kept pace with most of his peers. He had tried football and baseball, but had given up. He worked on his body, strengthening it with strenuous exercise, especially through wrestling. His muscles were taut and strong, and he was fearless as he gripped would-be challengers. He swam twenty lengths daily to keep fit. Peers respected him for his endurance. He would not take second place.

Eager to perform, and aware of his handicap, Jerry's mind was full of anticipation.

"Tell me about your Bar Mitzvah, Jerry. I mean, what you—we're—supposed to do."

"I was supposed to do the *Shema* . . . myself . . . on Friday night, and then chant the Kiddush."

"And on Saturday morning?" Sara asked.

152

"Saturday morning I have the last aliyah and my Haftarah."

"Good," Sara responded effusively. "Now do you have your . . . oh, yes. I see you brought your Hebrew Braille book. Good. Would you read it for me?"

Blind from birth, Jerry's eyes danced uncontrollably as he took the oversized Braille book, rested it on his lap, his knees tightening to form a desk. With roving, moving fingers, he searched for and found the place. He began to chant, then stopped.

"Should I sing it or say it?"

"Sing it, Jerry," Sara encouraged.

He sang loudly and clearly, and Sara felt a thrill race down her spine. "That was beautiful, Jerry, beautiful." Her voice was tremulous with emotion.

"Are you sure?" he beamed.

"I'm positive, Jerry. Now let's arrange to go into the sanctuary next week, and we'll practice from the pulpit. We'll go over the entire plan."

"You mean practice on the pulpit?"

"Of course, Jerry. I want you to have the greatest Bar Mitzvah in the temple. I want everybody to be proud."

"Gee, thanks. Thanks a lot. You're just as nice as Rabbi Weintraub."

Sara was touched. She bent over and kissed Jerry.

"Wait till I tell the guys," he exclaimed. "The rabbi kissed me."

The following Tuesday Sara met with Jerry in the sanctuary. She escorted him to the pulpit and led him to the seat he was to occupy, next to her, near the Holy Ark. She asked him to stand straight. He obliged eagerly. Together they counted the number of steps and judged the angle to the reading desk. He insisted that he come to the podium alone.

"It's not going to be easy, Jerry," Sara warned.

"But I *want* to do it alone. Please? Please?" he begged.

"All right, Jerry. Let's try it again. You stand straight. Here. Now, let's start. I call you; I explain that you will now lead us in

the Shema, our Affirmation of Faith. When you hear me, stand
up straight, and turn right at about thirty degrees. Understand?"

"Like this?"

"No, a little more to the right." Sara turned his body to the
right. "Understand?"

He nodded.

"Let's do it again."

He sat down.

"Now, I call you again. Up you go."

Jerry stood up, turned right. His angle was good. Sara smiled.

"Now let's walk. Ten steps. Short. And you'll be at the reading
desk. Ready?"

He nodded.

"Start." Sara held her breath and she watched the husky lad
count off ten steps. Reaching the tenth, he stretched out his
hands; the reading desk was there. He smiled. Success.

"Now let's go back. You finish chanting, turn left, about
ninety degrees, and walk. . . ."

"Can I walk backward?"

"Why?"

"It'll be easier."

"Fine. Let's try it. Ready?"

"Ready."

"O.K. Finish the last line and start back."

Jerry read the last line, hesitated for a moment, started backward, counting carefully. At the tenth step, his left hand
reached backward and the chair was there. He sat down. And
beamed.

There was an air of tension in the air Saturday morning. The
Courier had announced the Bar Mitzvah. No mention was made
of Jerry's blindness. His picture in the paper told the story
unmistakably.

As the service began, the organ provided the musical background. Rabbi Sara from one side of the pulpit, followed by Don

154

Shapiro and Cantor Markow from the other, walked onto the pulpit. Jerry Simpson walked confidently next to Sara. She seated him, as the congregation grew silent quickly, and whispered, "Good luck, Jerry." He smiled, seeking out the spot from which her voice came. Sara conducted the service as usual, though aware of added tension.

"Our Bar Mitzvah will lead us in the *Shema*, the Affirmation of our Faith."

At the mention of the *Shema*, the congregation rose, Jerry with them. He stood erect. Sara turned towards him. As if he sensed her look, he turned at a right angle and slowly started forward. A collective gasp sliced the air. From a few quarters, an inner compulsion to reach him and help him was almost literally felt, as if the entire congregation was edging forward. Jerry was deliberate, enjoying the sudden silence. He walked carefully, silently counting, the Hebrew Braille book in his hand. At the count of ten, his right hand reached forward and touched the desk. He smiled. The congregation released its breath. He placed his oversized prayerbook onto the surface of the pulpit, calmly felt for his page number in the upper right-hand corner. Two sets of four fingers began moving right to left, roving over the raised dots. His voice was clear as he sang "Hear, O Israel, the Lord our God, the Lord is One" in Hebrew. His hands shifted left to right as he continued with the English translation. Not an eye was dry.

At the Torah reading service, Jerry was summoned by his Hebrew name to chant the blessing, accepting responsibility.

"You have given us all courage, Jerry," Sara said as she spoke to him. "You, a thirteen-year-old boy standing here on the pulpit, have been our teacher, Jerry. Usually we look to age to teach us. Today, you—young, vital, strong—you have taught us the meaning of hope, faith, and courage. God bless you, our little teacher."

The theme reached its mark.

"You were wonderful, Jerry," exclaimed a worshipper.

In the social hall, Jerry chanted the blessing over the wine, as friends gathered around him, patting him on the back with congratulations.

"Stay with me, Rabbi," he called out, stretching his hands out for Sara.

"I'm right with you, Jerry." She glowed.

Children urged Jerry to read more from the Hebrew prayerbook. Happily he obliged. For fifteen minutes he read line after line of the Hebrew Braille. His nimble fingers searched and moved deftly. He answered a barrage of questions about Braille. How long had he studied? Did he like it? Is it different? Is it hard?

He rolled from prayer to prayer as children called out some of the more familiar selections. With his fingering eyes he moved gaily.

One child asked him about an old favorite. He searched page after page. Finally, he blared out a happy cry, "Here it is!" as if he had found a treasure. Then he turned to Sara, who was sitting next to him, and his whisper stirred the circle that had gathered around him. "I'm lucky I can read in the dark," he said.

Sara never forgot that pungent call of the courageous "I'm lucky I can read in the dark." She recalled it nights later. She identified with it, time and again. She had also been in the dark, for some four months, alone, without her husband. Repeatedly, her courage faltered. Outwardly strong and courageous, she released her feelings at night. Or tried to. Could she really love again?

She was in the dark, like Jerry. Was *she* lucky? Like Jerry said? He had never seen the light. She had. Her life had been full, happy, bright. Then, suddenly, in one inexplicable swoop, there was darkness. Was *she* lucky? Perhaps she was. She had two lovely children. They were loyal, devoted. She *was* lucky. The congregation had in the main responded positively to her. True, there were murmurings of anger and opposition. She had been concerned with reaction from women as from men, reactions that might force her to withdraw from her new role. Yet, she *was* lucky. Dr. Horner had been encouraging. She was spending every possible moment studying the materials Dean Kahn had given her. Immersion into the sources strengthened her resolve to achieve. She smiled in the dark. What's a smile in the dark? Who benefits from an unseen, unresponsive smile?

"Yes, Jerry did teach me a great lesson. I *am* lucky I can live in the dark."

The thoughts burst suddenly. Tears gushed relentlessly. "It's a lie. I'm lying," she cried. "It's so cold." Her mind raced.

"Forgive me, God," a thought called desperately as a picture of Hal formed and crushed the wall of control. She remembered the last Sabbath. "He's alive. Warm. I'm a woman; he's a man. Alive."

Guilt bore down relentlessly. She tossed and squirmed, pressing her head into the pillow to prevent violent outcry. She wept. It was dark . . . lonesome. . . cold.

Chapter Seventeen

CHRISTMAS IN WILMETTE began long before the day itself arrived. Beyond commercial enhancement, the season softened tempers, lessened animosities, removed irritants and allowed mellow spirits to pervade.

Like all affluent suburbs, Wilmette prepared mightily. Stores were spendidly and elaborately decorated. Green and red tinsel and paper dominated. Original creations won Chamber of Commerce awards. Merchants vied for the honors, and winners proudly displayed their awards. Some wondered what liquor stores or shoemakers or tailors had to do with Christmas. But in a spirit of good will, problems took a holiday, differences disappeared, friends were made. The air was full of love and brotherhood. Angry faces lost lines. Hostile eyes dimmed.

The jolly-fellow feeling of Merry Christmas was shared by Jews, and Happy Hanukah was similarly announced by Christians. Most meant it. Some mouthed it. Temple Shalom annually changed its bulletin board to read "Merry Christmas to our Christian neighbors." A minority of the congregation ob-

jected. But the majority held firm that in a Christian environment Jewish people should be sensitive to others' holidays.
Why not wish them well? Most persuasive was the assertion
that at Rosh Hashanah time, many churches noted on their
bulletin boards "Happy New Year to our Jewish Friends." Other
churches posted "Happy Hanukah" greetings.

This year, in addition to retaining the annual greeting on the
bulletin board, Sara wrote a letter to the editor of the *Wilmette
Courier*, wishing the Christian community the best for the season. It was a first, and the letter's prominent placement caused a
positive stir in the Christian community.

In Sara's home, the mood was brighter if not completely
festive. Simon, feeling guilty over past transgressions, wanted
to give his mother a new menorah for Hanukah, the eight-day
Jewish feast of lights. In the store, Simon looked and touched
several samples, admiring the skilled artistry and craftsman-
ship. Simon remembered his father telling him the story of
Hanukah. The Maccabees, a small group of Jews, successfully
thwarted the Syrian attempt to foist idolatrous worship upon
them. Seeking refuge in their temple, the Maccabees had
enough oil to burn the lamps for only one night. But by God's
miracle, the small amount of oil somehow lasted eight nights.
And that was why the festival of lights is celebrated for eight
nights, Sam had told his son. The words drifted back to Simon.
He could hear his father's voice, the soothing timbre, and he
remembered the nuances and smiles of love. Suddenly Simon
looked up and saw a man with a boy about Simon's age.

"I don't know, Dad," Simon heard the boy say. "Do you think
Aunt Leah would like a menorah like that one?"

Simon was surprised to feel tears in his eyes. He wiped them
roughly, then bolted out the door.

A few days later, Hal gladly accepted Sara's invitation to help
decorate for Hanukah. "The children will love it," Sara had
said. "I will too." Hal helped the children hang "Happy Hanukah" streamers across the living room. The suspended colored
dreidles, gold sunbursts, and blue and white strips crisscrossed

the room in the shape of the six-pointed Star of David. While they were decorating, Hal grew increasingly aware of Simon's reticence. Simon had always been talkative and cheerful in his presence, and Hal grew uncomfortable with the silence. Was it because Hal was helping them decorate, something his father had done every year? The awful realization that this would be Carol and Simon's first Hanukah without their father stabbed Hal. Sadness and guilt overwhelmed him.

Sara, on the other hand, seemed determined not to let the happy occasion be marred. She placed menorahs on the coffee table, for there would be one for each to light. "It's beautiful," she said, examining the decorations.

Hal agreed. "See you Sunday night. I'm looking forward to it."

"Thanks," the children said together. Sara's smile was a mixture of relief and happiness. "Thank God for Hal," she said in an undertone.

"What, Mother?" Carol asked.

"I said thank God for Hal, for helping us like this for the holiday."

"You know," Carol said mysteriously, "the more I see of Hal, the better I like him. What do you think, Si?"

Simon cast his eyes downward. "He's O.K., I guess." Sara studied her children. That talk about Sam's death was long overdue. But she couldn't bring herself to broach it now. "Come on," she coaxed, wrapping her arms around them. "Let's go into the kitchen and have some cocoa."

"I'll make it," Carol offered.

"Simon," Sara asked, "are you all right?" The boy still hadn't looked up."

"Yeah. I don't want any cocoa." He lifted his eyes.

The pained confusion in his face startled Sara. "Simon baby," she whispered, "what's the matter?"

He eased himself out of his mother's embrace. "May I go to my room?" he asked tonelessly.

Sara felt a growing concern about Simon. She had hoped his

uncharacteristic behavior would pass with time. It obviously hadn't. "Of course, honey. We'll be here if you need us." Simon shrugged and walked up the stairs listlessly.

It was a cold but clear Christmas/Hanukah night. Snow had not blanketed Long Island this year. Ski country, Vermont and New Hampshire, had welcomed six inches and people were praying for more. A snowless Christmas seemed almost sacrilegious, but Hanukah has no such historic weather connection. The busy season had ground to a halt. The quickening momentum eased as people rushed homeward laden with packages. The festive season was at hand.

Arriving with packages covered with special Hanukah wrappings, Hal looked dapper as he opened the door. He plunged into the foyer calling out a Happy Hanukah. The call brought the children. Carol ran to the door and unexpectedly hugged him. Simon stood back a little, so Hal made the first gesture and shook the youngster's hand.

"You look great," Carol said.

"Who looks great?" Sara called from the kitchen.

"Uncle Hal," Carol answered. Hal was wearing a light coyote fur coat with matching fur hat. His peppery sleek hair blended with the hat. He had dressed informally, a soft tan cashmere sweater over an open collar, a matching sports shirt, and dark brown pants.

"Where's Mother?" he asked.

"In the kitchen preparing latkes," Carol answered.

"Smells good; I haven't had homemade pancakes for a long time." He rubbed his hands in anticipation.

"Mom?" Carol called.

Taking her apron off as she walked into the living room, Sara revealed a slimmed-down figure covered by a soft white sweater and dark brown smartly fitted slacks. Hal looked approvingly at her. How attractive she looks, he thought. Sara kissed him on the cheek. The children seemed to accept the show of affection.

"Latkes will get cold," she declared. "Let's bless the candles."

Norman Rockwell could have painted a typical American-Jewish family, gaily dressed, faces aglow hovering over a living room table on which four unequally-sized menorahs rested. Each stood around the table holding a lit candle, and each of the menorahs held a candle waiting to be kindled.

Sara was radiant. In spite of herself, she couldn't help comparing Hal to Sam. Sam had gotten a little round in his later years; the angelic sweetness of his face had diminished, lines had deepened. If you looked at Hal, you knew he was successful, kind, in good health. His eyes were alive. Sam had looked like a successful but tired rabbi, unable to relax, ever on the brink of inner turmoil, which had affected even their most intimate hours. Sara could always feel Sam holding back, resisting, unsure. Hal exuded confidence and excitement. Sara could not help comparing even as Hal asked, "Who'll do the blessing?"

Sara snapped out of the reverie and said, "Everyone has a menorah, everyone together."

At the conclusion Carol called out, her face brightly eager, "Presents, presents now."

"Carol," Sara chastised. "Don't be so forward."

"That's all right," Hal said. "I've got presents for everyone." He distributed them, giving Sara a silk Pierre Cardin scarf embroidered with the initial S. Sara brought out the presents from the closet for the children and gave Hal a set of gold cufflinks initialed *H.K.* "Now we can have latkes!" Sara declared.

"Ummm," the children voiced as they tasted and thanked Sara for the delicacy covered abundantly with applesauce. She graciously accepted the praise, explaining that women had been blessed with the ability to make latkes because Hanukah was really a woman's holiday.

"What does that mean?" Hal asked, munching away.

"There was a time when the seventh night of Hanukah was dedicated to Jewish women because of the bravery of Hannah and her seven sons and of Judith, who was a heroine in those days. So Jewish tradition does pay tribute to women."

"A toast," Hal said, taking a glass of wine in one hand and a plate of latkes in the other. He rose and declared, "God protect our women!" Sara and Carol beamed, looking at each other.

"How about me?" Simon called.

"Right, Simon," Hal responded, pleased, "you offer a blessing with me."

Simon stood up and walked over to Hal's side. He lifted up a plate of latkes while looking at Hal. They chanted the blessings together.

Hal was not about to let Simon's unexpected gesture go by so easily. "Do you want to play dreidle, Simon?" The boy nodded. "Carol, how about you?" "Sure do." Hal looked at Sara, who returned a quick, approving glance. "Go on, kids. I'll clean up here. Enjoy yourselves."

Hal and the children proceeded to the living room. Carol showed Hal the various sized tops made from different kinds of material, all decorated with four Hebrew letters. She plunked down a batch of pennies, then flopped to the floor. Hal did likewise, patting the carpet, asking Simon to join them. "Here are twenty pennies for each of us to start with," Hal said.

They played zestfully. Simon took in the pot a few times as had Carol before and Hal before that. It was fun to watch the brightly colored tops spinning across the carpet. Players waited with bated breath to see where their "spin" would land. But even this game, as much fun as it was, couldn't last indefinitely. Carol stretched her legs. "Ooh, I think I'm getting a cramp." She stood up and took several steps around the living room. Hal looked at Simon intently. He cupped the boy's chin in his palm and was pleased that Simon didn't pull back. "Simon, what's wrong? Something has been bothering you for a while."

Simon looked into the older man's kind eyes. "Nothing, Mr. ... I mean Uncle Hal." Hal studied Simon's face. "You know, you and your sister have been calling me that for as long as I can remember. I always liked it, even though I'm not really your uncle."

A flickering light passed into Simon's eyes. "Are you trying to tell me something but don't know how to say it?" he asked perceptively. Hal admired the boy's intelligence. A sidelong glance at the sofa showed Carol tactfully leafing through a magazine. Such bright, sensitive kids, Hal thought. Just like their mother. And their *father*, he reminded himself.

"Yes, Simon. I'm trying to say a few things. I'm just not sure how to put it."

"Start at the beginning and just be honest without being insensitive. That's what Mom always says," he offered.

"Yes, well, your mother is right, Simon. And so are you." He tousled the boy's hair in a friendly way. "You're certainly making this easier for me." Simon looked at Hal, his eyes instructing Hal to continue. "I guess you know your mother has been worried about you lately, Simon. You're doing things not in your nature." Hal eyed the boy and continued cautiously: "The crowd you've been hanging around with is a little, mmm, rough?"

Simon colored. "They're bums, Uncle Hal, hoodlums. I knew it all along." Hal was caught unaware. He was not prepared for such direct honesty. "But tell Mom not to worry, and you too. I'm through with that gang." Simon looked at Hal evenly. "I was a dope. So don't worry, O.K.?" Hal breathed a sigh of relief.

"What made you realize you were on the wrong track?" Hal asked.

Simon bowed his head. "Dad wouldn't have been very proud of me," he whispered. "I want him to know that, Uncle Hal. That I stopped because I knew how it would have hurt him . . . and Mom. He hated it when Carol and I did something to hurt Mom."

Unabashedly, Hal let the tears swim in his eyes. When Judy was alive, he had been happy but missed having children. When she died, there was nothing left; emptiness was all he had. He wished they had had a son like Simon. Lucky Sara.

Sam, too, when he was alive. But he understood the boy's pain. So much worse for him because he couldn't understand it with the slight help that age with its added experience sometimes gave. "Simon," Hal said gently. "You're very much like your father, you know. In that way, he's never left you. And as Jews, you know we believe in some kind of an afterlife. I'm not sure I can explain it, or even fully understand it myself. But I know that, somehow, your father can see you and continues to help and guide you through life because he loved you so much. It's a very strong, sometimes mysterious force. But it's there."

"Love?"

"Yes, Simon. And giving and taking love is all part of God's plan too. Ask your mother about it. She can explain better."

With honest innocence Simon blurted out, "Do you love Mom, Uncle Hal? I mean the way my dad did?"

"Yes I do, Simon," Hal answered truthfully. He searched the boy's eyes for a negative reaction, feeling relieved that there was none. "But she needs time and I want to give it to her. She's been through an awful lot these past few months. I don't want to pressure her into anything. And, just as importantly, I truly want her to succeed as a rabbi. She's got to find her own niche." Hal stopped, drew a breath. "But," he stressed, "if we were to get married at any time in the future, I will never try to take your father's place in your or Carol's eyes." He paused again, and looked at the boy. "But I do hope we will be a family someday, Simon. I mean that with all my heart."

Carol had crept up on them unobtrusively. "I always liked you, Uncle Hal," she said kindly. "But Simon and I need time to sort out our feelings too. I think we've gotten used to the shock of losing Dad, but not the sadness. I don't know, maybe you never get used to it when you love someone that much, but the sorrow is too fresh, the pain too deep right now."

Hal drew the children close and hugged them tightly. Carol buried her head in his neck; Simon fought back tears.

Sara finished the dishes and later the children went upstairs to watch television. Now that they were alone, Hal shared the enlightening experience with Sara. Her eyes expressed her grateful warmth. She *was* falling in love with Hal, but couldn't admit it. She fought the rush of tenderness mixed with sexual attraction and rationalized the feeling as holiday euphoria. "Thank you, Hal. I truly appreciate your talking to Simon like that."

Hal had omitted the part about his mentioning to the children his comment on marriage. "It was wonderful, Sara," he said, toying with the dreidle and giving it one last exuberant spin. "Really, I feel so much at home."

"You *are* at home," Sara responded. "We feel so comfortable with you." She hesitated. "As if you've always belonged."

Hal moved quickly, embracing her tightly. Their eyes met for a moment; then they smothered each other with kisses and hungry caresses, allowing desires long suppressed and denied to awaken and stir.

"Hal, the children . . ." she protested weakly.

"They're upstairs," he said.

Sara breathed deeply, closed her eyes, and didn't resist. Her own embrace tightened around Hal's waist.

"You are a beautiful woman, Sara," he murmured through kisses. "I'm falling in love with you." He searched her face for a response. She kissed him warmly and sank into his arms welcoming his ardent caresses. . . . Finally they both became aware of the fact that they were not alone.

"We have to be careful," she reminded him. "If the children came down, what would we say?"

"You're so warm," Hal murmured. "So soft." He could feel her respond. Reluctantly, he concurred, "Yes, we will be careful."

Hal left, calling good-bye to the children who were too busy watching television to come downstairs. Sara combed her tousled hair and sat down in a lounge chair. She reached for a book, but her heart pounded. The memory of Hal's caresses lingered as her mind floundered in confusion. She tried to sort out her thoughts. The pathways of her life were no longer clear. She tried to clarify the meaning of what had happened. Had she succumbed or succeeded? Was she right? Wrong? God, if the children had seen. She broke into a sweat. I don't know what I would have done.

Does love mean taking chances? With Sam gone only five months should she feel guilt? She was no longer his. He was dead. Her expression darkened with anger. They had loved, to be sure, but Sam was not Hal. Hal was vital, exciting, alive. Sam had been dutiful, loving, true, and sensitive, but time had erased the memory of passion and replaced it with today's caress. Memory can never replace the reality of yesteryear. Live now, she thought boldly. And without guilt!

She opened the book. "It's no use," she said aloud. "I can't concentrate." Hal had left her tingling with excitement. "More than the calf loves to suckle, does the cow love to be suckled," she remembered a Talmudic dictum. "It's true," she mumbled. "What a beautiful Hanukah present!" Lulled by the warm euphoria of the evening, she fell asleep, the book open on her lap.

Chapter Eighteen

WILMETTE WAS ASLEEP Christmas and Hanukah Eve, except for a few churches open for special midnight services. Parents had shooed their children off to bed after the Christmas trees were decorated. In Jewish homes, families had blessed the Hanukah candles, exchanged gifts, enjoyed potato pancakes. Peace on Earth.

Suddenly, a thunderous bolt shot through the town, shaking it to its roots. A momentary silence and then lights went on almost by design—one, two, three, then a sunburst of lights.

Sara was torn from her sleep by wailing sirens and clanging of bells. She looked at the clock. It was only eleven. She had fallen asleep trying to read. Rising, she went to the little table and switched on the radio. "Here is the latest we have on the fire at the Baptist Church on Clinton Street," a male voice announced urgently. "According to Fire Commissioner Landy, the fire, which is still out of control, is of suspicious origin. . . . Stay tuned for further details."

Impatient, she switched to another station, hoping for more details. Reverend MacLeary was the pastor of that church. He'd recently spoken at a Thanksgiving program in the temple, creating a profound impact on the community. His dramatic theme was reminiscent of Martin Luther King, and had brought people to an appreciation of America as the land of opportunity. Now his church was burning. Suddenly Sara felt impelled to rush to the scene of the fire and find out for herself. Find out what? What could she do? Help put out the fire? She started for the door, and opened it. Carol was sitting up in bed. "There's a fire someplace," the girl called. "What happened, Mother?"

"I don't know, Carol. Let's see." At the window she saw the street beginning to fill with people. "Let's go, Carol."

People were rushing. "Let's go, Carol."

"Where, Mother?"

"Let's follow the people. There may be something to do. To help. Terrible! Terrible!" she moaned and muttered. "On Christmas Eve, too."

Carol looked at her in amazement. Sara understood.

"Christmas Eve is a night of peace, for all people, Carol. It should not be marred."

Rushing to put her clothes on, Carol called. "Wait, Mother." She sped into Simon's room. He was sitting up, rubbing his eyes.

"Simon, Mother and I are going out."

"What happened?"

"I don't know. Back soon."

"O.K."

Outside they saw people dashing toward the black section of town. The sky was bright, unnaturally bright. A flash of flame zoomed high. Then an explosion. Running people ducked; some collapsed to the ground. Sara and Carol held each other.

They got inside the Toyota, started the engine, and backed out, churning up a shower of cinders in the driveway. Down the tree-lined street Sara drove, past the one- and two-story elegant homes with their well-tended flower beds and vast lawns. Only ten minutes by car, driving fast, separated them from the black section and Clinton Street, where the church was burning. Two different worlds. She had mixed feelings about going to Clinton Street. She was a stranger there, an intruder, although in her childhood she'd lived in a black neighborhood on the South Side of Chicago. She still remembered the fear she had experienced when venturing out alone. Thirty years separated her from those days but the fear she felt, maneuvering the car into Clinton Street, wore a familiar face.

She had no intention of turning back; her conscience would not permit it.

An orange glow hung over the street. She could see the fire from a distance. Parking the Toyota, they started on foot, Sara pressing her bag against her side, an involuntary action for which she felt ashamed. A huge crowd watched the blazing church and the firemen who were trying to save the one-story wooden structure. But it was too late. She saw Reverend MacLeary.

With Carol behind her, she made her way through the crowd, the only white women. Her body tensed, as though expecting an attack. She held Carol's hand. They reached the tall black man, and she touched his sleeve and said: "Reverend MacLeary. Sara Weintraub. I'm sorry."

Tears poured down his face. "My church! My church! Christmas Eve." He looked toward the heavens. "God, why?"

"It's an insult to God Almighty," Sara comforted.

The minister exhaled heavily. "I was warned. I was told to desist, to shut my mouth, to avoid politics. I would not! I cannot! Why do they do this to us?"

His deacons arrived, gathered around him, each more dejected at the sight of their minister weeping than at the sight of the burning church itself. In the minds of his people, their big, burly minister, who only a few weeks before had brought them to great spiritual heights and confidence, was beaten. A dejected minister, depressed, was a sight they could not bear. "Brother! Hold on. Brother! Hold on." They were singing one of their minister's latest hymns. They quickly encircled him, protectingly, and joined in the mantra-like chant. Henry MacLeary forced himself to join. Slowly, tears dried on his face; the colorless drops left no mark. His eyes blinked away the wetness. "Hold on!" he sang in his deep, resonant baritone voice, and he straightened. Sara and Carol joined in too.

When the song ended, MacLeary turned to Sara. "Thank you. God bless you." Suddenly, "What'll we do? Where'll we pray?" Sensing desperation as she looked at the dispossessed flock of people, Sara suddenly shouted over the din of questions, "You'll pray in the synagogue. Our temple will open its doors to you."

MacLeary stared in stunned amazement. "At your church? I mean synagogue? You'll let us pray there? Us black people? Us Baptists? You'll invite us to use your temple?" Sara nodded affirmatively. Carol cried.

"Listen, all," MacLeary rose high. He waved his arms. A hushed silence settled over the heads of the standing people. "Listen all," he shouted. Only the sound of splashing water and crackling embers was heard.

"God has been good to us. God has blessed us." He turned to Sara, her face beaming now.

"Rabbi Weintraub, here," he said smiling with adoration, "Rabbi Weintraub has told me, just now, that we're not to worry about worship. We'll pray in her temple. Her synagogue."

"Merry Christmas!" he shouted happily.

He looked out for reaction. Quiet. And then a burst of applause, and a tumultuous shout. "Thank God. Yea, Lord. Thank the Lord." MacLeary, already transported, began his song again. Carol embraced her mother. "That was wonderful, Mother. Rabbi Mother." Sara's smile tokened her thanks.

Usually quiet, sleepy Christmas Day bustled this year. News of the explosion shook the entire community. Newspaper reporters were busy interviewing police and firemen. Odors of burned wood and cloth wafted through the town. It didn't *feel* like Christmas Day. "How vile and obscene!" was the unanimous expression of disbelief. How could anyone stoop to destroy a church, especially on the holiest day in the Christian calendar!

In the early afternoon, Sara phoned Don Shapiro.

"I was just going to call you, Sara," he began quickly. "I just heard what happened. Terrible. I can't believe it. Neither can Sue. It's incredible. What the hell is . . . sorry, what's this world coming to?"

Sara waited for him to finish.

"I heard you were there. I heard something that sounded like thunder but it didn't occur to me that this could happen. I was so doggone tired from business, I could hardly get up this morning. Then I heard that you were there, and were trying. . . ."

"Don," Sara interjected. "I have to talk with you and the board about the church."

"What do you mean?"

"I mean that I got more involved than most people know."

"Like what?"

"Well, it's something I had to do."

"Did what?" Don waited, sounding anxious.

"I invited the church members to worship in the temple."

"You what?" His voice rose. "You . . . invited . . . the church . . . the church . . . to worship in the temple." There was anger in his voice. "I don't believe it. Why, you're. . . ."

"Now wait a minute, Don. Wait a minute. Before you make any judgment. A church was bombed. On Christmas Eve. On Hanukah. We just had a tremendous Thanksgiving service . . . don't forget that. You thought it was terrific, didn't you?" She didn't wait for an answer. "In the spirit of ecumenism, I invited MacLeary. It's not the first time in history, Don. Churches have opened their doors to synagogues, too. And Hanukah celebrates religious freedom in history."

"But, but . . . black . . . boy, that's a new twist."

"I thought it was the decent thing, the right thing to do."

"You shouldn't have done it, Sara. Not alone."

172

"It's done."

"The board will never approve it."

"That's what I'm calling you about; I'd like the matter taken up."

"Fond as I am of you, Sara, I'll vote against it myself. Who wants them in our synagogue?"

Two nights later, responding to Don Shapiro's urgent summons, sixteen members of the governing board gathered at the temple auditorium for the emergency meeting; others were away on vacation. Sara sat in her study, adjacent to the auditorium, wondering when to venture into that lion's den. She had not been invited. The meeting was already in progress. She could hear the banging of the president's gavel. She hadn't heard such shouts in a long time. They penetrated the dividing wall. A hornet's nest had been stirred up—by her. She recognized some of the angry voices. Phil Elkind was furious. "What we are asked to do," he cried, "is to ratify her stupid offer to that black troublemaker! I am absolutely opposed to it! I will not have him in our synagogue! I also want to take this opportunity to remind this body that I warned you, to no avail, not to make her rabbi of the temple."

She trembled. In spite of herself, she opened the door better to hear. She heard Arnold Peskin speak; then it was Harry Servell's turn; Alan Steinberg's, Stuart Lodell's; all voicing their disapproval of what she'd done. Then who was for her? Had she really been wrong in inviting MacLeary? No, it could not be. She planned to defend her action. Let them fire her, if they wished. She started for the door. Her gaze wandered briefly to Dr. Horner's photograph on the wall. She hoped Rabbi Horner would not judge her harshly. She was doing it for God.

Don turned as she came in, started saying something, but changed his mind. Hal Kaplan smiled and nodded to her. A murmur passed through the board members.

Don, inviting Sara to sit, resumed the deliberations, striking the gavel hard, although the place was so quiet one could hear the chairman breathing. "Let's continue, gentlemen."

Gil Cowen, friend of Phil Elkind, asked for the floor. Cowen rose and directed his words to Sara. "It's about the offer you made to Reverend MacLeary," he began, his voice mild, reasonable. "Now, I'm a liberal-minded fellow, Rabbi. I believe in equality. One of the bakers working for me is a black man; he's my pastry man, the best I've had in years. Neat as a pin. When Miriam and I had our twenty-fifth anniversary celebration, I invited him and his wife to the affair. So you can't say I'm prejudiced. But here we have an entirely different kettle of fish. You invited MacLeary, who is known as a troublemaker, to bring his parishioners to our temple. Now, excuse me, Rabbi, MacLeary's parishioners are poor blacks from the Clinton Street area. Is it safe for . . . ?"

Don banged the gavel. "Get to the point, Gil; we haven't got all night."

"What I want to say is," Gil said, "I can't vote in favor of this offer the rabbi made, liberal as I am." Embarrassed, he sat down.

Arnold Peskin, the movie theatre owner, spoke in the same vein as Gil Cowen, more in sorrow than in anger. "Just last week," he said, "we admitted a black doctor to our country club. So you can't say I'm a racist. I'm for integration, which everybody here knows. I don't keep it a secret. But there is integration and there is integration. It's okay in a public school, but when it comes to my synagogue, I draw the line."

Harry Servell rose and made a very brief statement, casting an embarrassed glance at Sara. "The blacks turned against Israel, remember? I don't see myself inviting them to our temple. I'm sorry."

"Does anyone wish to speak in favor?" Don inquired.

"I do," Sidney Weinstein, advertising man, secret novelist, said. "I am *for* what our rabbi has done. Hers is a generous and courageous act. Reverend MacLeary, who we know has been making a career of attacking all whites, will have to modify his stand. A Jewish synagogue is giving him shelter. I have no doubt that it's a mitzvah for the Jewish people. And for Judaism. Not only is it truly a Jewish act of *rachmones*, compassion, but the national publicity Temple Shalom will get out of this will be worth a mint."

"You with your publicity!" Phil Elkind shouted.

"Publicity makes the world go round!" Weinstein countered.

"Address the chair, please!" Don scolded.

Hal Kaplan's turn came. Forgetting her position for a minute, Sara winked. She felt increasingly drawn to him, and her eyes now smiled with confidence. His handsome face was tanned, as though he'd spent a week in the Bahamas. "I could make a long speech about how it pains me that after we Jews suffered the loss of six million because Hitler claimed we were an inferior race, there are still many among us who cling to a philosophy of superior and inferior races. We Jews should be the last to do it. My vote is *for*."

Robert Smiler, the caterer, who had not said a word all evening, declared, "I have no use for MacLeary, but if he preaches in our auditorium three or four Sundays, will that hurt?"

"Call for a vote!"

"Vote has been called for," Don said. "But with your kind indulgence, I'd like to ask our rabbi if she has something to say."

"Point of order!" Elkind cried.

"What's your point of order, Phil?" Don quipped.

"If that *shwartze* is invited to come and preach in the temple, I drop out."

"You're kidding, Phil."

"I'm not."

Don, flushed now, disconcerted, turned again to Sara: "Have you anything to say before I call for a vote?"

She hesitated, was about to speak, but was prevented by Elkind, who cried: "I object! This is a board meeting, strictly."

"But, as a matter of courtesy," Don pleaded.

"I object!" Elkind repeated.

"I will desist," Sara said, reddening.

Don shrugged. "The motion made earlier by Harry is that we vote against inviting MacLeary to use the temple for his sermons. Okay? Is it clear? Now, all in favor of Harry's motion, signify by raising your right hand." Eight hands went up in the air.

"Eight," Don said. "All those opposed to Harry's motion?"

Hal Kaplan's went up, Sidney Weinstein's. Slowly, reluctantly, six more joined the two.

"Eight for and eight against," Don said, surprised. "So, it's up to me as chairman." The prospect of having to cast the deciding vote made him distinctly uncomfortable. He looked forlornly at his colleagues, examined his gavel, as though seeking to find an answer there, then gazed at Sara. Flustered, Don declared: "I'm for the rabbi's invitation. Meeting's adjourned."

Sara whispered, "Thanks," rose, and went back to her study. She regretted that Hal left alone.

Though satisfied with the decision, Sara wondered how parents and children would really react. Early Sunday morning after the schools' winter vacation, Sara arrived at the temple to see and to be prepared for any emergency. She felt tense as she stood waiting at the entrance.

Word of the board's meeting had stirred the community. Many views were offered, some violent, other conciliatory. This first day of the decision's expression would be telling. And Sara waited anxiously.

In a few moments, a beaming Reverend MacLeary, his wife, and the organist drove up. "Bless you. Bless you," he exclaimed in his booming voice. He wrapped his large hands around Sara's in a warm embrace.

"Welcome. Welcome," she responded, her eyes sparkling, "Shalom. Shalom."

"Shalom," the black minister exploded as Sara gestured a sweeping welcome hand toward the auditorium.

"Everything is ready for you," she said. A large congregation of happy-looking black people followed their minister; the choir members carried neatly ironed gold gowns.

"I do wish board members would have been here to see this," she mumbled.

She waited a few moments and watched children arrive for religious school.

"What's going on?" asked a bundled-up little boy as a group of black people walked toward the same entrance. "Holiday or something?"

"Search me," another responded. "I don't know of any holiday. Anyway, if there was a holiday we wouldn't have Sunday school."

A third commented, "They're all dressed up. Like going to church or something."

"They are." Sara walked up to them.

"They are?" the three asked at once as they looked at each other and at Sara.

"Where?"

"Here," Sara responded. "They're coming to church here."

"In our temple?"

"In our auditorium. Didn't your mother or father tell you?"

"No."

"They're coming to pray here? Why?"

"Did you hear about the church that was burned last week?"

"Yes. What does that have to do with us?"

"Their church was burned down, and so we invited them to have their services here, while they rebuild it."

"That's a nice idea, Rabbi. Whose idea was it?"

"Let's say that all of us thought we should do it," Sara glowed.

"How long will they come?"

"I don't know, as long as they have to."

"Is the auditorium like a church now, cross and everything?"

"Yes, that's the only way they can pray."

"But do we have to have a cross there? I mean, do they have to have it? Here?"

"We don't have to have one. But they can't pray without it. If this is the only way they can pray, shouldn't we let them have one?"

"I feel funny about it. In my temple—I don't know," the little

177

boy shrugged. "I just, you know, I just . . . I guess it's all right, but . . . you know, I don't . . . anyway, who cares?"

"I think it's important, Richie. It *is* important."

"Why?"

"Because we're trying to teach our children a lesson—to help people worship God, even though we don't worship like they do."

"I guess you're right. I still don't know why . . ." he shrugged. "Forget it . . . I . . . forget it."

"Look at it this way, Richie. We worship on the High Holidays. We blow the shofar, for example. Do you think it's right?"

"Sure, I do. I'm going to learn how to blow it myself when I grow up."

"If, God forbid, our temple burned down, and the church invited us to worship in their building, and we set up an Ark and a pulpit for the High Holidays, would you think it's right to sound the shofar?"

"Of course it would be. It wouldn't be Rosh Hashanah without it. It just wouldn't be . . . that's all."

"That's exactly the same thing. This is our way of worshipping. We couldn't without it. They can't worship without the cross, so they have it. Do you understand what I'm trying to say?" Sara looked intently into the little boy's eyes.

Richie's response indicated a slow realization. "I guess it's O.K." He was drawling the words. "I guess you're right." He moved away, and engaged in an animated conversation with two or three other children, as if repeating the conversation to them. He shrugged his shoulders as the others looked at him, and he was heard to say, "I guess. . . ."

Sara mingled among the worshippers, listening. She chattered with a few religious school teachers, suggesting that they discuss the program in their classes as an object lesson. It certainly was becoming a lesson for the entire congrgation.

Chapter Nineteen

CHRISTMAS VACATION allowed a brief respite, but the calm was quickly shattered with Ruth's visit from New York. Loving the flamboyant and luxurious lifestyle of the affluent East Side, Ruth rarely visited her sister in Wilmette. But now that Ruth had broken up her latest love affair, she had gotten it into her head that she wanted to get away to the suburbs to see Sara and the children. And Sara realized that she couldn't very well barricade her own door. Despite all the heartache Ruth had caused the family, she was nonetheless a blood relation. And Sara did feel sorry for Ruth. Ruth was simply the proverbial "lost soul," an unhappy woman aimlessly drifting through life, trying to grab at what she thought was happiness whenever she could. Sara often wondered why her own sister had turned out like this. Ruth had received the same love and attention that she had, went to the same schools, shared in the same Jewish childhood. Why was Ruth still so rebellious and unhappy?

Trying to put the bothersome thoughts out of her mind, Sara decided it was high time for a little fun and relaxation. She'd been devoting nearly every day to study during the holiday break, and religious school was not in session. "Why not have a little dinner party?" she asked aloud. "It would be fun." Sara began planning it almost immediately, and Carol helped.

"I think it's a wonderful idea, Mother," the girl said. "We haven't had one of your famous dinner parties for so long."

Sara smiled happily but was secretly elated for another reason. She wasn't quite sure why, but it almost seemed as if Hal had been avoiding her lately. After the warm togetherness they had experienced on Hanukah eve, this rather distressed her. So when he had readily accepted her invitation, Sara was more than pleased.

"And thanks so much for letting me come to this one, Mom." The teenager pecked Sara on the cheek.

"No reason why you shouldn't. You're a young woman now. I'm only pleased that you like my generation of friends almost as well as your own." Carol laughed.

"Carol, honey," Sara's casual mood suddenly darkened, "do you know where Simon will be? He didn't tell me."

"Simon likes to show he's independent lately, Mom. Don't worry. He really will be at Danny's house. I bumped into Mrs. Cohen at the drug store and she mentioned that Simon and Danny are planning an evening of video games in the den."

Sara breathed a sigh of relief. "Well, thank goodness for that." But relief was short-lived as Sara heard Ruth's high-pitched voice sail through the living room.

"Yoo hoo, anybody home?" she sounded tipsy.

"Damn," Sara muttered. "I was hoping she'd stay out shopping just a bit longer."

"What's that, Mom?"

"Nothing, honey."

A perceptive Carol eyed her mother. Although she rather liked her Aunt Ruth (who was an interesting oddity to the teenager) she was aware, nonetheless, of the shame Ruth had caused the family. "How old is Aunt Ruth, Mom?"

"Thirty-eight. She's the baby of the family."

"Is that why her voice still sounds like a little girl's?"

Sara looked at her daughter and broke into a grin. "She thinks it's sexy."

Carol laughed again. "I always thought men like deep-pitched sultry voices in women."

"What's that about what men like?" Ruth cooed, breezing into the kitchen as if she didn't have a care in the world.

Carol was staring at her aunt. "Aunt Ruth, that coat is absolutely *gorgeous*. Where did you get it?"

Ruth stroked the black mink as if she were caressing a lover. "Why this thing? Vinny got it for me in Beverly Hills. Needed it for these Northeastern winters, you know."

Sara scowled. "You don't have to flaunt your wealth like that, Ruth!"

Ruth, seemingly hurt at her sister's disapproval, answered dejectedly: "All the ladies in New York wear mink."

"All the ones on the Upper East Side at any rate," Sara quipped.

"Ruth," Sara chafed suddenly, "I hope you're not going to say or do anything to embarrass me tonight. To tell you the truth, you look like you've had a few drinks."

Ruth looked mortally offended. "Why Sara, I wouldn't dream of it."

Sara mistrustfully cast a side glance at her sister, then bowed her head, resuming the task of canapé making.

"And is Carol going to be there, too?" Ruth asked lightly.

"Yes. Mother invited me this time. She thinks I'm mature enough."

"Well, it's going to be awful tiresome for you without some young people. I hope you at least asked your boyfriend."

"Carol doesn't have a boyfriend," Sara said.

"Well, I do date boys, Mom. It's not as if. . . ."

"You don't have a boyfriend the way *she* means it," Sara nearly shouted.

"God rest Mama and Papa's soul!" Ruth retorted angrily. "What do you think I am, Sara? I don't live in a whorehouse, you know!"

Sara slowly wiped her hands on her apron. Her expression hardened. Outwardly calm, but inwardly furious, she clenched and unclenched her fists as if trying to control herself from striking her sister.

"You will *not* use the name of God in vain in my house," Sara ordered. Her tone was so taut and cold that Ruth actually took an uncertain step backwards.

"Secondly, what Carol does is her business and my business alone. And the sole job of supervision is *mine*. Now don't you dare insinuate anything about anyone tonight, Ruth, or so help me. . . ."

"I'm sorry," Ruth answered, abashed. "And I didn't mean anything bad about Carol either."

Carol looked at her mother. Ruth could arouse one's sympathies when she wanted to.

"Did you think I was saying something bad about you?" Ruth looked at her niece dolefully.

Carol was about to make a forgiving gesture when Sara interceded. "Forget it," she answered curtly. "Go upstairs and get ready for the party." Almost instantly, Ruth's expression changed into playful delight.

Don and Sue Shapiro were late, but the other three couples Sara had invited were right on time. They were about to begin the first course when the doorbell rang.

"I'll get it," Carol offered.

Sara made her way into the kitchen to get more wine, silently upbraiding herself for allowing Ruth to come. Ruth had been monopolizing Hal's attention all evening, hardly giving anyone else a chance to speak to him. Why are you so surprised? Sara asked herself. Hal was the only single man in the room. Ruth was just being Ruth.

"Congratulations, Sara," Don practically bellowed from the hall.

"What?" Sara exclaimed, coming into the dining room. "What are you talking about, Don?"

Sue maneuvered her bulky frame adroitly, practically running into Sara's arms to give her a bear hug and then a peck on the cheek. "You did it, Sara! You did it! You set the precedent!"

A flustered Sara set the wine bottle down, her eyes darting from Don to Sue, then back to Don.

"Ladies and gentlemen," Don began with exaggerated flair, "I would like to be the first to inform you that the Rabbinical Conference had a meeting of their . . ." Don stumbled, looking down at the floor. "Of their, um, what-do-you call-it, the committee that decides law. . . ."

"You mean the Commission on Legal Interpretation?" Hal burst in, enthused.

"Yes. That's it. They had a meeting and agreed that women rabbis are O.K."

"You mean they'll recognize women as rabbis officially?" Sara asked.

"That's what it sounds like Sara."

"Mother!" Carol cried happily.

Without thinking, Hal jumped to his feet and embraced Sara in front of everyone. Sara colored, but then recognized that the others regarded Hal as simply a long-time friend of the family. Only Ruth suspected that Hal and Sara's relationship went deeper than friendship.

The other friends broke in with warm words of congratulations. But Sara's moment of glory was quickly snuffed as she watched her sister slither up alongside Hal and casually drape her arm across his shoulder. The rest of the view was blocked, as the other friends rose to their feet, also wanting to show Sara their enthusiasm by embracing her and pumping her hand.

Ruth then slipped into the next room, alone.

"I'll help you serve, Mom," Carol said.

Sara looked askance. "Where's your aunt going?" she breathed in low tones.

"She says she has a headache. Asked to be excused. I think she's going upstairs to rest."

Just as well, Sara thought. The rest of the meal passed pleasantly and uneventfully. Sara left the friends to their own devices as Carol and she cleaned up afterwards.

"Well, I think we're just about finished in here, honey. Why don't you go inside with our guests? I'll be along in a minute."

"O.K., Mom. You know, it was really a nice party. Thanks."

Sara smiled. "Thank you. For all your help." Sara finished the last bit of straightening up, then walked back to join her guests. Her eyes swept the living room. Anxiety seized her when she noticed Hal absent.

"Where's Hal?" she asked.

Don looked at her curiously. "In the den with your sister. She said she doesn't feel well."

Sara choked back her anger. "Excuse me," she said in a tight voice, "but I better see what's the matter."

Don and the others looked after her with growing interest. Why was Sara so concerned about Ruth and Hal being alone together? But Sara didn't care about that right now. Ruth was her sister, but still a guest. This was *her* house, Sara reasoned. Ruth had no right to take Hal into Sam's study.

But as she yanked open the door, the sight that met her was even more upsetting. Ruth was crying, and Hal had his arm around her; he was stroking her hair while she leaned on his shoulder! Trembling with rage, Sara slammed the door. How dare she! Sara began to stalk away, when a red-faced Hal grabbed her arm and spun her around.

"Sara! It's not what you think. Ruth came right out and. . . ."

"And grabbed you," Sara flared.

"Yes," he defended righteously. "Honestly, Sara, I. . . ."

She might be a rabbi, but she was human too. She pushed Hal aside and stormed into the den.

"Now, Sara," Ruth wept. "Don't get all excited. Hal only seems to have eyes for you. So don't think. . . ."

"Get out," Sara hissed. "Get out of my house now!" If there had not been guests in the other room, Sara was sure she would have picked something up and hurled it at Ruth. But she kept her hands still, her voice so hard and cold that even Hal flinched. "And this time I mean it, Ruth. I don't ever want to see you again!"

"Sara," Hal tried to intervene. "Take it easy."

A granite-faced Sara looked at Hal, her eyes glinting like ice. "It's been like this a long time, Hal. What just happened is only the last straw." She faced Ruth, her voice deadly calm. "Get packed!"

Ruth started to protest but Sara turned her back. Hal was left standing there, ruefully shaking his head.

Chapter Twenty

S ARA, DETERMINED TO BLOT OUT the painful events of the last night, spent the entire day reading scholarly papers on the philosophical and practical aspects of women on the pulpit. She recognized the names of some of the rabbis who had written the papers, and noted that the negative opinions seemed to be in the majority. A Rabbi Levine quoted the Talmud: "An exposed hand of a woman's body, a woman's leg, a woman's voice, or a woman's hair, is a sexual excitement." The rabbi asked in his paper what would happen if a woman rabbi wanted to nurse her baby during Sabbath morning services. And what if the rabbi had to officiate while she were menstruating? Another rabbi, however, had answered the latter question in a different paper, stating that the matter was already settled, for sacred objects could not be defiled by a menstruating woman. This rabbi had a sarcastic quip to add as well, asking those who still considered this an obstacle if they would like to get back to the twentieth century and discuss some *real* problems.

Whether for or against the idea of women rabbis, the learned men were all in agreement about one thing: A revolution was about to be launched. Sara felt a secret thrill when she saw her own name mentioned in one of the articles: "Sara Weintraub, widow of the late Rabbi Samuel Weintraub, is acting rabbi of Temple Shalom in Wilmette, Long Island. 'Rabbi Sara,' as many call her, has caused a minor uproar by taking unexpected stands on several controversial issues. She's been written up in the papers; even *The New York Times* carried an article about her. 'Rabbi Sara' is putting us all to shame. And, according to Rabbi Friedman of the Seminary, who is in touch with the people of Wilmette, 'Rabbi Sara' is *still* waiting for recognition and ordination."

Sara read one positive article that greatly buoyed her spirits. One rabbi reminded his colleagues of the historical contributions made by women to Judaism. He mentioned the wife of Jacob ben Judah Mizrahi who continued as head of the yeshiva after her husband's death. And there was also Beruria, wife of Meir, who was a scholar in her own right; Miriam Shapior, who taught Torah to male students, separated by a curtain; Miriam, the sister of Moses, who brought deliverance from Egyptian bondage. Others included Deborah, the judge; Huldah, one of the seven prophetesses; and even the Maid of Ludomir, who served as a Hassidic *rebbe* and had many pious disciples.

Sara was so absorbed in her reading, that she didn't hear the phone ring. She picked it up on the second ring, her mind no longer in the present, but back, way back to the time of the Bible. Hal's deep-timbred voice jolted her back to the present.

"Here, let me take your coat, Hal."

Hal looked at Sara, trying to read her mood. The deadpan expression revealed nothing. "Thanks. Pretty soon we won't need them, hmm?"

A stonefaced Sara regarded him coolly. "Won't need what, Hal?"

"Coats. The weather will be getting warm again."

Sara didn't answer. Hal felt uncomfortable with her aloofness. Awkwardly, he remained standing in the hallway.

"Well, don't just stand there. Sit down."

Hal slowly walked into the living room, hating Sara's tight-lipped expression. She followed soon after, hands on her hips, and looked him squarely in the eye. "Coffee?" she asked. Her tone was curt, as if the question were a perfunctory obligation she'd like to dispense with as soon as possible.

"No, thanks," Hal grumbled.

She ignored his disgruntled expression and sat down, casually smoothing out the folds in her skirt. "You had some business you wanted to discuss with me?" Her tone was cold and matter-of-fact.

"Well, ah, yes," Hal began unsurely. "We know you've been studying diligently . . . now that ordination actually seems feasible, we were wondering, er, umm. . . ."

"You've never been one to stumble over your words, Hal. Get to the point."

"Now look here, Sara," he growled softly, "I know you've been upset since that scene with Ruth. But frankly. . . ."

"That's none of your business," she flung at him. "Get back to the topic at hand."

Hal was generally an even-tempered, affable man. But Sara was being unreasonable. What's more, he was in love with her. He wouldn't allow her to keep up this facade of cool detachment.

"Sara," he implored plaintively, "would you please listen to reason? You didn't even give me a chance to explain the whole thing last week. Everyone felt so embarrassed after hearing Ruth carry on the way she did after you told her to get out, they almost beat a path to your door to leave. You're lucky they're all such good friends. No one's mentioned it since."

"Another scandal averted?" she retorted bitterly. "Is that what you're trying to tell me, Hal? The town is *not* buzzing with the news that Rabbi Sara threw her very own sister out of her home because she tried to seduce the rabbi's. . . ." She faltered, not really knowing *what* Hal was to her. Potential lover? The good friend he used to be? Her enemy? Confusing thoughts assailed her, making her avoid Hal's gaze. She lowered her head, doubt creasing her brow.

"Sara," Hal urged soothingly. "Will you *please* listen to me?"

She didn't have the courage to look at him. "It's wrong, Hal. It's all wrong." Her voice was a hoarse whisper. "I'm the rabbi's widow. I might possibly become the first woman rabbi to be ordained. . . ." She jerked her head up, with guilt, ambivalence and affection conflicting in her eyes. "It's not Ruth. It's you and me. It's wrong." Seeing the hurt look in Hal's eyes, she shifted her gaze away from him. "In a way," she said gently, but not wholly convincingly, "I'm glad I saw that little scene with Ruth. It only made me realize. . . ."

Hal was on his feet, grabbing her shoulders roughly, shaking her into silence. "Don't say it," he breathed. "We're *right* for each other, Sara. If you'd only give things a chance."

She didn't break free of his hold. She just continued to look at him mutely, knowing deep in her heart that he was right. This was not a good time to fall in love, she thought. "Ruth," she whispered, treacherous tears forming in her eyes, "has always been such a problem to us."

Hal placed his fingers over her lips. "Don't you think I know how mixed up your sister is? Do you take me for an idiot? Do you realize that she dragged me in there to get me to snort cocaine? And then when I wouldn't, she started crying about her drug problem? How she's trying to quit and doesn't know how to tell you?" Sara colored. Of course Hal had done nothing to initiate the flirtation that Sara had walked in on. In fact, she was fairly certain that Ruth had planned it that way, knowing that ultimately Sara would find out. Sara had long suspected that Ruth was a drug user.

She sighed deeply, letting Hal gather her into his arms and hug her protectively.

"You know," he gestured with deliberate, dramatic intent, "if you take the whole incident into perspective, it's almost funny."

Had it not been the events in her own life, she would have seen the whole thing as melodrama. Now that the "threat" had effectively passed, she agreed with Hal. She looked up at him, relieved, his feigned expression of seriousness bringing a smile to her lips. The whole thing was utterly absurd, yet it *had* happened.

"Now what was it that you wanted to talk to me about?" she asked, stifling a grin.

"I made up that clumsy reason on the phone so I'd have an excuse to see you," Hal said.

They looked into each other's eyes for a moment; then suddenly, they broke into spontaneous laughter. Sara collapsed onto the couch. "Oh, Hal, we're acting like a couple of silly kids. If Carol and Simon could only see this!" Her tone was light and good-natured.

"It's good to act like this once in a while," Hal pointed out. "Who always wants to be a stodgy old fogey?"

"You're right," she laughed. "Now, how about that coffee?"

Hal loosened his tie and relaxed next to Sara. "That's more like it," he said softly.

As she rose, Hal called after her, his voice serious again. "Sara?"

"Hmm?" she asked, half turning to look at him.

"I hope we never have a misunderstanding like this again."

Her eyes filled with gratitude. "If we do, Hal, I hope you'll be able to make me listen the way you did just now."

"It could be *my* fault next time," he warned.

"In that case," she said smiling, "*I'll* be the one to straighten you out."

Easy laughter filled the room again.

Chapter Twenty-One

SARA FELT THAT THINGS were slowly falling into place. The Rabbinical Conference had apparently voted to lean toward positive action for women rabbis, and this restored her confidence. More important matters, however, had to be dealt with. Now that the principle had been recognized, she was more determined to study diligently.

Her thoughts of Hal occupied more of her time. Hanukah evening had been so wonderful, filled with warmth and happiness. She blushed as she thought of the recent incident and tried to push it from her mind.

The confirmation class was still her favorite base of operation. When vacation was over and they met again, Sara said: "Let's get down to business. We've been away for a few weeks. What shall we talk about?" The teenagers had become accustomed to class candor. Sara waited.

"Well," Susan Bolan began, "there was this program on television the other day about homosexuals and lesbians and. . . ."

A number of the young men shifted uncomfortably and a few girls looked embarrassed.

Susan stopped, looked around, now tinged with caution. "Is it O.K. to ask?"

Sara laughed gently. "Whatever you want to talk about is O.K. as long as we're interested in learning."

"I mean," Susan continued, "I mean, what do you think, you know, about Jews and people like that? I think one or two looked Jewish. I mean, what do you say?" Susan turned around to the others. "Didn't you kids see it?"

"I did," Henry Provost answered.

"Me too."

"My mother wouldn't let me see it," John Feldman said, slumping in his seat.

"Wouldn't let you?" Sara picked up on the disappointment.

"No, she said it was for grown-ups."

"Why?"

"Search me," he answered. "My folks said it wasn't for me. When I grow up, they said, I could read about all that stuff."

"I thought it was a wonderful program," Susan returned. "They were so honest, all of them."

"Honest, hell," Billy jumped in. "They're fags and queers, that's all." His feelings of disgust were revealing.

"But they can't help it; they're born that way."

"Like hell they are. They're sissies and fruits and they walk like this," Billy mimed in exaggerated, effeminate action. "They just like being girls and putting on dresses. I know a kid on the next block who dresses in his mother's clothes every day when he comes home from school. He pulls the shades down, puts on her dress, lipstick, and shoes. He's a fruit."

"I don't think that's fair," Carol reprimanded. "You have no right to condemn just because you think they're different."

"*Think* they're different! They *are* different!"

Sara felt satisfaction hearing her daughter defend.

"How would *you* like a girl kissing you and feeling you and all that?" Billy plunged back. "And what would you think if, if I danced with John?"

Laughter broke out. Susan and Carol seemed hurt.

192

"That's not fair," they said together.

"Fair, hell, it's just crazy." Billy's temples pulsed with rage. Like father, like son? thought Sara.

Sara allowed the reactions to crisscross the room. Voices outshouted each other. "I hate them," Billy yelled. "They disgust me. Gays, fags," the words came out rapidly.

"But they're human beings, Billy." Susan was almost in tears. "They're sick, they have to be helped."

"But they're crazy, going to bars and washrooms looking for men and women."

"Rabbi, what do you think?" Susan turned to Sara.

"I'm glad you asked," Sara said. "If you will all quiet down a little, we'll talk. I'm glad you're so open. Don't forget that we're living in a period of social revolution. It sounds like a big phrase, but it's true. Everything is changing, and almost every day, something else that has been closeted comes out. I'm sure that things will work out better in the open. Right? Fifteen or twenty years ago, less than that, no one even talked about it. And five or six years ago no one would have believed that there would be gay churches and synagogues."

"Synagogues? What the hell is going on?"

"Watch your language," Sara reprimanded. "Yes, gay synagogues."

"Where?"

"It's wild. Next thing you know, we'll have porno synagogues."

Sara stopped. "Let's be serious. If you will allow me, I'll tell you what Judaism says about the whole thing. After all, that's my purpose in meeting with you."

"I know," John asserted. "It's against the Bible. Abomination, right?"

"You're right, John," Sara said. "The Bible does say that if a man sleeps with a man the way he's supposed to sleep with a woman, it's an abomination." A number of the students squirmed, and a few grunts were heard.

"I could puke," Billy said.

193

"Are we, or aren't we going to conduct ourselves intelligently?" Sara's voice grew stern. "If you're going to react emotionally, we just can't learn anything. We'll stop." She waited.

"I don't feel well," Howard Epstein said, suddenly interrupting. "May I be excused?"

"Sure," Sara said. She turned back to the class. "Now, let's listen. The Bible does say that homosexuality is an abomination. An *abhorrence* is another way of saying it. As a matter of fact the Bible also says that a man should not wear woman's clothing. And a woman is not allowed to wear a man's clothing."

"If I wear slacks, it's against Jewish law?"

"I guess so," Sara laughed at the question. "Some say that the kind of slacks today are not the same type they wore during Biblical days." The girls wearing jeans looked at each other.

"There are many instances of homosexuality in the Bible."

"There are?"

"Yes, there are. There's the story of Sodom and Gomorrah, those evil cities. God destroyed them. Lot was saved, and his wife became a pillar of salt. Other commentaries add that a man who has sexual intercourse with a man should be stoned. That's been the general view throughout history. It's been different with women."

"Different? Why?"

"Well, the Bible itself doesn't prohibit female homosexuality. And the Talmud says that it's a religious violation but doesn't call it an abomination."

"That's not fair; it's unequal. They can't have it both ways," was a comment.

Howard Epstein came back into the room. "Feel better?" Sara asked. "Yes, thanks, Rabbi." He sat down and Sara continued. "Now today, even the Orthodox have made some changes. Because there have been so many demonstrations and it's been out in the open, there have been many television programs and plays and books written about it. There had to be a change, at least in understanding. You can't really disregard people. I don't care whether they're called gays or straights. You simply can't disregard people."

"You mean, it's O.K., Rabbi?"

"I didn't say that," Sara replied.

"It sounds like it."

"Now don't misquote me, again," she warned. "What I'm saying is, a Jew is a Jew, no matter what his sexual preference. But homosexuality is still against our heritage because it can't continue our people. It's that simple, that natural. Our Conservative movement essentially holds to the same position, but a few rabbis in the last year or so have begun to write articles and to plead for more understanding. They say that a homosexual should be accepted as a person, but without his homosexuality being sanctioned or condoned. Accepting is not condoning, or encouraging; that is, the homosexuality is a sin, but the sinner is still a human being," Sara emphasized. "But, and this is an important *but*, but I don't accept the idea of gay synagogues."

She was interrupted. "Gay synagogues? I don't believe it."

"Let me finish," Sara pleaded. "No gay synagogues because otherwise any person, any group which may be different from another would want to have their own synagogue. So you would have a 'blind' synagogue, or a 'deaf-mute' synagogue, or a 'retarded children' synagogue, and many more kinds, and that would splinter Judaism. For us, Jews are Jews."

"Who has gay synagogues?"

"Well," Sara responded, "the Reform movement out on the West Coast a couple of years ago helped to support gay synagogues; I think there are twelve or thirteen now. I was told there was to be a convention in Israel of an international organization of gay synagogues. There's one in New York, too."

"In New York?"

"Yes. If you look at *The New York Times* on Fridays, on the obituary page, of all places, there are always announcements of synagogue services for Friday nights and for the Sabbath. Many times there is a small ad at the bottom of the page which prints the caption 'Gay Synagogue.' "

"Can we attend?"

"I don't know. We're supposed to be at our temple. If some of you are ever in the city, maybe you can attend. I don't know. I've never really inquired."

"Is the rabbi a homo?" one of the boys asked.

"I honestly don't know," Sara responded, "but I seem to remember that the group expects their rabbi to be like they are."

"How about a lesbian rabbi?"

Sara felt a dagger. She disguised the momentary challenge to her femininity. "I really don't know," her forced smile faded. "I imagine she'd be acceptable there. Anyway," she continued, "they do have services. Their prayer book, as I understand, has symbolic themes. You know the two triangles of the Star of David? One triangle is pink, and the other is blue. In the center, where the two triangles converge, there's the lambda, which is a gay symbol."

"I think that's sick," Billy exploded. "Disgusting freaks . . ."

"Stop it! Stop it!" The shriek pierced the room. Howard Epstein burst into tears.

Faces whitened. Sara's heart pounded.

"What's wrong?" she jumped from her seat, rushing over to him. "What is it?"

Howard was sobbing uncontrollably, his head in his hands, face down on the desk. "I can't stand it anymore. They're not freaks!"

"What?" Sara asked, concerned, her arm on his shoulder. "What can't you stand?"

"I can't stand it," he sobbed. "I'm not like everybody. I'm not like the boys. I'm different. I'm gay, Rabbi."

"You're what?"

"I'm gay, I'm a *homo*." He continued crying.

Sara lost her composure momentarily. Mouths hung open. Shame and embarrassment showed on every face. She rose to the challenge. "You're a person, Howard. A human being. You're a. . . ."

"No, I'm not! They talk about me like I'm sick. I'm different! They call me a fag! A fruit! A sissy! I'm not! I'm gay. I can't help it. And you said I was . . . I was an abomination!"

"I didn't call you anything, Howard. I talked of a Jewish view."

"But I'm Jewish! And I'm one of *them*! I've never said it! I was afraid. I can't help it! I don't go to dances. No one ever asked me why. I don't like how girls feel. I like how boys feel."

"Wow," someone said softly. Others sank back into their seats.

"We love you," Susan pleaded. "We love you, Howard, for what you are."

"You feel sorry for me," he said hysterically. "You say I'm crazy. I'm a freak! Oh, God, what did I do? I should have kept quiet."

"You're honest, Howard. And you've got courage," Carol interjected. "Don't be afraid."

A stunned silence settled over the room. Sara knew that Howard would be shunned. Teenagers, especially boys reaching the height of their sexual proclivity, would be merciless. Howard shouldn't have come out, she thought. Was she responsible? Did she incite? The children had brought it up. But how was she to know? Did Howard's parents know?

"We will continue next week," she said firmly, casting a threatening eye on the young people. They walked out, subdued and quiet. Sing-song taunting followed: "Howard is a homo, Howard is a homo."

"See?" Howard cried.

"I'm sorry," Sara said. "They're cruel but they don't understand."

"I'm sorry too, Rabbi," Howard sobbed. "I'm so sorry. I've been wanting to be honest for a long time and I watched that program. I went upstairs. My mother and father didn't know. I cried because I couldn't say anything to them. I cried myself to sleep. I felt like the people on T.V. I'm different and it's not my fault. I don't want to be blamed."

"No one is blaming you, Howard."

"What will I say to my parents? They'll find out before I come home. What will I do then?" Howard was pleading.

"I don't know," Sara responded, searching for a solution.

"Oh, I'm such a freak," the boy said deprecatingly.

"You're not a freak, Howard. You have to believe in yourself."

"But you said *abomination,* didn't you? I'm like dirt and filth."

"No," Sara said, trying to comfort him. She felt angry with herself.

"Yes, now everybody will know." Howard's bitter crying intensified.

Sara had been holding Howard, pity overwhelming her. What do I do now? I'm torn. Religion versus people? This boy is human! Conflicts between ancient words and life? Between God and man?

"Howard," she said, not sure of her own direction. "I'll tell you what."

"What?" he interrupted, eager.

"Let's go home together. I'll go home with you."

"Oh, what did I do to myself?" he moaned. "Why didn't I keep my mouth shut?" He was grateful but hurt.

Howard lived in the Curtis Hill section of Wilmette, a comfortable upper middle-class area. A black-face figure at the side of the garage smiled and held up the wooden sign, Epstein.

It was six o'clock when Sara and Howard arrived. Howard nervously pressed the bell, Sara right behind him, her encouraging smile nudging him on.

"I'm so scared," he said.

"Don't worry, Howard. Everything is going to be fine."

Howard didn't wait for an answer. Using his key, he led the way in as he called out.

"Hello."

"Howard?" a woman's voice rang.

"Yes, Mother," the teenager answered.

"Good," she called. "Dad's on his way. We'll have an early dinner. Got a tennis game at eight. Want to wash up?"

"O.K., Mom." Howard motioned Sara into the living room. Chinese decor, vases, dividers, ashtrays, reflected modern trends. Paintings and lithographs of oriental themes coordinated with the furniture.

The lone Jewish symbol was an Israeli menorah resting half-hidden in the breakfront. The Epsteins belonged to the Jewish jet set. They did everything well. They were the best dancers in town, played tennis two or three times a week, twice in singles, and once a week they played doubles. They jogged religiously on Saturday and Sunday mornings. During the summer months golf was their favorite sport. Howard had learned to play tennis at the age of five. Dinner-table conversation revolved around tennis, the star of the day, and the tournaments which they watched on television.

"Mom," Howard called. "Could you come into the living room?"

Connie was trim in her fashionable gray slacks. A tight sweater in a lighter shade revealed her substantial breasts. Her hair was cropped short, a light straight trim over her forehead. She looked glowingly healthy as she bounced into the living room.

"What's the matter?" she gasped at the sight of the unexpected guest. She looked back and forth from Sara to Howard. "What's wrong? I didn't know you had company."

"Nothing's wrong, Connie," Sara had quickly risen and stood next to Howard. "I just thought. . . ." She changed the pronoun: "We thought that I should come over with Howard to talk with you and Richard."

"It's about Howard, isn't it?" Connie's glow turned ashen. Her voice reflected an incredulity that Howard had gotten into trouble in religious school.

"Yes, it is." Sara had to be assuring. "He hasn't done anything wrong. He's a perfect student, a wonderful student. Always has been. Maybe we ought to wait for Richard? When is Richard coming home?"

"He's on his way, any minute. Tell me what this is all about!" She turned to her son, "Howard?"

"Let's wait for Dad."

"What do you expect me to do in the meantime?" Connie challenged. "Sit down calmly and watch the news or read the paper? You come home with the rabbi and tell me to wait?"

"It's best, Connie. I agree with Howard," Sara said.

"What are you two cooking up?" Connie asked.

"Nothing," Sara and Howard answered together.

They turned at the sound of the automatic garage door opening. Connie rushed to the entrance of the garage.

"Richard, come quickly. Something has happened. Something terrible has happened."

"What's happened?" Richard called out, as he slammed the door to his car and rushed through the laundry room leading into the kitchen and the living room.

"Howard has come home with the rabbi," Connie declared flatly.

"Rabbi? What happened?" He turned to Sara. "How are you, Rabbi?"

"Fine. I'm glad you're home," Sara answered. "I came home with Howard from religious school because it would be better for him and easier for you."

"Sit down, please," Richard's voice quivered anxiously. He motioned to the sofa, leaving Howard standing. He took Connie's hand and sat her down at the edge of the couch. "Yes?" Connie said, waiting anxiously. Richard sat down. His face was contorted.

"I'll tell, Rabbi," Howard said.

"If you want to, Howard."

"I don't know," he hesitated.

"What's the matter? Why keep us in suspense? Howard? Rabbi?"

Howard began. "I didn't feel well in school today."

"Are you O.K.?" Connie asked, solicitously edging forward.

"I'm O.K. now. I felt sick."

"You were all right this morning," Connie said in disbelief while looking at Richard.

"In class I felt sick because of what they were talking about." Connie and Richard looked at each other. They shrugged.

"Well," Connie said. "What were you talking about?"

"Not me, Mother. They."

"Who's the they?"

"The class, all the kids and the rabbi."

Richard's jaw tightened. "Let's stop playing around. What were you talking about, Rabbi?"

Sara locked her eyes into his and said, "Homosexuality." The pause deafened.

"Homosexuality?" The Epsteins looked at each other incredulously. "In religious school?" Richard questioned. "I don't understand. So what?" He searched his son's eyes.

"Well, I got sick hearing about it," Howard said softly.

Their perplexity persisted. "Why?" Richard shrugged. "What does it have to do with you getting sick? I don't understand. Connie, do you?" She shook her head. "Rabbi, do you?"

Sara nodded. "Yes, I understand."

"Damn it, what the hell's going on?" Richard thundered.

"Please, Dad," Howard cried and fell into his father's lap. Startled to see his son crumpled like that, he looked up and caught Sara's unwavering gaze. His brow furrowed. With wide eyes, Richard looked at Howard, then back at Sara. His expression revealed that he understood the shocking truth. He didn't want to believe it.

"Howard?" He looked down at his son. Simultaneously, Connie reached the same conclusion. "Oh, my God," she whispered. Her hand flew to cover her mouth. Sara trembled for Howard.

The boy remained motionless. Richard and Connie violently shook their heads.

"No, no!"

Richard exploded, rising to his feet. Howard fell to the floor. "Rabbi, what are you doing to my son?"

"Nothing, Richard. It's what Howard feels." Sara braced herself.

"Get the hell out of here," he yelled at Sara. He moved threateningly toward her. Sara remained seated.

"Dad, please." Howard got up. "Mother, please!" he pleaded. "It's true. I'm gay."

"What are you talking about?" Richard shouted hysterically. "You're crazy. What kind of talk is this? Connie, am I going out of my mind?" Connie didn't answer.

"I've known it for three years. I don't like girls. I like boys."

"I don't believe this," Connie said, her eyes glazed. "What is this, a dream, a nightmare or something? What am I going to do?"

"You have to love him," Sara said so softly that they both turned to her. "You have to accept him the way he is."

Rage billowed up inside Richard, ugly and brutal. "Goddam fags. My son? Hell, no. I'll break every bone in his body." His fists clenched as he fought to control himself.

Connie was crying.

"Connie, control yourself," he ordered. "I don't understand, I just don't understand. My son like those nuts in the streets; I don't believe it." Richard felt hot and cold at the same time.

"Please, Dad," Howard grasped his father's hand.

"Don't *please* me," Richard shook his son off. He walked around the room as if he were running dazed. "We'll go to a doctor. You must be nuts. We'll go to a psychiatrist. Where did this all begin? God, my son, a homo? That's a hot one." Anger darkened his expression, the lower lip twisting into a snarl. "His father a golf pro, his mother a tennis pro and my son a homo. Rhymes, eh. . . ." Sarcasm laced his voice.

"Dad!"

"Richard, Connie!" Sara demanded. "You're not making things easier for him. You'll have to face it, sooner or later."

202

"Face it? I can't! I won't accept it," Connie said with determination.

"Mom, please," Howard pleaded, then rushed to Connie. She squirmed at his touch. Then she broke down.

"God, where did we go wrong? We gave him everything, Rabbi, everything. What didn't we give him?" Connie swayed.

"It's not you," Sara said. "Don't blame yourselves. No one knows why some of us are heterosexual and others homosexual. But they're human beings and they're our children."

"What do you want me to do?"

"He's your son. He needs you, now more than ever before."

Richard looked at Sara with disdain. "You're pretty smart and clever, aren't you," he countered. "It's easy for you to talk. Your son's not a homo! Or is he?"

"It never occurred to me," Sara replied.

"Well, it never did to us either. It's like being hit over the head with a sledge hammer."

"I'll kill myself," Howard's voice rang out. "That'll take care of everything. You won't have to worry about me. Everybody'll be happy. Lots of kids commit suicide!" The threat stopped the heated argument. He darted out of the living room. Connie lunged, caught him, and held him tight. They both looked frightened and white.

"Oh, no," Connie's feelings burst. She turned to Richard. "What are we going to do, Richard? He *is* our son. Richard, let's do what we can to help him."

Richard collapsed in a chair. "I guess. God!" he prayed. He looked up at Sara, spent. Dejection softened his voice. "I know you meant well. Damn it, Rabbi, why do you insist on talking about those goddam things that don't belong in a religious school? You brought this damn thing out."

"Maybe I did you a favor," Sara answered. "It would have come out, if not now, then later. I'm sure of it. It was only a question of time. Judaism is against it. Howard knows it. You know it. Everyone knows it. But we can't forget that they're also human beings. We brought them into the world. I have to be concerned with Howard and others like him."

"It's going to be so hard," Connie mumbled.

"Hard, hell!" Richard interrupted. "Impossible!"

"Nothing's impossible," Sara offered, then felt foolish over how trite her words sounded.

"What will I tell my friends?" Richard lamented. "What will Howard tell *his* friends, and what will they say? And God! I just can't believe it."

"You can't do it all in one night," Sara consoled. "It'll take time, lots and lots of time, and he's going to need help and you're going to need help, professional help. Howard is the one really on the spot. Don't forget that. You'll play your golf and your tennis, but Howard is the one who has the deeper anguish, who has to make a life for himself. And what do you think the other teenagers are going to do? He'll have a hard time with them, too." She turned to the frightened teenager. "You know what I'm saying is true. But you're strong. You've got to be strong and you've got to be able to stand up and talk back. You have to. I'll help you as much as I can."

"What will I do?" Howard pleaded.

"Well, right now sit with your parents and talk. Try to understand each other, and then we'll see." The parents' eyes met in utter despair.

"My son, God!" A heavy breath exhaled. "O.K. Rabbi, we'll try."

"Howard," Sara added, "you've been hurt, but remember, your parents have also been hurt. It's natural. You can't say you're right and they're wrong. You both have to be able to talk it out, to work it out together. You have to accept their feelings as they have to accept you. You want them to accept you? Well, understand them, too. It's not something they expected."

"I'll try, I really will," Howard cried. "What about the kids?"

"I don't know," Sara said.

"Shall I come to class next week?"

"Absolutely, Howard. You'll be taunted. Expect it, but you have to say to yourself, I'm doing the very best I can. I'm a human being. I'm going to try to understand myself. If the kids want to talk about it, I will. If I have to go to doctors, I will go. Maybe they'll help you but don't be afraid of life, Howard. It's going to be rougher on you than on others, but some of us have to fight harder. Look at me, I'm a woman rabbi. I have to fight harder to be successful than a male rabbi. We . . . we have something in common, haven't we?"

She stopped and looked at the tired parents, her expression begging them to do something. Richard hesitated, looked at Connie and stretched out his arms to his son. Howard ran into them, and with Connie responding, mother and father held their son tightly.

Chapter Twenty-Two

SHE WAS TIRED, needed time to relax, read, do nothing for a day. It had been a hard week. Sara had kept going from crisis to crisis. She parked the car and entered the temple by the side door. She expected to find only Ginny, the secretary. But today Ginny was not alone. Nettie Kornblatt was in the office, sitting in one of the modern, Danish chairs, her face a mask of despair. Nettie and her husband, Myron, were members of the temple, but Sara did not know them well and had never been to their palatial home on Crescent Hill. The Kornblatts, who owned the Supermarket on Route 9, were well-to-do, owned two Cadillac Fleetwoods and were consistent synagogue supporters.

Sara knew a little more about their daughter Stephanie than she did about the parents. The girl, who was Carol's age, but physically more developed, a pretty blonde, bright, spoiled and flirtatious, spent most of her time at religious school trying to attract the boys. She'd been one of the more vocal members of the confirmation class. Stephanie had prided herself on her reason for attending: "Because my father promised me a car if I do."

Sara could not bring herself to dislike the girl. She had intended for some time to get in touch with the parents and discuss Stephanie's schoolwork, but had put it off because of more pressing matters. Recently, Stephie's interest was more positive. Now, seeing Mrs. Kornblatt in the office, she had not the slightest idea what had brought her here.

"Good afternoon," she said to her secretary. "Good afternoon, Mrs. Kornblatt." Surprised at her visitor's failure to acknowledge the greeting, Sara asked: "Would you like to speak to me, Mrs. Kornblatt?"

As though coming suddenly alive, the visitor, who wore a pink suit with scarf to match, spoke, her body stiffening. "I certainly do. Private." There was a menacing note in her voice.

"Won't you come into my study?"

The woman sat down, facing Sara at the desk, underneath the photograph of Dr. Horner. A pleasant scent of expensive perfume filled the air.

"Now please tell me what's brought you here, Mrs. Kornblatt."

"A terrible thing's happened to us, a tragedy," the visitor began, tears appearing in the corners of her eyes. Sara waited.

"What's happened?" she tried to help.

"Our Stephanie, our little girl, is pregnant." The words burst forth.

"Pregnant?" Sara questioned, taken aback.

"What kind of question is that? Yes, pregnant!" Mrs. Kornblatt said, dabbing at the corners of her eyes with a little handkerchief. "And I hold you responsible for it."

"Me? Why?"

"Your teachings," Mrs. Kornblatt declared, raising her voice, "those heart-to-heart talks you hold with the students in your classes, those discussions about sex."

"That's not fair," Sara cried. "We discuss whatever subject the students request. They're interested in Israel, in Russia, in terrorism, and in sex, naturally. Do you expect fifteen- and sixteen-year-olds not to be interested? Isn't it better if we discuss such important matters in class, than for them to do it surreptitiously in the girls' room?"

"You tell them about sex and how beautiful it is," Mrs. Kornblatt countered. "So Stephanie went out to find out for herself. After all, the rabbi said so. The rabbi said it was beautiful, wonderful; the rabbi even mentioned the Bible to prove it."

"Now wait a minute, Mrs. Kornblatt. I never suggested to them that they have sexual experiences. I discussed family life, love between husband and wife, the purpose of sex, its significance in marriage, the duties and responsibilities involved. When questions about premarital sex are brought up—and they often are—I tell them that Judaism stresses monogamy and frowns on premarital sex. Love and sex are rooted in complete responsibility of action. Sex for gratification only is out."

"Who needs such discussions?" Mrs. Kornblatt demanded. "My husband and I sent her to school to learn Judaism, not sex. I never heard of such things in my life."

"They want to talk about it, Mrs. Kornblatt. They're vitally interested in the subject, particularly the girls."

"My Stephanie?"

"Why not your Stephanie? Is she any different from my Carol? Mrs. Kornblatt, have you noticed how Stephie dresses?— her tight provocative clothes with 'thou shalt' and 'thou shalt not' or 'satisfaction guaranteed' across her chest?"

"But your Carol didn't go and get herself pregnant, and my daughter did! What am I going to do? What am I going to tell my husband? He doesn't know. Stephanie only told me last night, like a bolt out of the blue. 'Mom, I have to tell you something. I can't keep it to myself any more. You'll kill me, Mom, but I have to tell you. I'm pregnant.' You could have hit me with an axe, Rabbi. I almost fainted. I didn't know what to ask first. Ask who was it? Or hit her. I said, 'How do you know?' and she said she

208

felt nauseous a few mornings in a row and missed her period. She went to the school nurse, who sent her to the doctor. She even went to a private doctor, on her own, and had a test. She's pregnant all right. My little Stephanie is pregnant! I don't believe it! Stephanie, the apple of my eye, her father's little girl, his Stephie, ai, ai, ai! Nothing was too good for his little girl! What she wanted, she always got. He even promised her a car when she graduated religious school. And if Myron finds out it'll kill him." She paused. "He may kill her."

"But he has to be told, Mrs. Kornblatt. You must discuss it with your husband."

"I can't tell him. He won't survive it."

"Do you want me to do it?" What am I getting into? she thought.

"No! My Myron has high blood pressure, over two hundred. He's on medication. When he gets upset, his pressure shoots up. He'll get a stroke yet. In addition, he has a very high cholesterol. Who could afford it? My parents, may they rest in peace, didn't have enough to eat to raise their cholesterol to a respectable level. Myron's only fifty-two. I'm not so well, either. I have a nervous stomach, gastritis; the slightest thing sets me off. But compared to my husband, I'm a tower of strength." She halted her long speech and wept. "What are we going to do? What are we going to do?"

"Well, you and Mr. Kornblatt might decide on an abortion," Sara said.

"Abortion?" Mrs. Kornblatt said, grimacing painfully. "My daughter? An abortion? It would kill Myron."

"Would you prefer she have the baby?"

"Oh, no!"

"Then if you and Mr. Kornblatt want to consider an abortion, I can be of some help to you."

Nettie Kornblatt shook her head. She slumped in the chair. "Please come home with me and talk to Stephanie," she begged. "Maybe she'll tell you who made her pregnant."

"Does that make any difference, Mrs. Kornblatt?" But Sara

accompanied the woman to her home that sat on top of a hill—like an aristocratic mansion, Sara thought.

"Stephie!" Mrs. Kornblatt called as soon as they entered. "Stephie!" There being no response, a look of panic stole into her eyes. "I hope she didn't do anything! Oh, my God! It'll kill Myron."

A moment later, Stephanie, dressed in a red Japanese kimono, her blonde hair combed neatly, her face composed, came down the carpeted stairs, a star-actress making her entrance. "Did you call, Mother? Oh, hello, Rabbi. Surprised to see you here," and she smiled a knowing smile.

"Thank God, you're alive," the mother said.

"What did you expect me to be, dead?" Sara detected a note of condescension in the girl's voice. "Calm down, will you, Mom."

"Calm down, she tells me! Wait till your father finds out!"

"Let's be grown up about it," Stephanie declared calmly. "It happens all the time."

"Oh, my God! What kind of talk is that?" the mother demanded, incredulously. "I've never heard any such thing in my life. Happens all the time? It never happened to me. I don't know anybody in the temple to whom it happened. Maybe it happens in other families, I don't know. Rabbi, pay no attention to her, she doesn't know what she's saying. That's not my daughter talking. A demon must have gotten into her. I don't know where she learned these things. In the private school we send her to? This is what we pay $10,000 a year for? We'll take you out of Willimantic and send you to public high school! Wait till your father finds out. You won't hear the end of it, my grown-up all-of-a-sudden lady!"

"Do you have to tell Dad?" the girl asked, concern setting in. "I can just go to New York to some hospital and get an abortion. It's safe, quick; they perform thousands of them."

"How do you know?" the mother demanded, staring at the girl as though she were seeing her for the first time.

"I've made inquiries. You don't even have to tell Dad."

Sara, who had sat quietly, marvelled at Stephanie's calm.

What if Carol were to act and speak like that? Nevertheless, Sara found it advisable to inform the girl that as a minor she would require her parents' consent for the abortion.

Suddenly turning to Sara, Mrs. Kornblatt cried: "Isn't it against Jewish law?"

"What?"

"An abortion."

"There's a difference of opinion," Sara declared. Both the Orthodox and Conservative are opposed. But when a mother's life is endangered, it's permissible. The danger need not be physical; if giving birth would affect the *mental* health of the woman, a therapeutic abortion is permitted. And that could be applied to Stephanie."

"I'm glad about that, at least," Mrs. Kornblatt said with a sigh. "Thank God."

Sara rose to leave, smiled reassuringly at the hostess, and waved to Stephanie. "Let me know what you decide to do after you've spoken to Mr. Kornblatt," she said. "If I can be of any help, please call me."

Driving back to the temple, she reflected on what had happened, as her mind turned to the question of religious school curriculum. Should they confine themselves to religion, historic subjects, Bible, history, customs? She was getting some answers by the rash of teenage problems. She didn't feel responsible. Other girls of Stephanie's age attended the class, joined in the discussions, but did not go out and get themselves pregnant, at least not to her knowledge. Stephanie's pregnancy was rooted in how she got along with her parents, how she felt about herself. Stephanie, she'd observed, did nothing to conceal the low esteem in which she held her mother. I hope that's not how Carol feels about me, Sara reflected. I scarcely spend any time now with Carol, with the children. At one time Carol had confided in her fully; they had talked things out.

Carol was in the living room when Sara came in. Simon was upstairs.

"Hi, honey," she kissed her daughter.

"What are you doing home so early, Mom?"

"Missed my children. So I decided to play hookey from work."

"I won't tell your boss."

"Good. Come, sit with me in the kitchen. Tonight I'm preparing supper, as in the good old days."

"That'll be a treat," Carol said.

"What would you like?"

"I can really have what I like?"

"Yes."

"Blintzes. All right?"

"Sure."

"It's not too much of a fuss? You've already put in a full day's work. You used to make fantastic blintzes before you became a rabbi."

"My mother is the one who knew how to make blintzes! She was a genius. She was the champion blintz-maker of Chicago."

"I'm sure you're just as good, Mom."

"Thanks; that's very sweet of you. Before I change and get started, let's just sit for a moment and sort of say hello."

They sat at the kitchen table. After a pause, Carol said: "Mom, why do you keep looking at me like that?"

Flushing, Sara replied: "Sometimes I forget what a lovely daughter I have."

"You're not so bad yourself, Rabbi."

"Myron," Nettie Kornblatt said to her husband after they'd finished supper and he'd swallowed his third Aldomet tablet of the day. "I have to talk to you."

"So talk," he replied, rising from the dining room table. "You don't need to make an appointment. What's up?"

Now that he was home, she had made up her mind about how to tell him about Stephie's pregnancy. She hesitated. What if the news caused a stroke? He'd had one a couple of years ago, but managed to recover without disabling, residual signs. His face was smooth, his mouth firm. He was short but had the build of a stevedore, solid, with the powerful arms of a wrestler. He gave the impression of physical strength to those who didn't know. But Myron was a sick man. His temper didn't help. Gentle as a breeze one minute, he came on like a tornado when he was angry. Nettie was terrified of what he might do to Stephie.

"Come in the living room, Myron," she said, rising from the table. She heard Stephanie close the door from the outside. Good. It would make it less difficult if she told him in the girl's absence.

"What's going on here?" Myron said, annoyed, following her. "I put in a hard day at the store. I want to watch a program. Let up."

She sat down. "Myron, we've got a problem."

"Who hasn't got a problem?" he demanded, looking at his wristwatch. "It is five-to-eight and I want to watch Bill Cosby."

"This is more important than your television, Myron, but promise you're not going to get sick on me."

"Spill it, already, for God's sake."

"Myron, your daughter is pregnant."

"You're crazy!"

"She is, Myron." Nettie watched the color drain from his cheeks, his lower lip trembling, his eyes popping.

"Get my Aldomets," he said. "I left them on the table, and a glass of water."

She brought him the blood-pressure tablets. He swallowed a tablet, drank some water, put down the glass. His hand trembled. "Now, say it again? Stephie is pregnant? I don't believe it. How do you know?"

"She told me, Myron. She checked it out with the doctor."

"What doctor? A reputable doctor?"

"Dr. Gordon."

"And Gordon said so?"

"I called him this afternoon. There's no doubt about it."

Instead of giving vent to his explosive temper, as she'd expected, he began sobbing like a child.

213

"Myron! Oh, my God!" she ran to his side, put her arm around his shoulders. She too began sobbing.

She watched him out of the corner of her eye. "Myron, please don't get sick on me," she pleaded.

Ignoring her plea, he asked, barely above a whisper: "How did it happen?"

"It happened," she shrugged. "What difference does it make? The damage is done."

The anger grew as Myron wrung his hands and spoke through clenched teeth. "I'll kill him. I'll . . . I'll break his neck!"

"Myron, it's over. What difference does it make who it is?"

He shook his head dolefully.

"Don't aggravate yourself, Myron."

But his mind was elsewhere. "You read in the papers about such things happening, but you don't believe they'll happen to your daughter. What's this world coming to? In my time, when I was a boy, I went to school, I was too busy trying to earn a dollar to go around making girls pregnant. I was a hustler. I knew the value of a buck. I sold papers after school, peddled ties on Sunday. At twenty-five I was already in business for myself. You *know;* I don't have to tell you." It was a story he'd told many times, his meteoric rise up the ladder of success. He felt betrayed. "You work yourself to death for your children, and this is what you get in return! What do I need my money for?" he demanded, turning to face his wife with tear-stained eyes. "Do I have to live in a big house with nineteen rooms and four bathrooms? Who needs it?" He sobbed uncontrollably.

"Myron, you can't lay down and die," she observed, stroking the back of his head gently.

"To me, it's the worst thing that could happen," he added. "I'll never live it down."

"We must have done something wrong, Myron."

"Wrong?" he demanded, flushing. "What wrong? We treated her like a princess. She had a nursemaid till she was six, and toys that filled a room to the ceiling. She went to camp all the way in Maine. She had piano lessons and learned how to ride horseback. Did *I* have a childhood like that? Did you? My parents were so poor, they couldn't even send me to camp for a week. Even when I married you, I didn't have a cent." He fell silent for an instant, then raised his head and regarded her searchingly. "Who does she take after?" he asked threateningly. "Not me."

"What do you mean?" Nettie accused.

"A thing like this, a girl getting pregnant, never happened in my family. All my sisters married . . ."

"Same with mine," she interrupted. "When I came to you, you know . . . I don't have to tell you. I don't like you casting aspersions, Myron."

"Who's casting anything? I'm only saying one thing I know. I'll never be able to show my face among people."

"Nobody'll know," she said.

"How can you keep such a thing secret?" he demanded.

"So far, only one person knows, the rabbi. I told her."

"The rabbi? That woman! She'll keep a secret? Nettie, how come you told her?"

"Because I thought she was to blame. But she's not. She said if we decide on an abortion, she can help us out."

"What are you talking about?"

"Stephie will have to have an abortion. Hasn't it occurred to you, Myron?"

"It has. But I tried to put it out of my mind," he replied. "A daughter of mine to have an abortion! How will I live it down?" Suddenly he was on his feet, a grim expression darkening his face, a murderous look in his eye. "Where the hell is she? I'll kill her!"

"Myron, you'll get a stroke!" she wailed.

"Where the hell did she go?"

"I think she went to Lucy Cowen's."

"Call her! I want her!"

"All right, all right, but calm down, Myron." She ran to the phone and summoned Stephanie. Myron paced, fist pounding into his hand with despair. Several minutes later, Stephanie

215

came in, gazed searchingly at her father and felt alarmed. She'd never seen his face so flushed. His hands were shaking, his lips trembling, but he could barely utter a word. The sight of his daughter changed his anger into pity and love. He finally managed to articulate. "Tell me how it happened," he pleaded.

By the way of a reply the girl began sobbing. He repeated the question. His moods alternated. He continued hurling questions at her. "How did it happen? I'll kill him. . . . Can't you talk? Talk, damn it!" Finally, he decided there wasn't any use going on and turned his back on her.

"Myron," Nettie cried, "get hold of yourself."

"What am I supposed to do? Just say thank you?" he asked sarcastically, a wan smile on his face grieving Stephanie's heart. "Thank you, my dear Stephanie, for bringing me a grandchild, a bastard. . ."

"Myron, stop that!"

"Stop it? Stop what?"

"She's suffered enough!"

"Suffered enough, has she? When? Yesterday? Today?"

"Daddy," Stephanie plunged into his lap, burying her head. "Please, Daddy," she shouted. "Please, I'm so sorry. I'm so sorry. Please help me. Please, Daddy!"

"Myron, let's stop shouting and talk about what we can do. Control yourself."

"God, what a mess." He suddenly felt spent, fell back on the back of the couch, Stephanie against him. He felt the crumpled girl on his lap, half at his side, watched her heave with sobs, her hair covering a pained face. He caught his breath, his heart pounded, his head flung from side to side. He looked to the ceiling and the door, at Nettie, and back down to his daughter's head throbbing with anguish. Tears poured from his eyes, "I don't believe it. I don't believe it." Yet he knew that it was true. Slowly, he attempted to fight his emotions, his reason returning. He stroked the buried head. The room was quiet for moments, long, tense moments. Nettie wept. Stephie was silent.

"Oh, Daddy," Stephie started to lift her face, searching her

216

father's eyes. He suddenly hugged her and she responded by clutching him tightly. "Oh, Daddy, I'm so sorry."

"All right," he began after minutes passed, patting her head. "All right." As Stephie sat up, he muttered. "Why Stephie?"

"I don't know, Daddy."

He didn't really expect an answer. Had he gotten one, it wouldn't have satisfied him anyway. He shook his head absently. "What's the difference?"

"Well! What now?" He looked at Nettie and Stephie, first one, then the other.

"Well," Nettie turned to Stephie. "We have to decide, Stephie too, if she wants to have the baby."

"Have the baby?" Myron exploded. "You mean, bring a little . . . bast . . . over my dead body." He was emphatic.

"But it's mine," Stephanie cried.

Myron stopped cold. "What?" Fear washed over Stephanie, reality setting in.

"I don't want the baby, Daddy. I don't want it."

"Whew!" Sweat beaded his forehead and dripped down his underarms. He shivered. His body recoiled.

"Then what can we do? Nettie? Come on, you talked to Sara. What shall we do?"

Slowly, Nettie said, "She'll have to have an . . . abortion."

"Abortion?" He exploded again. "Stephie?"

Nettie was deliberate. "Yes, abortion. Any other ideas?"

Myron repeated in a subdued voice, "Abortion . . . my Stephie . . . I know it's legal . . . but my daughter . . . my baby . . . my daughter."

"Daddy, it's going to hurt *me*," she blurted.

"Yes, Stephie," he responded, dejectedly. "Yes, it's going to hurt you. But you brought it on yourself. You're a big girl; you're not a baby. And how you allowed yourself to get into a pickle like this, I can't understand. Where were you? What were you thinking? You kids don't seem to believe that sex brings babies. It's that simple. How do we go about it, Nettie?"

"Sara said she could make some arrangements with a clinic

in New York."

"When?"

"I don't know. We wanted to talk with you, first."

"Daddy, will you come with me? I'm scared."

He looked at Nettie and Stephie. "Of course," he managed a wan smile. "Of course, I'll come."

"And I want the rabbi to come also," the girl pleaded.

The morning in February was bitter cold. Nettie had decided that they did not want Stephie's father to go with them after all. Nettie feared for his health. Myron insisted. "After all, she's my daughter," he pouted. "How do you expect me to go to the store and work with a clear mind while you're taking my daughter to . . . to have . . . I can't say it . . . I'm going with you," he asserted himself.

"I don't want you to go, Myron. It's too upsetting."

"Please, Daddy, it will be easier with Rabbi Sara," Stephanie interjected. "I don't want you to get sick."

"You're making it very hard for me, little girl," he said. "Nettie, please?"

"The answer is no," she said.

"Can I at least drive you? I won't bother you. I promise, honest to God, I promise I'll park two blocks away. After all, she's my little girl."

"She's a grown woman now, Myron," Nettie corrected.

"Yes, Daddy, it'll be easier this way."

Myron shrugged failure. "But don't forget," he demanded. "Call me as soon as it's over. Right away. Promise?" He looked at his child-woman daughter and shook his head in disbelief, muttering "ai, ai."

They picked Sara up at the temple, squeezed close together, Stephie in the middle. As the trip began, each was outwardly calm but inwardly anxious. Each searched for an impersonal subject to talk about during the next hour, but only meaningless interchange resulted.

Stephanie snuggled comfortably between the two women and

spoke openly about school, plays, dances, and even the confirmation class. "You make us think, Rabbi," she said. "That's why we like your course so much."

"Thank you, Stephanie," Sara responded. But Sara reprimanded herself. "Perhaps I've been too frank." Stephanie continued talking incessantly about her classmates: "Billy Elkind, he's a bore. Howard Epstein, he's so nice, a gentleman. Do you know him well, Rabbi?"

"Yes, Stephie, I know Howard very well. As you say, he's a wonderful young man."

Stephanie stopped, remembering the classmate responsible for her condition. Or was *she* responsible? The hesitation caused both Sara and Nettie to turn to Stephanie. Sara's eyes returned to the road. The teenager was blessed with fully developed breasts and wore tight sweaters to accentuate them. Her manner titillated and teased. She heaved her chest high when she walked past the boys. She knew what she was doing and enjoyed it. Boys sought to date her, and she was thrilled with the popularity. Nettie and Myron had seen how she was growing up and had cautioned her to be careful. "Oh, Dad," she would say, "I am a grown woman," and then offered those famous last words, "I can take care of myself." At Jennifer Brown's last birthday party, she had drunk some beer. Others were drinking scotch and vodka. Stephanie had felt free. There was dancing in the family room, pretzels and more beer. Collective games were tried unsuccessfully. Teenagers were learning instinctively the pairing-off game. She was dancing with a classmate named Stephen, who had also had a drink or two. He had touched her 'thou shalt and thou shalt not,' and she held onto him tightly, pressing body to body. She remembered only walking with him in the corridor, but later awakened unclothed in a bed somewhere with Stephen. He was kissing her. "What are you doing?" she had exclaimed, awakening. "You asked me!" he cried. "You brought me here." His tone was defensive.

"I don't believe it," she exclaimed. "I don't remember."

"You did!"

"God! What did I do?" She looked at him, frightened.

"What are you getting excited about?" he asked.

"I'll get pregnant!" she screamed. "Get off of me!" Stephen obliged. "What do I do now?" she wailed.

"It'll be O.K." Stephen said. "Don't worry; it doesn't always happen."

"Get dressed. Come on, get dressed. Let's get out of here. I don't want anyone to know what happened," she threatened. "Don't you dare say a word to anyone."

"I promise, I won't say a word." They dressed quickly, and self-consciously sauntered into the living room. They had not been missed. And now she was a woman, among women, between two women who had also experienced the ultimate in human relationships. We have one thing in common, she thought; we've all had men. For a moment she felt grown up. But then a quiver chilled her. It wasn't worth it, she sobered. She hadn't even enjoyed the experience. She didn't even remember it.

Stephanie shivered. Sara sensed the shiver and understood the feeling. She looked down at the young woman and smiled comfortingly. There but for the grace of God go I, she thought, looking at Nettie. It could have happened to Carol. It still can happen. And Simon? He was beginning to grow up. He will also be teased, titillated. He'll be Bar Mitzvah soon, and then girls will come into his life. Simon may be the kind of a teenager who would respond. Vulnerable. Why should he be different? Sara startled herself as she realized that she was thinking of a young teenager and sex. My, how the world has changed. Too fast.

The forty-five minute trip to New York passed quickly. As they crossed the Throgs Neck Bridge, Stephie asked, "What's it like, Rabbi?"

"What's what like, Stephie?"

"The abortion."

Sara squirmed. "I know only what I've heard. I guess it's like an examination."

220

"This is different; they take the baby out," Stephie responded.

"Not baby, Stephanie, fetus. There's a difference; a baby is alive, a human being. A fetus is not, in the religion. It's what they call a 'watery substance.'"

"Then it's not like killing a baby. I couldn't stand the idea of killing something inside me. But how do they take it out? Will it hurt? Will I be sick? I'm really scared."

Nettie's heart pounded. She glanced at her daughter. The car swerved.

"Watch the road, Mother," Stephanie warned.

"The doctors are fine people, who will do what they have to do as gently as possible," Sara comforted.

Stephanie shivered again and both Nettie and Sara felt the chill course through their own bodies.

Squeezed in between two brownstones on East 79th Street, the smaller building stood subdued, the town houses patronizing it. Drs. James Hamburg and Herman Jaffe had purposely sought a nonthreatening structure, warm, inviting, almost home-like. A small simple bronze plaque recorded their names, along with the words "private clinic" and "state regulated."

Sara had discreetly inquired of Dr. Harris Hoffman, a recognized gynecologist in a nearby affluent community, for a private hospital where Stephie's abortion could take place. "Nice fellows," Doctor Hoffman had said. "Understanding and gentle." Doctor Hoffman had called ahead to make the arrangements.

Although the town house had been completely remodeled, the high ceilings and heavily wooded side walls had been retained. Steps leading to the second floor had been scraped down to the bare wood and refinished.

They were welcomed by a young, smiling secretary who escorted them into a second room. Stephanie was suddenly frightened. "Don't worry, young lady, it will be over before you know it," the nurse smiled reassuringly. Stephie was not so sure.

"Would you wait in the foyer, please," the secretary said to

Nettie and Sara. They looked at Stephie and turned to the waiting room.

"I want my rabbi to go with me."

"Your rabbi, where is he?"

"She's here," Stephie said pointing to Sara. "She's my rabbi."

The secretary muttered, "Rabbi?" She paused. "Excuse me, I'll have to speak to the doctor."

"It's all right, Miss," Sara said. "I *am* her rabbi and I *am* a woman."

The secretary scrutinized her. "I should hope so. Excuse me."

"You don't want *me*, Stephie, your mother?" Nettie's lips trembled.

Stephanie hesitated. "I love you, Mother, but it will be easier with Rabbi Sara."

A moment later the doctor came out and asked, "Who's the rabbi?" Dr. Jaffe looked as Dr. Hoffman had described, fortyish, just the edge of full sideburns graying up. His horn-rimmed glasses gave him added dignity and maturity. An easy smiler, Sara thought. A good omen. "My secretary tells me about a woman. . . ."

"I'm Rabbi Sara Weintraub." Sara stepped forward. "The young lady is one of my favorites and we've come here at the recommendation of Dr. Harris Hoffman."

"Good man, Hoffman," the physician said, a slight smile forming. "But he didn't say anything about a rabbi like you." He turned to Stephanie. "You want to have your rabbi with you? It's not our practice, I'm sorry to say, to have anyone in the operating. . . ." At the mention of the word "operating" Stephanie burst out crying. The doctor moved over to her, as did Sara and Nettie, though Nettie still felt rejected. He placed his arm around Stephanie, patting her shoulder a few times. "Don't worry, young lady, it will be over in no time."

"I'm scared," she said, holding on to Sara.

"I'll have to take your history," the nurse interrupted.

"I'll take it, Jane," the physician said. He escorted his patient into an inner room, leaving Sara and Nettie standing anxiously.

He recorded the details. At times, his eyebrows raised and other times he hummed. "You have nothing to worry about, young lady. Everything appears to be in good shape. Would you come with me, please," he motioned to her to follow. Sara and Nettie stuck their heads into the room. "You can wait in the next room," he turned to Sara firmly. "I'm sorry, I really can't work with spectators." Sara and Nettie nodded and withdrew.

In a moment Stephanie disappeared into a second room. Listening and hearing moans and cries of "Oh, it hurts," Sara cringed in sympathy. The doctor's muffled voice filtered through. He was gentle in his probings, she thought, as she picked up the words, "Just a little more, Stephie." She heard, "One more second." Time dragged. "There it is," she heard. She pictured Stephie's anguished, tear-stained face.

"All over now," she heard the doctor say. Sara relaxed. Nettie wiped away her tears.

The doctor looked at Stephie lying on the table. "It's all over, little girl," he said. "You can relax now. Want to sip something?"

"No," she responded, her eyes blinking. "I'm tired." She closed her eyes and exhaustion lulled her to sleep. The doctor opened the door, stuck his head out, and called, "It's over, Rabbi. She'll need to rest for a little while. Tell her mother." He closed the door.

"Thank God." They hugged. "Thank you, Sara, for coming."

"Can I bring you some coffee?" the secretary asked.

"Thanks," the women responded, relieved at once. Rabbi and mother cried, shedding tears of bitter happiness.

Chapter Twenty-Four

L ATELY, SIMON HAD ABSENTED HIMSELF from the house during
supper altogether. As much as Sara probed, he would not
tell her where he spent the time. She was concerned about him.
But both children were home now. Sara felt determined.

"Simon and Carol," she called. "Come in here, please."

Looking at Carol's serious countenance, her long dark hair
falling neatly to her shoulders, and at Simon's boyish face
steadily becoming more and more like a man's, with blue eyes
reflecting growing maturity and body gaining muscular height,
Sara's heart skipped. These were her children, her babies. Yet
they were nearly grown. Tears filled her eyes for Sam who
would never see it.

"Simon, Carol, I've been wanting to talk to you about something for a long time now. It's quite overdue." She patted the
sofa, indicating that they sit on either side of her. She drew a
breath and looked at her children warily. "Simon," Sara began
slowly. "I know you haven't actually done anything wrong, but
you seem to be associating with the wrong crowd."

"I'm *not*," he interrupted angrily. "Didn't Uncle Hal tell you?

I'm finished with that bunch. If this talk is going to be about disciplining me, then . . ." he rose defiantly.

"Sit down, young man," Sara snapped. "This conversation is not about that. Yes, Uncle Hal did tell me that you confided in him. He said you were no longer friendly with those boys."

"And you don't believe me," Simon accused.

"I didn't say that, honey. I just wanted to hear it from you."

"Uncle Hal said it for him," Carol cut in. "Isn't that good enough?"

Her daughter's antagonism wounded Sara. "Of course I believed him. I just wanted Simon to tell me himself."

"Well, I'll tell you the same thing, Mom. I'm finished with that gang." An adolescent grunt punctuated Simon's impatient tone.

"What made you come to your senses?" Sara asked.

Simon bowed his head. "It's, um, hard to talk about," he mumbled.

Carol eyed her brother. "You told Uncle Hal."

Simon turned on Carol. "Stop treating me like a kid, Carol. I'm sick of the way you boss me around. Understand? I can't stand it. Who do you think you are anyway?" Red-faced, Simon jumped to his feet and pounded his fist on the coffee table. "I'm the man of the house now! So stop treating me like a little boy!"

Sara was stunned into silence. An understanding Carol looked at her brother with compassion. "Mom doesn't understand, Si. We've never been jealous of each other. You'd better explain."

"Explain what?" Sara asked.

Simon looked at Sara. Slowly, he sat down and held his head in his hands. When he looked up, his face was angry, hurt. "Carol and I talked about it, Mom. For months now, when you were at the synagogue or performing your duties as a rabbi, or out with Uncle Hal . . . we were kind of angry that you never did."

"Never did what?" Sara asked.

Simon looked down. "Talk about Dad," Carol finished. "At

225

first we thought you were too shocked to talk about it. Then we thought maybe it hurt too much. But then the months just went by, and you got busier and busier, and Uncle Hal came around more often. Well, we thought. . . ."

"We thought you didn't care," Simon blurted. "About Dad or us!"

An ashen Sara looked first at Carol, then at Simon. "Oh, children, I'm so sorry. I, I . . ." she wept.

"But then," Carol consoled her mother, "I told Simon about that night we started to talk about it a little. You remember? That was the night Simon told you about that gang and how one of the boys got in trouble with the police."

"Yes," Sara said, drying her eyes, still shaken.

"Well, that's when Simon realized that you *did* care. We figured it was probably even harder for you to talk about it. You were hurting for Dad and for us." Carol looked at Simon. "And one night," Carol's voice dropped to a pained whisper. "One night I heard you crying in your room. And then I understood." Carol rushed into Sara's arms. "Oh, Carol baby . . . I, I didn't know how to begin."

"When Carol told me all that," Simon continued, "that's when I realized how stupidly I'd been behaving."

"Go on," Carol urged, looking up.

Simon's face contorted with grief. But he held back tears. "I told Uncle Hal that when I realized how Dad would have felt if he knew what I was doing . . . how I was hurting you, Carol and myself. . . . Well, I knew he wouldn't have been too proud of me."

A heavy silence fell over the living room. Sara, sensing that the matter was still not entirely resolved, continued with her original thoughts. "That's why I wanted to talk tonight, kids. To get this all out in the open. Clear the air."

"It's cleared," Simon said flatly.

"No, it's not," Sara pressed. "We still haven't talked about how we really feel."

226

"We know how we feel," Simon countered. "Why do we have to talk about it? It's too, too. . . ."

"Sad," a perceptive Carol said.

"That's why we have to talk about it. And cry if we want to." Simon looked away. "In this way," Sara said gently, "women have it easier, don't we?" She drew Simon closer, keeping her arm around his shoulder. "There's no shame in crying, Simon, especially when the sadness is so deep. It's a lesson boys and grown men should learn."

"It scares me," Simon said.

"What does?" Sara comforted, cupping her son's chin in her palm. "Being vulnerable, opening yourself up to hurt? It's the only way we learn and grow, honey. It's all part of life, a very painful part. And in yours and Carol's case, a part that came sooner than it should have."

Simon didn't respond. Sara, looking at Carol, who seemed to be growing wiser with every passing minute, marvelled at the young woman who was her daughter. A slight shiver ran through Sara. Was it because of her and Sam? The way they loved her, brought her up? Or was it more? Something intangible, not quite visible?

"Does being a rabbi help you understand better?" Carol asked.

Warmth filled Sara's eyes. "In many ways, Carol. In learning, teaching, and practicing the ways of God, to be compassionate and helpful to other human beings. Yes, I believe you come to understand God better this way, and in this way it helps. Am I being clear?"

Carol nodded solemnly. "Simon, how about you?" Sara asked. The boy kept his head lowered. Carol embraced her younger brother. "Let it out, Si. You have to."

He looked up at Sara. The angry hurt returned. "Well I'm not a rabbi, and even though you're our mother and you are one, it doesn't help me understand any better!"

Sara was quiet for a long time. When she spoke, her voice was soft, yet even. "What would you have us do, Simon? Be angry with the world the rest of our lives? Be angry with God?"

"I'm not angry with God or the world," a dejected Simon said.

"Then with whom, Simon? Tell us."

Simon's eyes darted fiercely. "It's a sin to say."

"God forgives sins," Sara reminded him.

He looked at Carol, then back at Sara. "I'm angry with Daddy!" the grieving boy shouted. "To go and leave us alone like that!" Simon gulped air as he broke free of Carol. "To let himself die!" He ran across the room, shaking with anger and confusion.

Carol sobbed, long and hard. "Go on, honey," Sara comforted, holding her. "Let it out now. Let it all out." Knowing in her heart that Carol was the stronger of her two children, Sara went to Simon as soon as Carol's weeping quieted.

"Simon, honey."

The boy didn't look at his mother but rejoined Carol on the sofa, who was still crying, though more softly. He looked at Sara, who seemed to be waiting for something.

"Did you really cry, Mom? I mean we never saw you cry. Carol said she heard you but I never did."

Sara sat down next to Simon and stared into his eyes in a way that immediately answered all his questions. "I loved your father, Simon. Very much." She choked on the last words, feeling tears well up in her eyes.

"Oh, Si," Carol wept, "we don't have Dad anymore, but we still have the most wonderful mother. Don't you know that?"

Simon looked at Sara, then at Carol, then back at Sara. He let the tears come.

Chapter Twenty-Five

SARA HAD SET ASIDE Tuesdays and Fridays for visits to hospitals and convalescent homes. She did not particularly look forward to these visits. But it was another one of those duties rabbis had to perform.

She liked being a rabbi, but things were not working out as she'd expected. The editorials in the *Courier* commending her "ecumenical spirit" and "bold pioneering" afforded her little pleasure. The events passed too quickly for sustained gratification. Even a laudatory article in *The New York Times* failed to buoy her spirits. Some members of the temple had phoned to congratulate her on her successes. On a recent Saturday, when she entered the sanctuary, a large group of young worshippers rose. But there were mutterings of resignations too. The fact of the matter was that her congregants, by and large, were not ready to put aside their prejudices and concepts of an age gone by, to tear their bigotry out by its roots and serve God. She didn't judge them harshly. To serve God truly was not easy.

Her visit this morning would be to Happy Acres, a nursing home several miles from Wilmette. She had never been there;

nor had she even heard of it. But Mrs. Einbein, a member, had
called to say her mother was a resident who would appreciate a
visit. Sara started the Toyota, listened to a knock in the motor,
and drove down State Street. Five minutes later she gained the
highway and stepped on the accelerator. She loved to acceler-
ate. You'll get a ticket any day now. Not a nice thing—for a
rabbi. Briefly, the countryside, the farms, silos, the great red
barns uplifted her. Then she turned off the highway, and rode a
short distance on a dirt road until she came to a three-story
brick building. It was bleak in appearance, looking more like a
city school or a hospital than a nursing home with a name like
Happy Acres. It surprised her to see a high wire fence around
the property. The gate was half open. She blew the horn, but
getting no response, she put the Toyota in "park," emerged from
the car, and opened the gate wide enough to pass through.
Driving over a bed of gravel, she parked near the main building.
She tried the door, opened it, and went in. A uniformed guard,
a man with frizzy gray hair, sat on an old leather chair near the
door, asleep. Several old men, some wearing torn robes and
pajamas, wandered around in the lobby. One of them turned to
look at her, a vacant stare in his eyes, but the others ignored her.
Old women, hair uncombed, faces unwashed, clothes in disar-
ray, wandered around the lobby and the adjacent rooms. Some
sat on sofas, on chairs, dozing, reading, conversing in low tones,
some lifting lifeless eyes as she passed, bestowing on her a
quizzical gaze, a look of surprise that lasted only an instant.
Strong odors assailed her nostrils, odors of disinfectants, unwashed bodies, decayed food. She sought in vain for a member
of the staff, for someone dressed in white. Questions crowded
her brain. The place shocked and appalled her. She inquired of
a frail old man with a *yarmulke* where she might find the
director. The man shrugged, pursed his mouth, opened it, but
did not utter a word. She started up the stairs—Mrs. Bloom,
according to her daughter, occupied Room 209—her mind in a
turmoil. The odors pursued her, became even more pungent as
she reached the landing. A number of doors off the corridor

were open. Her throat constricted; she was on the point of vomiting. She fled down the hallway, only to stop at the next open door and the one after that, drawn by the ghastly sights, the overpowering odors, the lifeless eyes. She trembled, her knees shook. She barely made it to Room 209, where she stopped and tried to compose herself before entering. She didn't like herself. What kind of rabbi was she, falling apart at the slightest provocation? Get hold of yourself. . . .

"Mrs. Bloom?"

"Yes. . . ." An old woman, large, with a shapeless body, sat on a chair near the unmade bed. She was dressed in a quilted robe and faded torn slippers, and was gazing at the blue veins on her hands, as though she were making a study of them.

"Mrs. Einbein, your daughter, asked me to stop by to see you. I'm Rabbi Weintraub."

"Glad to meet you," Mrs. Bloom muttered, offering only a brief look at her visitor. Her eyes then returned to contemplate her veined hands. "I don't need anything."

"I'll just stay a while."

"I don't need a thing. We get everything we want. It's a good place. They treat us fine. I have no complaints. Why don't you go away?"

It was clear that Mrs. Bloom was afraid to complain. What could they have done to intimidate her so? What kind of place was this? Even a prison must be better than this. "Mrs. Bloom, you can tell me. I'll try to help you."

"There's nothing to tell."

"What's the director's name, Mrs. Bloom?"

"I don't know."

"Please tell me where I can find him."

"I don't know."

There wasn't any point in staying longer. She started for the door. Mrs. Bloom, who a moment ago had given the appearance of being welded to the chair, was suddenly on her feet. "Please, Rabbi, tell my daughter to get me out. They'll kill me here." But she would say no more; her eyes become hooded.

Sara walked rapidly toward the stairs. A man emerged from one of the rooms. In his early or middle forties, he was big, robust, potbellied and wore a brown wig. "Hey, what are you doing here?" he demanded, an angry scowl on his face.

"I beg your pardon."

"You don't belong here. This isn't visiting day. Who let you in?"

"Why, nobody."

"Leave! Go!"

"I'm leaving. I'm going now. But before I go, I would like to introduce myself. I'm Rabbi Weintraub of Temple Shalom. . . ."

"I don't care who you are, now go."

"I'm on the Governor's Committee on Aging. Who owns this place? Do you?"

"I don't own it; I'm the director. I don't know who owns it."

"I'll find out for myself. I'll report this to the proper authorities!" She stopped, drew a breath and shouted angrily: "I'll expose all of this!" She started down the stairs, walked past the guard who was now wide awake and gazing at her in astonishment, entered the Toyota and started back for Wilmette.

Driving in a mad fury, taking out her anger on the automobile, she returned home and immediately phoned Mrs. Einbein. Sara hadn't even stopped to remove her hat. She could barely contain herself. "You must get your mother out of there!" she exclaimed. Sara then conveyed to the bewildered woman what she'd seen. "We didn't know. We had no idea," Mrs. Einbein kept repeating.

"Do you know the owner of the place, Mrs. Einbein."

"No."

"How did you find out about it?"

"My husband found out."

"From whom?"

"From a member of the temple; actually, from Mr. Abrams. It happened at one of the Bagel Breakers' breakfasts. My husband was saying that we were looking for a nice Jewish nursing home

232

for my mother. Mr. Abrams said he knew of such a place and recommended it very highly."

"Did he say who owns it?"

"My husband asked him about that. Mr. Abrams said he knew the owner. He said he himself had a small interest in the business but was not involved in running it."

"Thank you, Mrs. Einbein. Please attend to your mother. I must hang up now. There are other calls I have to make." She phoned Hal Kaplan next. He was not home. But Don Shapiro was in. "Don? Sara."

"Oh, hi. What's up?"

"Don, I'm doing a little undercover work. Maybe you can help me."

"What about?"

"Don, do you happen to know who owns the Happy Acres Nursing Home over at Woodmere?"

There was a long pause on the other side of the wire. Finally Don, a note of hesitation in his voice, replied, "Well, yes and no."

"What does that mean, Don?"

"Jacob Abrams owns it, if you really want to know. But he's shy about letting people know about it."

"Why?"

"Abrams wants it left alone. A few years ago, there was some hanky-panky involved with a couple of Abrams' nursing homes—Medicaid overcharge, State Nursing Home difficulties—he seemed to be heading for trouble. But in the end it was all straightened out. According to him, he got a clean bill of health."

"That's what he told you?"

"That's right. 'I'm as clean as a baby's backside after a bath,' was how he put it."

"He was lying to you, Don."

She told him about her visit. She tried as best she could to conceal her agitation. Don, on the other end of the wire, clucked

233

his tongue, as she ran on, but made no comment. "This Jacob Abrams belongs in jail," she concluded.

"Sara, do you know what you're saying? Abrams put up a third of the money to build the new temple, five years ago."

"I'm aware of that."

"And another thing, he's pledged to finance the Sam Weintraub Library."

"I know that, too."

"Generous contributors like Abrams don't grow on trees."

"Don!" she cried, annoyed. "We're not on the same wave length! His nursing home is a *hell* on earth."

"But Abrams may not even be aware of it. He's got so many interests. You think he knows what's going on everywhere?" He paused briefly, then said: "I have an idea. Why don't you talk to him? Tell him what you saw. I'm sure he'll cooperate and make the necessary changes. You want me to call him, set up an appointment for you?"

"No, thanks, I'll do it myself. I'll call him." She hung up, and telephoned Abrams' place. He was not at home; his wife answered. They made an appointment for that same evening.

Towards the afternoon, she finally calmed down, spent a couple of hours on temple affairs, rushed home to be on hand for Simon's return from school. She made him a chocolate drink, helped him with his homework. But her mind wasn't on what she was doing; nor was her heart. While she was with Simon, another compartment of her mind was marshalling arguments for the meeting with Abrams. There was little conversation until Simon said bitterly, "How are you, stranger?"

Stung, she said: "Simon, honey, come here, sit here. I want to hear a little bit about your school work." Simon was not doing very well in school. She blamed herself. She must either cease being a rabbi and become a mother or learn how to be both.

But at eight o'clock, she announced it was necessary for her to go. The children voiced disappointment, and Simon, hostile again, said, in a stage whisper, "There she goes again!" Sara wavered. But she went out.

234

Outside, in the car, gradually thoughts of the children were replaced with the business at hand, Abrams. It was really amazing, she now mused, inadvertently crossing Washington Street on a red light, how little she knew about Jacob Abrams. Nor was she the only one. Abrams was the mystery man of Temple Shalom, although he was one of its most generous contributors. But, of course, it was all his own doing. He discouraged intimates, came only to services and to an occasional board meeting, stopped in now and then for a Sunday morning breakfast. Both he and his wife, Clara, rarely came to social affairs. No one even knew exactly what Abrams did for a living, though it was accepted that he had money, lots of it. Millions, some people said. How he'd made his money nobody seemed to know. From real estate, it was assumed, but he owned no property in Wilmette; didn't even own the house in which he lived. He rented. When asked—and people were curious and did ask—Abrams shrugged, smiled enigmatically, and replied: "What can I tell you? I'm not a poor man, but not a rich one, either." Only the fact that both he and his wife had been born in Hungary was known to temple members. During the war, the Germans had deported them to Dachau. Surviving, they came to America in 1948 and settled in New York. Several years later he was said to have borrowed twenty-five thousand dollars from an uncle and bought an old building in Brooklyn. Over the years he added to his real estate holdings. He did not dress like a wealthy man, did not own a car, and lived in a less than elegant apartment house on Euclid. Sara had met him on several occasions and didn't like him, though she couldn't, first as *rebbitzin,* later as rabbi, show how she felt. A soft-spoken man, he listened well, was not contentious. And one could not dismiss out of hand the fact that he'd been at Dachau, and had survived the Holocaust. It was his mysterious manner she disliked. His small eyes shifted. He's too sneaky, she mused. Or was she being too harsh? She didn't recall an instance when she'd been so agitated as now. The ghastly scenes at Happy Acres crowded her brain.

On Euclid, she parked, found the building and rang the bell. Upstairs, Abrams opened the door, put out a meaty hand and said, cheerfully, "Hello. Please come in." Although in his middle sixties, Abrams possessed a muscular body, short, compact, quick of movement. His red hair was sparse, the eyes gray, the lids hairless, a gold tooth gleaming in his mouth.

"Won't you sit down, Rabbi?"

A modest apartment, small, crowded with old furniture, mahogany, not particularly attractive, a little on the shabby side, in fact. If she didn't know him to be a millionaire she'd say, judging by what she was seeing now, that he was a businessman who had a modest income. Mrs. Abrams apparently was not home. On the tea table, in front of Sara, he placed a bowl of fruit—red Cortland apples, a couple of oranges stamped *Haifa*—and a paring knife with a pearl handle.

"You were never here," Abrams said, sitting down opposite her, "but your husband, Rabbi Sam, *olov hasholem*, may he have a bright paradise, was here often. A fine man, a great man, your husband. He died too young. Young people die, and we old sinners go on and on. It was a privilege to count Rabbi Sam among my good friends."

"My husband did appreciate your generous gifts to the temple, Mr. Abrams, and to the library, which I've used often."

"It was a pleasure, believe me. To give is better than to receive. In giving there is a *mitzvah*. Besides, you can't take it with you." He pushed the bowl of fruit closer to her. "Please, Rabbi, help yourself. Have an apple, an Israeli orange; Haifa grows the best oranges in the world. Should I peel a fruit for you?"

"No, thank you." She was aware of feeling more relaxed, of the turmoil inside her subsiding. Maybe I've been too harsh, misjudged him. He probably doesn't even know what's going on at Happy Acres, as Don said. A person who's been through Dachau, walking hand in hand with death . . . well, it just doesn't seem possible that he . . . consciously . . . is part of the neglect that goes on at that place. If he *knew*, he'd do something about it. . . .

"So, to what do I owe the pleasure of your visit, Rabbi?" he asked, eyeing her searchingly, a faint smile on his lips. "The library?"

"No," Sara answered. "The nursing home at Woodmere, Mr. Abrams. I assume you are the owner."

"I have an interest," he said with a slight nod and a touch of pink tinging his face.

"Then who is the owner?"

"Well, Rabbi, my wife has the controlling interest, and then there are partners. I'm one of them."

"To whom does one speak about conditions at Woodmere?" She couldn't bring herself to say Happy Acres.

"You can speak to me."

She tried, as dispassionately as she could, to tell him about her visit.

"I'm surprised," he responded.

"In the hall I was stopped by a man—I assumed he was the director—who told me in so many words to get out!"

"I'm surprised," Abrams repeated. "It's possible he was upset, Rabbi; today was not visiting day."

"Is that place livable *only* on visiting days, Mr. Abrams?"

"I'm not saying. He's a busy man, Feinstein, the director, with plenty on his mind. It's hard to get good help; nurses belong to unions; even a guard wants ten thousand a year. Do you have any idea what it costs nowadays to wash linen? The laundry bill alone runs into tens of thousands a year."

"But people have basic needs! They have to be attended to!" Her voice rose. "I happen to know what the Einbeins are paying you for Mrs. Bloom. Is the nursing home losing money?"

"Who says it's losing? But it isn't the gold mine people think, either."

She went on, "It's possible that your director does not inform you fully of what goes on there?"

"That could be."

"When did you last visit the place?"

"You think I remember, Rabbi? Maybe a month ago."

"And the place looked all right to you?"

"As good as any. Better than most. After all, these places operate according to state regulations. They send people to inspect. Very strict. If a place is not run properly, they close it up."

"When was it last inspected, Mr. Abrams?"

"You think I know? Maybe six months ago."

"I don't imagine you would have any objection if there were another inspection soon?"

There was a pause. Then he said, "Why should I object?"

"I'm on the Governor's Commission on Aging, Mr. Abrams. I plan to be in Albany next week and I'll take it up with the people there."

"Why not? We got nothing to hide. But if you take my advice, Rabbi Weintraub, we would be better off doing it ourselves. I'll go down to Happy Acres tomorrow, first thing, and have a talk with Feinstein. He's a reasonable man. He'll make all the changes, clean up the place, if that's what you say it needs. It's better than inspectors."

"From what I know of procedure, an inspection does not cost you anything. So why not have both? You talk to your director and I'll ask the people in Albany to visit."

"I wish you would reconsider it, Rabbi."

"Why?"

"It's a waste of your time and energy, a waste of mine. What do you think an inspection is? People can be bribed. I have a philosophy, Rabbi, and that is that everyone has his price. Even in Dachau I was able to bribe a couple of kapos, which is why I'm alive today. It's no different here. Why am I telling you this? I want to spare you a lot of trouble. You're a rabbi, likable, talented, conscientious, and young. You're also impatient and want to change the world—one, two, three. But change don't come so easy. It takes time. Justice moves slow. You and I are civilized persons, good Jews, believe in *tzedokeh*. I gave a million dollars for the construction of the synagogue; I was glad to do it. I'm prepared to underwrite the building of the Rabbi Sam Weintraub Library, to the last penny."

"You're proceeding on your theory," she said, trying to harness her rising indignation, "that *everyone* can be bought. Every now and then you may find that theory to be wrong." She rose. "Goodbye, Mr. Abrams. I plan to go to Albany next week."

It was too late to call Don when she came home from the encounter with Abrams. The children were upstairs, asleep. In the kitchen, she poured herself a scotch but doubted it would have the desired effect. Her problem, unfortunately, always pursued her to bed. She finished her drink and went upstairs, tiptoeing past Carol's room. She did not count on having much sleep.

She sat in her temple study, composing a letter to the governor. The morning sun streamed into the room pleasantly. Rabbi Horner, flowing gray hair on his noble head, looked down on her from the wall, a faint avuncular smile on his prophetic face; a smile of approval, she thought. She'd slept reasonably well last night after all, much better than she'd expected. She felt rested, pleased with herself. The phone rang; it was Don Shapiro. "Sara, I have to talk to you; it's urgent. May I come over?"

"Why not, Don?"

They hung up. She could well imagine what Don had on his mind. Abrams must have phoned him. A half hour later Don appeared, breathless, as though he'd raced to the temple all the way from the store. The usual sheepish smile was missing. He looked upset. She invited him to sit.

"It's about Abrams," he said, ignoring the customary amenities.

"Yes, of course."

"He called me."

"I thought he might."

239

"Sara, what do you think you're doing?"

She told him.

'You can't mean it, Sara. You simply can't be serious."

"I most certainly am!"

"Abrams offered to cooperate with you."

"He offered to *bribe* me, Don. *Everybody has a price,* he said. What a despicable man!"

"Well, all right," Don said, rising and pacing the study. "You don't have to like him. There are things about him I don't like myself. Spending two years in Dachau must have done things to him."

"That man is a jackal. . . ."

"He happens to be the biggest contributor to our temple. Without his aid there wouldn't have been a new building. He offered to build the Sam Weintraub Library. To put it to you bluntly, the difference between Temple Shalom and all the other synagogues in the area is Jacob Abrams. The other synagogues would give an arm and a leg to have him as a member. They're probably working on it already."

"It's a sad day for religion if our survival depends on the likes of Jacob Abrams."

"Look here," Don pleaded, leaning over Sara's desk. "We've been through a lot together. I'm talking to you as a friend. This thing you're about to do—it's futile."

"Man is supposed to be made in the image of God, not the devil," she countered.

"Okay, okay, but do you have to write that letter?"

"If I'm to go on living with myself, yes."

"I'll tell you quite frankly, Sara, you'll be cutting your own throat." He hesitated, tightened his jaw, "I won't always be around on your side."

He left her stunned.

Chapter Twenty-six

"I'M CIRCULATING A PETITION among the Board of Governors and members of the temple to terminate her contract as rabbi!" Phil Elkind declared. They were in Don Shapiro's living room, sumptuous, vast, like a hall, with picture windows, white and yellow sofas, and a shaggy pink rug, over which the gynecologist almost tripped when he came in. He'd called Don after reading the article in the *Courier* about Sara's trip to Albany, regarding Abrams' nursing home. As if to bolster his case, Elkind appeared at the Shapiro home with Gil Cowen and Helmut Allen.

Expressing amazement, Don was startled as he greeted the men. "You didn't tell me you were bringing a committee, Phil."

"No," Phil said. "I thought, after I called, we'd make our point stronger and impress you with the seriousness of this problem."

"I didn't think we had a problem," Don said as he ushered them in.

"She's crazy, Don! All my prophecies are coming true. I was opposed to having her as a rabbi in the first place. Now I hope I can get a majority of the board and membership to see it my way." He pulled out a paper from his inside jacket pocket and thrust it at Don. "Will you sign it?"

"Wait a minute, Phil. Sue, please bring Phil a drink. The usual, Phil? Sue, make it a scotch and soda."

"Double scotch, please," the guest said.

"How about you fellows?" Don asked the others. They refused.

Mrs. Shapiro, heavy, like her husband—crash diets didn't do a thing for her—went to mix a drink for the irate gynecologist.

"Since Sara became rabbi," Phil said, "she's put her foot in her mouth every time. First she started to talk to our kids about sex, and, Don, I've been hearing some wild things happening around here; then she invited the *shwartzes* to hold their services in our temple, which almost made me resign; and now, Abrams. The last straw! Abrams gives away in one year more in philanthropy than you and I earn in ten! Look here, Don, attempts have been made in the past to drag his good name through the mud, but they failed. Fact is, Abrams' been cleared each time." He reached for the drink and swallowed. "Thanks, Sue, you saved my life."

"Of course, you're right," Don soothed. "But you know that Abrams has been accused of, let's say not a few improprieties over the years—like giving his sons-in-law Royces paid out of the 'courtesy' of fraudulent Medicaid money."

"But he paid it back."

"After they caught him."

"Don, everybody cheats a little. Can you honestly say you pay the government every last cent you owe on income tax? It's human nature to take advantage."

"But between you and me, Abrams has been known to go overboard."

"He's only flesh and blood."

"True, but Sara's a woman. Women are more sensitive to suffering than men. She was shocked at what she saw at Happy Acres. The neglect, the crap. She described it to me. It's unbelievable."

"It's not easy to keep old people clean. They get to be like babies. All nursing homes are the same. Why pick on Abrams? He's our biggest contributor. I talked to him this morning. He's quitting."

"It's a big loss," Don conceded, mournfully. "How many big givers do we have after all? That Sam Weintraub Library which was going to be the showplace of the East Coast . . . down the drain." He shrugged.

"So, will you sign the petition to get rid of her? A lot of people are going to sign this time. I got some promises already."

"From whom?"

Elkind ignored the question. "The way I see it, getting rid of her should be a cinch. Keep in mind that she hasn't even been ordained."

"I know that, Phil. The Rabbinical Conference has been taking its time. But let's look at our situation here for a minute. If we get rid of Sara, we'll be the laughing stock in the Conservative movement. Sue, please get me a drink too," he said, turning briefly to his wife.

"First, Phil, we put on an intense lobbying campaign to get Sara as a rabbi. Now you want us to go in the opposite direction, to abrogate a solemn contract, and get rid of her?"

"Admit a mistake, Don. Cut your losses."

"To abrogate, suddenly? I'm opposed," Don countered. "If you want to talk about nonrenewal at the end of the year, that's another matter. But to put her out in the street with the two kids is not *menschlich*. Besides, I doubt you'd get a majority of the board to go along with you. The same goes for the membership of the temple. The young members will line up solidly on her side, as they always do. And, in this instance, so will the women. Mrs. Einbein has been talking to the women, telling them hair-raising stories about her mother's experiences at Happy Acres. She's taken the poor hysterical woman out of there. They've had her under sedation the whole week, trying to calm her down. Sue here can tell you more about it."

Sue Shapiro, trussed in her foundation garment, one thick leg crossed over the other, nodded. Don always said she shouldn't wear a skirt with a slit. But she ignored him. "Abrams' name is mud among the women," she said. "I saw Mrs. Bloom yesterday and she's in a state of shock."

"It probably has nothing to do with what is going on at Happy Acres," Phil responded. "I want to get back to Sara. Frankly, I think she needs a man, not a pulpit. And what we need is a rabbi who minds his business, not a sob sister. I see no alternative to getting rid of her."

"A lot of members don't go along with you on that, Phil," Sue declared. "Especially the women. For awhile, there were a lot of women against her, jealous I'm sure, but they've come around. Sara somehow has gotten to the ladies and she's proven that she's strong."

"The men are the ones who pay the dues and contribute," Phil countered. "A lot of them are really disturbed. They may be afraid to talk individually, but get them together and you'll see, they'll open up, I know. I've talked to some of them."

Don went back to his pleading. "An action like yours will split the temple, Phil, right down the middle. It'll ruin us. Worse than Abrams' quitting will ruin us. You wouldn't want that to happen. Not after all the work you've put in these many years."

"I'm sorry, Don." Phil rose. "I'm going ahead with the petition, whether you sign it or not."

"Phil, please. I never gave you a bum steer. Let her serve out the year."

"Sorry, Don. At the next board meeting, I'll take it up."

"I won't put it on the agenda, Phil."

"Fine," Phil continued. "I'll bring it up under New Business or Good and Welfare." He paused. "Someone has to bite the bullet."

Though the agenda did not indicate unusual subjects, the board of trustees meeting was well attended. Phil Elkind had

done his homework well and had called those he thought
would support him.

Don Shapiro, convinced that Phil meant business, did his
own caucusing. He contacted Hal and was convinced he would
come. Hal's response was, "That sonofabitch. He doesn't have
the faintest idea of what's going on. Sara's working like a dog to
help people. I know first-hand."

"I know you know," Don interrupted. "But you can't speak."

"What does that mean?" Hal quipped.

"You know. You're involved. I mean . . . with her."

"I don't know what you're driving at, Don, but I'll be damned
if I won't defend her. She confides in me. So what? Don't forget I
was once president of the temple. I know from the inside what a
rabbi does and how hard a rabbi really works."

"I'll bet," Don breathed.

Hal's defensive flow stopped short. He pondered Don's reaction and then let it pass. "Just because I've been a friend of the
family doesn't mean I'll keep quiet. I'll fight Phil all the way."

"Don't get so excited, Hal. You'll be giving yourself away."

"Truth is truth, Don. She's gone to bat for so many, she's
established a national reputation. She's given us real pride,
Don. We're on the map, and I know that she's exhausted. In
addition to everything, she's studying hard. We've got to help
her, not throw up roadblocks."

"I know, and Phil's gonna use that ordination business
against her too. He'll get it in somehow that she's not really a
rabbi. He'll try anything."

"I'll worry about that," Hal answered. "I'll report her association with Dr. Horner, the only case in history in which the
president of a seminary asked a woman to prepare herself. I
believe that he's getting ready to ordain her. That'll mean a great
deal, not only for her and for the community, but for the world
too. I think that when I explain it, it will sort of put Phil in his
place."

Don ended the conversation by muttering, "I need this like a hole in the head. I'm glad my term is coming to an end. This year has been hell."

"Don," Hal concluded, "you better speak to more people, prepare them for what might come up. If they know what's going on, they'll come."

Don surveyed the twenty-eight member group, considering the probable outcome of a vote. It was one thing to plan preliminary maneuvers on an issue, and another to meet it head on.

"Any old business?" Don asked.

"We've been having a problem with the morning minyan," Sanford Stein said, rising. "We've had some days without a minyan and so we couldn't have a service. Where the hell can men say Kaddish if not here in the synagogue?"

The board members looked at Don for direction. What an inane subject to bring up when a major issue was lurking in the wings! But Sanford, unbeknown to himself, was creating an issue when he said innocently, "The rabbi hasn't really helped us. She hasn't come at all hardly, I mean. Hell, if she wants to be like the men, she has to feel responsible and come at least once in a while, to set an example, you know."

Phil smiled smugly. Someone had done the dirty work for him. Don looked at Hal. It amounted to additional nails in Sara's coffin. Many temple members felt strongly about the daily minyan. Whether *they* attended was another story, but the *rabbi's* got to come.

Stanley Aronsen waited for Sanford to finish. "I appreciate what Sanford said. He's right. I come, you know, once in a while. When I said Kaddish for my mother, I was grateful that I could come to my own temple, didn't have to go to the Ortho-dox synagogue. They got problems, too, getting a minyan. But once you go there, they pressure you to join the synagogue. We've lost a lot of members that way. But do you know how hard a rabbi works? He's, I mean, *she*, she's out almost every night, keeps going all day. Most of us don't know many of the things they have to do. When my mother died, Rabbi Sam was

246

with me all that afternoon and all night long until everything was arranged. Hell, they're human, they can't do everything. Don't forget, you guys, a rabbi counts for only one person. You need a minyan? Hell, send cards out, call people, assign days; all you need is ten. If you can't find ten men or women of the whole congregation to come once in a while we're in bad trouble. Let's not kid ourselves." He sat down, carried away, Don relaxed. Here was one for his side.

Phil looked uncomfortable. "Don," he began, standing up. "I was going to wait for either New Business or Good and Welfare. But since Sanford and Stanley have spoken about the rabbi, I'd like to discuss her."

"We're in old business, Phil," Don knocked the gavel.

"What's the difference, Don? Anything about the rabbi is really old business. Don't be so damned technical. You know what this is all about."

"Let him talk," came a cry from the rear. "Since when are we sticklers for protocol?"

"Yeah, let him talk."

Don looked at Hal, who shrugged.

"Okay," Don said. "Go ahead."

"Doesn't give a damn about anything," was heard.

Phil turned around to the sound of the voice, "What did you say? Were you talking about me?"

"Yes, I was," Robert Glass flung back. "You're nothing more than a goddam troublemaker. Why the hell don't you let things be? Ever since you got on the board all you do is stir up trouble. What is it this time?"

"Maybe I'm the most valuable member here," Phil responded, his anger mounting. "I care. I care about the temple. No one is as dedicated. The temple is very important to me. That's why I play devil's advocate. If I didn't care, I wouldn't waste my time."

"Like hell," Robert answered.

"I give more time to the temple than most of you fellas. If you don't like it, I'll quit. I don't need this."

Phil looked for the signal from the president. Don banged his

THE RABBI IS A LADY

gavel and raised his voice, sweat heavy around his neck. "All right, let's keep it down. Let him talk. Let's get on with it."

"I have a petition, Mr. President," Phil began, "which I want to present."

"You don't need a petition, Phil. Tell us what's on your mind."

"I circulated a petition to prove that there are many like me who think that the time has come," he hesitated, swallowed hard, looked around feeling like Daniel in the lion's den, "the time has come to . . . to change rabbis." He stopped. Those unaware of the issue reacted in shock.

"What? What the hell is going on?"

"What's he talking about?"

"I don't understand!"

Phil allowed the expletives to be expressed. "I would recommend, as I present this petition, that the board consider a change."

"You mean now, in the middle of the year?" a voice asked.

"Yes," Phil felt his time of glory had come. "Now! In the middle of the year, before Rabbi Sara does irreparable harm."

"What's he talking about? She's done a great job."

"Like hell she has."

Everyone vocalized an opinion. No one was seated solidly in his chair.

"I agree. Let's make a clean break." The responses were sharp. No middle road was apparent. Sara had either friend or foe.

Pandemonium drowned out Don's gavel. He looked at Hal, stretched his hands out in despair. Hal sat coolly, waiting for the commotion to subside. Don was standing, his jaws tightened, anger seething. "Damn it," he yelled. "Quiet down. Everybody. Everyone will have a chance to speak." He banged viciously until the pounding drowned out the voices. When quiet resumed, Don sat down, but his gavel went on abusing the table. "Please. I don't like this any better than you do, but now that it's out, let's be gentlemen." He turned to Phil. "All right, Phil, make your statement."

"I got a petition signed by twenty-seven people."

"How many?"

Phil turned around. "Twenty-seven," he repeated. "And that's enough to represent a respectable number who believe that Sara, I mean Rabbi Sara, should be stripped, I mean . . . defrocked." He was flustered. "I mean cancel her contract." He regained composure. "We believe that she's created more trouble than good. We believe. . . ."

He was interrupted. "What are you talking about?" came the challenge.

Phil turned sharply. "Well, she's gotten our teenagers all excited about sex and abortion. Many parents are up in arms. The kids talk about sex and abortion and homosexuality and they got it all from the rabbi. It's incredible. She should be teaching Judaism; you know, *religion*. Do you guys know about some of the problems the kids have had? I know. Sex is my field, my business."

"Come on, Phil, sex isn't your field. What are you talking about?" The group laughed. Phil continued, "You men don't even know. As a physician I have to keep this confidential, but I know what's been going on with the families and the mothers and the girls. Believe me, if your kids, especially the girls were involved, you'd agree with me."

"What's he talking about?"

"To top it all," Phil continued, "she's gone too far with the community, with Jacob Abrams. She's out of her cotton pickin' mind thinking she could put him out of business. Hell, he's given us a wing and he was going to endow the Rabbi Sam Weintraub library." He paused. "She doesn't even have respect for her own husband's memory." He paused again. "I move that we make her resign." He sat down self-righteously.

Don looked around for someone to second the motion. The room was deathly silent. Phil turned to Cowen, who squirmed. "Aren't you going to second it?" Cowen faltered. Phil pressed, calling him "chicken." Meekly, his head down, Cowen said inaudibly, "I second the motion." It was now an official matter of business.

Disappointed, Don gavelled, "Discussion?" The lull of quiet was overwhelming. Don looked at Hal. Hal nodded.

"Yes," he said calmly. "I want to speak against the motion. Everyone has a right to recommend any action to help the temple," he began. "It is equally our right to differ." His faint smile was disarming: his eyes stopped at Phil and lingered. He continued, "It's certainly true that Sara has been in the forefront of our temple activities. You have to give her credit for her fighting spirit. Isn't that what you want of a rabbi? Some of our youngsters have found a new, what shall I call her, guru. They've come to services. Isn't that something we've always wanted? She speaks candidly, but from a Jewish point of view. Isn't Sara honestly doing what we always expected a rabbi to do? The nursing business? Abrams?" He turned to Phil, saying, "Isn't she taking the only honest position a woman of God or a man of God can take? Some oppose Sara. But in the main she's done a superb job. The Seminary has guided her in a study program which may, I stress *may*, lead to official recognition. The Rabbinical Conference has already said that there is nothing in Jewish law that prohibits ordaining a woman as a rabbi. I happen to know only because, well, let's say because Sara has told me that Dr. Horner indicated it to her. And, don't forget our synagogue has gained a national reputation because of her." He stopped and sat down slowly.

"Look," Phil stood up. "You're pretty smooth, but you don't have to deal with all the people and hear all the complaints like I do. You get up in the morning and you're a commuter. You go to New York."

Hal stood his ground. "Why should you be the one to hear all the complaints, Phil? You're not even an officer."

"I don't know; they just come to me and confide in me. I still say she's disturbing our families and community. What she is on a national level is fine, but we're living right here in Wilmette." He paused, hesitated. "And I haven't been personal."

Don looked up as other startled eyes did. He interjected, "And you won't be, Phil."

"If I have to make my point, I will."

"No!" Don decreed, "I won't permit any personal references."

"Hal knows," Phil blustered. Faces turned to Hal.

"Knows what?" Hal asked coldly.

"You know, Hal, you and Sara . . . I meant Rabbi Sara." Hal rose slowly, calmly, a touch of anger emerging on his face. He walked several steps to where Phil was seated. Phil froze. Wordlessly, Hal bent over, grabbed Phil by his tie, raised him to a standing position and swung, his fist smashing against Phil's chin. Phil went reeling over three chairs, landing against a collection of other chairs. Dazed, he felt his chin. He looked at his hand for blood, astonished to find a dab of redness. He shook his head in disbelief. The other members were astonished. Some rose to stop the fight. Don's mouth was agape. Hal adjusted his jacket, turned around, and calmly asked: "Is there anything else you would like to add, Phil?" He then sat down.

Phil's recovery was quick. "You can't scare me off like that," he shouted. "I'll expose everything." Hal started towards Phil again. Don rushed between them.

"Cut it out, you two."

"I don't have to listen to his insinuations or anyone else's," Hal flared. "And I won't!"

"Easy, Hal. Phil got carried away."

"But not at my expense or Sara's."

"That's all right," Phil raged: "I'll tell the whole goddam world about you and Sara, you kissing her and all that." Hal shook off Don's hold, pushed him aside and started for Phil again. Phil raised his left arm. "You can hit me, Hal," he said, "but truth is truth. My brother-in-law drove past Sara's home and saw you in the doorway kissing her. Who the hell knows what else you do." He turned around. "I say get rid of her before she disgraces the temple."

Hal stopped, contemplated, looked at the board members who had gathered around. "So that's what you're talking about," he said, relieved that this was the only incident Phil was aware of. "I drove Sara to the Seminary to meet with Dr. Horner, and I kissed her good night. Sure. How many of you kiss people good night when you leave a hostess! And you, Phil, took that evening and built up the whole picture of Sara and me?" Hal sounded convincing, except to Phil.

"There's more but I can't say what, not now," Phil countered.

In a flash, Hal was at him, flinging more devastating punches. Phil went down again. "You're getting me angry, Phil. I don't usually lose control, but be careful."

"Stop them. Call the police."

"Shame, in a synagogue yet."

"Move we adjourn," Don heard this last recommendation pierce through the others. He announced the end of the meeting.

Phil's few friends gathered around him and pulled him away.

As they walked out Don said to Hal, "You shouldn't have done that."

Hal answered, "You have to fight fire with fire, Don. And, nothing happened with the motion. Remember that."

Don smiled, "I guess that's one way to defeat a motion, isn't it?"

Chapter Twenty-Seven

No sooner had Rabbi Friedman returned from lunch than the buzzer on his desk sounded. He tried to ignore it. Busy, busy, busy. Why hadn't he stayed rabbi of a congregation instead of taking this thankless job as secretary of the R.C.? It ruined his stomach, robbed him of sleep. Not that there weren't compensations. The movement was growing. You met some brilliant rabbis. You matched rabbis and pulpits. A real *shadchan*. You changed the course of many lives by your decisions in this matchmaking process. What power you held! The infernal buzzer again. He pressed. "What is it?"

"Mr. Harold Kaplan to see you, Rabbi."

"Already?" An instant later, contrite, he said: "Okay, show him in, Libby."

This Mr. Kaplan, who came at you like a Sherman tank, was just an example of it. What did this man want of his life? For months now, Kaplan had been pestering him about the Weintraub widow who wanted to be a rabbi. A Jewish Joan of Arc. Personally, he didn't object. He was favorably disposed toward her. He was, in fact, pro woman rabbis. It would be good for the movement, like a breath of spring—new, exciting, challenging. It would also be good for the congregation to appreciate the vitality of Jewish tradition; tradition and change. The door opened and Hal Kaplan came in, carrying a topcoat and attaché case. He looked tall, robust, handsome, strong—a combination Rabbi Friedman ordinarily admired but now he regarded Mr. Kaplan as a pest.

"Sit down, Mr. Kaplan. How have you been?"

"Fine. And yourself, Rabbi?"

"As well as can be expected of an old man." Why do rabbis demean themselves? he asked himself, too late.

Hal sat in the soft leather chair facing the rabbi. The desk was large with white telephones, a dictaphone, and piles of papers. "As you suspect, Rabbi Friedman, I've come to find out about Rabbi Weintraub's ordination."

"Of course. What else? I wish I had some news for you, Mr. Kaplan. As you know, the Commission on Legal Interpretation has voted to admit women into the rabbinate."

"Yes, you told me that, some time ago."

"I did? Well, now it is up to the Membership Committee to act on the particular matter."

"And when will that be, Rabbi? I have the feeling I'm getting the run-around."

Rabbi Friedman shrugged. "Your guess is as good as mine. Soon, I hope. It's in the hands of the gods, you might say." He tried to be funny but failed.

"Rabbi Friedman, we should be old friends by now. Can't anything be done to prod them? It's become quite urgent."

"Justice, sir, is notorious for moving at a snail's pace."

"But this has been dragging, Rabbi. We can't afford to wait much longer."

"And why not? According to the reports we receive, Mrs. Weintraub has already been functioning as a rabbi."

"It's not fair to her or to the congregation. How well can she function if she's kept guessing about whether or not she'll be ordained? It's like being on probation."

"In a way it is a probationary period. What's wrong with that? Shouldn't provision be made for the congregants to find out how they feel about a new rabbi? And shouldn't the rabbi, by the same token, see how she feels about the post, whether she likes it, can handle it?"

"Rabbi Weintraub has been doing an outstanding job," Hal announced proudly.

"Has she, really?"

"You doubt my words, Rabbi Friedman?"

"Not really. I'm sure she's doing exceptional work in certain areas. But according to reports we've been receiving, all is not peaches and cream."

"What do you mean?" Hal asked surprised.

"There are difficulties, problems. . . ."

"Who doesn't have problems? We have our share, but no more than other temples."

"True, true, Mr. Kaplan. It has come to our attention that a petition is being circulated against her."

"Oh, it's come to your attention?" Hal's eyes narrowed. He wondered how the news had spread so quickly.

"Yes, it has."

"A tempest in a teapot, Rabbi. It'll blow over."

"That's not the way we hear it, Mr. Kaplan. We've gotten reports of a . . . volatile meeting of your board. You say it'll blow over? Maybe. Still, Mr. Kaplan, a petition is a very serious thing, not to be taken lightly. She's antagonized some of the older members."

"Mostly the male chauvinists and the reactionaries. She's stepped on some sensitive toes; sure. She's made some people uncomfortable; she's made some people think. Mr. Abrams, the nursing home operator, to give one example."

"Yes, we read about that in *The Times*."

"She's really incorruptible, Rabbi."

"Since the Sara Weintraub matter came up, almost eight months ago, you've sort of been arguing her case before us. You don't have an official position do you?"

255

"No, not now. I've held positions, on and off, over the past fifteen years. I was president, but drew back after my wife died almost three years ago."

"Oh, I'm sorry. Are you still a . . . widower?"

"Yes."

"And as a good Jew you will, of course, remarry. It's a mitzvah, you know?"

"I'll do my best. What does this have to do with what we're talking about?"

"You've known Rabbi Weintraub a long time, haven't you?" Rabbi Friedman seemed to persist in his own line of thought.

"More than a decade. We're old friends. I'm very attached to the Weintraub children."

"Do you spend much time together?"

"That's a personal question, Rabbi, but I'll answer it. No, we don't spend much time together. Sara, excuse me, Rabbi Weintraub . . . is busy with her work, the children. Hers is a twenty-four hour job. I see her occasionally, on holidays and so on." He stopped. "What are you getting at?"

"Well, nothing really. But yes, I'm intrigued. You're a most eligible man. Rabbi Weintraub is young and attractive. A married rabbi has his or her mind more thoroughly on his or her work than a single one. I'm thinking of the benefit to Temple Shalom."

Hal chuckled. "So not only are you a rabbi and an amateur psychologist, a pulpit *shadchan*, but you're also a people *shadchan*, trying to make a match. Before you draw any conclusions, let me tell you that it's nothing like that between us. Oh, no. As I said, we're simply old friends. That's the way it's been all these years." Hal's voice turned matter-of-fact.

"But it needn't be, Mr. Kaplan. You two would make an ideal couple."

"Thanks very much for the compliment. The fact of the matter is—and I don't know why I'm telling you all this, notwithstanding the fact that you are the nosiest rabbi I've ever met—the fact of the matter is, I'm really attracted to Sara Weintraub, but

256

discern no reciprocal feelings on her part."

"Well, you know best," Rabbi Friedman continued, not bothered that Hal had called him nosey.

Hal looked at the rabbi, who seemed to know everything and was ever ready to analyze and advise. "We haven't settled Sara's ordination, or at least, the question of membership. If we could work that out, Rabbi, it would knock the sails out of that petition and catapult Sara onto the national scene. Everyone, I mean, would rally behind her. Probably even Elkind, who originated the petition."

"As I said earlier, Mr. Kaplan, the Commission on Legal Interpretation has acted favorably on admitting women to the rabbinate. Now the Membership Committee is to vote *specifically* on Rabbi Weintraub. And then, there's the Seminary." He paused. "Of course, I know of Dr. Horner's *special* interest in this case." He paused again. "Haven't you been driving Mrs. Weintraub to the Seminary?" Hal decided to ignore the question.

"Which probably means another six months," Hal said. "Can't we speed it up, Rabbi?"

"I admire your determination. I'll do what I can with Dr. Horner."

Chapter Twenty-Eight

DEAN KAHN WAS SITTING in Dr. Horner's study when Sara was ushered in.

She had studied diligently these past months, and had conditioned herself against the stresses of her profession, the unexpected challenges, and the daily regimen of discipline. She had written papers, sent them and received corrections and comments. It was time to visit Dr. Horner again. Hal, of course, offered to drive her. "I want to make sure you get there on time. I've a personal interest in this program, you know."

Sara began to feel an inner confidence that showed on her face. She had learned not to take each incident so seriously and personally. Many more episodes would surely demand her attention; it was in the nature of her profession. Concluding one matter, solving another problem, she drifted with ease to the next one. She could shift concentration from a baby-naming ceremony, to a hospital visit, to a funeral, to a wedding, to a *bris*, to an unveiling, to an engagement party and a lecture—all in a day. She was sleeping better these days, awakening more relaxed. Even the Elkind petition and the Board of Trustees' imbroglio, while shattering to her rabbinic equilibrium, did not depress her. Taking an overview of each situation she bounced back, with a serenity sensed by her secretary and her children. She was glowing, healthy-looking; the children witnessed a new mother-rabbi.

For his part, Hal had been thinking deeply these days. Why had he reacted so violently, uncharacteristically, at the board meeting? What did Phil really say that merited such uncontrolled anger, his attack on the smaller man? And then Rabbi Friedman's repeated insinuation. Was it so obvious? He concluded that he had indeed been sending signals. He was in love with Sara and the realization radiated a sensation of warmth all over. What should he do now? How to express that feeling and cautiously? A woman may be loved by a man, but when the woman is a rabbi, discretion is certainly the better part of valor and judgment. He was delighted when Sara called to say she was going to the Seminary to see Dr. Horner again.

When he honked, his eagerness was like that of an adolescent. His heart beat rapidly as he waited. Sara dashed out of her house, closed the door, and darted briskly down the few steps toward the car. Carrying a small attaché case, her dark blue topcoat flung open, she was, as Hal observed, dressed in the height of fashion. She wore a soft, flowered silk blouse, with a little bowtie at the neck. Her long, brown hair was neatly coiffed. A healthy happy smile caught Hal's eye. She's beautiful, he thought. God, why does she have to be a rabbi? He opened the door for her with a satisfying flourish and abandon. He thought of Phil Elkind and muttered, "The hell with him."

"What did you say?" Sara asked, as Hal returned to the driver's seat.

"Nothing," he answered, his face brightening. "You look gorgeous, Rabbi. Going to meet someone special?"

I heard what you said, she mused. As a matter of fact, yes, I'm going to meet someone special. Her smile broadened. Her face was open, beaming, her teeth glistened. Hal repeated, "I must say, you do look great."

"I feel great, Hal. I've learned to take each step at a time. I've got to do it. For me. I've studied and I hope Dr. Horner will be pleased. I intend to prove my knowledge and impress him. I really do."

"Good for you," Hal encouraged. "You've really gotten hold of yourself."

"I hope it's easier today. I feel as if I'm in command, so it should be. Nothing's going to stand in my way. I won't even say anything negative about that terrible board meeting. But I must confess I was thrilled," she sparkled, "when I heard that you came to my defense."

"Rabbi!" Hal admonished. "A rabbi glad a man was hit?" The reprimand was half-serious.

"Yes," she continued, "I *was* glad. I was excited because I knew you cared enough for me to shut him up."

"What language," Hal laughed. "I'm shocked."

"What excitement!" she countered.

"You're like your old self," he said hesitating, "and I'm glad." He turned the ignition. "I'm so glad I fell in love with you," he said, looking straight ahead. Sara's smile faded. "Let's keep the day light, okay?"

"Okay," he said. She wanted to concentrate on her meeting.

"Good morning," she smiled as she came into the office, stopping short as she saw Dean Kahn. Unbeknown to Sara and other faculty members, Dr. Horner had asked Dean Kahn personally to supervise a program of study for her.

"I asked Dean Kahn to join us," Dr. Horner announced, motioning Sara to a chair. "He's been quite interested in you and your progress. I must say, Sara," Dr. Horner noticed approvingly as she took off her hat and placed it on the side chair, "you hardly look like a candidate for the rabbinate, highly unusual."

Sara smiled. "Thanks." He had noticed. "Are you pleased?"

"Yes, yes," he returned to the subject, "Very much. You are doing very well indeed. I've read your papers after Dean Kahn studied them, and while I can see room for improvement, you have a real insight into our tradition and literature. What would you like to discuss today, from your studies?"

Sara hesitated. "I thought you might question me," she answered. "Unless I may make some observations on a subject which affects me personally and women generally."

"Of course," Dr. Horner encouraged. His expression softened into a smile. She didn't notice him wink at Dean Kahn. "I'd be disappointed if you didn't speak about *women*." Sara took a deep breath, opened her attaché case, took out a few folders and calmly selected the one marked WOMEN. She glanced at the pages as the two men waited patiently. With the same calm she now felt delivering a sermon or lecturing to her confirmation class, Sara traced the role of women in Jewish history. She touched on the Bible, recalling women who were of primary importance. She spoke of the Talmudic period, the era of the commentaries and the codes, the Middle Ages. For each of these periods she noted women who had been recognized for their achievements, religious or secular. She brought her analysis to the present, speaking of women's roles and their attitudes and the attitudes of men and tradition towards them. She stressed her appreciation for the Bible's sense of equality for women, for God's creation of both men and women. "True," she explained away, "equality is a hard term to define. There are deprecatory references in Biblical and Talmudic literature, but no literature is monolithic.

"Isn't it true?" she asked rhetorically, "Are there not denigrating references to men? I know," she said, "that historically women were viewed with a measure of disdain. I don't think women should have been. Many areas of life are viewed negatively, but we must take the best of the past for our present understanding. Search the distilled essence of tradition and infuse it into this volatile world of change."

Dr. Horner interrupted, a smile resting on his face. "You're delivering a sermon, aren't you, Sara?"

Sara relaxed, smiled, and continued. "It is true that women are not obligated to fulfill positive Biblical commandments based on a time factor. I find this exciting, unlike some of my female contemporaries, because it tells me of the importance of women's role in life. I find it positive. If times have changed, then we can change with them without violating our heritage. If women today want to participate in those positive duties, they're not prohibited, are they? They *may*. There are enough scholarly authorities to support this position."

From the overview, Sara moved skillfully to specifics. She spoke of women donning tephilin and prayer shawls. She analyzed some Biblical passages and rabbinic interpretations. She discussed women as witnesses to divorces and marriage documents, practices not permitted by Jewish law. "I can challenge interpretations, but the interpretive process is traditional and I'm not quick to discard even the rules of interpretation which have been used for thousands of years. Tradition means too much to overturn quickly; it has kept us alive." Dr. Horner and Dean Kahn nodded; they glanced at each other, wondering how long the dissertation would last.

Dr. Horner interrupted, "You *do* know your subject. I'm impressed. Aren't you, Dean Kahn?"

Dean Kahn nodded. He said, "I wouldn't expect less." Sara smiled broadly. "Thank you," she said, and turned to her papers.

"It won't be necessary to continue, my dear," Dr. Horner said. "I didn't intend to examine you, but you've really examined yourself. I was confident from the beginning and now I'm very much impressed." He hesitated. "Even students who spend five or six years here are not expected to have complete knowledge. They study basics and then they learn where to go for further research. But they do learn where to find the law. You've made a very good beginning."

He continued slowly. "I am very pleased. You're doing well. You've managed to study while carrying on a difficult role. I commend you and I hope that some day soon you'll be happy with your achievements." Sara looked deeply into his eyes and thought she understood. Without spelling it out, Dr. Horner was telling her that he would soon consider a positive step.

"Oh, thank you," she jumped up, ready to kiss him. The Chancellor responded. "We'll keep our joyous expression for another time. Now, Sara, you'll continue working with Dean Kahn, and in a month or two we'll meet again. Keep up the good work." He smiled.

They were standing. Flinging her coat over her arm and holding her attaché case, Sara said good-bye and started out.

"My, my, how rabbis have changed," Dr. Horner mused.

"Oh, by the way. . . ." Sara turned around at his words. "Would you want to join us for lunch?"

Sara responded quickly: "Of course; I'd be delighted."

In the cafeteria-style lunch room, Sara stood in line with Dr. Horner and Dean Kahn. Professors and students seemed to share the same gastronomic tastes. She noticed some of the younger men looking at the three of them as they walked into the lunch room. She heard a stage whisper, "Who's she?" Another response came to her ears as one of the younger men covered his mouth and whispered, with a smile, "She's the rabbi of Wilmette." Dr. Horner looked about as he heard, "Who's the old man sporting around with? She's pretty."

Sara felt an excitement she had never before experienced. Standing outside the Seminary building, she felt exhilaration mingled with self-satisfaction. She smiled openly, not caring who noticed. She had succeeded; things were looking up. She was moving into a new era. With trim body erect, she walked with a more confident stride.

Glancing at her watch, she was startled. She had been with the Chancellor for almost two hours. She had promised to call Hal when the interview was over. But standing outside the Seminary, she decided not to, thinking that she needed a little time for herself. She noted the steady flow of walkers rushing to keep schedules, and she wanted to be anonymous, lost in the shuffle of humanity. She wanted her mind to clear, to feel good and enjoy the moment without obstacles or problems . . . just to be herself. She walked lightly, almost dancing in her exuberance. The sun shone in full force. No cloud disturbed the sky's perfect blue.

Next she took a cab to 59th Street, where she walked past the Essex House, the Hampshire House, Rumpelmayer's famous coffee shop. She marched on, paused to glance into the beautiful restaurants, some new, some old. She looked into lavish entrances of magnificent hotels and apartment houses. Long sleek cars with bars and television sets stopped to let out their guests. At the Plaza, she stopped. The doormen were busy welcoming new arrivals. She walked in slowly, savoring the beauty of the renowned hotel. The elegance captured her. Like a new tourist, she looked about in the inviting flat-domed lobby, scanning ceiling and shops. Heritage, tradition, history reached out to embrace her. At the same time modernity was evident. In the wake of the morning's experience, tradition also meant change; the blend foretold strength. The theme was everywhere, in Judaism, in her life. She was a new woman—today's woman, breathing new vitality into Judaism.

She walked slowly into the large open-air Palm Court, corridors of charming shops on either side, the soft melodies of a string orchestra filtering through the air. A feeling of peace overtook her. She saw happy and contented couples chatting at the small, round marble tables.

Sara stopped. Felt a twinge. She was alone. A single. Career? Yes. But she was not modern enough to get used to the absence of coupling, marriage, relationships. She felt the bitterness of her private reality. The happier the couples appeared, the more envious she felt. She struggled with her inner self. The void she suddenly felt turned into panic. Compulsively, she sought the telephone. She pictured Hal, as her nervous fingers dialed.

"What's the matter, Sara?"

"I, ah . . . nothing actually."

"You sound nervous," he noted. "Didn't it go well?"

"Everything went beautifully, just wonderful." She spoke quickly, trying to cover her anxiety.

"You don't sound right," he began.

"Are you busy, Hal?" She asked hurriedly. "Could you come now?"

"Now?" He hesitated, sensing the panic in her voice. "Of course. Where are you?"

"I'm at the Plaza in the lobby."

"The Plaza? What are you doing there? Are you sure you're all right?"

"I'm fine, Hal. Please hurry. I miss you."

"What?" he asked, his eyes blinking as he looked in the telephone.

"Please hurry. I need you."

"Be right there. Twenty minutes."

"I'll be here." She broke into a fit of perspiration, angry that the luster of the morning's success seemed to have disappeared so quickly. I've got to get hold of myself before Hal comes. I can't let him see me so distressed.

She wiped her face again, looked at the mirror, startled. She looked at herself again. It seemed so calculated—her dress, Hal's almost boyish joy, her success, Dr. Horner's approval, the sight of the happy couples in the Palm Court. The scenes melted together, then sharpened into focus. She *was* in love with Hal Kaplan! Her face brightened. She had come full circle and pondered the meaning of destiny. She felt like a young girl eagerly waiting for her beau. She must look foolish, she thought, but she didn't care. Rabbi or not, she was a woman of feeling and she had no need to feel ashamed.

"What's the matter, Sara?" Hal was half out of breath. He embraced her, kissed her on the cheek. "Are you okay? You look great. But you sounded terrible."

"I know," she responded quickly. "I did feel terrible, but I feel wonderful now. I love you," she whispered as she kissed him on the mouth.

"What? Have you gone crazy? First, you're excited, then you call me and you sound terrible, you scare me half out of my wits, and now you kiss me and tell me you love me. You sure you're all right?"

"I'm fine, just fine. Let's sit down in the Palm Court. Just you and I."

"For lunch?"

"No, I had lunch. Just coffee. I just want to be with you." Without fully understanding, she led Hal to the Palm Court where the maitre d' seated them near the orchestra. They were hidden by palms and colorful plants, finding themselves almost alone in an alcove. Sara scanned the room, now feeling she belonged. They ordered coffee and finger sandwiches.

"What's this all about?" he asked. "I just can't. . . ."

"I just want to sit and look at you, talk to you."

Relief cleared away Hal's concern. "You certainly look fine. Now what happened?"

"First I want to look at you." She looked deeply into his eyes, her gaze unwavering.

"You sound like a little girl."

"I am," she said. "I'm a little girl in love." Hal shook his head, took her hand on the table. "I can't understand what's going on," he whispered.

Sara turned around as the music began. "Dance?"

"Dance? In the middle of the day?"

"What difference does it make? People are dancing." Sara held Hal tight and he felt her love flowing through her hands, fingers, and body. She pressed her head against his chest.

When they returned to the table, a happy equilibrium sustaining her, Sara calmly described the interview, the signals Dr. Horner had sent, her strolling on Central Park South, her feelings and thoughts, the Plaza, the sight of happy couples—"then I realized Hal, at that moment, that what I missed most was you. Everything is going well but I need love too. I need you."

"I've been trying to tell you the same thing for a long time, Sara. Helping you with the board, the first meeting with Dr. Horner, Hanukah at home, and then punching Phil the way I did. And then, this morning, but you never really gave me a chance."

266

"I heard you, Hal, but I didn't realize until today and I. . . ."

"You were supposed to call me as soon as the interview was over."

"I'm glad I didn't. I wouldn't have realized anything."

"I'm so glad," he said. He looked around, and then whispered, "I love you, too." They held hands. "You can say it louder," she encouraged.

"Sara, I want to say it only to you."

"Let's walk today. Can we? Can you?"

"I'll call the office and tell them I won't be back. Where to?"

"On Fifth Avenue. Let's just walk and look, okay?"

They walked briskly, together, arms around waists, bodies close, speaking abstractly about the inanities of the street, the fumes of the buses, the waiting shops, people window shopping. They stopped to stare at department store windows, boutiques, and bookstores. Customers filed in and out of the stores.

Sara snuggled close to Hal as he drove home. "You get me all excited," he said. "Some rabbi."

She blushed. "O.K.," she said, "I'll move away."

"No," he protested. "Please don't." Hal's mind whirled and thoughts clashed. Sara's mind was equally tumultuous. Reality set in as they neared Wilmette. Had she finally let herself go? she pondered. Woman or career? Would Hal want her if she were not a rabbi? Did he want her for herself or for her role? Trying to sense his feelings, she concluded that he looked upon her as a desirable woman. What the children would think was another question.

As the car neared Sara's street, Hal didn't make the customary right turn. Instead, he continued in the direction of his own house. Sara kept silent.

"I know it's been a long day, Sara, but I have to be with you a while longer. Will you come in?"

Conflict continued to mount. She had admitted to herself and to Hal that she loved him, yet she continued to feel torn. "All right, but only for a bit. The children will wonder."

Hal's manner was easy, relaxed. Sara looked around the large, comfortable living room which exuded an ambience of understated elegance. There were the tasteful contemporary furnishings, teakwood tables exquisitely carved, interesting pieces of sculpture and original Chinese silk screen paintings on the walls. Sara imagined Hal alone, rambling about the big house. There were three bedrooms upstairs as well. She wondered why Hal had never sold the house and moved into the city.

"Can I get you anything, Sara? Some coffee?"

"No thanks. I've had enough coffee. What do you want to do, keep me awake all night?"

"Is that such a bad idea?" he smiled. "How about a drink?"

"No, thanks."

He poured some scotch for himself and took a sip. "Mmm, that hits the spot. Sure you wouldn't like one?"

"No, but I'll taste yours."

Hal offered the glass to her. He watched the sensuous lips open as she sipped. She swallowed and made a face. "A little too strong for me."

"Something else, then? Maybe some white wine?"

"No, thanks, Hal. I'm fine."

"You're a real drinker!" he teased.

"Mmm." But the pleasant sensation was already in her blood, relaxing her, making her feel slightly giddy.

As Hal sat down next to her, she was drawn by the aroma of his cologne. His closeness flustered her. His hand brushed against her thigh as he took the glass from her hand, his touch sending a pleasurable tingling through her body. "Don't you think it's time for me to go, Hal?" He didn't answer, but moved closer.

Hal was aware of a certain vulnerability Sara had not displayed before. In all the years he'd known her, she had been almost intimidating, formidable. Seeing her with her defenses down aroused and excited him. He took her hand. "Feels so soft. Like this afternoon at the Plaza."

"My hands haven't changed," she said, though she didn't withdraw.

"Your heart?" he asked softly.

"No," she replied, "that hasn't changed either."

"I'm glad," he responded, turning to kiss her. At first, the pressure of his lips was light. But then he grew passionate, and Sara found herself responding. She didn't resist but crumpled against him—wanting him, needing him. His fingers moved gently to caress her breasts. "I love you, Sara."

She wound her arms around his neck and pressed closer. She felt him massage her tense shoulder muscles. "And I love you." Hal scooped her into his arms. He carried her upstairs effortlessly, placed her on the bed with gentleness.

He removed her clothes slowly, stopping to brush back a stray hair that fell across her face. She responded, finding renewed pleasure in stroking his naked body. "Hal," she murmured.

"Ssh," he assured her. "We're together now. We'll work it out." Seeing the unmistakable look of tenderness in his eyes, Sara lay back at ease, allowing her senses to take over.

She enjoyed the lovemaking, more than she believed she could. It had been so long. She heard Hal whisper her name over and over, caressing her, massaging her, giving her pleasure.

A strange silence filled the room afterwards. Hal tried to think of something to say. "I enjoyed it, Rabbi," he said with kind humor. A million thoughts rushed through her mind, forming but never developing totally. Flashes of pleasure, guilt, and doubt streamed in and out of consciousness. "So did I." She drew a breath and averted her eyes. "But I have to go home."

"So soon?"

"I can't spend the night," she said quietly.

"No. Of course you can't."

They dressed. Hal's excitement in watching her dress nearly matched his ardor when he had watched her before. He wanted to reach and touch her again, but didn't.

They rode in silence. Sitting close to the window, Sara felt the space between them uncomfortable. Was Hal feeling guilty? Was she?

They passed Washington Street, halfway between Hal's place and her own. Still no words had been exchanged. As though we were strangers, she thought grimly. Hal kept his eyes fastened on the road, his hands gripping the steering wheel. It seemed as if he were on the point of speaking several times, but changed his mind.

Conflict tore at her heart. Judaism favored sexual union as a part of *married* love. Had she been a hypocrite? She slid a look towards Hal. She *was* in love with him. Somehow, that eased the guilt. But deep down she knew the nagging question would plague her. She was, after all, a rabbi, a leader to her people, a woman of God. The word jabbed her. Was Elkind right? Perhaps she didn't deserve her position. She'd been vulnerable and had given in to temptation. Somewhere, she didn't understand why or how, a tiny voice whispered: But even a rabbi is not above human weakness. Only God is perfect. With an inward smile, she lay her head back to rest. Who was *she* to judge anybody, for that matter? She felt she had been given another test and that in some strange, ironic way had passed.

Chapter Twenty-Nine

EXHILARATED AND EXCITED, Sara was eager to share her experience at the Seminary with her children. They listened as she detailed the story. Inflated with her success, Sara's feelings flowed outward. Her children watched. She was not aware of their reactions, expecting only accolades.

"Mommy," Simon said softly when she concluded, "my Bar Mitzvah is coming and we haven't even talked about it." He looked at Carol. She encouraged him by her sympathetic look.

Sara sat on the couch, her face aglow with excitement. Her son's words didn't penetrate at first. She sat stunned. What had happened to her? Had she become so engrossed in herself? Was this what she wanted? Self-fulfillment? She had succeeded in her rabbinate; success was beckoning to her as a woman—but she had failed as a mother.

Tears spilled out. She rushed to embrace her children. Simon retreated. Sara called: "Simon?"

"Yes, Mother," he answered, dutifully, coldly.

"Simon?" she choked. The boy remained motionless.

"Mother," Carol interjected, voice controlled. "Simon is supposed to be Bar Mitzvah, and we haven't made any plans."

"Why . . . I, ah. . . . ," Sara's defense crumpled.

"Mother! Simon and I have been talking. You're never home anymore. You go from one meeting to another. You're not like a mother anymore. We don't do anything together anymore."

"I . . . I . . . didn't realize . . ." Sara muttered. "I've been so wrapped up with . . . the synagogue . . . and. . . ."

"And churches. . . ."

"You've cared more about everybody and everything else. You talk about family . . . family life. You've helped some of the other kids with their problems. And you . . . oh, Mother . . ." she cried. "I don't mean it . . . I don't mean . . . I," she sobbed. "It's. . . ."

"Yes, you do," Sara helped. "Yes, you do." She was crying too. Simon looked on to see his mother and sister, sobbing.

Sara moved quickly over to the other side of the couch. Without giving her two children a chance to resist, she pressed in between them and embraced them.

"I'm sorry. Really, I am. I'm so sorry. Forgive me? Won't you forgive me?"

Carol raised her head, seeking Simon's on the other side, asking whether they should.

Simon's face retained its hurt.

"Please, Carol, Simon. Please forgive me. I've let things run away with me."

"They're more important than we are," he had said to Carol earlier that night. "She. . . ."

"Who's she?" Carol challenged.

"Mother. Mother is always talking to the other parents. She meets with them before the Bar Mitzvah. Mr. Edelstone and she set up Bar Mitzvah dates. But she . . . she . . . never even thought about me . . . about my Bar Mitzvah . . ."

Carol had tried to be mature. "She's so busy, Simon. With the temple and the other things and especially the. . . ."

"I don't care, Carol," he blurted out. "Mother just doesn't

care. I don't care if she *is* the rabbi. I don't care anymore. I wish Dad were here. He'd care."

"Don't say that, Simon," Carol cautioned, maturely.

"Why not?"

"That'll hurt Mother."

"She's hurt me, Carol. She's hurt me bad."

"She doesn't mean it, Simon. You have to believe that. She's working hard. For us."

"I don't care. She hurt me. Doesn't even care about me." He waited for a second or two. "I don't want to be Bar Mitzvah."

"Don't say that either, Si. Every boy has to be Bar Mitzvah."

"Why?"

"Well, it's tradition, that's all. It's gone on for thousands of years."

"So what if it *has* gone on for thousands of years. Nobody cares about me."

"I'm going to tell Mother."

"No, you won't!"

"Yes, I will. I'm going to tell her as soon as she comes home."

Simon listened to his mother pleading, her arm tightening around his shoulders, her fingers burrowing in his hair, his flesh.

"Please, Simon. Please forgive me."

Carol coaxed. "Please. Let's forget it."

Simon glanced over at Carol. "O.K.," he said, but still dejected, pouting. "I forgive you."

"Thank you so much, Si. I promise, from now on, I won't be only a rabbi. I'll be a better mother."

"I don't want you to be a *better* mother. I want you to be *a* mother."

The remark stung. Sara covered it with a forced smile.

"Sunday morning, I promise I'll check with Mr. Edelstone on your Bar Mitzvah, and we'll make arrangements. You'll have a beautiful Bar Mitzvah, Simon. A beautiful Bar Mitzvah."

But she had doubts. There would be an unfillable void. Was

she unconsciously avoiding it?

Her thoughts troubled her as she lay awake in bed. Her children's confrontation had wounded her deeply, threatening the reality of her exciting fulfillment. Life was again difficult. Slowly, she grew resentful. They *should* understand, she thought indignantly. I undertook this not just for myself, but for them too. Their lives have changed but so has mine. They'll grow up, marry and leave. And me? Alone? Her thoughts returned to Hal for the second time that evening.

How selfish can children be? They want me. All the way. Well, I'm also a human being. I have needs too. Weary of the same thoughts going around and around, she sighed, switched off the light. Deep down, she recognized her resentment was defensive. After all, Simon would have only one Bar Mitzvah in his life.

Slowly, the Bar Mitzvah day arrived. The congregation had been asked to attend.

"Mother, you're nervous," Carol said a few moments before the service.

"Yes, I guess I am, Carol," Sara admitted.

"But . . . but you've had so many Bar Mitzvahs!"

"I know, Carol, I know. I've seen . . . oh, hundreds, I think, but it's different . . . now." She tried to smile. Being a single parent is devastating. It must be worse at a wedding, she thought. No union of *nachas*, of delight. No one to share it with. She thought of Hal.

God! Why?

Simon sat on the pulpit, next to Sara, with Don Shapiro on the other side. Hal sat in the front row with Carol. The service proceeded smoothly. Sara felt her heartbeat quicken, her breath shorten. She conducted with controlled emotion. It's not easy, she said to herself, repeatedly. I belong down there with Carol.

Sara spoke to her son.

"This is a great day for you, Simon. A very great day for you, for your sister Carol. I have stood in the presence of many Bar Mitzvahs. This one is different. I am not only your mother. I am also the rabbi of this congregation, as your father was for fifteen fruitful years." Women dabbed at their eyes, men blinked their tears away. "I feel this moment more like a mother than anything else. And I shall, Simon—I promise you—I shall never forget *this* duty." She continued, "This official act, I perform, Simon, as your mother and as the rabbi of the congregation with pride. I am proud of you, and of Carol." She asked him to bow his head. Placing both her hands on his head, she chanted the priestly benediction.

"God bless you, my son. God bless your sister. Here is your Bible. Hold it dear and close to your heart."

Unashamed, Simon lunged forward and fell into his mother's arms. He wept, and the whole congregation wept. Sara stood at her pulpit, clasping her son in her arms.

Later, they assembled in the social hall. Here the cantor obliged them with some songs. There were snacks and a few bottles of liquor which Hal Kaplan had brought for the men who wished to make *Kiddush*. There was a little dancing, a Hora, in which most of the guests joined in, even those who didn't know how to dance. "It was very nice," Simon said to Sara after it was over. "Thanks very much, Mom. I love you."

Chapter Thirty

THE INTERVIEW WITH DR. HORNER and her new relationship with Hal had so invigorated Sara that she felt completely new. She plunged into her work with relentless drive to achieve her goals.

Sitting with her students again, she brought up the issue of the danger of cults. She discussed more than one specific cult and delved into the "philosophies" of many others. "Jews for Jesus" struck a particularly sensitive note with Sara. She suspected that Bruce, Carol's on-again-off-again friend, was more than a curious onlooker in this movement.

"In fact," Sara stressed, "there's a law in Israel that anyone who willfully tries to convert a Jew is guilty of a crime."

"Mother? I mean, Rabbi!" Carol's voice sounded shattered.

"*Mother* is all right here," Sara responded.

"I don't know what to say. I think you're being very unfair Mother." The teenagers looked at each other with questioning eyes.

Sara leaned back.

"What do you mean, Carol?"

"Well, you're getting overly excited about this. I think you're losing control."

"I don't know whether I'm losing control. But it's true—I *am* excited," Sara answered. "But I get excited about everything that's Jewish."

"Maybe you do, maybe too excited . . . maybe you ought to think more about people, and not about their religions."

Sara looked unbelievingly at Carol, wondering what had brought this on. Carol was certainly striking out. But publicly? "Should we talk about it at home?"

"I don't know," Carol said. "I want everyone to know that I don't always agree with my mother."

Sara wondered how to handle this. She felt defensive. "I've always been interested in people but I don't just think about their religions. How could you say that?"

Carol flushed; her face seemed impenetrable, angry.

"I'll think about it," Sara continued. "We'll talk about it at home." She stopped.

The class ended in turmoil. None of the children gathered around Carol. They walked out talking, looking at her, then at Sara. Carol walked out alone.

Carol's bombshell thoroughly unnerved Sara. Simon was asleep. Carol said she wanted to talk about Bruce.

The request took Sara by surprise. "Of course, honey, sit on my bed. I'll join you soon."

Changing slowly, she regarded Carol searchingly, trying to guess what was on her daughter's mind. Carol appeared agitated, flushed. She fidgeted on the bed, entwining her fingers. Sara felt a tremor pass through her. Was Carol in trouble? Carol *wouldn't*. She'd talk to me first, before sleeping with a boy. She rethought her answer. How can I be so sure? She knew Carol once had had a crush on Bruce Fogel, who was three years her senior. They had virtually grown up together. Bruce was an only child with well-to-do parents and had been an "A" student in college.

277

As a boy, he had come on occasion to services, sat in the back of the sanctuary and listened intently to Rabbi Sam. But basically Bruce grew up ignorant of Judaism. His parents were rationalists. "We'll make a Jew of him," Rabbi Sam used to say. Bruce had been through Zen Buddhism, the Hare Krishna movement, and had also tried drugs. Running away from home several times, he was now back with his parents. Shouts were often heard across the grassy lawn that separated their home from the Weintraub place. Carol felt a secret fascination in Bruce's worldliness.

Sara, clad in rose-splashed pajamas, sat down on the bed and said: "All right, let's talk."

"Mother, it's about Bruce," the girl began.

"Yes, what about Bruce? And that outburst in class today!"

The girl hesitated, on the verge of tears. "Well, I'm worried about him. You know how close we are."

"Oh, are you?" Sara's reaction was acerbic. Her eyes shifted involuntarily to Carol's belly.

"Oh, Mother!" Carol was shocked. "I'm not pregnant! It's not anything like that!"

Sara threw her arms around the girl's shoulders.

"Of course not," she said, relieved. Tears came to her eyes. She was ashamed of herself.

"Mother, how *could* you?"

"Forgive me, honey."

"Mother, Bruce plans to convert to Christianity."

Sara moved away from Carol as though she'd been struck. Her face was drained. "You're not joking! So that's it!"

"That's what he told me. He plans to convert, and then study for the ministry."

"He's mad! What do you *mean* convert to Christianity and study for the ministry?" She grasped her by the hand. "Bruce has a gift for shocking people. He likes to get a rise out of them. Once, I recall, when Bruce was ten or eleven, he said to his parents, out of the clear blue sky, 'I think I'll jump off the terrace.' Just like that! Trying to get a rise out of his parents.

278

Shock them. I remember Rose saying, 'If you must, Bruce, go ahead and jump.' Well, of course he didn't. But you get the point."

"Mother, Bruce isn't joking."

"Of course he is. Has he told his parents?"

"No, he hasn't."

"They'll raise the roof. Al and Rose won't stand for it."

"He'll tell them," Carol replied.

"When?"

"Any day now. Soon as he's finished taking instruction from his minister."

"Who? What minister?" Sara demanded. A numbing fear seized her.

"Where do you stand, honey? Or, let me put it to you this way—apostasy is a dreadful thing. *Meshumed* is the most horrible word I know. *Death* is preferable to apostasy. To leave the faith is *unthinkable*. Hitler decimated our people. We treasure every Jew. We will not give up even *one* Jew, if we can help it! We can't afford to!"

"Bruce knows all that, Mother."

"Bruce knows nothing!" she struck back, reddening. "With Bruce it's a fad, one more fad, after all the other things he's tried. But that's Bruce. It's *you* I'm concerned about. If Bruce goes through with this suicidal thing—and I don't believe deep down that he will—I don't want you to continue talking to him."

Enraged, Sara closed her fists, as though to strike. But in the next instant she regained composure. "Oh, my God!" she muttered. She, who scarcely ever said a cross word to them, had been on the point of striking. She collapsed in a chair, crushed.

"Mother, aren't you overreacting? I know at least two kids in my school who dropped out of Judaism and joined the Jesus movement."

"I know of no such persons," Sara countered. "And my daughter is not an admirer of one of them."

"It's only a matter of time, Mother. . . ."

"*What's* a matter of time?" she shot back. "What are you talking about? What kind of poison has this boy been giving you?"

"Mother, please. To you all this is a life-and-death matter, like it used to be in Russia or in grandpa's days. I still remember the stories you told me. If someone converted, the parents sat *shivah*, and said *Kaddish*, as though they were dead. That was Russia, almost a hundred years ago, Mother. But this is America."

"I know what you're saying," Sara countered. "I myself am an example, I suppose, of the changes taking place in our religion. A woman rabbi. I'm for changes. I believe Judaism should adapt itself to modern life. But I can't accept apostasy. I'm not that liberal. Apostasy means the death of Judaism."

"I think you should talk to Bruce, Mother."

"I certainly will!"

"Which is the reason I brought it up."

"Of course," she hesitated. "Is this why you accused me of being narrowminded?"

Carol fought back her tears. Sara embraced the girl and kissed her fiercely. "I'll talk to him."

That night, unable to sleep, Sara berated herself for losing control. In the dark, groping for the switch of her table lamp, she thought: Carol isn't involved with him. She's too level-headed. I don't give her enough credit. Her good sense will win out. And besides, she's too Jewishly grounded to emulate Bruce.

Out of bed, she began pacing. Although the rug was thick underfoot, the floor creaked. There wasn't anyone below, but Carol was in the next room. She didn't want Carol to hear. Who was the minister instructing Bruce? She would have to find out. There was tacit agreement among the clergy of Wilmette not to proselytize. She intended to find out who was guilty of the breach and raise the issue at the next Ministerial Alliance meeting.

Chapter Thirty-One

A L AND ROSE FOGEL walked hurriedly across their well-kept lawn. Sara took them into her study and shut the door. There was no need for amenities; they were old friends, in spite of their religious differences.

Rose Fogel's flower beds were the most attractive in the neighborhood. She had a way with growing things, though she confessed failure with her son. The Weintraubs were privy to the loud and frequent arguments between the Fogels and their son which sometimes lasted into the night. Aside from these occasions, however, the Fogels were a quiet couple.

"That pride and joy of ours is going to convert," Al Fogel said bitterly. It was a curious way for a psychologist to speak, Sara thought.

"The point is," Rose Fogel added, "Bruce doesn't really care about converting. His telling us he's going to study for the ministry is really to get back at us, Al and me. All his life he's been trying to hurt us, as though we're his enemies." She began to sob.

"He's getting even with us for some imaginary wrong we've

done him," Al declared. "Though I'll be darned if I know what it is. What have we denied him? Bruce was the only one on the block who had a car at eighteen." Al took his glasses off and began wiping vigorously.

Rose, a plump woman in her mid-forties, a head shorter than her husband, fidgeted nervously in the chair. "He warned us," she said. "If we try to stop him, he said he'd leave home. This time for good. What if he goes through with it?"

"Has he told you the name of the minister who's instructing him?" Sara asked.

"He wouldn't say," Al replied. "We tried to get it out of him, but he wouldn't tell us." He reached into the pocket of his faded khaki trousers and took out a pipe. Filling it from a pouch of tobacco, Al tried to light it, but his trembling hands forced him to give up. "I can't get over this," he added, speaking to no one in particular. "I'm not an observant Jew; for a time I was a Unitarian altogether. Is what's happening to me rational? When Bruce declared he was joining the Hare Krishna movement, I wasn't particularly perturbed; I thought it was a stage. Then he became a Zen Buddhist. That was okay with me. If he came to me and said, 'I'm going into Ethical Culture' or 'Humanistic Judaism,' would I fuss? Hardly. But his declaring he was converting to Christianity and planning to study for the ministry . . . well, that hit me like a ton of bricks. Why? Is it because I feel he's renouncing us? Does it have anything to do with the Jew in me? How would our lives change if Bruce went through with it and became a minister? Life at home might even become less contentious. He might settle down. Get married. It wouldn't change Rose's and my life one iota. Then why am I so excited? Why does it keep me awake nights? Why is all this driving me crazy?"

"You've said it. It's the Jew in you. Why deny it?" Sara answered. "My father, of blessed memory, summed it up very well in Yiddish. *Dos Pintele Yid*, he called it. The Jewish essence. The soul. The Jewish experience is another way of putting it."

Al Fogel shrugged. "But how do I come to be burdened with

it? I was born in Rhode Island. My parents were both born in New York. I was never exposed to anti-Semitism or threatened by gas chambers. So where do I come off having it?"

"I believe it's in the genes," Sara answered. "It entered our genes when our ancestors were driven into the Diaspora."

"You think so?" A pained expression came over his face. "It's all very confusing."

"We came to ask a favor," Rose Fogel said to Sara. "Talk to Bruce. You can come up with more reasons than we why he shouldn't go through with it. Besides, he won't listen to us anyway. To you, he might. Bruce has always liked you. More than once he said to me: 'Why didn't I have Sara for my mother?'"

"I will; I'll do what I can." She had intended talking to Bruce even if his parents had not asked it of her. Saving a single Jew is tantamount to saving the universe, the Talmud said. And she had an additional reason for trying to dissuade him; her daughter was emotionally involved.

"Will you do it soon?"

"Of course." Sara was overwhelmed with work but this matter had priority. A sense of urgency possessed her.

Bruce came on his own, as though summoned. He seemed eager, dressed in a pair of jeans, wearing sneakers, his brown hair unkempt. A scraggly beard barely covered his lower chin, and his shirt was open, revealing a hanging cross and a Mogen David. "Well, here I am," he said defiantly, sitting down opposite Sara in the study. "You want to talk to me?" he said, shifting in his chair. "Go ahead and talk. But you won't change my mind; nobody will." His nervousness belied his brave words.

"I'm glad to see you, Bruce," she lied. The sight of both the cross and the Star of David unnerved her. Her first impulse was to reject him outright.

"It's really a waste of your time," he answered. "I would like to please you. Your approval means a lot to me, always has."

Sara eyed the disturbed youth. What does Carol see in him?

"I'm going through with the conversion," Bruce interrupted her thoughts.

"Wait a minute, Bruce," she pleaded. "The least you can do is tell me about it. As old friends. . . ."

"It's a long story," he said, perspiration beading his forehead. His initial bravado seemed to melt. "It has a lot to do with how I feel about life and death. About death, particularly. About myself, about sin, about love. You see, Jesus died so that those who believe in him would inherit eternal life. Jesus loves people, especially sinners like myself, whom he loves most of all."

"For my sake," she said, overwhelmed by the hot flow of words, "let's take these things one at a time."

But his mind was too full of what he had to say, and he would not let her speak. "Ever since I was a little boy I was terrified of death. This fear of dying has been with me. For a while, I hoped that by the time I was old enough to die, a discovery would be made that would do away with death. . . . The Apostle Paul was also terrified of death. I identify with him strongly. He came to Jesus and was saved."

"Paul was not saved from death," she corrected. "He was saved from the *fear* of *death*."

"That's what I mean, fear of death. Judaism offers me no such thing. I made a study of it. '*He who goes down to the grave shall come up no more,*' it says in *Job*. But Jesus offers you Life Eternal. All my life I've been trying to escape from mortality. This time, I will!"

"Bruce, darling. . . ." She observed him shaking as though with the ague. His eyes were filmed over with tears. She brought him a glass of water. He'd been into drugs in the past. Had he taken something before coming? He reached for the glass with trembling hands. "What were you going to say?" he asked. "I dare you to. . . ."

"There's no need for that," she said gently, not wishing to upset him further.

"What has Judaism ever offered?" he demanded.

"Not easy and simple solutions," she replied. "Our Bible does not offer you a simple life after death. All of us must die. It isn't easy to accept, but it's futile to spend one's life trying to find ways of cheating it. Paul, himself, a most fervent believer, was buried, like all mortals."

"Paul will rise," Bruce declared. "He may already have risen. We don't know. He will declare himself when the time is ripe. I believe it, Mrs. Weintraub. I *have* to believe. There is nothing else. I've tried everything else—drugs, psychiatry, Zen, Hare Krishna. This is the last stop for me. If this doesn't come off, I don't know what I'll do." He paused, regarded her, and said: "Why don't *you* try Jesus?"

"Let's be serious, Bruce."

"I *am* serious. Carol is interested."

She flushed. "Carol is *not* interested. Judaism provides a way of life that serves her well. She knows there are no easy solutions, that human beings are mortal, and that someday she too will have to die. Judaism teaches her how to *live* fully."

"It didn't teach *me* that."

"You never gave it a chance. Your parents, good people though they are, are strangers to Judaism. Our religion, you see, calls for study, for effort. 'And now go and study,' Hillel said. Judaism does not appeal to everyone. Many desperate people look for easier, quicker solutions. I've read statements by evangelists who tell you that the essentials of Christianity can be learned in *one evening*, mind you. You don't have to work or study. The essentials are: you are a sinner. Jesus died for you. If you accept him as a savior, God will forgive you. Pray. Read the Bible. Is there anything I've left out?"

"No, I don't think so," Bruce said. "But that's what makes it so beautiful—the simplicity, the directness."

"But what happens when the quick solutions don't turn out to be solutions at all? Don't throw your life away, Bruce. You have a good mind. You once talked of becoming a physicist. Go back to it. Your parents will back you to the hilt. They love you."

"Stop soft-soaping me," he said, pushing back strands of hair that fell over his face. "My parents don't love me, never have. Nothing I've ever done pleased them. I've been a disappointment to them since the day I was born."

"Oh, no! That's not so. You don't know what you're saying, Bruce."

"I know very well what I'm saying," he countered. "But it hardly matters how my parents feel about me. Jesus loves me, and that's what counts. I don't have any bones to pick with you. You believe you're doing the right thing. But my parents are hypocrites. They're making a big fuss, my father in particular, about my decision to convert. Why? They never practiced Judaism, never took me to a synagogue. They prided themselves on being rationalists. When I was eight years old they read Voltaire, George Bernard Shaw, and Bertrand Russell's views on religion to me. And Marx, too."

"These men didn't provide the answers," Sara said, watching Bruce drink greedily from the glass. "One can survive only when one has faith. Especially now, when we're threatened by nuclear bombs, Star Wars, terrorism. . . ."

"I agree," he said. "But only Jesus has the answer. My mind is made up. My parents are planning to stop me, but they won't. And you won't either, Rabbi. It's a life-and-death matter to me. Do you understand what I'm saying? Don't any of you try to stop me. My friends have taught me. They love me. They help me. We sing. We dance. We touch. We hug. We kiss. They've taught me how to express love."

"They've brainwashed you, Bruce, like thousands of cults. They're relentless. You lose your own ability to think. They harp on your insecurities and weaknesses, and you've responded without really understanding. But the decision is yours to make," she finally relented. He's sick, she thought, unstable, in worse shape than he's ever been. Since the age of twelve he'd been going to psychiatrists. The Fogels spent a fortune on his therapy but apparently with little effect. A little less psychiatry and a little more religion, Sam used to say. Was it too late now? She wondered what strategy to use. She saw Bruce rise.

"There's nothing more to say," he declared flatly.

"Would you do me a favor and read a book I believe might help you?"

"No, Rabbi, it's too late for that."

"Do you mind telling me who's instructing you? The name of the minister?"

"Why? So you can tell him to lay off? My parents wanted his name for the same reason. Goodbye, Rabbi, I hope you change your mind and decide for Jesus."

"Bruce," Sara said firmly. "I'm going to forbid Carol from seeing you. You need more help than you think."

Bruce stopped, listened, and walked out, leaving Sara alone.

Left there to think, she grew furious. One of her colleagues in the Ministerial Alliance had to be instructing Bruce. She scanned the list of names but couldn't imagine who the culprit could be. She fumed, reaching for the phone to call Reverend Gribens. Her voice was taut. "Gene, I'd like you to do me a favor and call an emergency Alliance meeting."

"What's the emergency, Sara?" Reverend Gribens was surprised at the urgency in his colleague's voice.

"Someone's been proselytizing one of our people—the Fogel boy, to be specific—instructing him, preparing him for conversion. I want this out in the open."

"Of course, Sara. But I *am* surprised," Reverend Gribens replied.

"You don't happen to know who it is?"

"Oh, no, Sara."

"How soon can we have the meeting?"

"Let's see. Today is Monday. How about Wednesday? Some people are out of town so tomorrow may be too soon. Wednesday okay?"

She agreed.

Then that evening she received a telephone call from Jack

Kirkwood, pastor of the Evangelical Presbyterian Church on Madison Avenue. Reverend Kirkwood asked if he might come over for a few minutes for a chat.

"It's about young Bruce Fogel," Reverend Kirkwood said after the amenities. "He came to me some weeks ago and said he wanted to convert to Christianity. I said, 'No Bruce, I won't do it. I don't believe in conversions.' I also advised him not to try any of the other ministers either."

"It's what I would expect of you, Jack," she said.

"But that's not the end of the story. He said if I didn't help him to convert he'd slash his wrists. He's a sick boy, this Bruce."

"I know."

"An obsessive fear of death. He wants to be *saved*."

"What did you tell him, Jack?"

"I said no, but he came back. Demanded that I instruct him, prepare him for conversion. Wants to become a minister. 'Tell me about Jesus,' he demanded. Well, Jesus is my *favorite* subject, which you well know. . . ."

"Jack, what are you trying to tell me?" she demanded. "That you *are* instructing the boy?"

"Well, yes and no."

Her face grew hot. "How can it be yes *and* no?" she pressed, her anger mounting. "You, of all people? Racking my brain, trying to figure out who it might be, I didn't suspect you were the one!" She was aware of her voice rising, her pulse racing wildly. "Leave him alone!" she cried. Sara pounded the desk until her palm hurt.

Reverend Kirkwood leaned back in the chair, silently gazing at her with sad eyes. "You need a rest, Sara," he comforted.

"I'm sorry, Jack," she replied, her voice level barely above a whisper.

"I deserve it, I suppose," he said. "How I get myself into these scrapes, I don't know. They all beat a path to my door—the psychotics, neurotics, dope fiends, petty criminals, pimps, prostitutes; they come to me to be saved. This Bruce Fogel is a very mixed-up boy. He's desperate and crazy. Both. He virtually started slashing his wrists in my study when I tried to turn him down. I came here to talk to you, to find out what to do about him. If I send him away, he'll kill himself. I don't want him on my conscience. I put it to his parents. . . ."

"When did you see the parents?" she asked. "I spoke to them this morning. They didn't mention seeing you."

"I stopped to speak to them before coming here. I told them what I'm telling you. I asked them, should I send him away? Their answer was they'd rather have a live son who's Christian than a dead Jew."

"Then there's nothing more to be said on the subject," Sara said, rising.

After Reverend Kirkwood had gone, she said *Kaddish*, the prayer for the dead. The Fogels wouldn't know how.

Chapter Thirty-two

"I'M SERIOUSLY THINKING of selling my house and moving elsewhere," she said to Hal. "I don't think I can handle it anymore."

She was with Hal in his living room. It was almost midnight. The others had gone home soon after the meeting had broken up. The meeting had been called by Don and Hal to plot strategy that would counteract Elkind's petition to remove Sara as rabbi. Elkind hadn't given up. At a recent board meeting he had been more determined than ever.

"She's stepping on everybody's toes," Elkind fumed. "Now she's attacking the Christian community. We lived here peacefully before she took over, and now she'll make more anti-Semites than we need. She has no regard for the Jewish people here. I'll call the Anti-Defamation League and report her."

About twenty persons had shown up to listen to Hal's ideas, and he had asked Sara to come. She'd declined at first, but he had prevailed upon her to put in an appearance, if nothing more. It had been a lively meeting. Many suggestions were offered.

"My mind is made up, Hal. I suppose I should have more confidence. But I can't stand it any longer."

Hal shook his head. "Sara," he admonished. "Where's that exuberance, that spark of yours? You were excited about the future, and you felt so good about looking ahead. Everything was perfect. You're allowing yourself to be dragged down. Don't! You can't! We'll work this out."

Sara noticed that he said "we."

Hal continued. "Where will you look for a house? If you must move, why don't you move here, to my place? I'll get myself a small apartment till things simmer down."

"No, thanks, Hal, it's very sweet of you. I appreciate your offer."

"Why not?"

"That's all Elkind needs. Oh, I'm not concerned about people talking or anything like that, Hal; you know me better than that. I'm worried about more important things."

"Then why don't you consider it? A big empty house. It's here. I would enjoy nothing better than for you and the kids to make use of it, at least until we lick this Elkind petition and you're ordained."

"*If* I'm ordained," she sighed.

"Of course you'll be," he said confidently.

"I don't know, Hal."

"What's the matter with you, Sara? How long have I known you? I don't remember you ever so lacking in spirit. You've changed overnight. You're not the same woman."

"I *am* tired, Hal, and weary in spirit."

"I understand why you might be physically tired. It's been rough on you. But as to the spirit being weary, that puzzles me."

"I'm a failure, Hal. As a rabbi, I mean."

"You are not!" he countered, rising and going to sit near her. "You're the most exciting thing that's happened to our temple since its inception."

"Apparently they prefer to do with a little less excitement. No, Hal, I've really failed as a rabbi, I know it. I lack diplomacy, flexibility, a sense of humor. I take everything too seriously. I'm a woman—and they're not ready to accept me. They want me out."

"A small minority," Hal declared. "The great majority is on your side. I have no doubt that if you just hold on a little longer, we'll lick this petition. We'll do it together. Hey, come on, Sara. As for the ordination, that's a matter of time, but it's inevitable."

"I don't know, Hal. And there's the relationship with my children. Simon's been acting up. And now Carol."

Hal nodded. "The children need a father, I suppose. Don't you think so?"

"Oh, definitely. But fathers don't grow on trees."

"They're not as hard to find as one imagines."

"Help me, Hal," she said, her gloomy countenance relaxing. "The rabbi appoints you a committee of one."

A brief silence intervened. Finally Hal spoke. His voice was serious, yet warm. "Sara, I want to ask you something. What I want to say . . . that is, ask . . . should be the easiest thing in the world. After all, we've known each other for years. But it's not easy, in fact . . . very difficult . . . and I've never been so nervous in my whole life."

"What is it, Hal?"

"Sara, I'm asking you to marry me."

"Oh, Hal," she smiled. "I'm . . ." she spun around and kissed him.

"You don't have to give me your answer now. You may want to think it over, talk about it with the children."

"The answer is *yes*, now, Hal." she said, radiant. "The children, I know what they'll say; they'll be as happy as I am. The answer is *yes*." She kissed him again.

"Careful," he said. "Big Brother Elkind may be watching."

They laughed.

"You came home late last night, didn't you, Mother?" Carol asked as they sat down for breakfast the next morning. Sara searched her daughter's face but sensed nothing. "I waited till

11:00 before I went to sleep," Carol added.

"I watched TV," Simon chimed in.

"Yes, I was late," Sara agreed. "We had an important meeting at Hal's house and it didn't break up until almost midnight."

"What was the meeting about?" Carol asked innocently.

"You know . . . problems, finances," Sara answered. While answering evasively, Sara wondered whether she should talk to her children now or wait till evening. She glanced at the clock over the cabinet. There was plenty of time before they had to dash off for school. She was not eating. Carol looked up from her cereal.

"Not having anything, Mother? Are you O.K.?"

"Yes. I'm O.K., children. After the meeting, Hal and I talked. I told him how hard things were. Fact is, I've even been thinking of moving, giving up and moving."

"You were? That's not right," Carol answered.

"Yes, Carol, it's been too much. But Carol, Simon. I have something wonderful to tell you." The children looked at each other, then at Sara. Sara took a deep breath, looked deeply into the eyes of her children, and said, "Uncle Hal has asked me to marry him." She released her breath and waited. A long moment of shock and quiet. Then Carol, her eyes sparkling, pushed her chair aside, spun around to her mother, and they embraced.

"Oh, Mother, I'm so happy," she cried. "I'm so happy."

Sara wiped her tearful eyes.

"And you, Simon?"

"I think it's great, Mom. I like Uncle Hal. He's great; he really is."

"Me too," Carol joined in. She nearly jumped while she clapped her hands.

"I'm so happy," Sara beamed. "We've known each other for such a long time. And now two old friends are going to get married!"

A momentary sadness swept Carol's face. She was remembering her father.

"I know," Sara responded. "You were thinking of Dad." The silence bore down on all of them for a moment.

"When's the wedding?" Carol asked, suddenly brightening.

"Yeah, when's the wedding?" Simon repeated.

"We haven't decided yet. Hal sprung the big question last night."

"He sprung it? You didn't know?"

Sara winked, "We women have a way of knowing, don't we?" Carol nodded.

"Where will we live?" Simon asked. "I like Uncle Hal's house better than this house."

"We'll see."

"Are you going to be a rabbi, Mother?"

"I don't know. I'm thinking about it. I think I might just want to be a wife and a mother, all over again."

"You mustn't, Mother. You mustn't . . ." Carol insisted. Sara withdrew from the embrace.

"You mustn't stop. You mustn't give up."

"Carol!"

"No, you mustn't give up now, Mother. You've worked so hard; *too* hard to give up now. We won't mind, will we, Simon?"

Simon agreed, shaking his head.

"What will Uncle Hal say?" Carol asked, persistent.

"I really don't know. I think he'll want me to at least finish out the year. Not quit. After the year, we'll see."

"You *have* to Mother; you *have* to continue." Carol changed subjects. "Are you going to be ordained?"

"That's the next question," Sara answered. "It all ties in. Everything is dependent on everything else."

"I'm so glad you told us, Mother," Carol beamed.

"I am, too. But kids," she cautioned, "not a word to anyone. It's still something between us, okay?"

"All right, Mother," Carol promised.

"Simon?" Sara looked at her son.

"Okay, Mom." He shook his head, "Not a word."

Chapter Thirty-three

TENSION HAD NOT RUN SO HIGH since the board meeting in August when Sara Weintraub was selected as rabbi. Anticipating a large crowd, Don Shapiro had moved the meeting to the junior auditorium.

The usual chatting was absent. Every board member came; none wanted to miss the excitement. Sides were drawn. Friendships seemed to have dissolved. Perfunctory exchanges revealed anxiety by some, guilt by others. Heavy cigar and cigarette smoke filled the room. Elkind took a seat on one side of the aisle. Hal judiciously joined some of his friends on the other. Sara would not be coming.

"All right," Don banged his gavel. "Fred, close the door. Let's get this show on the road. I'm going to dispense with everything and get right down to business. I'll be happy if we get through this without breaking heads." His smile didn't carry; nor was his humor effective. Blank faces stared at the president. "Before we begin, gentlemen, will you please stop smoking. I'm getting nauseous." Some complied by pressing out stale butts; others continued to puff. Don looked at the others. "Please?" A few more stopped. "All right, let's get down to the issue." Don turned to Elkind. "Make your presentation, Phil," he said.

Elkind rose, looking sideways at Hal. "Okay." He appeared calm. He glanced at his cards and began. "My position is well known, so it's not necessary to repeat."

Don interrupted. "It *is*, Phil. This is a new meeting. Not everyone was present at the last one. Present all your facts and reasons so that we can act intelligently." The doctor looked around. "Okay. I've jotted down a number of . . . of . . . reasons why I believe we ought to discharge our rabbi." He gained confidence.

A shifting in the seats and murmurings disturbed the quiet. Don pounded the gavel five times. Then suddenly the rear door to the auditorium opened and a stream of people started to walk in. The editor of the *Courier*, Ed Fitzpatrick, led the way, followed by Reverend Gribens and Reverend MacLeary. They were followed by ten to twelve adolescents in jeans, jerseys, and tennis shoes, some with their parents and others in groups of two or three. The Kornblatts, Epsteins, and Einbeins appeared, striding confidently. They were solemn, walking slowly toward the back of the auditorium where they sat down. Don tried to compress a smile; he winked at Hal. Elkind's face paled. He shot a suspicious look at Don.

"What the hell is this? Mr. President, what is going on?"

Don looked straight-faced at the questioner. "I guess we have visitors."

Phil sought his friends, questioning. Their eyes widened as each shrugged a "search me" look. "Why you son-of-a-bitch," he fumed.

"Watch your language, doctor; your son is here." Phil wheeled around, saw his son meekly hiding behind Stephanie and Howard.

"What are you doing here?" he shouted.

"Tell him!" Stephanie urged. "Tell him!"

"Yeah, tell him."

Billy's voice shook. "I'm here," he said defensively, "I, I'm here to defend our rabbi like the other kids."

"You're what?" Phil shouted.

"I'm here, too," Reverend Gribens offered.

"So am I," Nettie Kornblatt announced.

"Amen," intoned Reverend MacLeary.

Don, obviously pleased, banged his gavel. "You're all welcome. We have nothing to hide."

"This is a synagogue," Cowen called out. "Private!"

"Right," Don said. "But our rabbi is part of the community too. This matter has been talked about outside, even in the *Courier.* That makes it a community affair." Mentioning the newspaper, he acknowledged the presence of the editor.

"Everyone wants to be part of this issue. Most of our guests are our own people, our young people. Isn't it wonderful that they're interested?"

Elkind growled.

"Go ahead, Phil," Don nudged.

Hesitating, Phil started to speak. But his voice sounded less secure. "As I was saying, there are many reasons why this board should be courageous and act for the betterment of the temple. We should elect a new rabbi!"

"New rabbi?" came the response.

"Yes, new *rabbi,*" he responded to the voices, getting stronger. "It's absolutely essential that the temple take a proper course and remove a rabbi who is so infatuated with sex, who contributes to the delinquency of minors. . . ." There was hissing and booing from the rear of the auditorium. He continued doggedly. "A rabbi who undermines our fund-raising projects, who embarrasses us in the Christian community, who talks about things that don't belong in a synagogue." The stamping of feet and hand-raising continued. MacLeary was obviously distressed. Gribens courteously raised his hand. Don pounded his gavel firmly. "Everyone will have a chance," he said, enjoying his role now. "I move, Mr. Chairman," Elkind's voice shouted above the din, "that the board dismiss Sara Weintraub."

He sat down abruptly, self-satisfied. "Second?" Don asked.

"We need a second to put the motion on the floor." Cowen's loud second was stronger than his support had been at the first board encounter.

"All right," Don announced. "The motion is on the floor." He looked at a cool Hal Kaplan.

"Discussion? Board members have priority," Don declared. Back and forth members reacted, each repeating reasons for or against the motion. Feelings rose higher and higher.

"Donald, I'd like to say something." The voice came from the group that had marched in. "Yes, Nettie."

"It's not easy. When you selected Sara as rabbi, I was against it, remember? I couldn't see a woman as a rabbi. When she began talking to our children," she glanced at Stephanie, "I was concerned. And then," she took a deep breath, "then I had a personal problem, a real problem in my family, and I want everybody to know that Sara went out of her way to help us. She really saved my life. She's been wonderful to me and my family and I would be very disturbed if we hurt her in any way." She sat down.

"I want to second Nettie's comment." Another woman rose. "You know that confirmation class that we were so worried about? Well, even Rabbi Sam couldn't bring them to the temple. Sara did. She talks to them like they are human beings, real people. She understands their problems as adolescents and isn't afraid to meet the problems head on. They all admire her. Don't you, kids?"

As if by signal, the teenagers shouted affirmatively. "Yea, Rabbi Sara," as they stood up and applauded.

"My father and I disagree," Billy Elkind said. "You want me to be honest, don't you, Dad?" He looked at his father. "You accuse Rabbi Sara of talking about sex and abortion and homosexuality and all that. But we know what it's all about, Dad. Come on, we're living in a different age and we're growing up quicker. Rabbi Sara makes it all real. You talk about sex. Well, I read the other day about a town in New Jersey where they're selling sex magazines and some people are against it, trying to stop it. Well, you know what the owner said? He said that the *adults*, that fathers and mothers, had been keeping that business going, not the kids. That's hypocrisy, isn't it?"

Elkind's fury shook him. He muttered to Cowen, who tried to calm him. "Take it easy, Phil, don't lose control. Kids can't vote."

"May I speak!" MacLeary's voice boomed. "A few words. I must."

Don hesitated. "Of course."

The big black man rose. His eyes glistened. "I can't understand anyone," he repeated, "anyone speaking against my dear, dear friend. I hope you haven't forgotten what she did for my church. She saved us. She's a real sister to our people and we don't want anything done to hurt her. She's done marvelous things, like the Bible says. Bless her, don't hurt her." He sat down. The teenagers exploded with applause.

One after another, pros and cons were spoken.

"Call the question," came the summons after more than an hour.

"Wait a minute, before you vote," Phil called out. "You're letting the kids run this temple. You don't understand what this is going to do to us, believe me. We'll never be able to grow. The other synagogues will run away with us. Let's start a new period, a new era. On a proper level."

"I've had enough," Hal interrupted. He stood up and faced Elkind. "I've been very patient, Phil." The tone was carefully measured.

"You can't shut me up, Hal; I'm not through."

"Yes you are, Phil. You're through." He slowly looked around as all eyes watched him. "It's different now; you're talking about my fiancée. Sara and I are going to be married."

Stunned silence. Phil looked startled as if hit by a sledge hammer. Don dropped his gavel. "Well, I'll be damned," he murmured.

The teenagers applauded, rupturing the silence. Phil sat down. "Withdraw the motion, Phil," Cowen whispered. "You'll make an ass of yourself."

Phil shook his head. "No way; it's principle."

"Yes," Hal said, all smiles. "Sara and I will be married. I don't know if I want her to be the rabbi of a group of people who don't appreciate her. It's up to her. And also, I want to let you in on another secret, even Sara doesn't know yet." One man whispered to another, facetiously, "God, is she pregnant?" Hal continued, disregarding the stage whisper. "No, she's not pregnant. . . . What I was going to say is that I'm fairly certain that the Seminary will ordain her. Let's keep it a secret."

Another round of applause burst out. "Phil," Hal said, looking contented. "I promise you, my wife will never visit you professionally."

"Let's finish."

"Call the question."

"All right," Don called out. "Any comments? Phil?" Elkind was sullen. The vote was taken. Only three voted for Sara's dismissal. Then pandemonium broke out. The group rushed to congratulate Hal.

The next day the *Courier* carried a red boxed statement. "Rabbi Sara Weintraub gets almost unanimous vote of confidence. Board stirred to solid support as impending marriage to Harold Kaplan is announced."

Chapter Thirty-Four

"**W**OMAN RABBI, INDEED!**" Dr. Horner rolled the phrase off his tongue, testing its sound. "Rabbi Sara . . . Sara?" He had been examining its flavor ever since their meeting. Sounds so strange, he thought. He waved his head left and right, his eyes gesturing. He smiled, then frowned, then said, "Not bad. Mother Sara, Rabbi Sara. It sounds good."

He knew, however, that this was mental play. He was getting used to the idea. Sara had impressed him. The idea was alive. But he would not decide on the basis of his own personal response. His conclusion had to be rooted in traditional sources. A stand on such a volatile issue required the support of his faculty members and board of trustees. Together the men of knowledge and the men of business would have to be involved. The movement had to stand as a bulwark behind the decision he wanted to make. There could be no schism: he needed the endorsement of the traditionalists as well as the liberals.

Dr. Horner walked along the walls of books lined high, his head scanning, his mind associating. "Where? This book? This tractate?" He hummed as he strode by the books, and stopped.

"Oh, yes, I'll start with this one." He lifted it out of the packed group, saw another, then a third. Finally he assembled a stack of books. He placed them alongside his leather chair, nestled in it, and started to flip through the pages, singing now a Talmudic, now a Hassidic melody as he thumbed.

A pad of paper rested on the lamp table. Occasionally he jotted down notes he would need for his presentations. When the hours rushed past midnight he finally was convinced. "There's enough theology, ideology, what have you, in Jewish sources," he muttered to himself, "to go ahead."

"Let's look at it the other way around," he conjectured. "There are no strictures *against* women rabbis. Yes." He agreed with his conclusion. "Yes, we must live with the times. We must dare to be courageous."

The Seminary faculty and the board of trustees gathered in the library at Dr. Horner's summons. The board members were meticulously dressed executives, their faces healthy, reflecting their daily routine of calisthenics and jogging. The others looked like scholars. Their dress was casual, faces wan. The contrast was marked but both groups were needed now. Malcolm Friedman and Dean Melvin Hahn were present.

"Gentlemen," Dr. Horner began slowly, his eyes scanning the men seated at the library tables. "I have called you to this meeting because of its historic purpose. I have asked two groups of men, each wholeheartedly committed to our Seminary and to Conservative Judaism, to consider a very important proposal, a watershed crucial issue. We are asked to consider ordaining a woman. Our rabbis have agreed to accept women into their organization. Ordination, however, is a condition precedent to membership."

He stopped. Some faculty members turned ashen.

Professor Steinhart's face reddened. *"Chutzpah!"* he exploded, turning away. "Why, it's unheard of. It's a death sign."

But many of the trustees were delighted. "Good idea. Great.

302

Right with the times. We'll get more money and support for the Seminary."

Dr. Horner looked out. "I would not expect all of us to agree. The lifeline of our existence as Jews is discussion and debate, even disagreement. Our rabbis have set the pattern for our style of decision. Let's not be hasty. Or afraid. Our sages never feared an issue. Let's be deliberate and not allow our prejudices to get the better of us. Think of Judaism, our people, our synagogues, our youth. And our future."

The faculty members relaxed, but Steinhart's head still bobbed with fury.

"I am not suggesting that we adopt a resolution to ordain women carte blanche, for the sake of ordaining, or for publicity value, though God knows, we can use so many more rabbis. We could fill many empty chairs of Judaic studies on college campuses, Hillel Foundations, and religious schools if we had the men . . . or women. This would give us the shot in the arm we need. It would carry our message, the relevancy of tradition *and* change, tradition *in* change, change *in* tradition. Are we better off not having enough rabbis in the field? Including women? We have to look to the future and consider the issue from that vantage point."

"He's got something there," Jonah Federen agreed. "Good idea. Beautiful."

"What I ask of you at this meeting is to break the ice. Consider one specific case. True, the one case may establish a precedent. I have here a biographical résumé of Sara Weintraub and an analysis of her accomplishments and her studies."

He passed out the papers and watched anxiously as the distinguished group devoured the pages.

"She's tremendous," said Herbert Frankel, a rich investment banker. "She's brought us more glory, if you'll excuse me, Dr. Horner, than many of our other rabbis!"

"She's more publicity conscious," interjected Steinhart.

"I don't care, Doctor," Frankel retorted. "Even if it were true, what difference does it make? Hasn't she brought glory to God and man, as you would say? Why, it's simply magnificent. My wife and all our friends have talked about her. We have fallen in line calling her Rabbi. It's not bad, really. It sounds pretty good. Try it, Dr. Steinhart. Try it." The objector turned his head away.

Dr. Horner gently tapped his fingers on the desk. "It is true that many limitations are placed on women in our tradition. But I also know that we have had many women who were leaders, scholars." He pulled a sheet of paper from the side and placed it in front of him, reading, "Twelve percent of our prophets were women. Let me quote from a recent volume. 'How great were our women and how much we have to admire and love them. Sarah was the mother of prophecy; Rebecca, Rachel, and Leah, mothers of prayer. Miriam, mother of deliverance, women in the wilderness, mothers of faith, Ruth, mother of royalty, Esther, mother of Israel's rescue. Daughters of Mattathias and Hannah of the seven sons fame, mother of sanctification of the Divine Name. In every age there have been righteous women by whose merit we are destined to be redeemed. The Talmud says that the Holy One, blessed be He, endowed women with greater understanding than men.'"

Dr. Horner continued, "I don't have to tell you that many other women in Jewish history have distinguished themselves as well. Even in our day."

There were nods of agreement.

"Mrs. Weintraub's background and education reveal to me that she has studied diligently. Do you agree, Dean Kahn? Of course, she is not familiar with all the Codes as some of our men are. However, her knowledge is certainly, unquestionably, sufficient for her position. I really believe that in her case we should bestow the title of rabbi on her. Our ordination is Rabbi and Teacher. We should give her that title, dignify her and dignify the title. What will we lose? What will we gain? Weigh the balances. The Jewish world, perhaps even the Orthodox group, might think we have done the right thing.

"I have studied the sources and I find nothing against ordaining a woman. There are really no legal obstacles. Emotional? Perhaps. Legal? No. I ask you to recommend that I be authorized to bestow the title of rabbi upon Sara Weintraub."

After a heated debate on the recommendation, the vote was affirmative.

Chapter Thirty-Five

MANEUVERING THE TOYOTA into the spot marked "Rabbi Parking," Sara already felt more relaxed. The marriage proposal had done it. Let the storms rage; she felt unaffected by them. The Elkind threat dissipated. It had backfired. She had made up her mind. She was quitting. I'm going to lead a normal life again, attend to the needs of my children, my husband. The mention of "husband" brought a wave of warmth. A rabbi has no life apart from the job. Not only are you a spiritual leader, which is in itself a full-time job, but you're also consoler of the ill, advisor to the perplexed, arbiter, guide, marital counselor, participant in birth celebrations, Bar-Mitzvahs, weddings and funerals. Your phone rings day and night. You see your children on the run . . . it's a killing job. How congregants forget; there's no satisfying them. And in addition, if you're a woman, the first woman rabbi, you have to prove yourself again and again. Who needs it? You've got two strikes against you. Even the women ordained by the other seminaries have not really been accepted by the congregants. "I'll give notice," she thought. She had no intention of leaving before a replacement was sent in. And she hoped to be active in the congregation, teach a class or two in religious school, if they asked her. Could she change roles? Why not? The family would claim the rest of her time, and the house. Hal's was a baronial house, an estate, more properly speaking. Did a small family need all that space? I'll have to dust off my recipes and start cooking again. Be a homemaker again. Reading was what she'd missed while busy with her rabbinical chores. Her readings had chiefly dealt with heavy subjects, philosophy, theology. Now she'd have time to catch up on bestsellers.

Rolling up the window of the car—a fine rain had begun to fall—Sara went inside the temple, aware with every step she took that a subtle change was taking place. She felt differently about the synagogue, the objects in it, the doors she passed, her study. I love this place but it's no longer mine. I'm giving it up for a better life.

Approaching her desk, piled high with unfinished sermons, unanswered letters, she averted her gaze from the Horner photograph. She knew there would be disapproval in his gaze. But why? She wasn't abandoning her post. She'd given it a good try. She would have liked nothing better than to stay on as rabbi. Yes, there were satisfactions but it was mainly a collision course. She sighed. We've been on this track before. *Farfaln,* as Mamma used to say. Lost cause.

The buzzer sounded. Sara pressed the button. "Rabbi, Mr. Kaplan is on the phone."

"I'll take it," she said, her pulse quickening. "Hal? Where are you?"

"Where should I be? In New York. I. . . ."

"That's what I thought. You all right? What's up?"

"Plenty is up!"

"You got that Belgian account you were hoping for?"

"The Belgian account? Oh, no, that's not what I'm calling about. Something much more important than that. Sara, I'm at the Seminary. Rabbi Friedman's office."

"Seminary? Rabbi Friedman's office? What are you doing there?"

307

"Attending to some urgent business. They called me to come here."

"What business?"

"Your ordination as rabbi, my dear."

"Hal, honey, it's too late for that. I'm at my desk, working on my statement of resignation. My mind is quite made up." Hal's announcement hadn't penetrated.

"Well, un-make it," Hal said, his words sounding clipped and metallic through the wires. "You're getting ordained. Rabbi Horner is going to ordain you. Got it from the horse's, I mean, the rabbi's mouth."

There was a pause. Then she said: "He is? You serious?"

"If you don't take my word for it, you can ask Rabbi Friedman. He's right here with me."

Sara sucked in her breath. Her voice trembled. "Oh, Hal. I . . . I can't believe it. Could it be?"

"It already is," Hal beamed.

"Hal, I'm going to faint."

"Not now, Sara. And," Hal emphasized, "I've told Rabbi Friedman that we're going to be married. He's sending you a *mazel-tov*. And so does Dr. Horner."

Tears came to her eyes. "Tell me everything," she urged, a catch in her voice.

"We just got through meeting with Dr. Horner. That's why I'm at the Seminary. Dr. Horner is going to personally ordain you. He had a special conference with the faculty and they agreed. Not unanimously, but they agreed."

"What? Dr. Horner is going to *personally* ordain me? I *am* going to faint."

"He says it will be a privilege to ordain you."

Emotions bubbled over, tears poured from her eyes. "Why?" she whispered.

"Sara, are you there? I can barely hear you."

"Yes, I'm h-here," she managed.

"Dr. Horner says he followed your work at Temple Shalom and thinks you're doing beautifully. You impressed him deeply.

You're an asset to the movement, he said. Sara, I just want you to know how proud I feel."

She felt as if she would burst. The unexpected news caught her unaware, not unlike the unexpected tragedy of Sam's death. But this was different. It was a joyous, momentous feeling. An inexplicable deep welling of her faith washed over Sara. It was one of the most profound spiritual moments of her life, reminding her of the same experience that had swept her months ago when she asked for guidance at the Holy Ark. Utter peace filled her being. "Hal, I'm speechless."

"And to set your mind totally at ease, Dr. Horner knows all about Elkind and his group. Read about it in the *Times*. Obviously it didn't make any difference because he's coming to Wilmette to ordain you at your temple, Sara—Temple Shalom. What an honor for you, for the temple!" Hal added with warmth, "And for me."

Silence. Sara reached for some water and drank.

"Sara, you okay?"

"Hal, what shall I do?"

"Get ready for your ordination."

"But didn't we decide I was quitting to become Mrs. Kaplan?"

"You can become Mrs. Kaplan without quitting. I think you'll be happier staying on as a rabbi."

"You're right. I really do want to stay on. It's in the genes. My great-grandfather, my grandfather, my father—all rabbis. Abraham Horner himself will ordain me? God! What an honor! I'll die of fright. In all my wildest dreams. . . . But does the congregation want me?"

"You know they do."

"You really think so?"

"Of course."

"What about my qualifications?"

"Abraham Horner would not have enthusiastically volunteered to come to Wilmette and ordain you if he didn't believe you had the qualifications. After all, the prestige of the Seminary, of the Conservative Movement, is behind him."

She nodded into the phone and dabbed her eyes. "I suppose what you say is so. Then you think I should go ahead?"

"Definitely. If you want to."

"Oh, I do Hal. I *do* want to. You know I do. There isn't anything in the world I'd rather do than be a rabbi! Thank you, Hal. And thank Rabbi Horner and Rabbi Friedman. Oh, I'm so excited. I . . . this is the happiest. . ." She really was speechless.

Chapter Thirty-six

A ND SO IT CAME TO PASS that Rabbi Abraham Horner jour-
neyed to Wilmette to ordain Sara Weintraub as rabbi. The
sanctuary was crowded when the hour came for the ordination,
on the holiday of Shavuot, Feast of the Weeks. The sanctuary
was packed to capacity and the electronic doors to the auditorium were opened so that additional chairs could be set up.
Sara's confirmation class turned up en masse. A slightly self-
conscious Ruth slipped into the last row. Even Elkind and his
wife came. He was no longer fighting. Doubts about Sara's
ministry had dissipated. She had proven herself. Never before
had Wilmette been so honored as to have Rabbi Horner all to
itself. The Men's Club took charge of the ushering and the
Sisterhood prepared an elaborate *Kiddush* to follow the service.
The aura of the High Holy Day season permeated. Sara had
never been so anxious. She arrived at the temple early, accompanied by Hal and the children. She wore a white gown
trimmed with gold. Carol and Simon sat proudly next to Hal in
the front row. Hal's face was radiant. That pleased Sara as much
as the ordination. She felt elated, but terribly nervous.

311

Rabbi Horner stood on the podium, his head crowned by a shock of white hair. Tall and impressive, he towered over the stand. Pain and joy seemed creased into his brow. Deep blue eyes penetrated his audience. Abraham Horner's voice was strong and vibrant, charged by some inner flame.

"This is a great day for our people," he said. The instrument of his voice quivered with the emotion of a prophet. "This day celebrates Moses giving the Torah to our people on Mount Sinai. In a sense, Moses ordained us as children of God and has imposed upon all of us the duties and responsibilities as leaders of humanity. On this holiday, my friends, we read the story of Ruth, of her devotion and love. Because of this, we felt it proper to select this day to ordain the first woman as rabbi in Conservative Jewry."

After repeating the words he had read before the Seminary officials, he turned and motioned for Sara to come forward. Heart pounding, Sara walked up to the great man. He placed his hands on her shoulders. Her head bowed, she heard his words, each one articulated slowly: "I perform the ceremony of *Semicha*, of laying of the hands, as did our master Moses to Joshua, as our elders performed in their days. And I declare you rabbi in Israel. Lift up your head, my colleague, and accept the blessing and the welcome of your people, as their rabbi."

His voice, filled with emotion, sang the priestly benediction: "May the Lord bless you and keep you. May the Lord turn His countenance to you and be gracious to you. May the Lord turn to you and grant you peace."

Her eyes glistened with tears when she looked up. Rabbi Horner leaned forward and kissed Sara on the forehead. "God bless you, my colleague." A thrill ran through her as a happily weeping congregation shared her pride.

She stood before the lectern, her head slightly bowed, facing her congregation, her children, Hal. She was aware that they were with her, united now behind their rabbi, and expected her to address them. Nothing came to mind; no words that formed in her mouth could express how she felt. One of the reasons she hadn't slept the previous night, in addition to trying to decide whether a special memorial prayer, Kaddish, should be recited for Sam, was because of the statement of acceptance she'd written out. It was a good, sound speech, but she felt that it would not do; nothing she might say would do. She recalled now, standing in front of the lectern, gripping it with her fingers until the tips and knuckles hurt, that morning many months ago, when she'd come alone to the sanctuary, on tiptoe, as though she meant not to be caught visiting there. She recalled how utterly alone she'd felt, how like an interloper. . . . "And God tested Abraham," the phrase now recurred to her. As then, she was being tested. Isn't that what living was all about? But she no longer felt like an interloper. The lion on the pulpit did not intimidate her. Then why did she tremble so? "I pledge to you," she heard herself saying, "that I will serve you, serve all people, as rabbi, with all my heart and strength."

Temple Israel
Minneapolis, Minnesota

IN MEMORY OF
DOROTHY BANKS
FROM
NANCY & LARRY SHILLER